Lord Uthe, a member of the Vampire Council, was a Templar Knight centuries ago. Even up to the present day, he has attempted to honor the spirit of the Rule, despite the volatile and highly sexual nature of the vampire world. Yet now he's caught the attention of the Fae Lord Keldwyn, liaison between the Council and Fae Court. Keldwyn challenges Uthe's emotional isolation and dominant nature. When a quest from Uthe's past requires Keldwyn's help to protect both their worlds, Uthe will have to decide whether the Fae male is a gift from God to be cherished and trusted, or a curse that will make Uthe fail the Order he promised to serve all his life.

Night's Templar

Copyright © 2015 Joey W. Hill

ALL RIGHTS RESERVED

Cover Design by W. Scott Hill

Print Publication: October 2015 by Story Witch Press.

This book may not be reproduced or used in whole or in part by any means existing without written permission from the publisher, Story Witch Press, 6823 Neuhoff Lane, Charlotte NC 28269.

Warning: The unauthorized reproduction or distribution of this copyrighted work is illegal. No part of this book may be scanned, uploaded or distributed via the Internet or any other means, electronic or print, without the publisher's permission. Criminal copyright infringement, including infringement without monetary gain, is investigated by the FBI and is punishable by up to 5 years in federal prison and a fine of $250,000. (http://www.fbi.gov/ipr/). Please purchase only authorized electronic or print editions and do not participate in or encourage the electronic piracy of copyrighted material. Your support of the author's rights is appreciated.

This book is a work of fiction and any resemblance to persons, living or dead, or places, events or locales is purely coincidental. The characters are productions of the author's imagination and used fictitiously.

The publisher and author(s) acknowledge the trademark status and trademark ownership of all trademarks, service marks and word marks mentioned in this book.

The following material contains graphic sexual content meant for mature readers. Reader discretion is advised.

ISBN: 978-1-942122-17-3

Night's Templar

By Joey W. Hill

Book XIII of the Vampire Queen Series

Acknowledgments

My eternal thanks to my critique partners, both old and new—the patient and amazing Sheri Fogarty, who has been with me since my early Ellora's Cave days, and the incomparable Angela Knight, who has more recently been inflicted with my manuscripts. As she was one of the authors who inspired my original writing style, it is an honor to have her as a critique partner. I sort of keep pinching myself to make sure it's not a figment of my vivid imagination. Thank you both for giving me content insights that made this complex story a better book.

Readers are the gifts that keep giving throughout an author's career. I am thankful for all of mine, and want to mention some in particular who helped with this book:

Thank you to Judy and Lauren, who made sure this book was up to the standards my readers expect from me. I thank them also for invaluable proofing help.

Thank you to my readers on the JWH Connection fan forum for their musings and questions about Uthe and Keldwyn. You made me consider their relationship and world from different angles, which resulted in a richer story. I also wanted to note some specific contributions in that regard:

To Shi for the idea that led to Uthe's personal conflict in this story (no spoilers!). Her questions and comments on this topic took Night's Templar in an unexpected but exact right direction.

To Meki for the discussion of Sufi poetry that led to an exploration of the word *Yaar* and its multiple meanings.

To Alicia for the insights about and pictures of La Couvertoirade.

As always, any mistakes or flaws in this manuscript are entirely the fault of this author. Even after my proofers go through it, I'm usually still tweaking and massaging, therefore increasing the likelihood that some gaffes will still slip through. I hope nothing is so jarring that it distracts you from enjoying Keldwyn and Uthe's journey.

Finally, last but never least, to my husband. The decision to start self-publishing some of my titles was a way to diversify my offerings to my readers. However, I could not have taken that path without his willingness to work alongside me in this crazy career choice and take over the "publishing" end of things. In a very short time, he's come up to speed on all aspects of publishing, including cover design, as the gorgeous cover to this book attests. Yet another way he has demonstrated he is my tenacious partner on this life's journey. You're my heart, darling. Thank you!

Author's Note

In my research on the Templars, I found three different spellings for the name of the founder of the Order, Hugh of Payns. I chose to use Malcolm Barber's version, as he is considered one of the top authorities on the documented history of the Templar Order. I didn't want those of you who are used to a different spelling to think that I had it wrong (wink).

A note on the use of historic figures in my book, like Hugh of Payns, Grand Master Gerard de Ridefort and St. Bernard of Clairvaux. I'm always leery of making such people part of my story, especially if they're painted as a villain. As we all know, history is only as objective as the people who write and research it. On top of that, they're often basing their research on the accounts of historians who came before them. In short, documenting history is an enormous game of "grapevine", and it gets additionally twisted by politics, ignorance and carelessness.

So I apologize now to any of those "non-fiction" folk if I did you any injustice. In the end, my story is fiction, so I ask the reader to take whatever I've learned about these characters with a grain of salt. None of us really know if we're good guys or bad guys until we face the end—and most of the time we're usually something in between.

Bibliographic Note

In most of my research, three texts were cited as the guiding principles for the Templar Order. Since Uthe quotes from them in his story, I wanted to credit these specifically, though I'm grateful for all the scholars who have researched and documented this fascinating Order. Their sources were also invaluable in writing this book.

The Rule of the Templars : The French Text of the Rule of the Order of the Knights Templar (Translated and introduced by J.M. Upton-Ward, Boydell Press)

In Praise of the New Knighthood (De Laude novae militiae) by Bernard of Clairvaux (Translated by M. Conrad Greenia OCSO)

"The Letter of *Hugh peccator*" circa 1130 (author unknown)

Chapter One

"For a member of a species that considers itself superior to all others, you spend an inordinate amount of time on your knees."

"None are superior to God. And on one's knees is where salvation and answers are found," Uthe responded.

His tormentor shifted in front of him. Though his head was bowed and eyes closed, Uthe felt the shadow of his presence. Either the Fae Lord was trying to be as disruptive as possible, or he was blocking the view of the horizon, where the sun was seconds from making an appearance. Uthe could feel it, like the fires of Hell rising up to claim him.

He preferred to think Keldwyn's intent was to disturb his meditation, rather than shield him. The Fae being protective of him opened the door to thoughts Uthe didn't wish to have. What was behind that door already strained its hinges.

Why now? Why all of this now?

He banished that thought in a blink. One didn't question the Lord's designs and plan. One obeyed and served His Will.

"You are on your knees before me," Keldwyn pointed out.

"I am on my knees to God. You inserted yourself into the conversation. If there is justice, a lightning strike will reduce you to a smoking pile of fancy clothes by the time I open my eyes."

"I'm not certain if a lightning strike would be fatal to me," Keldwyn mused.

"If it was the hand of God, I'm certain it would be."

Keldwyn leaned over him, because silken strands of his long, thick hair brushed Uthe's neck. "I hate how you do this," the Fae said.

"No one asked you to watch." Uthe kept his own hair severely short, shearing it frequently. One of God's sheep.

"You know, Uthe is not really a name. It's a piece of a name, a connecting word, like 'the' or 'and.' Was it the noise your mother made when she pushed you out of the womb—oof—and the doctor misheard her?"

His mother. Uthe had never known her, though there was a time he'd wished he could lift the veils of his mind that hid the memory of being inside her. His father had never spoken of it, but Uthe was sure his sire had killed his human mother moments after his birth. He'd given Uthe first blood from his own vein.

He no longer wished for a memory of her. If a woman's emotions laced the womb of her growing child like the grasses of a bird's nest, his nest had been lined with terror, pain, despair. It had not been a place of safety or warmth, an echo of the Virgin Mary's love that St. Bernard had suggested was the resting place above all resting places.

There is no rest for the wicked.

He stiffened at that voice, smooth as a serpent's tongue. Concentrating so hard that perspiration trickled along his temple, he shut out the voices of the past, present, and his absurd future, to focus on the one thing that mattered. The sun crept out from the horizon, thinking itself a stealthy hunter. He was stealthier. The key was being alert to every passing second, every change in the air around him, in the feel of the earth below him.

Night's Templar

But what if he wasn't? He usually used Keldwyn's buzzing around him as a beneficial test of his discipline, but these unexpected thoughts of his past could throw him off. There were so many things the kiss of sunlight would end. His death would stop them before they could come to fruition, a deep relief. Yet his ease was not an option, since there was one vital thing his death would leave undone.

How much longer would it take? Will it be too late?

Keldwyn straightened. Uthe tried to ignore the featherlike retreat of his hair along his nape. It was only marginally less difficult to do that than to dispel the unsettling vision Keldwyn had planted in his head—Uthe kneeling before him.

So many secrets were bound inside Uthe, layered like fossils in the earth. It should hardly take any effort to conceal his reaction to being on his knees in front of the male who always smelled of autumn leaves and pale sunlight. Fall was a transition season, from the life and birth of spring to the death signified by winter, endings. How apt.

Now. The fingers of flame closed over his skin. As always, his heartbeat and adrenaline surged, trying to push him into headlong flight, a base survival instinct. He held fast, forcing himself to calm, even as his skin felt like it was about to erupt. Then he moved.

He sprang from the kneeling position and was running, his vampire speed making him all but invisible to the human eye. He pushed himself to the limits of his endurance and beyond, legs scissoring across the ground, arms pumping, every muscle rippling in smooth motion. Off of the grassy knoll, through the short stint of woods, then across the meadow. He thought he could detect Keldwyn's scent around him, but it was autumn here, so he told himself that was what he smelled.

The thundering of his heart was like horses' hooves in a Templar cavalry charge, sending up plumes of gritty sand while the bright sun blinded him. His hand light on the reins, sword tight in his hand. The fluttering snap of the black and white beauseant, the screams of the dying. The touch of a grateful pilgrim's hand on his calf...

By the time he reached the manicured lawn, Uthe felt like he was inside a ball of fire. He accepted and endured, never losing sight of his goal, never losing control. Only a matter of seconds between life and death. All the will of God.

He shot across the threshold of the side entrance to the Savannah estate. It was a stone structure appended to the main house, an enclosed rock patio that provided a pleasant place in summer for those who wanted to enjoy the view of the side lawn and the forest beyond it. It also had a trap door that led to the underground rooms housing guest vampires, like himself. As he fell back against the cool wall, which enclosed him in shadows, a shard of sunlight speared the ground at the archway like an enemy lance, falling just short of its mark. Uthe narrowed his eyes, watching the spread of the light. Vampires could see the individual motes, threads, bands and bars of sunlight in a way humans couldn't. It was a language a vampire couldn't read for long, though, unless he wanted to burn out his retinas. He averted his eyes.

Keldwyn was leaning against the stone wall to his right as if he'd been there all along, waiting for him. While the Fae Lord had an exceptional ability to blend into his environment, such that he could seem to appear or disappear at will, he was also capable of a swiftness that surpassed even a vampire's.

"Would you like me to open the trap door?" Keldwyn asked pleasantly, though there was a sharpness to his onyx eyes that reminded Uthe of the sun's threat to wrap him up in flame.

"If you are planning to stay on this side of it after it closes."

It was always safest to keep Keldwyn in his peripheral vision, because gazing directly upon the Fae Lord could be as hazardous as staring at the sun. During Council meetings, he usually eschewed his assigned seat, wandering through the spacious chamber as the meeting was conducted. Despite his restless behavior, they'd learned they had his full attention, for Keldwyn wouldn't hesitate to interject a pertinent comment when needed, whether it was while he sat on the edge of the koi pond with its gurgling fountain or from a perch on one of the crisscrossed ceiling beams.

His preferred spot, however, was the stretch of wall behind Uthe's chair. It was an unexpected choice. At social gatherings, a vampire's servant would stand behind their Mistress or Master. Uthe's third marked servant, Mariela, was a quiet presence behind him at such events. Even if he could not see her, he always had a connection to her mind. He had no such connection to Keldwyn, yet he was as aware of the Fae's presence behind him during Council meetings as he was of his own servant's breath and blood.

Keldwyn was no servant. Not even in Uthe's imaginings, though he'd tried once or twice to put him there, with some very disturbing results.

He'd learned to treat his growing reaction to the Fae Lord as another challenge to his discipline and resolve. He compartmentalized his response, handling it the way he handled Council business. Steady, thoughtful, with an eye to short and long term results. No anger, always calm. No harmful passions.

To test that discipline and resolve now—or so he told himself—Uthe looked directly toward his troublesome companion.

The male was a temptation to any species. Lord Keldwyn, liaison to the Seelie and Unseelie Courts, first ever Fae liaison with the Vampire Council, was of high Fae birth. Years of exposure to perpetual vampire beauty should have made Uthe immune to a handsome face, but a high Fae eclipsed even a vampire's appeal, because their beauty was mixed with an unearthly quality that was unsettling, dangerous, irresistible. Keldwyn's face and form were a blatant reason for every cautionary tale about crossing into the Fae world and never being heard from again.

His nose and cheekbones were like honed blades, his black hair thick as a curtain. It fell to his waist, tangling over his arms when loose. The pointed tips of his ears parted the flowing strands, though sometimes they were concealed, like when he leaned over a table to study a document, his long-fingered hands braced on the wooden surface. Or if he tilted his head up to look through the domed ceiling of the Council chambers to study the moon and stars through the skylight.

His body was just as distracting. Right now his arms were crossed over his chest, which was broad and well developed despite his lean form.

A reaction to physical features was mere lust, easily dismissed. It was the deeper qualities that he sensed in Keldwyn, elements eluding definition in his soul, which tangled up Uthe's mind. The only thing that should be indefinable—that *was* indefinable, he corrected himself— was God. Curiosity was not a sin, but when his interest in those qualities heightened his awareness of Keldwyn's physical features, then there was a problem.

The introduction of Keldwyn as liaison to the Vampire Council had been an historic moment between two species who were sworn enemies. Lady Lyssa, the current Council head and last of the vampire royalty, a Queen of the long vanished Far East clan, had made that possible due to her half-Fae blood. As her right hand on the Council, Uthe knew he would have the most interaction with the male, beyond the Fae Lord's relationship with Lyssa herself, but Keldwyn had taken a disconcertingly keen interest in Uthe from the beginning. At first, Uthe had been amused. Of late, it had become a challenge to the core of who he was. He wasn't sure of Keldwyn's intent. But then, that was the nature of the Fae. Elusive, hard to pin down.

Night's Templar

The thought produced an intriguing vision of pinning Keldwyn to a board like a butterfly by his stunning golden, red and yellow wings, which he mainly brought out for formal occasions, having the ability to summon or cloak them at will. Uthe thought of him like the surface of a lake, hinting at an array of concealed exotic wonders. All he had to do was step into the waters, let the cool currents take him forward, under...

"I should like to see your wings." He'd never seen them when they were alone, like this.

His own words startled him like the touch of electricity, for he'd had no intention of speaking them aloud. Where potential incineration by the sun couldn't rattle him, such a transgression sent his heart rate into a panicked sprint. Keldwyn's eyes narrowed. The irises were the color of onyx, but the sclera were vivid as the light of the moon, a glittering contrast. According to Lyssa, each Fae fell into the realm of an element and often a season. Keldwyn was most certainly of earth and autumn, his skin a light golden reflection of fall's melted afternoon sunlight.

"You have never asked anything of me, vampire. Except to go away."

"Perhaps I've decided a different tactic is necessary to accomplish that goal. I shall be just as annoying to you as you are to me."

A vampire's reflexes were keen, such that the slightest movement, even a breath, could draw his attention. So Uthe could have easily anticipated and drawn out of range when Keldwyn reached out. But he calculated a lack of reaction was safer, no matter what odd things it did to him inside as Keldwyn stroked long fingers along Uthe's short cap of dark hair. Once, a long time ago, it had been long, the dark brown reflecting sunlight in bronze strands.

"You have always worn it thus."

"A Templar does not adorn himself in flowing locks, or clothes of silk or velvet," Uthe said, deliberately sweeping his gaze over Keldwyn's appearance.

In contrast to Uthe's monochrome dark trousers and white tailored shirt, the cream-colored gossamer shirt the Fae wore had layers of ruffles down the front and billowing sleeves with draped cuffs. Lacings showed glimpses of his skin beneath the ruffles. The shirt was open at the throat. Keldwyn's lower body was clad in front flap brown trousers, laced on either side, the garment tight and thin enough to be considered hose or leggings. They displayed the musculature of haunch and leg well, until the snug hold of supple thigh-high boots took over, laced up the back and adorned with the faint impression of leaves. The style framed his groin conspicuously, for Fae males had little modesty about such things. It was clear he had a substantial enough cock to please a lover.

Kel made a noncommittal noise at Uthe's implied deprecation. He was using only his fingertips, yet every stroke sent a ripple of reaction along Uthe's scalp and down his spine, making his buttocks clench and his stomach coil. He hadn't reacted to touch, not without calculation, in a very long time. Since Keldwyn was demanding nothing of him, all it left him was the openness of feeling.

Keldwyn leaned closer, shifting along the wall. He appeared slim, but it was the svelteness of a cheetah. Power emanated from him, and it wasn't all from magic. When Kel wore a sleeveless jerkin on Savannah's hotter days, Uthe had been impressed by the carved musculature of his arms. Muscle mass didn't define the strength of a Fae, however, no more than it did a vampire. High Fae were more powerful than vampires, and that was before their magical abilities were called into play. Uthe had no doubt Keldwyn could pin him to the wall and hold him, though he was equally sure he could make it a difficult and interesting fight.

The startling lick of bloodlust that came from the thought warned him that he'd made the wrong move. Studied disinterest was the key to defeating Keldwyn's effect on him, and voicing a desire to see his wings was certainly contrary to that. But what was done was done.

Keldwyn's wings unfurled above his shoulders. At first, they looked like brown leaves that drifted to the ground in fall, edges curled, but as they spread out, the delicate inner web of veins was gold thread against smooth russet silk. Touches of red and yellow glittered among the gold, a melding of hues.

His shirt wasn't disturbed by the transformation. Managing the emergence of wings without disrupting one's wardrobe was a paltry magic to a Fae of Keldwyn's stature. Yet Uthe wondered at the texture of the wings. If he loosened the lacings, drew the shirt over his head, would the wings fold and twist like thick ribbons as the garment was pulled free of his body?

Uthe's gaze slid up to Keldwyn's. Keldwyn's breath was caressing his own parched mouth.

"You asked something of me, vampire. Now you give me something in return."

The Fae had very specific protocols on such things, not unlike vampires. Uthe would honor that protocol, prove he could do so with fixed control. Yet as Keldwyn drew ever closer, Uthe took in a breath a vampire didn't need. When Keldwyn's lips touched Uthe's, he stood firm. Though water surged up against a dam of feeling, he made the wall stand. He kept his eyes open, staring into Keldwyn's. As the tip of Keldwyn's tongue slid along a fang and the Fae male's hand curved behind his nape to hold him fast, he quivered, a heated breath escaping into Keldwyn's mouth.

"Kiss me back," the Fae said. "Or your selfishness will offend me."

Carefully measured offense wasn't a bad strategy. It might dissuade Keldwyn from this inexplicable obsession he had with Uthe. Yet Uthe couldn't bring himself to deny the Fae, and it wasn't because of the critical need to maintain good relations with the Fae world.

He didn't move his mouth, too much risk there, but he

slid a hand over Keldwyn's upper arm, the taut biceps beneath silken fabric. He tunneled his fingers under the waterfall of shining black hair covering it. Softer than an animal's pelt, even thicker than Mariela's blonde hair. A vampire's beauty wasn't random; it was a predator's tool. While Fae didn't need to attract prey with their beauty, Uthe was sure Keldwyn's allure held even more risks than that of his own kind. A human might walk away from a vampire's touch, disoriented and weak from blood loss, but his soul would be intact. With Keldwyn, he wasn't so sure his own was as safe.

He became even more aware of the blood rushing through Keldwyn's body, the pumping artery at his throat. He wondered how a pure Fae's blood would taste.

If he was having such thoughts, he was hungry. His fingers were tangling in Keldwyn's hair, grip tightening on his arm, and his fangs were starting to lengthen. He needed to get to his chambers, summon Mariela to him to break his usual three-day fast between feedings.

Keldwyn drew back, hand moving to Uthe's shoulder. He had a silver and gold ring on his forefinger. The oblong amber stone in the setting had a curled rose petal captured in its depths. The petal was a dark blood red. Would his blood be the same color?

"You are intelligent and insightful," Keldwyn said. "Generous with your knowledge and advice, a male valued by your queen and the rest of the Council. Despite that, you keep all at arm's length. Yet today you have left a door unlocked you always guard so zealously. What has changed?"

Uthe jerked back. Keldwyn's expression flickered at the abrupt motion, but Uthe stepped away from him, moving to the trap door and lifting it on smooth hinges. This time when he met the Fae's gaze, his own was courteous and remote. "You are the liaison between our two species, Lord Keldwyn. Despite your own considerable ability to mask your intentions, I know that relationship matters to you.

The Fae pastime of uncovering and twisting vulnerabilities for idle amusement should be subordinate to that charge. If your current intentions lie beyond our chess games and friendly debates, I would ask you to leave me in peace when Council business does not require contact between us."

It was a gracious nod to his own blame for the current situation. Over the past few months, he'd fallen into the habit of enjoying the Fae's company for meals, for debates of theology and philosophy, and the sharing of all kinds of books. It was a challenge not to reveal too much of himself during those discussions, but in that, Uthe was well-practiced. Even if the Fae was far more clever than most he usually had to fend off.

It had started with the best of intentions. Though the Rule, the guiding principles for the Templar Order, counseled silence with the admonition, "To talk too much is not without sin," it also acknowledged the importance of wisely chosen words: "Life and death are in the power of the tongue." He'd justified talking to Keldwyn as the requirements of his office, to learn more about the Fae. When he'd found Keldwyn a stimulating and interesting companion, Uthe had recalled the additional warning that the Devil had a way of inserting himself into the best intentions.

The Fae was even more of a risk to his senses in potent silence. Keldwyn had asked Uthe about Templar practices he still observed. When there was no business to be conducted and he had a rare night to himself, Uthe embraced the habitual silence from evening compline to early morning matins. One far too memorable night, Keldwyn had observed the practice with him. He'd stayed with Uthe through his meditation and prayer, and had walked the forest with him, all in silence.

The Fae explored many things about the vampire world to increase his understanding of it. Through their discussions, Uthe knew Keldwyn had done similar things to understand other species he'd encountered through the years. He might have observed the evening silence with Uthe to get a better grasp of the Templar history and culture, because the Fae had that kind of keen, inquisitive mind. He was an interesting mix of scholar, tactician and warrior. However, when Uthe made the mistake of asking Keldwyn if that was his intent, Keldwyn merely said, "It teaches me more about you, my lord."

They also played chess and a variety of strategy games. Uthe taught Keldwyn those he'd learned over the years, Keldwyn offering up those played in the Fae world. *Merelle*, one of the few games the Templars had been permitted to play, didn't differ much from what Kel called *shigreni*. They both preferred chess, a game the Rule had forbidden, but chess between him and Keldwyn was far less likely to involve wagering or result in a fist fight. Sometimes they played the Fae version of it, *juste*.

Keldwyn had just pointed out why it was important to bring those seemingly innocuous pastimes to an end. They'd increased Uthe's pleasure in his proximity and resulted in this. Now, instead of merely imagining it, Uthe possessed the actual memory of the male's lips on his, the tease of his tongue. The unwelcome tightness to his loins was something he'd need Mariela to assuage with her lovely mouth so he didn't make an even greater transgression on his oath than her ministrations would be.

Non nobis sed nomini tuo da gloriam. Not to us but to Thy Name give the glory. Including the glory of maintaining a sacrosanct oath. Once he lived long enough, a man realized that his determination to honor an oath could turn into the sin of pride, especially if the oath became more important than the ultimate good he was supposed to be serving. Yet Uthe knew the difference between dispensations on the chastity oath to maintain his commitment to his primary charge, and rationalizations that allowed him to indulge in forbidden pleasure. Keldwyn was definitely a forbidden pleasure.

Uthe descended the curved stone stairwell, the door closing on silent hinges above him. He ducked and spun, bringing up his fist as a shadow swooped upon him, but it captured the fist, twisted it and shoved him against the wall. The stone scraped his cheek, taking skin so he left a smear of blood there. Uthe forced himself backwards in the narrow corridor, slamming Keldwyn against the wall behind him. They tumbled down the remaining stairs. He was back on his feet in an instant, but by the time he pivoted, Keldwyn had him again. He still had his wings out, which was a mistake. Uthe caught the edge of one, intending to tear it off if necessary.

He had time to register it was far more substantial than he'd expected, thick and resilient as a leather cloak, before a current rocketed through him. It illuminated the stairwell, making Keldwyn's dark eyes flash. The jolt yanked every nerve ending so hard Uthe thought they'd pierced his skin, and his muscles knotted in painful reaction. When it passed, Uthe was lying on the steps, the stone edges pressing into his shoulder blades and buttocks. His fist gripped the front of Keldwyn's shirt, his other wrist pinned to the stairs as Keldwyn leaned over him, body pressed against Uthe's chest and hip.

Uthe bit back a groan as Keldwyn completed the motion so he lay upon him, groin to groin. Keldwyn's knees pressed into the step below Uthe's hips, the Fae's body inserted between his legs. Keldwyn's noticeable assets had grown in size, his erection now insinuated against Uthe's cock, which refused his discipline. It was twitching to an even fuller size against Keldwyn's friction.

"You frustrate me," Keldwyn said pleasantly.

Uthe took that for the threat it was. He curled his lip, showing the tips of his fangs. "Is this about a sexual conquest, my lord? Will taking a Council member satisfy your need to feel superior to all of us?"

Keldwyn's eyes glowed in the dark. "I seek a true kiss

from your mouth, Lord Uthe. The kiss you actually want to give me, not the one you permitted yourself to offer. I want inside that open door."

"You have no right to that."

"If you use that cold, courteous tone on me once more, you will offend me beyond where your God can help you." Power rippled through the Fae's body, forced so intimately against Uthe's.

Uthe wasn't the strongest vampire on the Council, but he knew he was among the top five of his species. As such, power games didn't come into play for him the way they once had. It had been a while since he'd received a challenge for dominance from another. And while that kind of challenge from another vampire always had a sexual component, dominance meant a great many other things in the vampire world. To Keldwyn, too, he expected, based on what he'd sensed about Keldwyn's sexual orientation for some time. Which was why Uthe had initially thought he'd have no trouble resisting him.

He had no room for any of this, particularly in his current circumstances. Yet an alarming part of him didn't care. It needed to give, to break loose. God help him. No, he was being weak. This wasn't something with which God should have to help him. Never before, not until recently. He'd always been able to manage it. But...

With a snarl that echoed through the stone stairwell in hollow mockery, Uthe broke open a valve in the dam. The rush was sweet, icy cold, bringing pain and the desire for more. He thrust both hands into Keldwyn's hair, lifted up off the stone and crushed his mouth against Keldwyn's, tasting the heat of his lips, the moist slickness of his tongue. He inhaled the base scent of him, something indescribable, something not of Uthe's own world, yet still vaguely familiar. Perilously familiar.

Since when it came to sex, a vampire's nature was unquestionably all about dominance, he obeyed the charge now, rolling them so he was on top. Keldwyn allowed it, though Uthe knew the Fae's strength could have denied him. The male's hands left a trail of heat over his shoulders, his back, over his hips, long fingers gripping Uthe's buttocks. The sensation brought indescribable pleasure. When Uthe thrust his cock more firmly against Keldwyn's, the shudder of desire through Keldwyn's lean, beautiful body was a garden of temptations.

A garden he could not visit. Riding desperation, Uthe took control in a very uncontrolled way. He let his fangs lengthen and slashed Keldwyn's tongue, his succulent bottom lip.

Keldwyn's reaction was violent enough to lift Uthe off him and catapult him into the wall, slamming the back of his skull into the unyielding surface. It was a good thing the wall was stone; else he'd be explaining the need for repairs to Lady Lyssa. He bounced off the bone jarring surface and landed on his feet, but the close call with unconsciousness meant it took him a second to acknowledge his feet were braced, one on a higher step, another on the lower. He had his hand tented against the rock to give him a necessary third balancing point.

As he'd intended, there was no more need for physical combat. Keldwyn's wings had disappeared and he was standing several steps above Uthe, staring down at him with angry dark eyes.

Fae considered themselves vastly superior to vampires. While they obviously weren't averse to fornicating with one, Uthe knew there was a hard and fast line on the feeding issue. Being a vampire's food was a reprehensible degradation to them.

"If you can't handle the consequences of a vampire's kiss, then I expect you should stick with your kind, Lord Keldwyn," Uthe said, wiping the smear of blood off his mouth with the back of his hand, resisting the desire to lick it off. Even though Keldwyn was difficult to predict on his most congenial days, Uthe suspected he'd consider this incident a personal affront, not a diplomatic catastrophe.

But he wouldn't push it or add to the insult by tasting his blood in front of him.

Regret speared him at having to take such an extreme tactic to dissuade Keldwyn. While he didn't trust the Fae, he respected him and, yes, even had an affection for him he couldn't deny. Keldwyn might be frustrated by Uthe's control, his courteous tone, but Uthe wondered how he'd react if he knew how Uthe himself felt stifled by it these days, in ways that disturbed him down to his soul. If only Keldwyn would back off. He needed to quit trying to corner Uthe with emotions Uthe couldn't afford, now more than ever.

The reasons for that were more important than even the relationship between Fae and Council, though Uthe might be the only one in the world who knew it. Maybe Uthe should have licked the blood off his hand. The brief taste he'd had was an intriguing mix, like lightning and sweet honey, tinged with chocolate. It had been an echo of what he'd felt when he'd done the live wire grab of Keldwyn's wing.

"I will see you at the Council meeting at nightfall," Keldwyn said. In a blink, his expression had returned to dispassionate indifference. He was like a statue whose perfection could compel every eye in the room, but who gave nothing back to honor that regard, because a statue was too remote to respond to the desires of others.

Though Uthe knew himself to be far from such perfection, he understood that feeling. He gave Keldwyn a courteous bow, his own mask back in place.

"So be it, my lord."

Chapter Two

As Uthe strode down the hall to his sleeping quarters, he fought the needs of his own body, but he already knew he wasn't going to win. He was aroused, flushed with heat, and his fangs had no desire to retract, his blood lust fully provoked. He'd learned to accept his weaknesses, manage them with control and denial as much as he could, but Keldwyn was just too much to be denied.

Mariela, I have need of you before I sleep.
Yes, my lord. I am already here.

Of course she was. Unless he told her otherwise, she always came to his room at dawn in case he needed blood. Six feet tall, built with the curves of a goddess and the strength of an Amazon, she was an intelligent, warm and steady servant, offering him everything he needed from her, yet never asking for more than he could give. If he'd ever sensed otherwise, he would have had Lyssa re-assign the Inherited Servant to another Council member. He had no desire to bring her pain. She'd given him too much to hurt her so carelessly.

Yet today he needed more from her than he usually demanded.

I want you undressed when I get there, Mariela. He wanted to feel her skin under his hands, see her body vulnerable to him. *His.*

Blessed Virgin. He stopped himself in the hallway, despite the protest of his dual hungers. He could do better than this. He usually did. But lately... His jaw firmed. Damn his soul to Hell, he had to do what he had to do, and these arguments with his conscience were pointless. The Templar vow of chastity had always been something different for him, far more in keeping with the spiritual meaning than the functional one. *Keep your intentions pure, so that you may stand in the light of the Lord...*

The tenets of the Cistercian Order had guided much of the Templar Rule, thanks to St. Bernard, one of the original authors, being a member of that Order. Uthe recalled the words of Guerric of Igny on poverty: "...truly blessed poverty of spirit is to be found more in humility of heart than in a mere privation of everyday possessions, and it consists more in the renunciation of pride than in a mere contempt for property. Sometimes it might be useful to own things..."

He wondered what Guerric would think of his words being applied to a vampire's carnal needs, or the ownership of a third marked servant's soul.

All Council guest rooms were suites, with kitchenette, bathroom, bedroom, living room. His had little in it beyond the provided furnishings, his small collection of books and a locked chest of belongings. His few items of clothing were solid black, white or brown. The garments had simple lines, but the tailoring and fabric were excellent quality. Despite their lack of ostentation, they ensured he represented his position on Council appropriately. Due to the conscientious care they received from Mariela, they did not require replacement often.

On the dresser next to his bed, seven candles were lined up on a silver tray. When he retired for the day, Mariela would light one of them, and it would burn until sundown. Its sputtering was his nightly alarm clock.

She'd turned down his bed and laid his nightclothes on

the foot, a T-shirt and cotton drawstring pants. In accordance to the Rule, he always slept dressed. Mariela knelt at the foot of the bed. She'd unwrapped her long blonde hair, which she usually kept plaited, and it was falling over her bare shoulders. He paused beside her, put his hand upon it. Soft and thick, not as silky as Keldwyn's, but still pleasing. He trailed his fingertips down the curve of her spine, watched her shudder at his touch. The mark that indicated her link to him cut a diagonal track across the firm flesh between her left shoulder blade and hip bone. It looked like a spear, tipped like an arrow but with no feathered fletching.

The shape of the mark that appeared during the third mark binding was not dictated by the vampire, but by Powers beyond understanding. He understood the message in that mark, though, and had always been grateful for the reminder, especially on a night like tonight.

He could be inside her heart, mind and soul to whatever depth he chose. There was no place for a servant to hide from her vampire, inside or out. The bond was absolute, which was why one of the few vampire laws to protect servants required that a human's decision to become a servant must be a willing one. Enforcement of that was too lax for Randoms, those servants chosen by vampires from adult humans who weren't part of the Inherited Servant program. However, the issue didn't exist for an InhServ like Mariela. She and those like her were raised from the age of six to serve vampire masters or mistresses. The children were provided by human families who had generational ties to the vampire world, reminiscent of feudal loyalty to liege lords.

As he touched her, he saw the curiosity in Mariela's mind, a pleased surprise. He didn't often engage in a drifting caress like this, exploring her lovely skin. In the twelve years he'd had her service, he'd never even shared a bed with her. But he looked after her well-being, made sure she was honored by his protection and care as her service deserved. He permitted her to have human lovers if she desired them, and so he knew she had an ongoing arrangement with Torrence, Lady Helga's servant. He also gave her several vacations each year. Though he always had to order her from his side for the prescribed time, he knew she benefitted from those respites from the demands of being a Council member's servant.

As his fingers trailed downward, she anticipated his desires and moved from her knees to all fours, lifting her ass to accommodate his touch there. Curious at his own reaction, he traced the seam of her buttocks to her cunt, stroking as she opened her knees wider. Her lips were slick, ready for him. Inherited Servants were trained extensively in sexual arts. She'd likely become aroused when he'd ordered her to get undressed, or even before that. She was schooled to stay in a state of readiness.

He respected their dedication to the demands of their order, which resulted in a deserved pride in the skills they honed. Yet it was balanced with their steadfast humility, their joy in serving their Masters and Mistresses, however was required.

As a Templar Knight, he understood that dichotomy well.

He was taking too much pleasure in this. He should open his trousers and take her quickly, empty his seed and relieve the pressure in his cock and balls, currently intense enough to beat on the back of his brain. Then he could give her a prolonged and intense climax with his fingers or mouth, a reward for her devotion that allowed him to stay emotionally in control but not unkindly detached.

An image flashed through his mind. Keldwyn on all fours beneath him, naked and savage. That slim, taut ass waiting to be penetrated, the male's head turned, those glittering eyes focused on him. Strands of dark hair would spill forward to tease his knife blade cheek, his sinfully tempting lips.

That scenario was even more improbable than the Fae

allowing Uthe to take his blood. Uthe thought of Keldwyn's attack in the stairwell, the way he'd pinned Uthe against the wall, holding him fast, proving his ability to overpower him. His palm had been hard on Uthe's chest, his other one spread over his throat. He could almost feel Keldwyn's nails digging into the arteries, constricting the flow of Uthe's blood.

Mariela gasped as he dropped to a knee behind her, snaked his arm across her chest and brought her up against him, so forcefully he had her body arched and her knees off the floor. She had to rely on him to hold her upright. Fisting his hand in her hair, he pulled it out of his way and sank his fully lengthened fangs into her throat. As she let out a startled cry, a growl rumbled from him.

The sound, the act, was so unlike himself, it should have shocked him. It might later, but now he unleashed his hunger. Despite her initial shock, Mariela had caught up with him, swaying with the vibrations of his body. Her hand dropped, curved over his thigh. He could have forbidden her touch, but when her fingers convulsed, a physical reaction to the rush of responses in her mind—that sweet taste of fear a vampire enjoyed, coupled to her intense pleasure at serving him in this way, her willing surrender to him no matter what—he wanted to feel the pressure of her fingers. He wanted to feel openly, no restrictions, no safeguards.

The kiss you really wanted to give me...

Whereas vampires were all natural sexual Dominants, the Fae were more like humans. A Fae might be Dominant or submissive or neither, according to their desires. Yet Uthe had known from the beginning Keldwyn was pure Dominant, in, out or across species. That awareness made something tremble deep inside Uthe now, thinking of the male's mouth so close to his, that unveiled threat.

If you use that courteous tone on me once more...

He understood the danger of locking down impulses too long. It was why he had made the concessions he'd made over the centuries. It had worked, for so very long. The knowledge of why it wasn't doing so now was a barb in his gut, a weight on his shoulders. He was an exceptionally intelligent male, yet that would mean nothing in the end. It made him so angry, and yet anger wasn't an option. He was supposed to accept any contingency, be prepared to surrender all.

As his fingers tightened on her throat, Uthe realized he was cutting off his servant's air. He couldn't kill her this way, but he could render her unconscious, causing her the wrong kind of discomfort. He eased the touch with effort, but the blood was leveling him out. Sweet Mariela's blood, so rich and pure.

As he let his fangs retract, he shifted and lifted her in his arms, something he also rarely did. After a hesitation, she curled her arms around his shoulders. She was a tall woman, built strong, but he was far more powerful. Feeling her arms around him made him lay his temple against hers. He drew in a steadying breath, her female scent.

Bernard of Clairvaux, who had endorsed the Templar Order and given it momentum, had revered the Virgin Mary. That reverence gave the Templars leeway to embrace her nurturing power and strength, though their Rule forbade them to kiss women, even their own mothers or sisters.

His lips curved at the thought as he pressed a kiss to Mariela's forehead. He laid her on his bed, her knees bent over the edge, and stood above her, studying her naked body. Her brown eyes flickered up to his face, then down again, awaiting his desires. He didn't typically forbid her to speak until spoken to, but he could tell she thought herself in uncharted waters right now.

It was further evidence of what Keldwyn had said, about how Uthe held himself away from everyone. Yet for good reason. Reminding himself of that, he took a settling breath. Laying a hand on either pale thigh, he knelt between her dangling feet.

Night's Templar

"How was your day, my dearest servant?" It was how he greeted her every sunrise.

She propped herself up on her elbows and smiled tentatively before she responded in her usual way. Sincerely. "It was a blessing, my lord. Every day I am yours is. May I...please you?"

In her mind, he saw she wondered if he would reverse their positions, put her mouth to use on his cock. It was the usual way he availed himself of her sexual charms, and even that not nearly as often as other vampires did. He was able to stave off the relentless vampire sex drive with the act once or twice a week. Most vampires craved sexual release almost more than they craved blood. He was no exception, but abstinence was a discipline. Constant practice helped, but "practice makes perfect" was never going to apply to a vampire. He'd learned to accept that, as he'd learned to accept many things, to fulfill his role in his strange straddling of multiple worlds. He'd learned to indulge in a controlled manner.

That control, maintained by countless paternosters and other types of penance, returned him to the center line of the road each time. However, maybe that success was because he'd never been knocked all the way off the road and into the weeds by a desire for someone in particular. He thought of Keldwyn's taste on his lips, the primal need that had gripped and led him to take his own servant's blood so passionately.

"You never do anything but please me," he answered her. "I want you to lie back."

She obeyed, with that lovely little trembling. Even after twelve years, she was affected by his touch and demands. Yes, it was InhServ training, but the remarkable thing about that training was that the reaction was genuine. An InhServ like Mariela desired to serve her vampire, and every option he gave her to do so was welcomed with enthusiasm and fervent pleasure.

A shadow darkened that thought as he recalled Alanna,

an InhServ who'd been bound to a treasonous Council Member. Thanks to the scientific prowess of Lord Brian, they'd been able to separate her from her Master before he was executed, but the girl had been tortured almost to the point of madness before it happened. As he thought of anyone doing such a thing to Mariela, his bloodlust rekindled.

Lord Mason had proposed a policy to grant more protections to servants. It was the first to address the welfare of servants in decades, introduced by Mason as a result of how his own servant, Jessica, had come to him, a story even more horrific than Alanna's.

Uthe had always been ambivalent about vampire-servant issues, because the structure of the relationship had been in place for a long time, and had proven more beneficial than catastrophic. He wasn't inclined to endorse new policies based on the needs of an exceptional few cases. Reactionary legislation only overloaded a governing body, and the Council had far more pressing issues that affected the majority of vampires. Yet when Alanna had been brought before them, nearly broken in mind and body, but still doing everything she could to serve the Council, he couldn't help but respond to her courage and loyalty. If she'd been a Templar Knight, she'd have never left the field of battle.

Fortunately, she had a far better Master now. The highly trained echelon of the servant class were usually given to powerfully placed vampires, but because of the extenuating circumstances, the Council had made an exception. She'd been allowed to stay with the vampire who'd protected her while her Master was being hunted down. Evan was an artist, with no political standing at all, yet he had recognizable potential. He also had the patronage of the Council, because Uthe had sired him when Evan was a nineteen-year-old dying human.

People, vampires, Fae...they could all become something different and unexpected when needed, couldn't they?

If he was thinking of Council business, his meal had achieved the desired effect, restoring his control. He gazed down at Mariela, enjoying the view, fondling her white thighs as he collected his thoughts. Perhaps he'd been hungrier than he expected, suggesting he needed to start feeding more often. Another voice interrupted his sudden tension.

A missive is coming. Are you ready to sever all ties, if that is what God demands? Go beyond the things you know, back to that which you once knew...

This voice was filled with God's purpose, no serpent's smoothness. The gravelly throat had been burned by the heat of the desert and the stress of God's might. Uthe always respected that voice, prayed for its owner, but that message, with only slightly different words, had come to him repeatedly over the decades. Right on cue, the seductive voice came in right behind it to mock.

Like Armageddon, Madman. Everyone is sure of its coming, but does not even your own revered text say no one will know the time? Stop your raving. You're giving me a headache and making me wish for the End of Days in truth.

That voice might personify evil, but he had wit. Uthe shook his head, offering a respectful prayer to the bearer of the first voice before he attended to his present task. He'd learned to not be distracted by those voices, though it had taken several decades to learn the way of it so he didn't appear like a madman himself. Vampires couldn't afford to appear weak in mind or body.

He staved off his worries about that, about the missive never coming, about a whole basket of things he couldn't control. *Trust in God's will. And celebrate the beauty of His creation, spread before you now.*

Mariela arched into his touch as he leaned forward, placed his lips on her sweet cunt and tasted the honey there. He'd read her desires from her mind and body, and take her to the pinnacle he wanted to see her reach. Whenever his heart was raw or his mind uneasy, immersing himself in giving rather than taking restored them. He could spend a sleepless day in a prayer vigil, work out a Council problem...or give his servant mindless pleasure.

As Mariela began to writhe under his ministrations, he clamped his hands around her thighs, holding her still, driving her ever higher by denying her a climax until she couldn't hold back her begging cries. Sometimes giving could be a sharply sweet taking.

Come for your Master, Mariela.

She obeyed with vigor, her lovely nipples tight and dark rose, her stomach and thighs taut with her response, her sex suddenly dewed with moisture within and without. He brought her down with gentle licks, a few nips that had her shuddering. A whisper of a smile crossed her pale pink lips at his teasing. Her hand moved toward him, but he closed his around her wrist, kissing her palm before she could touch his head as Keldwyn had done.

Rising over her, he stripped off his clothes. He could have resolved the issue with his hand at this point, but bringing her to climax wasn't what gave an InhServ true contentment.

Taking a seat on the bed, he directed her to her knees on the floor between his feet. *Service your Master, Mariela. Bring him ease.*

He closed his eyes as Mariela's soft hands slid up his thighs, her mouth closing on the head of his cock. As he moved his grip to her hair, he tried not to think of dark tresses or a male's firm mouth sucking him the way she was doing it now, but he knew some fantasizing was necessary to reach climax. It wasn't essential to think of that particular male, but his mind was giving him no choice. He supposed that was fine. There was no universe other than the one in his imagination where a Fae would kneel at his feet and suck his cock. He envisioned

Keldwyn's reaction to the fantasy. All that fine black hair would stand on end, wouldn't it? What would Kel's retribution be for such an outrageous insult?

His cock got harder, his fingers constricting on Mariela. She made a noise of encouragement in her throat, her clever mouth driving him even higher.

What was the Fae's end game with Uthe? There was no end game. There never was with the Fae. It was all about the game itself. Uthe should be far beyond such games.

Mariela nipped him and he let out a breath. "You seek punishment."

He would give it to her, because he never left her aching or wanting. It was an attempt to make up for all the things he couldn't give her. Like his body inside her, his seed. It had been some time since he'd actually joined with another.

Damn Keldwyn for making him miss that. Damn Fae.

§

Evil cannot be destroyed. It will always resurface, a root that runs deep beneath the earth. Even if you kill the plant, it will sprout elsewhere. Whereas Good is like the plucked flower. There are endless flowers, yes, but so fragile, so temporal. Why do you think He made it that way? Why do you think your religions exhort you not to ask why? Never question, only serve...

A bouquet of flowers. She'd plucked them from around the front door, as far as her chains would allow her to reach. She'd been thinking...what had she been thinking? That she wanted to summon something of who she'd been. An appreciation for beauty might balance the horror that had happened to her. As she sat at the table, watching the flowers, her hand on her swelling belly, Uthe could feel the pressure of her hand. Through the cushion of her nourishment, the liquid of her womb, he tried to put his hand up, touch hers.

Flowers, scattered over a table. Washed with blood.

Uthe surfaced, the wooden dagger beneath his pillow tight in his grip. The candle had just stuttered out, for he could still smell the smoke, the faint scent of the wax. It was sundown.

My lord? You are well?

Mariela was kneeling on the floor, for she started his night the same way she ended it. There was a touch of concern to her mind-voice.

"Of course." He put his feet on the floor, scrubbed a hand over his face and gave her an absent smile. "Go see to your household duties, Mariela. Tonight will be busy for all of us. I will meet you in Council chambers. They are requiring the presence of our servants to discuss the arrival of Queen Rhoswen."

Had that been part of what had driven Keldwyn's own thrumming energy to such an edge yesterday? Knowing that tonight the Unseelie Queen was coming to the human world for the very first time in years?

Those in her entourage would be the oldest and strongest of the Fae, for politics and appearance. Though younger Fae were quickly drained of energy by too much concrete, iron and other trappings of the human world, the Council's headquarters outside Savannah had plenty of undeveloped woodland and marsh property. Nearly a thousand acres of it cushioned the mansion, the driveway a winding mile from the closest rural road. The surrounding forest contained a portal between the Fae world and the human one, so that was where the receiving ceremony would be. There'd be a short honorary meeting in the Council chamber, followed by a soiree in the grand ballroom. A few carefully chosen vampires, beyond Council members and their servants, would attend.

The current Queen of the Unseelie Fae was Lyssa's half-sister, so the sisters would take some private time together after that before the Fae Queen returned to her world.

There was no official business planned for this visit, but

it was an important one. Lyssa had indicated a planned lack of controversy and her familial connection with the Queen were no guarantee things couldn't go to hell in a blink. The Fae had done their best to murder Lyssa's vampire mother after Rhoswen's Fae father impregnated her. He'd been turned into a rose bush and banished into a wasteland for fraternizing with their species. Though that had been over a thousand years ago, relations between the Fae and vampire had advanced very little until recently.

As one of the humans might say, today would require everyone's "A-game."

Given that, Uthe decided to start the evening with a short but intense workout. Since their hierarchical world was unapologetically built on the idea that might made right, all vampires set aside time to keep battle skills sharp. Normally he might have engaged Lord Belizar for a sparring match, because the two were well matched in weight, height and weapons use, but he wasn't ready to be around any other members of Council after that disturbing dream. Plus, Belizar would want to dissect the latest Council decisions in his gruff, heavy-handed way, and Uthe wasn't in the mood for that.

Opening his chest, Uthe chose the sword he'd carried centuries ago. He needed the closer connection to his past tonight.

The marsh side of the house had a quiet courtyard with enough space for sparring maneuvers. When he was relieved not to meet anyone along the way who would engage him in conversation, he realized how much he needed the exertion to steady his mind. There were more second mark servants on the grounds right now, but though they offered him a respectful nod and bow as he passed, they would not speak unless he engaged them. From their harried expressions and quick steps, they were occupied with preparing the estate to Lady Lyssa's specifications. All surfaces gleamed with cleanliness, and fresh flowers were arranged. No risk of offending the Fae

Queen was too small to be overlooked.

"If you think I am easily insulted, you have not met my sister." Uthe had overheard Lyssa say that to the small army of servants she'd addressed earlier in the week. She'd then turned them over for more detailed instructions to Jacob, her own servant, and Elijah Ingram, a second mark who had majordomo responsibilities for all her properties.

Uthe smiled a little. Lady Lyssa had always had a dry sense of humor, but it had become a little easier of late. Much of that had to do with her relationship with Jacob, and the birth of their son, Kane. Uthe could not deny it. Vampires and servants. He thought again of Mason's proposed policy, but today other things would take priority, which suited him fine. Complex problems needed time and study to determine the most sensible decision, not the most politic one.

Once he reached the courtyard, he started as he always did, on one knee, offering a quick prayer for his training to serve the Lord's purpose. Then he launched into the exercises. After so many years, he had no problem imagining his opponent's possible strikes and going through the stances. The blades were old-fashioned weapons, but training and a vampire's speed and strength made them formidable still. The swords the Crusaders had brought initially from France were not as well-tempered and balanced as Saracen blades, but the knights had learned from their metalworking skills. Though he could have upgraded to even more modern versions of those now, Uthe practiced with these blades for different reasons—to remind him of his purpose, who he was.

He pushed himself, but never lost an awareness of his immediate surroundings, because a vampire who did that didn't live long. Hearing the whisper of air over a weapon not his own, he spun, and his sword met the edge of Daegan Rei's katana. The chime of the two blades echoed as he held the stance. Daegan did the same, a warrior's greeting he reinforced with an approving look. Uthe knew the Council's enforcer was lethal and near invincible with that Japanese weapon, so he'd measured his stroke to match Uthe's. He didn't take it as an insult, but as a sign of respect.

Daegan let his blade slide free and backed up a step, though he kept a sparring position. "May I help you with your workout, my lord?" he asked.

Uthe's vampire senses told him that Gideon, Daegan's third mark, was with him. The muscular, sharp-eyed male shifted into his peripheral vision, confirming it. Anwyn, the other vampire of their threesome, was not, but both males bore her fragrant scent, suggesting they'd left her bed only recently. Since she was still a fledgling, she would stay below ground until full dark around nine p.m., but Uthe was certain one or both males was monitoring her wellbeing. Gideon could do it with his third mark connection to her, whereas Daegan could use the blood link he'd chosen to have with her, or the access that the two of them sharing Gideon gave him.

Even at the Savannah estate, one of the safest locales against outside attack, they wouldn't relax their vigilance. Vampires rarely trusted one another fully, but in addition to that, Gideon was a former vampire hunter, and Daegan was the Council's executioner for vampires who'd overstepped their laws one too many time. Alertness was a more comfortable state for both of them. Plus, there was very little they valued as much as the lovely sable-haired woman who'd been forcibly turned by a rogue vampire.

Anwyn had been and still was owner of Club Atlantis, a BDSM establishment in Atlanta. When the Mistress became a vampire, her Dominant streak had simply been enhanced, but she and Daegan did not share Gideon as equals. There was no such thing as equal partners in the vampire world. One was always top. In their case, there was no question it was Daegan. Out of all the vampires in their world who could challenge Lyssa's strength, Daegan would have been one of them, with Mason following a close second. Fortunately, both were loyal to her, as was Uthe. She deserved their loyalty on every level. It also didn't hurt that Jacob, Lyssa's servant, was Gideon's brother. Two former vampire hunters serving as servants, one to the head of the Vampire Council, and the other to their assassin. The world was an unpredictable place.

He brought his mind back to Daegan's offer to spar. "I fear this old vampire would be a poor match for your skills, Lord Daegan."

"Then I will be happy to improve yours to ensure you stay ahead of danger, my lord. Your counsel is worth ten vampires with my fighting skills."

"Well spoken." Uthe signaled his intent, and re-engaged. He didn't try to challenge Daegan's far greater skill; he merely worked on his own and let the male adjust as needed to push him a little harder, a little further. Blessed Virgin, they should have the male train all their vampires to fight.

It was difficult not to get distracted by the smooth, deadly grace of his opponent. Daegan was tall and compact, every muscle honed in the service of his assigned role. He'd worn his hair almost as short as Uthe's for some time, but since Anwyn had become a vampire, he'd let it grow so it feathered across his brow and had some silky thickness to the short layers. Uthe thought of Keldwyn's hair tangling in his hands, and how much he liked its length. He almost missed Daegan's next counter, and increased his speed and deftness to catch back up.

Daegan slipped back in and out, swift and flashing like a needle through fabric. Uthe didn't think, just parried and responded with more elaborate footwork, faster jabs and arcs from his own blade. The flicker in Daegan's eyes gave Uthe a quick jolt of reminder, but the reminder was too late. Daegan lifted his blade, a formal request for a pause, and stepped back. "My lord Uthe, I would ask a favor."

Uthe put the tip of his blade to the ground, folding his fingers over the pommel. If he closed his eyes, he could imagine the weight of his mail, the ripple of the tunic over it as a desert breeze touched him. He jerked himself out of the memory, recognizing it for the danger it was. "Any favor within my power to grant you is yours, my lord."

"Do not hold back. Show me your true skill set, so I don't waste your time offering you guidance you don't need."

Uthe noted Gideon's face remained impassive, but the servant's midnight blue eyes had been tracking him as closely. While Gideon's preferred fighting technique was blunt force, hammer against nail, rather than the elegant brutality of sword play, Uthe expected the servant was well-versed in reading an opponent. Humans had no chance against vampire speed or strength. They had to rely on surprise, strategy and calculation. Even if they had exceptional skills in that area, most human vampire hunters didn't live long, because the odds were always stacked against them. Gideon had not only survived, he'd been more successful than any other vampire hunter they'd encountered.

As for Daegan, he'd read that slip in Uthe's footwork for what it was. Any other time, Uthe wouldn't have revealed too much, even to eyes and senses as sharp as Daegan's. It wasn't unusual for a vampire to be cagey about what fighting skills he had, so Uthe knew it was not a serious faux pas. Yet it was a disturbing indication about his state of mind tonight.

Daegan would allow him to gracefully decline the invitation, and Uthe should. Knowing the skill set of friend or foe in their world was a vital advantage, because one could easily cross the line from one to the other in a blink. The thought made Uthe inexplicably sad. He started to bow and offer a polite but firm dismissal.

Instead, an impulse surged up from his gut, so strong he couldn't deny himself. He gave a short nod, and then he moved.

It was not hard to remember, not today. Today it was so

clear. The blood and dirt as they engaged the raiders. The scent, the heat. The thin screams of the horses, since the cursed enemy would target them, knowing they were the most difficult weapon for a Templar to replace. Uthe spun, thrust, swung, crashed. His sword was a cutting tool, made for close quarter fighting, and the boon of such a superior opponent was he didn't have to hold back. Daegan was still better at this, no chance of Uthe doing him real damage. Plus they were using metal blades. Unless he tried to sever Daegan's head from his body, the assassin could come to no mortal harm.

Uthe's muscles strained in fierce pleasure. His feet knew the steps, a dance he'd done over and over. Adrenaline rushed through him, the light of battle firing his blood, his gaze. It burned all the way to his roots. He felt like he was breathing after holding his breath for centuries.

He didn't realize Daegan was calling his name, not until the vampire moved in aggressively. Using a move too fast for even Uthe to follow, the enforcer slipped under his guard and knocked the blade clattering from his hand, shoving him back with his other hand so Uthe had to plant his feet, regain his senses.

Even the crickets had stopped singing. He realized he had a feral grin on his face, and his heart was roaring. Though Daegan's eyes were sharp as twin knife points, his sensual lips curled. "You do me honor with your trust, my lord," the vampire said. "I fear there is little I can teach you that wouldn't threaten my job security."

"Fucking Christ," Gideon said before Uthe could respond. "Maybe you should tell Lyssa not to have Uthe sit so close when they're disagreeing about Council policy."

His blood was pounding in his ears, singing with savage pleasure. It propelled him toward Gideon, closed the ground between them. In a heartbeat, he had the male's throat gripped in his hand and his body up against the courtyard wall, slamming him there so a plume of dust rose from the brick.

"She is Lady Lyssa to you, servant," Uthe said. His fangs were bared, and he relished the slick, sharp curve of them against his bottom lip. "To insinuate I would ever raise a hand to her is an insult so deep I should take your head for it. After flaying the skin from your body. You will also not blaspheme the Lord's name in my presence, nor interrupt when one vampire is speaking to another, unless you are invited to join the conversation."

Gideon's eyes flared to rage when Uthe laid hands on him. If Uthe had not moved so quickly to pin him, he was sure the former hunter would have resisted in some way, no matter that Uthe was in a position to beat him into a heap of bones and blood.

He had no plans to do violence to Gideon, and not just because Daegan was breathing down his neck, the long fingers curling over his shoulder in warning. It made Uthe think of Keldwyn's touch. The two men had a similar way about them. He expected when Daegan put that hand on Gideon, his gut coiled and uncoiled the way Uthe's did now, remembering Keldwyn's demanding hold. Daegan's sensual mouth, held firm and stern as he'd sparred, heralded all the dark pleasures he could inflict on his servant, ones that would make Gideon suffer and beg for more.

Need and desire rose inside his own breast in edgy conflict. It could slice him up like the edge of Daegan's sword. The vision Uthe had of blood slipping from his body brought an agonizing relief so strong his mind countered the image with alarm, a reminder to draw back, rein in. Control himself. Be who he was expected to be.

Both the Rule and Bernard's written endorsement of the Templars had emphasized the need for a tempered reaction to everything. Unlike other warriors, Templars did not charge into battle with battle cries. They engaged silently, never exulting in the death of the enemy but only in service to the Lord's will. They did not raise voices, curse or speak in anger to one another, not without facing penance. While such enforced calm might seem restrictive, there was a level peace to it, a tranquility he knew well, even if it was eluding him at the moment.

Releasing Gideon, Uthe stepped back and away. He drew a deep breath, forcing the calm he didn't feel into his voice. "I will do your servant no harm, Lord Daegan. Though I could certainly demand a punishment from my hands as a lesson in minding his tongue."

He shifted his unblinking gaze to Daegan. "You value my counsel. I offer it now as repayment for your sparring instruction. The primary concern the Council has about formalizing more rights to our servants is that they will forget their place in our world, to the detriment of themselves and their vampires. If you want him to live long and well, and if he values you as you do him"—he let his gaze flick over Gideon's tight expression—"teach him the rules before someone forces your hand in the manner you thought I was about to do. No policy the Council passes will punish a vampire's justified reaction to your servant's careless tongue. Do we have an understanding?"

Gideon had been a controversial decision as a human servant. But controversial didn't mean wrong. He'd probably be surprised to know Uthe believed the former vampire hunter was a good match for Lord Daegan and Anwyn. His loyalty to his vampires, and the courage that backed up his great love for them both, compensated for his rough edges. Daegan and Anwyn merely needed to smooth some of those edges before they were forcibly sheared off.

"I understand, my lord." Daegan dipped his head, though his eyes did not leave Uthe's, nor did he withdraw his hand. "I will attend to it." His gaze shifted to Gideon, and Uthe sensed the intent conversation there. A muscle flexed in Gideon's jaw, threatening to crack bone. Uthe sheathed his blade and stepped back, allowing Daegan to release him.

"You wish to ask me or your Master for permission to

say something, Gideon?" Uthe said.

If the human could have spit nails, he would have. The vampire hunter cared little for saving his own skin, but putting Daegan in an untenable position was a different matter, which was why Uthe had deliberately inserted that implication into the discussion. But as Gideon fought his natural aggression and consistent disrespect for authority, he looked toward his Master, and Uthe saw more than that at work.

Commanding submission from Gideon was a challenge, but it was a challenge that Daegan had well in hand. The slight altering of Gideon's face told Uthe the truth of it. Whatever complicated makeup the alpha hunter had in him, something in the male recognized Daegan as his ruler on matters of justice and balance. Uthe had no doubt Gideon kept the relationship lively with challenges. Daegan and Gideon were yet another pairing that did not fit the traditional vampire-servant mold in the way that Uthe and Mariela did. While Daegan was not as open as Lord Mason was about his feelings for his servant, they were still nevertheless there.

Gideon inclined his head with grudging but genuine respect. "I didn't mean any offense, Lord Uthe. Sometimes sparring like this, I forget we're not just a group of guys training, if that makes sense."

He wasn't a pretty speech maker. Uthe understood that. As the moment passed, he was more concerned about his hot-blooded response to what he'd known all along Gideon hadn't intended as a slight. But it had been so long since Uthe had unleashed himself like that. He'd wanted to act on the power boiling through his blood.

Why control your impulses at all? Your father knew how absurd that was, yet you resist it still...

He shut that sibilant voice down with a resounding clang. His fingers twitched on the sword hilt as he heard distant, mocking laughter. Daegan's eyes flicked to the motion.

The Lord is my shepherd, I shall not want. A Templar was required to say sixty paternosters a day, thirty for the dead, thirty for the living. It wouldn't hurt to do one now. He reached the end of it quickly enough, though the pause had drawn out long enough both men were staring at him, wondering what he was thinking, doing.

Steadying himself. Mission accomplished. He looked at Gideon.

"To the Templars, the use of archery or spears to take out an enemy was considered cowardly, in most circumstances. It seems foolish in retrospect, with all we've learned since about battle strategy and weaponry. It was also hypocritical," he mused, "because our ultimate charge was to defend pilgrims, not to cling to pride in how we accomplished that."

Daegan cocked his head. He was over seven hundred years old, so the turns and twists a vampire's mind could take, even in a tense moment like this, were not unknown to him. Whereas Gideon looked as if he thought Uthe had wandered off topic like a doddering uncle. Uthe was not amused. His gaze sharpened on Gideon like Daegan's katana.

"In your years as a vampire hunter, with your skills, you could have taken out more with a high powered cross bow at a distance, like a sniper."

Gideon gave him a wary look. "Yeah, but a vampire's reflexes and instincts are too sharp. They hear it coming and move, most the time."

Uthe nodded. "That may be so. But I don't think that was it. You needed the close kill. You are a knight at heart, Gideon, like your brother. A knight must straddle a fine line between honor and pride. You still have too much of the latter, and anger. A knight can easily become a brigand, if he does not learn self-discipline and humility to something far larger than himself. If you have no belief in such a thing, then the next best thing is realizing what you fight for and against, and how to reconcile the two."

Uthe returned his attention to Daegan. "I know you will not be present for the activities involving the Fae Queen, due to the need to maintain as much anonymity as possible among our kind, but Anwyn has been invited to the soiree afterward, yes?"

"Yes, my lord."

"Your servant will not attend with her. Too much is at stake to risk him giving offense. He has a limited ability to behave properly around vampires, let alone Fae royalty."

Regrettably, that would likely make it impossible for Anwyn to attend. Due to the volatile nature of her forced turning, the young woman was susceptible to seizures that Gideon's proximity helped meliorate. It was another reason Uthe knew one or both of the men's minds were always in contact with hers. However, a fledgling's desire to attend a party wasn't Uthe's primary concern.

He glanced at Gideon. "Why are you looking at me, servant?" he snapped.

He was pushing, but he had cause. After three seconds too long, Gideon shifted his gaze to the far wall, but he didn't lower it. Uthe didn't expect miracles. Plus, he had no desire to break him—simply to temper the steel.

Daegan shot Gideon a look as the vampire hunter shifted. Uthe kept his eyes on Daegan's face, and he saw what he intended to see. The vampire assassin understood Uthe's intentions. Disappointing his Mistress was a lesson Gideon would not soon forget. Daegan inclined his head, conveying respect, though his own eyes never lowered. While the vampire was technically subject to the Council's rule, Daegan was an authority unto himself, so there was no purpose to jerking that chain beyond necessity.

"My thanks for your guidance, my lord," Daegan said evenly. "And for the workout."

"The pleasure and benefit were mine. Thank you, Lord Daegan."

Uthe left them without further comment, striding back toward his quarters. Gideon was all muscle and flashes of rebellious temper. Uthe suspected it was a pleasure to Daegan to take his body, hold his soul and heart in his hand. To possess, or be possessed that way...

He turned his mind to related Council business, a way to ease himself out of hazardous waters. The debate over Lord Mason's policy to formalize certain rights for servants had been ongoing for a month now. While Uthe still straddled the middle ground on it, Lord Belizar, the former head of the Council, headed up the stringent opposition. The Russian vampire was certain the universe of vampire kind would be destroyed if anything changed. Ever. Uthe allowed himself a smile. For all of Belizar's flaws and his propensity for violence, Uthe had stood at Belizar's side as his right hand for many years, and he knew the male's strengths. Despite his stubbornness, it was good Lyssa had kept Belizar on the Council.

Uthe's apprehensions on the subject were more aligned with Lyssa's. For all that she loved her servant openly and deeply, she knew the vampire world was ruled by blood and power, far more than the human one, at least in the human societies which claimed to be civilized. Order and a known structure were extremely important in keeping the vampire world balanced, and the role of servants in that balance was critical. Otherwise, the world of the Trads would rule. Uthe knew exactly what that kind of world looked like.

Trads, or Traditionalists, were an extremist splinter of the vampire world, though there was a certain romanticized regard for them by vampires like Belizar. Trads lived as pure predators, rejecting most of the technology and domestic comforts the human and vampire worlds both preferred. They viewed mortals as prey alone, with no rights accorded to their sentience or wellbeing. While Trads kept their kills fairly close to the maximum allowed, thirteen annually, Uthe suspected that was a common sense decision and a way to avoid the irritant of Council involvement in their lives, rather than any respect for Council laws.

When made vampires had staged a coup against the born vampires recently, some of the made who had fled justice had reputedly become Trads. Trads weren't known for organizing in force. Mostly they wanted to be left alone by non-Trads. They were like rabid bears who never sickened and died. However, there was no telling what an infusion of made vampires in their ranks would do. There'd been more frequent reports of female vampires disappearing. Uthe, as well as other members of the Council, was concerned the mostly male Trad population was trying to reproduce, to increase their numbers and maintain their blood purity. Even that was rumor. Rumors were nigh impossible to substantiate in a world where vampires could disappear for long periods of time, for their own reasons and purposes. Usually it was only noted when a tithe for a Region Master or overlord wasn't delivered on time. If that amount was small, it might not even be pursued.

He paused in a breezeway, lifting his face to the touch of the evening wind. The crickets were out in full harmony tonight. Servants' rights, made vampires, Trads…there were so many things to resolve, but they were the usual kind of problems. It was easier to think on that than on the things that could spiral out of his control more quickly. Like his reaction to a Fae Lord. He shook his head at himself. Out of all the things that could cause him serious problems, that one should be at the bottom of the list. Instead, because of his preoccupation with the arrogant male, it slipped into his mind at the least provocation.

He sighed. He'd given his heart and passion to many things. To God, to battle, to protecting what was important to protect. Despite his wayward mind and suddenly overactive libido, he knew how to prioritize. He valued Keldwyn's friendship, and within those boundaries was where he needed to keep it contained.

He'd had friendships he'd prized deeply. Like Daegan's

mother. She'd succumbed to Ennui, the one incurable disease that vampires faced. One dawn, she'd chosen to wander out of her room to meet the sun. Lord Brian, who headed up all scientific research involving vampires, had explained that Ennui could manifest itself in many ways, depending on the vampire. There were those who gave in to their impulse control like a rogue fledging, pursuing ever greater violence to assuage the raging pain that such loss of control caused inside them. Others, like Daegan's mother, experienced an almost gentle slipping away of the mind, becoming ever more childlike. Vampires could experience symptoms all along that spectrum. The only common thing about Ennui was that it was more of a risk with advancing age, and seemed to connect to a loss of interest in life. Though Lord Brian, ever the practical scientist, had been quick to say that should not be assumed. It was still a chicken and egg question – did the Ennui incite the loss of interest, or did the loss of interest make the vampire more vulnerable to the condition?

The Council had protected and watched over Daegan's mother until she embraced the sun, part of why Daegan gave them such loyalty now. Uthe had sat with her in the gardens at night, listening to her rambling talk of the flowers, of the stars, of an angel who visited her once and conceived a beautiful son upon her. No one knew who Daegan's father was, and she'd never spoken of him before the Ennui, so an angel was as good a reference as any. Uthe supposed it was a vampire she didn't want to be an active father for her son. It happened. Some vampires made good parents. Some shouldn't be trusted with a dead bug collection.

Like his own father.

Shaking his head, Uthe shut down all the open topics in his head and started to work on those fifty-nine remaining paternosters. He should finish them in the time it took him to shower and arrive at Council chambers. They had a Fae Queen to meet tonight. He would need his mind fully locked in the present—and focused on anticipating any problems before they happened.

That was why he was Lyssa's right hand, the role he would serve until God called him to answer the purpose he'd been waiting centuries to complete.

A missive is coming...

Chapter Three

The Council meeting was swift. Lyssa ran down a few details on Fae protocol, then Uthe returned to his quarters to clothe himself in a manner suitable to meet Queen Rhoswen and her retainers. Lyssa had said there was no vampire complement to the finery a Fae male would wear for a formal occasion, so black tie was the best option. Mariela helped him with the tie, which, to her amusement, still baffled him. She was already dressed, in a strapless chiffon dress of blue, teal and purple, with a floral rhinestone clasp at the hip. Her blonde hair was dressed in a chignon with a waterfall of blue sparkling stones dressing it.

"You look quite beautiful, dearest. You are a credit to us, as always."

She glowed as she arranged the tie. "I admit I'm nervous, my lord. You hear so many things about the Fae. Lord Keldwyn has tended to live up to those unsettling stories."

"He is no different from the rest of us males. We pretend to be complex only to impress our sexual conquests, but under those trappings we are decidedly dull."

"I believe he attempts to impress you quite often then,

my lord."

At his look of surprise, she lifted one smooth shoulder. "It is the way he looks at you when you are not looking at him." She pressed her lips together as if she thought she'd said too much, but Uthe touched her face, lifted her chin. Since she was six feet tall, and tonight she wore three-inch heels, they were eye to eye.

"Speak to me of your concerns, Mariela. I value your thoughts. You know this."

"I do not know his motives, my lord. When he is near you, I am concerned for your wellbeing. It is as if he could simply make you disappear for his amusement."

"Well, he is Fae. But considering his queen and Lady Lyssa would like to see some advance in the relations between our two species, and I do believe he has that same wish, perhaps he'll hold off. He'll wait for a more expedient time to put me in a box, tap it with a wand and produce a rabbit."

Her full, moist lips twisted. "I cannot tell what he wishes, beyond his desire for you. And I think desire to a Fae is no simple thing."

"Desire rarely is a simple thing, for any of us."

"Hmm." She suddenly was very focused on the tie again. "My lord, I hope you know I would never allow my concerns to interfere with my service to you. Should you have an equal desire for him, and wish me to be part of what you want from one another, I will not shame you."

"I would never think you would, even if you told me he repulsed you and you had to imagine someone far more handsome than either of us to get through it. Like...who was the actor in the movie you were watching the other day in the servants' common room?"

"My lord." She pushed at him. "A Council member should have far more weighty concerns than spying on servants."

"Now my servant is chastising me." He chuckled. "Another reason to punish her later. Right now, I would do nothing to muss your beauty. I will have that name from you then, though."

She shook her head, her reserve returning as she completed the task of helping him dress. He enjoyed teasing her, but he could not indulge the easy informality like what was between Lyssa and Jacob, or other vampires who enjoyed greater intimacy with their servants.

He'd never considered that a burden, and he didn't now, but it made him think about how often of late he woke up with a feeling as if he were bound in heavy chains. The sensation sometimes lingered throughout the night. Because of it, he prayed more, worked out harder, pushed himself further on Council duties. Which was what could have led to his slip earlier tonight, he mused, where Daegan had seen Uthe's fighting skills were greater than most knew. He needed to figure out the right balance to restore his equilibrium, but the problem was the fulcrum of that seesaw was moving daily.

He could not give in to the fatigue. Or the fear of what it all meant. Too much remained to be done. One moment at a time. For tonight, Lady Lyssa and the Council were depending on him to be who he'd always been for them.

"My lord, did you review the mail I left on your desk today?"

He tuned back in to Mariela. She had a voice like a flute, haunting like a dove's coo. It soothed. At times he allowed her to read him to sleep at dawn. Perhaps he'd do that tonight. "I didn't realize I'd received any."

Though many things were communicated electronically, correspondence requiring excess discretion was usually couriered. He searched his mind for what might have come from the Berlin office, but came up with nothing.

"It was just a postcard. I should have propped it up on your desk and made it more noticeable. I was going to throw it away, because it was from a tourist attraction." Mariela grimaced. "Even vampires end up on marketing lists."

"Evidence of the Devil at work, for certain." Uthe shrugged into his coat.

"Hmm." She smiled at him. "However, this card had a first class stamp and it's handwritten in Arabic. It may be inconsequential, but..."

Mariela moved to his desk, her skirt flowing out from her like peacock feathers, the light in the room reflecting off her blonde hair. Picking up the single postcard, she brought it back to him. "Discover the Holy Land Experience" was in bright red letters on the front of the card, and layered over what looked like a map of the exhibits one could see there. It appeared to be a Florida tourist attraction. His brow creased. Solomon's Treasures, the park's gift shop, was circled with a black marker. When he flipped the postcard, there was only one handwritten line. In Arabic, as Mariela had said.

Your gift is ready!

It is ready. He should know what that meant. It was the missive. Heat flushed through his body beneath the confines of the tuxedo, and a tremor went through his fingers. His mind strained, panicked, as the information eluded him. By the Holy Relics, this was important. So important.

"My lord?" Mariela was staring at him. "You have gotten...paler. Are you..."

"Leave me." He spoke brusquely and turned away from her. "I will see you on the back lawn."

"Yes, my lord." He heard the hesitation in her voice, the worry, but she was ever-obedient, his beautiful Mariela. She closed the door behind him.

He stared at the card, passed his fingers over the writing. Damn it, damn it. Closing his eyes, he dropped to one knee by the bed and began to pray, fervently. But he was trying too hard, he knew it, and he could not open himself to God's will. The information eluded him.

§

A couple hours later, he stood on the back lawn of the Savannah estate, facing the forest perimeter. He'd tucked the card into his jacket, hoping the proximity to his body might jog something loose, but right now this had to be his priority. Keldwyn had indicated the Fae Queen preferred to be met at the forest portal only by her half-sister and the Fae Lord. She and her entourage would then proceed to the house, which was why they were all assembled on the lawn, awaiting the Queen's arrival so she could greet them formally there.

Jacob had accompanied Lyssa. Though Mason and others of the Council hadn't been pleased by Lyssa meeting a Fae entourage so unprotected, it was a reminder that this was supposed to be a social visit, peacekeeping observed on all sides. Vampires were far too used to an evening ending in blood among their own kind, let alone a species with whom they'd had less than friendly relations since...ever.

At one time, the blood triggers for a vampire social event could have been anything from true insult to an idle desire for lethal sport. Considering their population was not large, intelligent vampires like Lyssa had realized channeling the energy into sexual play with servants at such meetings kept more vampires alive. The evening might still end in blood—just of the less fatal variety.

He thought of Keldwyn's mouth so close to his own, the Fae Lord's whispered words. *You frustrate me.*

A shift in the assembled Council vampires and attendants brought his attention back to the forest edge. As the Fae court made their appearance, firelight flickering off their trappings, the line between past and present blurred. For an instant he was on a battlefield years ago, and horses were emerging over the ridge, the sun catching the glitter of weapons, helmets. It felt odd, not being on horseback, ready to meet them, waiting for the call to charge.

It was not Saladin's army. Nor Turkish raiders. He yanked himself back to the present, more forcefully this time. Only two of the entourage were on horseback, the Fae

Queen and Lyssa. Jacob was leading her horse and another Fae male was leading the Queen's. The man was clad in a light armor that molded to his broad-shouldered body, a sword at his hip. His dark hair shot with silver—actual silver, not gray—was pulled back in a braided queue, exposing an unexpected scar on his face. Apparently not all high Fae had the healing ability vampires had, making their beauty eternally flawless. This must be Cayden, captain of the Queen's Guard. Lyssa had spoken favorably of him.

The Fae Queen was in a white and silver dress with streaks of blue. It shimmered like a combination of ice and water. Her white hair poured down her back past her hips. A dozen Fae accompanied them on foot, six men and six women, and they were garbed no less spectacularly. They looked exactly as the fables said. Uthe heard the Council members murmuring among themselves. Even Mariela allowed herself a quiet whisper to Jessica about the beauty of the two queens, side by side. Rhoswen was on a snow white stallion, Lyssa on a glossy black palfrey. The horses seemed to tolerate her unusually well, since horses were normally fractious around vampires. Mason was a rare exception, as he kept two Arabians at his South American estate.

Lyssa and her sister were speaking, Lyssa gesturing as if they were discussing the grounds. So far, so good. Everyone looked congenial. However, the sheer power emanating from the party was causing some uncomfortable glances and movement among the Council members.

"Is that all coming from the Fae Queen?" Belizar muttered, shifting to Uthe's side.

"I expect so. It may be a simple show of strength, to remind us of our place." He gave his former Council head a look without rancor. "Our current Council head has been known to do something similar at politic moments."

Belizar snorted. "You ever keep a salt shaker on your person, my lord, so you can rub it into my open wounds."

"I know how tough you are, my old friend. You do not hold onto such things in favor of the greater good. It is why I continue to have high regard for you, despite your stubborn unwillingness to see anyone's point other than your own, unless it's at the tip of a wooden stake."

"Change of any kind is a critical decision for vampires. Proper incentive is necessary."

Uthe hid a grin at that. It was always unexpected how well Belizar presented in a tux. His hot-blooded demeanor and muscular body mass suggested he'd be more at home in the long coat and tall fur hat of a Cossack. But with his shoulder length hair sleekly combed, he looked handsome, if not entirely approachable. Though he'd always been more warlike, Belizar had once excelled at the political maneuvering necessary to lead the Council. Even Lyssa had supported his appointment. Belizar had only embraced his less admirable leadership traits in the last few years, losing patience for political machinations and becoming far less tolerant of change.

Uthe wondered if Lyssa should have suggested Belizar and Gideon engage in a nice evening of poker and vodka together. But though Belizar got along well enough with Vincent, his current servant, he decidedly didn't cross the traditional vampire-servant lines.

Though he'd been aware of his position in the entourage all along, Uthe only now allowed himself to shift his attention to Keldwyn, who was walking a few feet away from the Fae Queen's mount. Uthe suspected it was a politically chosen, neutral position, for the Fae did not look shunned, and Rhoswen tossed a couple comments his way that seemed friendly. He responded with an amicable half-bow in response.

The Council members might be drawn to the beauty of the queens, the exotic newness of the other Fae, but it was Keldwyn who held Uthe's gaze. The outfit he had chosen was less embellished than what he normally wore. While Uthe wondered why, he didn't disapprove of the choice, for it only enhanced his physical attributes, no ruffles, embroidery or jewels distracting from them. His short white tunic was belted with a rust-colored sash over matching hose and black boots that stopped below the knee. He wore a gold ring, a simple band, on the middle finger of one hand. His hair was braided in two short plaits on either side, the slim pieces pinned back with a gold clasp, keeping the rest of his loose mane out of his face. It enhanced the precise cut of his features. Uthe pressed his lips together as his gaze drifted over the sensual mouth, held in a slight curve of polite interest that revealed nothing, yet intrigued one to the point of obsession.

He would have issued a prayer to control his thoughts, yet Keldwyn's gaze shifted to him and the prayer that came to mind had little to do with control. The Fae's smile disappeared. It was a personal acknowledgement to Uthe, one that swept heat through his body and reminded him of their last encounter. Sometimes he wished vampires didn't heal so quickly. He might have liked to feel those bruises longer, the ones Keldwyn had inflicted when they tumbled down the stairs together.

He didn't remove his gaze from the Fae Lord, not until Keldwyn's own attention had to shift at something the Fae Queen said to him. Uthe managed that prayer then, and forced his gaze back to Lyssa.

She'd dismounted into Jacob's arms. Rhoswen accepted the same help from her captain. Interesting. Uthe noted there was more there than guardsman and queen, if her lingering touch on his biceps and the heat under what was otherwise a respectful gaze on his part were any indication.

As the entourage came their way, Uthe began to move forward, drawing the other Council members with him. Cayden spoke a word to the horses. The animals turned, breaking into a trot to disappear back into the forest. It dispelled Uthe's wonder about whether Jacob and Ingram had made provisions to stable horses. Lyssa's servant and her majordomo were rarely caught unawares, so he was sure it had been considered.

Lyssa gestured Uthe forward. "My sister, may I present my right hand on the Council, Lord Uthe. I'm sure Keldwyn has spoken of him."

"With high regard," Queen Rhoswen said. Her blue eyes were multifaceted, as potent as magic crystals. She put out a hand and Uthe moved to take it, bend over it with courtly courtesy. His grip closed gently over the pale fingers and...

Desert heat. A battle. Jacques at risk, and only one choice. The dagger was in his hand. It must be thrown, no matter the consequences, even though Hugh's words were screaming through his mind.

You must always stand apart. Never give your heart and soul to any other but God, for you are the guardian of life itself, of the future of our world and any other...

A woman whispered in Uthe's ear, her voice an unexpectedly masculine rasp. *He is right. When the time is right, you will remember again, you will know all in a blink, and your way will be clear...*

His left knee buckled beneath him. Fortunately, he neither tightened his grip, which might have yanked the Queen down with him, nor did he let go, so it passed as a somewhat dramatically polite gesture of bending to one knee before the Fae Queen. Curious but not wrong. He was sure Lyssa's brow raised in surprise at his excessive courtesy.

But while his own queen might let it pass as mere eccentricity, the person he was touching was a creature of great magical power. She noticed far more than that. Rhoswen's hand was on his face, lifting it, her blue eyes staring into his. Ah, blessed Savior, she recognized him, of course she did. By the Virgin Mary, why now? Why all these centuries later?

He knew exactly why. *It is ready.* The internal earthquake he was experiencing knocked the meaning loose from his mind like treasure from a jagged crevice, bringing a shower of gravel with it, stray bits of thoughts and words that only increased his disorientation. He had to use his formidable discipline to sweep it out of the way, to stand atop the heaving mass and appear as if he were standing on solid ground. Maybe that was how Jesus had done it with water. Sheer will, though he didn't think the Great Teacher had been motivated by the concern Uthe had now, that he was about to set Fae and vampire relations back irrevocably.

Keldwyn was next to him. With the Fae Lord having such an excellent poker face, it was a matter of identifying his different masks, seeking tells which told Uthe the true feelings happening beneath. Right now, Keldwyn was probably wondering what the hell was going on with him. That made two of them. His knees were like water. If he passed out at the Fae Queen's feet, the breach of etiquette would be unclassifiable.

Even more importantly, he'd have passed the salt shaker to Belizar and the Russian would use it liberally. The humor helped steady him.

Keldwyn stood at his back now, his hand on Uthe's shoulder giving him the energy to rise without looking like the Fae Lord was hauling him back to a standing position.

"We shall have a conversation later tonight, you and I," Rhoswen said. Then she turned away, to answer the other introductions Lyssa was making. Uthe saw Lyssa's speculative look before she turned her focus in the same direction, thankfully. Keldwyn did not. He shifted closer to Uthe, thigh pressed to the side of his own.

"You are well, my lord?" Keldwyn spoke low. When he brushed his hand against Uthe's, Uthe realized his was clenched. As he eased the grip, he found his fingers were shaking.

"Yes, Lord Keldwyn. Perhaps I did not feed well enough, with all the work involved in your Queen's arrival. I'll attend to it as soon as possible."

He stepped back, leaving Keldwyn with the two queens. He should stay in the midst of the introductions, absorbing all that was happening. But if he was forced to choose a moment to collect himself, he was not as essential right now as he would be when they had their honorary session in Council chambers later. Right now his mind was a movie reel turned on fast forward, a flash of images rushing through, things he knew but had been locked away.

The dagger. Though he was certain it was where it always was, he needed to verify its whereabouts, close his fingers on it, let it steady him in his purpose. Muttering a quiet explanation to Lady Helga that he needed to check on something, he excused himself to return to the house. He would have used vampire speed to get back to his rooms, to give him the maximum amount of private time, but he found that dizzy sensation wasn't going to permit that unless he wanted to risk bouncing himself off a few solid surfaces between here and there. So he hurried as best he could and, once he was in his suite, he closed and locked his door. Going to the chest, he opened it, removing the interior compartments until he reached the false bottom. Carefully, he withdrew the item he sought. It had been wrapped in black silk with reverence, and he opened it the same way now.

As soon as he closed his hand on the wire- and leather-wrapped hilt, the thrum of that power and knowledge went through him, steadying him, holding him. His mission, what God had charged him to do. It made him feel strangely desolate, though. The flash of images he'd received when he touched Rhoswen's hand had unfolded the years, the remembered and not-remembered things. Yet what if he was still missing something critical, something that had left a hole in his heart and mind? If there was more that had been hidden from him by design, the pieces of the puzzle dropping into place at the appropriate moment, he could accept that as God's will and have faith that things would be provided when needed. But he worried there was a factor none of them had counted upon. Had his mind lost those pieces, never to be returned?

A dark dread filled him. To think he had had knowledge not long ago, that was now missing... That could affect many things, too many things that were important. He could no longer put it off. It was time to leave before he caused irreparable harm. His reaction to Keldwyn was proof of it. He saw Keldwyn's eyes watching him, the set of his mouth as he tried to understand Uthe. Uthe had begun to take too much pleasure in being that puzzle for him, and indulging the same fascination with the Fae.

As he'd always done whenever he was conflicted, he stayed on his knees and opened his heart, asking for guidance. But what if he didn't remember tomorrow what he was told today? *Lord help me, if it be Thy Will. Let neither fear nor pride keep me from Your path.*

Do you speak to your God out of fear of your past, or out of true love and belief?

Does it matter to Him, as long as I serve His Will?

It had been years since he'd remembered that conversation with Hugh. The founder of the Templar Order had called him to his quarters. King Baldwin II had given the Order the section of the Temple Mount presumably built over the ruins of Solomon's Palace. Before the First Crusaders took back Jerusalem, it had been the al-Asqa mosque. Since the Templars had no other lucrative benefactors then, there'd been no money for the Poor Knights of Christ to maintain the structure. Hugh had been sitting on the stump of a broken pillar, using a slab of jagged rock as a table.

Though he'd asked Uthe to join him, he'd said nothing to him for nearly an hour. He'd sharpened his sword, cleaned his armor, and written some correspondence. Then he'd sat back and studied Uthe as if he was a wall of incomprehensible text. Yet Uthe remembered Hugh didn't look concerned that he couldn't immediately decipher the mystery that was Uthe. Because of the penetrating power of that regard, the strength of the faith behind it, Uthe had eventually been the one who spoke. He told him everything.

He'd wept, asked for mercy. The torment of his soul was unrelenting and, since he did not have the resolve to take his own life, he had to find another solution. As he knelt in Hugh's presence and made his spontaneous confession, he'd felt a sliver of hope. It didn't matter if Hugh decided to stake him there or had other plans for him; his quiet listening had been a balm to Uthe's soul. That sliver of hope was like what he'd felt when he'd first closed his hand on the dagger he held now, as if its original owner had left that quality sealed into the blade and hilt. He'd left other powers in it, but that was the one that Uthe had valued the most.

It is ready. He now knew what that meant. He saw the sorceress's aged face in his mind. How long had it been since he'd seen her? Ten years? He had to leave, not because of his fear, but because it was time. He would start the preparations. He could do that without abandoning the responsibilities expected of him tonight. The two things were not incompatible.

Calmer now, he put the dagger away and rose, straightening his clothes. Without Mariela, he couldn't tell if anything was mussed that only a mirror could show, but when he returned to the others, she would let him know if anything was out of place. God bless her.

§

"Lord Brian." Uthe gave the blond-haired, green-eyed vampire a cordial nod as he moved to stand beside him. Brian looked like he was studying for an exam, his eyes narrowed on the scene before them. "It's rather remarkable, isn't it?"

Together they watched the elegant swirl of those dancing in the ball room. So far the vampires and Fae had swapped off dance styles. The Fae version of the waltz was

Night's Templar

similar to theirs, albeit a bit more acrobatic. If Helga introduced them to disco dancing, Uthe expected it was going to get even more interesting.

"The chance to observe the Fae up close like this, even a subset of them, is all that and more." The vampire couldn't contain his enthusiasm. "I wish I could obtain a sample of their blood. Lord Keldwyn has graciously given me a strand of hair, but there is so much more I could do with blood."

"Have you asked him for it?"

"No." The vampire male was young, not even a century old, but he'd convinced the Council of the necessity for scientific research for the survival of their species. Rather than being interested in politics and power hierarchies, Brian pursued remedies for their few weaknesses, like their inability to expose themselves to sunlight. While he'd made no advances on that yet, he'd already figured out how to safely separate a third mark from a vampire when the vampire deemed them incompatible, a problem that in the past could only be resolved by killing the servant. He'd also made some intriguing connections between the fertility of vampires and the depth of relationship between vampire and servant. He currently headed up the research facility that was based out of the Savannah estate and oversaw the sister center in Berlin.

His exceptional maturity was occasionally flavored by a charming academic obliviousness, evident now in the frustration creasing his fair brow. "I know it's a debasement to them, to give blood to one of us for drinking. I thought it might be considered an equal insult to ask for it as a sample. Though from Lord Keldwyn's expression when he gave me the hair, I think he expected me to make that misstep."

"Perhaps he has already deduced your love of knowledge often outpaces your good sense," Uthe said genially, putting his hand on the male's shoulder. Brian's servant and fellow researcher, Debra, stood a few paces away. The servants stood equidistant along the ballroom walls, waiting in patient attendance if their vampires needed anything. Over the past few months, it seemed Debra and Brian's relationship had changed in some key way, for Uthe thought she looked happier, more content. Less tired.

Brian seemed to have a heightened awareness of her as well. A vampire did not have to look at his servant to know her whereabouts, because their blood connection made him aware of that at all times. Still, Brian seemed to enjoy glancing her way more often than usual. His almost possessive regard showed blatant male appreciation for her slim form, clad in a sequined blue sheath that stopped at mid-thigh. Debra always wore classic fashions, less revealing than most servants, but ones which highlighted her attributes well.

Uthe had noticed the change in their relationship soon after she and Brian had made the discovery there was an undeniable correlation between fertility rates and the closeness of the bond between vampire and servant. Though the more formal, traditional vampire-servant relationships like his and Mariela's had resulted in pregnancies, Brian and Debra's research had shown the birthrate was greater among vampires and servants like Lyssa and Jacob who shared a far deeper bond.

Well, it would make sense that the scientist would act on his own research, though Uthe suspected if the feelings between Brian and his servant hadn't already been there, dormant but waiting, they couldn't have been acted upon so quickly.

He didn't indulge sentiment often, which made it strange that he was glad for the new bond between them, that closeness. He also experienced a yearning he couldn't quite define, as if he were lonely for the same experience. Which brought a desire to see where Keldwyn was.

He put that aside. Complicating the questions didn't make the answer any less simple, or the consequences less severe. He brought himself back to why he'd approached

Brian.

"Lord Brian, I wish to break the third mark bond with my servant. As soon as possible."

Brian's gaze snapped from his absorption with the Fae to Uthe's face. "My lord? Are you unhappy with Mariela? She seems quite devoted to you and you have seemed content with her service." He paused at Uthe's expression. "My apologies. I know I have no standing to question you, and I certainly didn't mean to pry. For...non-Council vampires, I am required to determine the reasons. You do not have to give me yours, but if you are willing to volunteer that information, it does help me hone my current efforts to develop compatibility guidelines between vampires and servants on the front end, so we have less reasons to use the separation serum."

Uthe respected the scientist's thoroughness, so allowed his expression to relax. "I have been very happy with her service, Lord Brian. So much so, I would owe you a debt if you would share that with your servant when the time comes, so it may be spread throughout their ranks and Mariela suffers no censure for it. I must regretfully request the separation for personal reasons, which I must address with Lady Lyssa as soon as feasible. How quickly does it take effect?"

"Once administered, it is a matter of minutes now, my lord. But it's best to do it during the early afternoon hours, when the vampire is in his or her deepest sleep. It is less difficult on you both."

Uthe regretted hearing that. He would have preferred to be at Mariela's side while it was done. As if detecting his concern about that, Brian continued with an assurance. "Debra is experienced with the process. You should have no lasting physical effects, but even without the memory wipe we do on Randoms, your servant will have a period of weakness and lethargy that lasts a few days. We will monitor and help her through the initial disorientation."

"Thank you for that. I've not yet spoken of this to

Mariela, so I do not wish it shared with anyone else, until I indicate to you that it is all right to do so."

"Of course." Brian glanced across the ballroom. Following his gaze, Uthe saw Mariela had been called upon to dance with Lord Belizar. While vampires had no reservations about orientation, such that it would not be unusual to see same-sex pairings on the ballroom floor, Belizar liked to dance with a woman when he wanted to dance. Uthe had suspected for some time that Belizar preferred male servants primarily because it was easier for them to tolerate and interpret his bullish nature. Glancing toward Brian again, he saw the young vampire's focus shift from Mariela to Debra, his handsome expression softening.

"Something amiss, Lord Brian?"

"No, my lord. It's simply... I hope you won't interpret this the wrong way." He lifted a shoulder. "With the proposed changes for servants currently under consideration by Council, and the research I've done of late about fertility, and...some changes that have occurred between me and my servant, I have a heightened sensitivity to their feelings."

His green eyes reflected his personal struggle with that. "Detachment is important not only in science, but in the vampire-servant structure of our world. However, I admit I am wrestling more often of late with the moral implications of too much objectivity."

"You think me cruel."

"No, my lord. We are not a compassionate species, but you are the least sadistic of those in the upper ranks of our kind. There are those in our world who would take that as a near insult, and I hope you will know that is not how I intended it." Brian offered a half smile. "You do not flinch at making tough decisions, ones that might be seen as cruel, but are for the greater good of our species. I respect that."

"But?"

Brian grimaced. His father was a well-respected Region

Master in the UK, so Brian had no difficulty balancing deference with honesty. It was part of what had helped him make his case with the Vampire Council. An audience with even a single Council member could catapult most lower-ranking vampires into stammering silence. "I am sorry for Mariela, my lord," Brian said simply. "I think she loves you well. I know you will care for her feelings in this matter, though, and I am glad of that."

"Do you love her, Lord Brian?"

Brian looked startled. "Mariela?"

"No. Debra. Your servant. Do you love her?"

Not very long ago, the question would have been taboo. It was still unthinkable in much of the vampire world. The changes happening at the Council level had not left that level officially, because the Council didn't have a majority resolve on the matter. But two sitting Council members, Lyssa and Mason, had openly declared their devotion to their servants. Being two of the most powerful vampires made it difficult to castigate them for something that had always been considered forbidden. On top of that, Lyssa had given birth to Kane, and Mason and Jessica had recently celebrated the arrival of their daughter Farida. It was visible and well-timed proof of Lord Brian's fertility findings, that birthrate might be related to the depth of emotional connection between vampire and servant.

The dwindling birthrate for born vampires was a far greater concern to Council than even the relationship of human servants to vampires. It had weakened the arguments of dissenters like Belizar, Stewart and Carola who disliked the idea of emotional parity with servants.

There was a third on the Council who, while not as open about it, was just as committed to her servant. Uthe located them now. Lady Daniela was dancing with Dev, him holding her close in his arms, her leaning into his body. Sex and intense intimacy was part of the vampire-servant relationship, but when intimacy became love, it was fairly evident, if one looked closely enough.

"I am not trying to trap you, Lord Brian," Uthe said absently. "Are you in love with your servant?"

"Yes, my lord. I am." Brian turned to face him. "From an objective standpoint, I'm not sure if that will skew my research results on matters related to the vampire-servant relationship, but Debra and I are working on ways to minimize subjectivity."

"No one would expect any less of you, Lord Brian. As such, none of us have those concerns. Thank you for your honesty. If Lady Lyssa approves, I will have Mariela come to Debra for the procedure tomorrow."

When Uthe turned away, he pivoted into Keldwyn, standing beside him. Uthe brought himself up just short of putting a hand on his chest to stop his forward momentum. It disturbed him that he hadn't noted the Fae's proximity. Keldwyn sketched an oddly formal bow, considering their earlier interaction on the stairwell. "Queen Rhoswen wishes to speak with you. She is in the gardens. I will take you."

"All right."

Keldwyn lifted a brow. "You look relieved, Lord Uthe. Afraid I was going to ask you to dance?"

"If you do, you need to be wearing something other than those." Uthe glanced down at the Fae's soft-skinned boots. "I can do a passable waltz, but nothing else without breaking toes."

"I shall teach you some of the dances we do in the Fae world. It's more like fighting than dancing." Keldwyn gestured toward the gardens. "The Queen does not like to be kept waiting."

"None of them do." Uthe pushed down the sudden trepidation, recalling how it felt to take her hand. If he did it again, what else would he see or discover? Would she allow it?

He was preoccupied with his thoughts and the walk was short. Keldwyn, either respecting that or lost in his own musings, didn't disturb him with conversation, but Uthe was aware of how closely he walked at Uthe's side, their arms occasionally brushing as they navigated the narrow walkways to where the Queen was.

A low hedge and artfully arranged layers of fall mums made a circle around a cluster of stone benches, a rose bush the center feature. The ground beneath it was dotted with decorative stepping stones, stamped with Celtic knot designs. Sitting on one of the benches, Rhoswen looked like the moon come to rest. An ethereal light bathed everything around her in a silver glow. While Keldwyn was a creature of autumn and earth, his Queen was winter and water. Uthe remembered Lyssa explaining that the Queen was wont to express herself through the combination of the two, and he saw that now. There was a limning of frost on the hedges nearest her, and a dusting of snow along the silver-grey concrete of the bench.

He was relieved to see she'd restrained herself enough to spare the leaves of the rose bush, since Lyssa was protective of her roses. In winter, during the occasional frosts, they were covered with light blankets during the night. Viewed from inside the house, they looked like old people hunched against the cold.

Cayden stood a few feet back from his Queen, watching over her, though Uthe wondered what the man thought a few vampires could do to a woman who put out a power signature like a nuclear explosion.

"My lord Uthe." Her pale eyes fastened on him as he approached and bowed. She didn't offer her hand this time, though she did gesture to him to take the bench across from her. Keldwyn drifted away, though not far. He meandered along the garden path that spiraled around the low hedge circling this area, studying it as if he were planning a career in landscape design.

A brief flash of irritation crossed Rhoswen's face as she glanced his way. "He never sits or stands in attendance on me. His way of making it clear he owes no one any allegiance."

"Allegiance is earned day by day, Your Majesty," Keldwyn said absently, bending to examine a plant. "I have not yet stopped serving your well-being, so I'd say that is its own answer, is it not?"

Rhoswen's face was as cool as the ice on the hedges. "He does prove useful enough that freezing him into a permanent ice sculpture isn't an intelligent option," she said. "Though I keep warning him the day may come when I am not feeling quite so intelligent."

"I've seen you on those days, my lady, and your acuity is still ten times sharper than most."

Cayden shifted behind her. Uthe saw him and Keldwyn exchange a look. Cayden's contained an admonishment, an easy-to-read suggestion that Keldwyn try not to be such a pain in the ass. Keldwyn's expression showed bland puzzlement, as if he were unaware of any problem. Apparently, he could be as irritating to his own kind as he was to vampires.

Rhoswen examined Uthe thoroughly from head to toe. "You have not changed so much. But then you are a vampire. Any changes would be in your eyes and more mature body language, not physical appearance. The sun gave you those handsome creases on your face, something a born vampire cannot experience. But you have."

"God has given me a full and interesting life, Your Majesty."

"Hmm. What do you remember of our last meeting?"

"When I took your hand, I recalled some of it. But there are other things that are still shadowy. I think Lord Reghan, your father...I think he intended I shouldn't remember until it was important that I did."

Curiously, that had captured Keldwyn's full attention. The Fae Lord gave him a sharp look and exchanged a glance with the Queen laden with meaning.

"So you think the information has been spelled all this time, held away from you?" she asked Uthe, pulling her attention away from Keldwyn.

"Yes, Your Majesty." He hoped. "It may be something your father and I agreed upon."

"So why now? Why did my touch unlock it?"

He thought of the postcard in his jacket. "Because the time has come for me to finish what was started." The moment he said it, he knew it as truth, which reassured him. He could feel Keldwyn's attention on him now, but he held the Queen's gaze. He needed to ask her permission to touch her again, and he despised the fear in him that made him want to hold his tongue. If he didn't know what had been lost to him, he would not have to mourn it. But that was a delaying tactic. He firmed his resolve and opened his mouth to speak.

She extended her hand before he could. "Take my hand again, Lord Uthe, and revisit our first meeting. Make sure you see all you need to see."

Did she know what was at stake? It was the only reason he could see her allowing him to take hold of her twice. Mindful of the honor, as well as his reaction last time, he slid off the bench onto both knees before her. Taking a steadying breath, closing his eyes, he bowed his head. Issuing a quick prayer for guidance and clarity, he closed his hand around hers.

And was pulled back to the Crusades.

§

What the Grand Master had ordered was insane. They all knew Gerard de Ridefort's pride had overridden common sense. They were a few hundred men, facing thousands of Saladin's. They had no strategic advantage in terrain, for instead of waiting for Saladin to come to them, Gerard had marched across the desert in the heat of the day, depleting the men and the horses.

Saladin must be considering his good fortune the blessings of Allah. Blessings of Allah, the stupidity of a man's ego...today it was difficult to tell the difference.

When the word was passed down that Gerard said battles were not won by numbers but by faith in God, Leonard scoffed an expletive that needed no interpretation and earned no admonishment from any of them. He was merely echoing what they all felt.

Uthe's destrier moved restlessly beneath his knees. Nexus became more aggressive before battle, but it wasn't anxiety. He'd never seen the horse cowed. Because of Uthe's abilities, Nexus had survived more cavalry charges than most of his equine brethren. Most of the horses that did survive the battles were only effective for a few of them before they began to fear the charge and had to be exchanged for different mounts. However, his steed became fiercer with each battle, as if Uthe's own bloodlust fueled him. He loved Nexus, caring for the blood bay stallion like a baby when they weren't on the field. Now, when the order came down the line to prepare for the charge, the horse pranced forward, arching his neck and shrieking a defiant whinny.

The Templars around Uthe grinned, despite knowing they were all sweaty and doomed. Maybe *because* they knew they were doomed. Though St. Bernard had indicated dying in the service of the Lord's Will was a free pass into Heaven, Uthe wondered if many were thinking as he was. If the commander of the battle was directing them for his own interests, were any of them fighting for the Lord's Will?

Ah, well. Death was not something any of them feared. If it was time to meet the Maker, at least they could say they were following orders. As Bernard had said, God loved nothing so much as obedience.

"*Charge!*"

The roar reverberated through the line, cutting them loose. Nexus led the way toward the wave of Saracens, thick as the sea. As they thundered across the ground, Uthe was aware of every Templar with him, the pump of adrenaline, the pounding hearts, the rasping breath. *Lord, we fight for the wrong thing today, but have mercy on us all.*

It twisted the fury in him, and he broke the Templar's traditional silence with a bloodcurdling yell. They picked it up, every one of them, and the cries were punctuated by an additional defiant scream from Nexus. They hurled themselves into that sea of humanity.

From there forward, all was blood, the clash of metal, the horrifying screams of men and horses. He briefly glimpsed the beauseant flying and had no idea how it stayed aloft as long as it did. It wouldn't matter. Even if it fell, the only reason a Templar could retreat from the field, they were surrounded. There was nowhere to go. Too many. Uthe hacked, slashed. Despite Nexus's teeth and hooves, they pressed too close around him, and the horse threw up his head, shrieking. Uthe cried out as if he felt the knives going into his own unprotected belly. Nexus faltered beneath him. Uthe was dragged from his dying horse, dragged away from the loyal animal. His last glimpse of Nexus was the noble beast still doing his best to fight off his attackers, head thrashing and eyes rolling as he tried to see Uthe.

Rage took the place of fury. A Templar was supposed to fight without bloodlust, taking no pleasure in the death of his enemies, all the will of God. He let go of all of that, and fought like the monster he knew he was, no thought or reason. He cut down foe after foe, until his sword was taken and he was fighting with his bare hands, unleashing his vampire strength to crack men like kindling, strike their heads from their bodies. As they became aware of the swathe of destruction he was creating around him, the Saracens started backing away from him. It wouldn't matter. Gerard's ego had killed them all. Uthe wasn't leaving this field alive. Eventually someone's blade would take his head.

A cry amid the cacophony pulled him out of his blood haze. Jacques, his squire, was fighting like a tiger. He'd taught him how to use the sword he was using so ably now, back when the boy could hardly lift it. Tears ran down the squire's face but Uthe doubted Jacques was even aware of them. Such things could happen in a fight, all emotions either shutting down or spinning into a tornado that fueled one's sword hand and reflexes with a manic energy.

Another Saracen was coming up behind the squire fast, his blade flashing. Uthe drew the short dagger from his belt. He didn't use it for fighting—that wasn't its purpose. However, he couldn't imagine a situation that called for it more than this one. As if God agreed and showed him His Will, a clear path opened up between him and the Saracen bearing down on Jacques. It was a good way to die, perhaps the only righteous kill he'd made today.

Uthe threw the dagger, straight and true.

It buried itself into the Saracen's back, for the blade could penetrate any mail, any shield. Uthe had time for one spurt of grim satisfaction, then heat scorched him through his helm, his chain mail. His protection from the sun was gone, his body on fire. A scream of pain fought its way from his throat, but he turned it into a roar of defiance and tried to launch himself at another Saracen. He saw fear in the man's eyes, but it was no use. He never reached him. The sun drove him to the ground, took his strength. All he knew was pain and darkness.

Until he woke.

He was in a tower of silver stone, for he could see the sky outside a slit window and sensed he was far from the ground. Coolness had a smell, as did peace and quiet, the trinity forming a healing aroma that restored the soul. He expected to see his limbs blackened, but his bare body was under white sheets, and unmarked. He was startled to see the dagger, cleaned and sheathed in its scarred leather scabbard, on a side table next to his bed. Those two pieces of furniture were the only things in the round chamber.

A male came into the room. Uthe stopped himself from reaching for the dagger, but the man's power signature

Night's Templar

pressed into every corner, took up all the space. His dark hair lay loose on his shoulders, and his eyes, a peculiar mix of green irises and silver sclera, studied Uthe with an impassive expression. While his clothing wasn't ornate, an embroidered tunic belted over leggings, the quality and the way he wore it told Uthe he was dealing with a person of authority.

A woman was with him, with pale hair, eyes and skin. Both of them were unnaturally beautiful, even more so than any vampire he knew. When the woman looked toward the male, he saw her pointed ears. Incredulity warred with other feelings. Fae. He was with the Fae. While they and vampires weren't outright enemies, there was no love lost between them. They did not associate.

Uthe closed his eyes, uncertain if he was dreaming. He remembered the battle, seeing the carnage all too vividly. But he also remembered more now. A cloak being thrown over him that immediately cut the sun's piercing effect on his body. The battle had disappeared, as if he'd been born away in a swirl of magic. He remembered opening his eyes briefly to see this woman, a quizzical, distasteful look on her face. He'd heard her voice, quiet and muffled like the falling snow. *"Father, why are we helping a vampire..."*

"What became of the battle?" Uthe rasped.

"Your battle was lost," the male Fae said. "Decisively. No surprise to you, I am sure."

"My brethren?"

"Some died in the battle. Those who didn't, their heads were removed by Saladin's orders. Your Grand Master allowed himself to be ransomed. He gave away Gaza in exchange for his life."

The fury from the battle field echoed through him. Saladin depended on Egypt for supplies for his army. Gerard had put a high price on his worthless life, and a Templar wasn't permitted to be ransomed. It was against the Rule. It didn't surprise him to hear that Gerard had refused to adhere to it, though it didn't make Uthe's anger over it less sharp. He imagined the men he knew, Manfred, Leonard... all of them lined up, the sword coming down. Jacques...

"I am glad my brethren did not live to see that act of cowardice and shame. What of the squire I tried to save?"

"He made a good accounting of himself. He died with honor, without fear."

Hearing that shamed Uthe. It shamed him to be here. Shamed him to be alive. Shamed him to be glad to be alive.

As if the Fae could see it, he cocked his head. "They are not your people, vampire. You do not belong on the ground with their headless corpses."

"They were my brothers. Are my brothers. They watched my back, shared my beliefs and ideals. That's family. Blood means nothing."

"An interesting thing to hear a vampire say, on many levels. I am Lord Reghan. You are in the Fae world."

Uthe frowned. He knew little of the Fae but that they considered vampires crass and weak enemies. "Why did you save me?"

"That dagger provided you protection from the sun, gave you an advantage over your enemies. Yet you sacrificed yourself to save a friend, a comrade in arms. It intrigued me. That is all." The Fae nodded to the sheathed dagger. "Where did you get it? It does not seem to have any spell work attached to it, though it bears considerable power. Which means that its magic came from the original wielder."

"Yes. Another vampire gave it to me, before his death. It was given to him by the original wielder. Why did you not take it for yourself?"

In Uthe's current condition, the Fae could still do that. It was possible he'd left the dagger near Uthe to taunt him. But the Fae didn't look interested in playing such games. The woman with him was a different matter. She looked at him with a detachment devoid of empathy. If she had her way, Uthe expected he would even now be a pile of ash on the field.

"The Fae already have enough power," Reghan said. "And stolen power is a punishment waiting to happen. Which is how I knew you did not take the blade away from someone unwilling to relinquish it. That type of gift must be bestowed to retain its power. There are those in the human world, magic wielders, who know of you. They claim you were never supposed to be in that battle, that you are committed to a higher purpose."

It was a secret that had been zealously guarded for decades now, since those first days with Hugh in the al-Asqa mosque. Uthe considered the Fae suspiciously. "That purpose is known to very few. Especially not to the current Grand Master. He ordered me into battle and I obeyed, because I would not leave my brethren to die alone."

"Despite your higher purpose."

"I prayed upon it. I believed it was God's will that I be in that battle."

"Perhaps that is true, because our paths have crossed, have they not?" Reghan studied him. "The sorceress wants you returned to your world, but not from where you left. You will be returned through the portal that puts you in France. She needs you to come to her at La Couvertoirade. She has home repairs that need doing. She says it will occupy you better than these endless foolish Crusades."

He could hear the irascible old witch saying it. He wanted to protest, but Reghan's implacable look said Uthe was not being offered a choice. Besides which, she was right, was she not? There was nothing left for him in the Holy Land now. The truest of the Templars had died at Hattin. They'd lost Jerusalem and they'd lost their way. Their Grand Master was despicably living proof of that. Hugh had made clear what Uthe's primary charge was and always would be, until it was done. It was time to honor that fully.

Reghan was back to studying him with his penetrating green eyes. In certain lights, they were like jade.

"You have my thanks for my life," Uthe said formally. "I am ready to leave whenever you wish."

"It shall be done," Reghan said. "Fare thee well, vampire. We will see one another again."

Chapter Four

Uthe came back to the present. Mortified, he realized he was collapsed against the Queen's legs, his head in her lap. Fortunately, Keldwyn's hands were upon his shoulders, easing him back.

"So did you see more than you did before?" Rhoswen asked.

"Yes, Your Majesty. I..." He needed to stand, back away, but had to accept Keldwyn's help for that. The Fae moved him efficiently to the bench again, but instead of moving away, he sat down next to Uthe, hip to hip, shoulder brushing his, a sturdy brace. "I cannot remember if I properly thanked you for my life, all those years ago," Uthe said to the Queen.

"It was my Father you thanked, quite properly. It was his doing." Rhoswen shrugged. "I had no reason to save a vampire. He had been watching you for some time, finding you an interesting anomaly. My father had obvious interests in the vampire race that most of us Fae do not have."

While her voice was neutral, disinterested, Uthe felt a ping of danger from the casual words. The slight shift of Keldwyn's body next to him was a warning of the same. Since Lyssa's father had been executed for his association

with Lyssa's mother, it didn't take a wealth of intuition to know it would be a sore spot for his Fae daughter, even now when the sisters had apparently reconciled.
"So what is it you need, Lord Uthe?"
"I'm sorry? I thought you requested the audience, Your Majesty."
"I did. When you touched my hand the first time, at the edge of the forest, you said 'I need your permission to...' And then you fell silent."
Uthe ignored the reactive clutch in his lower gut. "I apologize, Your Majesty. I think I spoke while gripped by the first vision. It is not clear to me what I need your permission for, but as soon as I determine its nature, I will certainly attend to that." Yes, he was sure the Fae Queen would grant him multiple audiences until he could flounder around and figure out what he needed from her. The coil of anxiety grew, refusing to be blocked. "With your permission now, I will leave your company to see to my lady—"
Rhoswen reached out, clamped a hand on his arm and slapped the other palm against his forehead, a shockingly familiar gesture. But Uthe didn't have a chance to draw back or mouth a protest. It was as if he'd been sucked straight down into a tunnel and was falling through it like an insane vertical amusement park ride. Had Keldwyn ever ridden a roller coaster? A Ferris wheel? Had Uthe? He should remember something like that, if he had.
Lyssa's father materialized before him, mostly translucent but clear enough Uthe saw him pointing to a shimmering wall of gray nothingness. "There, Templar. The Shattered World. It will be safe there until your sorceress has found her answer. That is all. You will not see me again. Just as in your own world, the fewer connections you have, the harder it will be for any other to trace the path you must follow when it is time."
The Fae shimmered. Scarlet fabric wafted between the two of them, obscuring him from Uthe's vision. A spray of

Night's Templar

sand, and then the fabric broke into pieces, floating through the air. No longer cloth, they became petals. Rose petals. Uthe was staring at a rose bush in the desert. The red of the petals dissolved like blood, drying up into dust and blowing away.

Uthe turned and looked in the direction the Fae had been pointing, that massive grayness. He realized he was wearing his Templar mantle, his mail and armor, all his weapons. The short dagger was sure in his grip.

Yes. It was time. He knew where it was, and what he had to do.

This time when he surfaced, he threw up Mariela's blood and the few things he'd sampled in the ballroom. Thank the Lord, Keldwyn roughly spun him around so he vomited into the hedge. If he'd splattered Rhoswen's dress with blood and tea cakes, he wasn't sure how he would have fixed that. That gauzy, moon glow fabric probably didn't dry clean.

Keldwyn held him until he nodded shortly, indicating he was done. The Fae handed him a handkerchief from somewhere on his person so Uthe could wipe his mouth. When he looked over his shoulder, he was surprised to see the Queen still there. She didn't seem out of sorts with him. She and Cayden were speaking in low tones, but she cut off the conversation when she saw Uthe was with them again.

"I have some ability to bend time backwards to recall memory," she said. "Though it can have some unpleasant effects when done so quickly. I've been told I'm impatient."

Her gaze shifted to Keldwyn, who had that bland look once more. She narrowed her eyes at him, but the expression became neutral when she turned it back to Uthe.

"Your patience and tolerance overwhelms me, Your Majesty," Uthe assured her. "You have my thanks for your assistance."

"Perhaps you could work on teaching Lord Keldwyn manners." Rhoswen tilted her head toward Keldwyn. "Your vampire friend is much better at talking to a Fae Queen."

"He's had limited exposure to you."

"Your Majesty," Uthe interjected as smoothly and swiftly as he could, to Cayden's visible relief when Uthe drew the Queen's attention back to him. "I know what I need your permission to do now. Are you aware of a place called the Shattered World?"

She was not quick enough to hide a startled look, but Keldwyn stiffened. "It is a place within our world," the Fae Lord said. "But no one goes there. No one who wishes to survive or be heard from again."

"That is not relevant to my goal." Uthe held the Queen's ice blue gaze. "Your father put something there for me years ago for safe keeping, until the time came when I could address its ultimate destiny."

"What was it?"

Uthe had been at a disadvantage throughout this interchange, and this part wasn't going to help matters, but he knew anything less than honesty would be a grave error in judgment. "I am oath-bound not to reveal that to anyone until I have no other choice left, my lady. It is important to both our peoples that I do not. To the human world also. Throughout this quest, the less who have known about it, the better. I do not wish to abandon that wisdom now, particularly if it might repay Your Majesty with anything less than kindness for your forbearance."

She stared at him, long enough he felt the piercing pain of a stare made of ice. "I am aware of the warnings and constraints of magic and would not push them out of mere curiosity, Lord Uthe. What if I forbid you passage in my world? What will you do then?"

"Do what I can to change your mind."

"And if I tell you I am done with this and will not speak of it again, on pain of death to the one who dares to defy me?"

"My death is God's will, my lady. I must serve it as long as I'm able."

"Your method of evasion indicates you are far too clever for your own good and cursed with an overabundance of stubbornness. No wonder my lord Keldwyn is fond of you."

She didn't mean it as a compliment, her displeasure unfurling like a frosty wind. Uthe owed the Vampire Council and Lyssa his allegiance, and disrupting the tentatively mending relationship between the two species would definitely conflict with that. But unfortunately, this was more important. His mind was still in disarray. Rhoswen forcibly shoving him into the past had left a painful vibration through him, as if a foot wide strip of skin had been torn from inside his chest wall. Regardless, he reached past it for his usual diplomacy, looking for something that wouldn't make his refusal seem like defiance.

Keldwyn spoke instead. "Your Majesty, might I request a private audience with you after I escort Lord Uthe back to his chambers? I think it best if he recovers his strength and sensibilities before you continue this conversation. He's fairly disoriented right now and I'm sure he doesn't wish to insult you."

Being escorted back to his room like a feeble old man. Uthe wanted to snarl, but Keldwyn didn't give him much choice, hauling him up and propelling him into motion. Since Uthe couldn't yet walk a straight line, resisting would be an awkward and humiliating one-sided fight. "Let me see what I can do," Keldwyn muttered as he took them out of range of the Fae Queen and her bodyguard.

"I don't require you to do anything. I'm capable of managing this."

"You are quite capable, Lord Uthe, but there's a reason I'm a liaison." He gripped Uthe's arm through the tuxedo coat. "Shouldn't I earn my considerable salary?"

"Your liaison role is for Council business, and we don't pay you a salary."

"Well, you should. And this is Council business, in a sense, if it concerns the wellbeing of all of us."

"When did I say that?"

Keldwyn stopped him in the hallway. "A few moments ago, to the Queen. You'd recall it if the Queen hadn't dunked you into your past like a puppy in cold bathwater."

Uthe was ready to fight with him, accuse him of telling Uthe he'd said things he never had, trying to confuse him, but Kel's explanation made sense and calmed his racing heart. He had to get control of the panic. The panic made it worse.

"Lord Uthe." Keldwyn's voice was firm, his glance even more so as he directed him into his room. Cool, blissfully cool. He shouldn't be craving the touch of his own sheets the way he did right now. "This is not a matter of pride but of practicality. Lie down until the effects of your vision wear off. Even the lightest touch of Fae magic can be very powerful when you're not used to the effects on your mind. Until you regain your bearings, you are like a spinning top with no direction."

Uthe started to peel his lips back in a fang-baring response, but Keldwyn touched his face, distracting him. "Uthe," he said quietly. "Let me help. Showing the Queen what is in all our best interests is something I do better than most. Certainly better than a vampire."

Uthe snorted. "She likes you only marginally more than she likes my kind."

"That may be true. But I'm still family, in a way. She has to put up with me. As you heard, I haven't outlived my usefulness yet." He sobered again, held Uthe's gaze. "I will not betray you in this."

He didn't have much choice, did he? Somehow, while he was mulling that over, Kel eased him to the edge of the bed, helped him remove the coat. As he opened Uthe's shirt, the male's fingertips slid against his bare skin, since vampires had no chest hair to interfere with the sensation of contact. He took off his own shoes and slacks, though the Fae stood close, as if he expected Uthe to topple over like a three-legged chair. Since Uthe wasn't sure if he was right, he maintained a sullen silence and stretched out on the bed in his shorts. It was less than he normally wore to bed, but he was recuperating, not sleeping.

"I'll lay down for a short while, but I need to attend to other business. How long a recuperation will this require?"

"Probably an hour at most. Maybe a half hour, given you have a strong mind and constitution." Keldwyn adjusted the pillow beneath his head.

"I have been putting myself into bed for some time, my lord."

"Indeed." But Keldwyn trailed his fingers over Uthe's short crop.

"What she wants to know, I can't give her." Uthe spoke to derail his mind from the direction the Fae's peculiar behavior was taking him. Keldwyn's touch drifted from his scalp to his naked shoulder, over the curve of his pectoral. Uthe's nipple became taut in anticipation of a caress. He grasped Keldwyn's wrist, stopping him. "But what can I offer that will help you convince her?"

"Your motive." Keldwyn withdrew and took a seat at the foot of the bed, his hip pressed against Uthe's leg. "You may be easy on hers. She is not trying to take from you what you are seeking. Whatever Lord Reghan placed in the Shattered World would not be beneficial to the Fae world. She has enough confidence in his memory for that not to be an issue. Her main concern is allowing a vampire into her world whose purpose she does not understand."

"Hmm." Uthe closed his eyes. "Would she understand who the Templars were? Who they were meant to be, no matter what they became?"

"Perhaps. What did they mean to you?"

"Pure service. The mercy of that is almost a forgotten memory. To serve simply because it is just and right, for the higher good, not for any purpose of your own." Uthe mumbled the last part, but opened his eyes before he could get lost in the rumination. The disorientation, the need for Keldwyn's assistance, had made him feel like a child. Yet the Fae seeking Uthe's counsel reminded him of who and what he was. It returned his sense of order and let him focus on the truth, the best thing he could offer the Unseelie Queen. "Tell her that is my intent. I was charged to do something centuries ago, and I must finish it, to honor my oath of service."

"Hmm." Keldwyn pursed his lips and ran a fingertip along Uthe's jaw. "I hope you will remember those words when I return to you, my lord. They intrigue me no little amount."

"I will be here," Uthe said. "Until I am not."

He didn't remember Keldwyn leaving, but when he opened his eyes again, it was forty-five minutes later. His mind was once again settled and clear, though beset by a sense of urgency. Everything was coming together quickly. Perhaps it had been planned that way all along, which was comforting, the idea of a Grand Plan driving him. It might be in conflict with the inexplicable chaos of other outcomes bearing down on him, such that he wasn't sure how to process the whole picture, but he would deal with it the best possible way. One painful thing at a time, and he knew what was next.

Mariela, please meet me in the garden, at your favorite place by the moonflowers. Best to be done with all of this at once. Though he cared deeply for his servant, he was still surprised how the prospect of what he was about to do sent shards of pain through his heart like emotional stakes. But he wasn't likely to return from this quest. It was rare a man had the opportunity to say farewell to all that was important to him before Death claimed him. He could say what he needed to say now, before he was beyond the ability to say anything.

Yet he wondered if it might be better to be like young Jacques, where Death took the soul away before such goodbyes were anticipated. Perhaps the heart wasn't equipped to bear this much sorrow at once.

He was past any logical way to silence the denial that it

had to be done. The postcard and the memories the Fae Queen's touch had unlocked had brought that to an end. He couldn't simply go on as before, pretending that nothing had to change.

When facing the end, the child often rose inside the man. But he wasn't a child, and there'd been a time when he faced the possibility of meeting the Grim Reaper every day. That proximity had made him insensitive to his own death. Now he had no shields to defend himself against what it truly meant. It seemed he had far more to miss now than he'd had previously.

Lyssa's array of nighttime blooming flowers were whorls of white silk against their green leaves. The garden on this end of the estate was remote from the ballroom, where guests might still be milling. Mariela was kneeling. If she hadn't been told what he needed, she assumed that patient, waiting position. It was how an InhServ put her mind fully into service mode, an almost meditative state until her Master made a demand upon her. Taking her hand, he lifted her to her feet, and brought her to sit next to him on a bench carved out of oak. Lady Lyssa loved moving water, so there was a fountain with a pair of sculpted swans crowning it. Their necks were intertwined, arcs of water spurting from their slim beaks.

As he explained his departure and what it would mean for her, Mariela's expression initially lacked comprehension. When understanding dawned, it was followed by puzzlement, hurt. Pain.

"My lord, have I—"

"You have done nothing but be an exemplary servant," he told her firmly, reaching out to capture a delicate curl of blond hair framing her face. "I forbid you to think otherwise. This has to do with a task I was assigned many, many years ago. It is something I must do on my own, without the benefit of my valued servant. I want to know you are safe, happy and in the care of a vampire who appreciates you as I do. Perhaps even better."

It was difficult for an InhServ to process being released from service through no fault of her own. He was not a man who normally tolerated repeating himself, but she deserved his patience and far more. He told her in several different ways. Since she was wrestling with her emotions, he expected she wasn't really hearing the words, but she would recall them later. Or rather, he hoped she would.

"May I ask a question, my lord?"

He caressed her silken cheek. Lord above, she was truly lovely, inside and out. "You may speak plainly to me, Mariela. Ask anything, and I will answer it as best I can."

"When...will Lord Brian do this?"

It was past midnight. He steeled himself against the shock she experienced when he answered. "Today. The best time to do it is daylight, when I am sleeping. The process is less strenuous on you that way. The bond is stronger when I'm awake, you see. Without that logic, he would not have kept me from your side while it was occurring." He cupped her chin. Blessed Virgin, this was more difficult than he'd expected. He cleared his throat, removed his touch from her face but continued to hold her hand.

"He has said you will be disoriented for a short time. You are welcome to speak to him or Debra about it and he will not consider it inappropriate. I think he enjoys the opportunity to talk about the process they discovered."

Mariela didn't return his faint smile. "So soon."

"Yes. It's best that way. I'd rather you not have to dwell on it."

She said nothing further, though the misery in her face, the way she was staring a hole in his chest, inspired him to lift her face to his again. "You have been a gift to me, Mariela. I think you know just how much. I cannot change my mind, but if there is anything within my power to ease the decision for you, I would gladly offer it."

Pressing her cheek into his palm, she kissed the heel of his hand. "You have always had calluses," she said. "No other vampire I know has those. A strong man's hands."

Night's Templar

It was one of the most personal things she'd ever said to him. He knew she wouldn't ask him for anything. As an InhServ, she would deny wanting anything, faithful to her Order. However, unapologetically taking advantage of the dominance he had over her mind, he saw her wish dwelling there, a sad and forlorn kernel at the center of her churning emotions.

He had never sensed Mariela longed for the type of relationship with him that Jacob and Lyssa had with each other, but Uthe had denied her certain intimacies that could have enriched her service. While it wasn't something in his control, given his other priorities, he could give her that, as a thank you for her years of unfailing care for him.

"Yes." He drew her against his chest and wrapped both arms around her, inhaling the scent of her hair, her skin. "You may go to bed with me at dawn and sleep in my arms. When it is time, you will rise and go to Brian, but I will have you drink from my throat so that I send you to him strong and well nourished."

A tiny sob caught in her throat. A stake wouldn't have hurt as much. When had he become so sentimental?

Yet during her twelve years of service she'd probably been closer to him than anyone else. It was that way for most vampires and servants. The binding of the servant's mind to the vampire's through the three marks introduced an intimacy of thought that allowed the vampire to trust the servant like they trusted no other. Whether a vampire and servant had a traditional bond like his and Mariela's, or a unique one like Lyssa and Jacob's, that link was a critical and undeniable part of every vampire-servant relationship. Even if it wasn't acknowledged or valued by the vampire the way it should be.

His internal choice of words surprised him. *The way it should be.* Perhaps Mason was having more influence on him than he'd realized.

"I would...I would like to give you pleasure once more, however you require it," she whispered.

"Your very existence gives me pleasure, but yes, we will do that." He would give her the same, bringing her to orgasm several times, depleting her body, giving her heart a chance to purge through the physical release.

"My lord...you won't take a servant again, will you?"

"I do not see that in my future."

She nodded against his chest. It was easy and pleasant to keep holding her. She didn't seem disposed to move. "I think that's good."

"Why? Because I'm such an odious Master, and you're glad that no other servant will have to suffer me? Like your Torrence?"

He'd gotten her to smile, the pull of her lips a light pressure against his shirt. "Torrence could do with some suffering. Lady Helga spoils him."

"I'll tell her you think so, if you don't tell me why it's good that I won't take another servant."

A flash of uncertainty went through her mind, but he reminded her via their link she could speak plainly. "I don't think you need a servant, my lord," she said at last, slowly. "I think you need someone... I think you need love. I mean, someone in love with you, who you can be in love with as well. Someone...equal to you."

The hesitation was curious, but the thought that slipped through her usually impeccable mental discipline startled him to the core.

Someone who is as much your Master as you are mine.

She felt his stiffening and realized he'd heard it. She drew away, her face flushed. "Forgive me, my lord. I should not have...I didn't mean it exactly like that. There is a freedom of thought and feeling in the service of a Master. Your service to God, the way you describe it, it is somewhat like that, yet based in more earthly joys. I think you deserve joy and pleasure, my lord. I think you deserve to laugh freely, to act like a lover with another. After all these years, I think you deserve the right to enjoy your life. You are so self-disciplined; I thought maybe, sometimes, you need permission to allow yourself that. The desires of a Dominant lover can do that. Even if you don't call him Master."

She knotted and unknotted her fingers as he said nothing. "If you will grant me permission to do so, I will take my leave, my lord. I realize I've overstepped myself. I will beg your forgiveness for my wrong thoughts as your parting gift instead." Her throat thickened over the words, and he realized she was close to tears, thinking she'd done something unforgivable as her last act as his InhServ.

Ah, hell. Despite the reputation of vampires for being touchy about anything that didn't fit with their view of themselves, he had never been that kind of vampire. He analyzed everything from empty compliments to hostile criticism for whatever value they provided. Mariela's thought had not been laced with resentment or negative feeling. She truly believed it, and the motive behind her explanation, whether or not the explanation was accurate, was based in her regard for him, which he had no reason to question.

Plus, he couldn't deny those last two statements had called to mind one very troublesome yet undeniably Dominant Fae Lord. *The desires of a Dominant lover can do that. Even if you don't call him Master.*

His Order didn't approve uninhibited laughter, or joy except in the service of God, which was supposed to be sufficient. It truly always had been for him, until recently. A few hundred years was a good track record for self-discipline, but the problem was he couldn't relax that now. Not when he needed it now more than ever.

"I will dismiss you, Mariela, but only because I seek an audience with Lady Lyssa. At dawn, I expect to have your company in my bed, as we discussed." He rose, drawing her to her feet before him, and lifted her fingers to his mouth, pressing his lips there. "You are my servant tonight, Mariela, but your honesty tells me you will also ever be a worthy friend and ally. I thank you for that, and things too numerous to count."

Another little sob escaped her, and he folded her into his arms once more, giving her an admonishing squeeze. "None of that now," he said. "You will break my heart."

"I know. I'm sorry. But I will miss having you in my heart and mind, my lord. I will miss you greatly. You always made me feel...safe."

"You will always be safe." Her reaction sent a ripple of bloodlust through him, the weapon a vampire could call to hand so quickly when violence was needed. "You may not be my servant after today, but your well-being will always be mine to guard. While I'm away, if you have cause, go to Lady Lyssa. Do not hesitate, because I know you will not bother her for something minor. If you are harmed because of your unwillingness to protect yourself with the resources at your disposal, I will not be pleased."

"Yes, my lord." Her arms were around his back and waist, strong and sure. She would be all right. He knew she would be. She'd always been capable and independent. The perfect servant.

§

Uthe stepped into the Council meeting chambers. In Berlin, it had been an intimidating place, even without the world's most powerful vampires seated in it. The dark stone and torch lighting conveyed menace, as if the room had been a torture chamber before it had been converted to meeting space. Since the Berlin headquarters was an ancient castle, it wasn't entirely impossible.

The Council room at the Savannah estate had a high ceiling crisscrossed by decorative timbers. The timbers were wrapped up in night blooming jasmine vines that received sun from a circular sky light. When they met here at night, the skylight gave them a view of the moon and stars. One of Lyssa's many fountains gurgled in the corner, several koi swimming lazily amid the rocks. The tapestries

Night's Templar

on the wall, depictions of battles and histories of the vampire race, had come from Berlin, but here they seemed more heroic and praiseworthy, less sinister and monstrous. Lyssa preferred torchlight in the wall sconces, the only similarity between the two chambers, though there was electricity if needed. Tonight, firelight flickered off the tapestries, making the images on them seem to move in small ways. It was as if the events depicted were happening somewhere else still, in another dimension, and he was looking at them through a window.

This chamber and the whole of the Savannah estate reflected the message of Lyssa's leadership. Respect and obedience to her rule, and that of the Council, weren't the result of trappings or surroundings. It was the fairness of the decisions they made, and the power they had to enforce them consistently. The strength and authority to rule a species as volatile as vampires rested inside the mettle of the Council members themselves.

In Berlin, the Council table and chairs had been placed on an elevated platform, so any petitioners were looking up at the Council when they came before them. Here the solid dark wood chairs, cushioned in rich gold velvet and carved with decorative engravings, were arrayed around a matching crescent-shaped table positioned on one level floor. At five feet, Lyssa was not a tall woman, but she had no need of height. One look into her jade green eyes, and any vampire with a scrap of sanity would recognize the ancient power there.

He'd seen her call it forth, when she wrested control of the Council from Belizar in one astonishingly brief fight. She could have staked him, but she was as much diplomat as warrior. She'd known Belizar almost as long as Uthe had, and understood the same thing Uthe did about the former Council head. Power and blood drove Belizar as it drove most vampires, but it wasn't true evil or maliciousness, like that which had infested Alanna's Master, Lord Stephen. Plus, Belizar had a keen intelligence and a brutal directness to him that were assets to the Council, as long as they weren't at the rudder. He was better at the prow, for when a battering ram was needed.

"You are much in your mind these days, Lord Uthe."

She'd come upon him unawares. Most vampires had a proximity alert to other vampires, knowing when one was within as much as a quarter mile of them. When many were staying in one house, awareness took a more practical form: a cognizance of movement, of scent, of a change in the air. He supposed he must trust Lyssa like no other vampire, because it seemed an unconscious choice to accept her approach without any awareness of it. He recalled Keldwyn had done the same earlier, though Uthe had attributed that to careless distraction.

"I am, my lady. I apologize if it has caused any dereliction of your needs."

"You think I would be circumspect in telling you so if it was?"

He smiled. "No, my lady. I always appreciate your directness."

As a result of Lyssa's wary relationship with her Fae half-sister, Uthe had already known Lord Reghan was Lady Lyssa's father, but until Queen Rhoswen touched Uthe's hand, Lord Reghan had only been a name to him. Now that he had more to go with it, the regal resemblance was unmistakable. Neither father nor daughter had minced words when it mattered, and both had that vivid jade coloring in their eyes.

"On that note..." She moved to the fountain, took a seat beside it and gestured him into a chair across from her. He realized he'd expected her to sit in her Council chair, with him before the table like a petitioner, but that wouldn't have made any sense to her. The formality was a reflection of his state of mind, not hers.

Jacob was with her, a quiet shadow along the wall. He was unobtrusive, but Uthe knew the servant wouldn't leave her alone in any vampire's presence unless she specifically ordered it. He approved of the servant's protectiveness. Now more than ever.

"Tell me what's been troubling you," Lyssa said. She was watching him with her jade eyes that saw so much. He couldn't get distracted by the possibilities of what she knew or didn't know.

"I must leave, my lady. I do not know for how long." He adjusted his slacks to cross his legs. A palm frond from a plant draping over the fountain teased the tips of his fingers as he rested them on the chair arm.

"Can you tell me why I must do without your company?" she said after a long moment.

"I wish I could tell you all of it, my lady, but it is old business. Vital, but old."

"Does it have to do with what took place between you and Queen Rhoswen?"

"It was related to that, yes. But it is nothing that has an impact on the Council or the future of our species." No worse than it would impact any other living being on the planet if he failed.

"Is she aware of the nature of your business?"

"Somewhat, but not all, my lady. It was best that way."

Lyssa studied him. Uthe waited. She was considering the variables. She knew he wouldn't withhold information from her on a whim.

"Will you be taking Mariela with you?" she asked at last.

"No, my lady." He straightened and leaned forward, clasping his hands between spread knees. "With your permission, I will ask Lord Brian to separate us and free her to be assigned to another. Where I am going, she cannot follow, and there is grave risk to what I do. I would not have her lost to the Council. She has been an asset to me and the Council in her every action, so I would ask the favor of your personal involvement in her future, to make sure her next assignment is someone who will properly value and care for her."

Despite his earlier ambivalence, suddenly he wanted

Mason's policy in place, so Mariela would have as much protection as possible. His judgment was obviously being impaired by his personal preferences, but it didn't stop him from adding, "Helga's servant has been her lover for some time, and I think their relationship has grown quite serious over the years. It would never interfere with their responsibilities as full servants, but if she can continue to have access to him, I think it will contribute to her happiness and soothe this decision."

"Torrence?"

Uthe gave her an amused look. "Lady Helga enjoys watching them together immensely. As to the other Council business under my auspices, I will make sure I tie up the loose ends before I go or assign them appropriately. May I offer you some parting advice about Belizar?"

Her brow rose. "Of course. He has been difficult in Council meetings of late, particularly on this servant issue."

"Which I'm sure you expected." Uthe smiled. "However, since you deposed him as head of Council, he has an even greater regard for you. It is his nature to respect violence and strength. He is a battering ram, but if you point him in the right direction, he will understand the nature of the door better. He also represents the less enlightened thinking of many of our kind, so if you heed his perspective, you'll find the right balance to ensure change doesn't happen too swiftly."

"I don't disagree. Thank you, my lord. But returning to the issue of Mariela, perhaps I should temporarily assign her as a second mark to Helga, until your return?"

"If another appropriate vampire isn't available for her service now, that would be welcome. But I will not take her as mine again." This was a tricky point. There was so much he had to keep hidden.

"You tell me you must go on a trip, and that you do not know when you will return. I think you are softening the blow of this conversation. *Will* you return, Lord Uthe?"

When he did not respond, she leaned forward and clasped

his hand in slim fingers, an unexpectedly intimate gesture. "Not too long ago, when I had to choose someone for the Queen's dance at the Vampire Gathering, you took my hand and offered to dance with me. You wanted to help me manage the loss I was feeling over losing my husband Rex and my former servant Thomas. And though you did not know it, you were helping me deal with the certain death I thought I was facing at that time. We are vampires, and yet your compassion and honesty have always set you apart, Lord Uthe. It is not your vampire blood that drives you, but things far deeper and more powerful. Those things have been a foundation for me and this Council, and I am unspeakably loathe to lose them or you."

Her expression was sincere, her eyes telling him the truth of her deep affection for him. "We have fought the Territory Wars and built this Council together. We have experienced loss, frustration and victories. Set aside formality, and let's speak plainly. What can I do to prevent the tragedy of losing you? Is there nothing?"

By the Cross, he was getting hit by a surfeit of emotion tonight. He should have stayed away from the women in his life and ducked out like a thief in the night.

Instead, he shifted further forward and rested his forehead against hers. There was a comfort there he couldn't deny himself or question the act. The familiarity brought back those times of which she'd spoken. He remembered a night during the Territory Wars where they'd been outnumbered in a skirmish. They'd defeated their opponents regardless.

Due to her slender frame and short stature, the femininity that emanated from her like a bouquet of delicate roses, it was hard to see her as a savage and exceptional warrior, until one saw it firsthand and never forgot it again. It was why when she'd challenged Belizar for Council leadership he'd known she was going to win, and the power structure of Council was going to change.

On the long ago night during the Territory Wars, she'd

sat on top of a corpse she'd created, using the fallen's shirt to wipe off the blades she'd used to hamstring him before she staked him. She'd been humming something like a lullaby. Uthe understood she was using the haunting tune to center and distance herself, from the horror of having to kill their brethren to ensure the survival of them all. At a recent Christmas gathering in her home, he'd heard her hum the same song to her son Kane when she was rocking him to sleep.

She stroked the back of Uthe's head, much as she'd done to her son then, offering comfort. "Stay here," she murmured. "Let me help. I would care for you and protect you however is needed."

It startled him, the insight so close to what he already knew and had barely acknowledged himself, but he squeezed his eyes closed, and drew strength from her love and his own resolve. He lifted his head and straightened, attempting proper decorum. "My lady honors me," he said in a thick voice. "It is difficult beyond description to resist the offer of being forever in your presence, but my regard for you is part of why this quest must be done."

She studied his face with shrewd eyes. Uthe recalled Lord Reghan looking at him much the same way when they'd made the decisions that had led to this moment.

Squeezing her hands, he rose, clearing his throat. "I will take my leave within the next couple days, as soon as I see to Mariela. If I may presume upon your friendship, please make my good-byes once I depart. I'm more susceptible to emotion about this than I expected. I cannot lose my resolve."

"Your honesty tempts me to be dishonorable and drown you in sentiment to keep you here, but I know you, Lord Uthe. Even if your heart broke in pieces, you would never allow it to keep you from what your honor and your God demand of you. It is why I've ever trusted your counsel."

Allowing herself a tight, sad smile, she rose with him. "Very well. It will remain our secret...and Mariela's, until your departure." She placed her elegant hand on his face. "You are a great friend, Lord Uthe. I pray you have a safe journey and safe return, for you will always be welcome in my home. *Always.*"

Her many years showed in her face like the timelessness of smooth rock, worn by water's flow and polished. One might miss how many compressed years and experiences lay behind that remarkable beauty. He felt her stature like a towering Goddess.

"You asked if you might do something for me. It will not keep me here as you wish, but it will aid my quest." He sank to one knee before her, keeping his eyes on her face so he saw the flicker of surprise. "If you would bless my journey with your favor, and allow me to kiss the hem of your gown, I would deem it a far greater gift than this poor knight is worth."

It was rare that a vampire took his eyes off another, for it made him vulnerable. So he did it deliberately, lowering his eyes and bowing his head, awaiting her decision. Her finger tips whispered along his hair. "Lift your head, Lord Uthe," she said after a moment. "But keep your eyes closed."

He did, and quivered as her lips pressed against his throat, her fang sliding along the pulse there, a tiny needlelike sensation. Then she laid her hand on his head. "You have my blessing, Lord Uthe, and my command that you return to my side and service as soon as your conscience permits."

He didn't lift her hem to his mouth. No honorable knight would do such a thing. Instead he bent all the way to the floor and kissed the edge of her dark gown there. When he straightened and rose to his feet, for both their sakes he ignored the glistening in her right eye that suggested a threatening tear.

"'Our Lady was the beginning of our Order," he said. "In her and in her honor, if we please God, will be the end of our lives and the end of our Order, whenever God wishes it to be.'"

Lyssa arched a brow, and Uthe explained. "A quote from St. Bernard, who supported the Templars. Having that subconscious desire for a Goddess to worship, as so many do in a patriarchal religion, he was a devotee of the Virgin Mary. When I am in your presence, seeing your wisdom guide this Council and all our kind, his words come back to me."

He met her gaze then, as an equal, as a mentor, as one whose advice she'd valued. "In you, I see the strength and endurance, the suffering and ferocity ascribed to every feminine face of the Divine since the beginning of time, my lady. It has been a privilege to serve a queen worth serving."

The flash of emotion crossing her face was an even broader stroke this time, but he saved them both embarrassment with one last quick squeeze of her hand and looked toward her servant, standing silently in the shadows. "Care for your Mistress, Jacob. As I would and even better, as you always do and always will."

Jacob's blue eyes were steady as he bowed. "God grant you peace, my lord."

Uthe nodded and started toward the door. He'd almost reached it when Lyssa spoke. "My lord Uthe?"

He paused. "My lady?"

"Before I allow you to depart, I demand at least one piece of the puzzle from you."

"I will never lie to you, my lady."

"I mean I must have this truth, whether you wish to reveal it or not. A courteous refusal to tell me is not the same, is it not?"

"No, my lady." He would miss her clever tongue.

"How old are you, Uthe? Truly?"

She made him smile. In the answering glimmer in her eye, he saw she intended it. It eased his heart in ways he couldn't explain. "You are not the oldest among us, my lady."

Night's Templar

That she'd posed the question meant she'd suspected, but she would be wondering how he'd been able to conceal it, because a vampire's strength correlated to his approximate age, and vampires were able to detect the relative strength of potential friend or foe. When asked about his Templar background, he'd always intimated that he'd been inducted into their ranks in the early 1300s, right at the time the Order was disbanded, but that he'd continued to serve in various capacities as the scattered members relocated. Most thought that put him close to the eighth century mark, and he was able to mask his strength to match that impression.

That strength-to-age parity was one of the things that made Evan, the vampire Uthe had sired, vulnerable to other vampires. His protégé had the strength of a hundred-year-old vampire, and was therefore often mistaken for being that age, though he was over three hundred now. Lord Brian thought it was because of lingering effects of the wasting disease that had come so close to taking his life as a mortal.

"Do you have an exact count? Or a guess?" Her eyes twinkled. "I can't remember mine anymore without effort."

"It was around 950 A.D. I believe. Give or take a couple decades."

Her lips pursed. "One day, I hope you'll tell me stories of your life at that time. We can find how close and how often we came to crossing paths."

Playing seven degrees of separation was a favorite pastime of vampires of advanced age, but the chance he and Lyssa would have that opportunity in this lifetime was slim.

"Perhaps God will be merciful and we'll share a garden in Paradise together. We can sit and share all, like old humans in their rockers at a nursing home." Would they be content, knowing the Lord's Will had been well served in their lives? Or be tormented by what had been left undone? In which case, he expected it wouldn't be Paradise at all, but some form of Purgatory.

Her mouth thinned. "My preference is to have your company on this side of the Veil again, Lord Uthe, before we face what lies beyond it. However, wherever I meet you again, I will look forward to it. And remember what I said." Her gaze locked on his face. "Whatever you need after your quest, I hope you will know you can find it here."

He could not answer that, for the thickness to his throat had returned. Offering her another short bow, he took his leave.

§

Mariela was waiting for him in his chambers at dawn. He allowed her to undress him, and then he took her into his bed, a twining of naked limbs and torsos. When he pressed her to her back, he saw the tears shining unshed in her eyes before she hid her face in his shoulder, her arms holding him urgently. He gave her the gift he'd promised, holding nothing back. He spilled his seed in her wet heat, making sure she came to a pinnacle with him. He brought her to another orgasm with his mouth, and a final with his fingers, enjoying the slippery sensation of her clit and labia spasming under his fingers. Women were endlessly responsive, something he'd always enjoyed watching. He made her drink from his throat, then let her sleep. He'd exhausted her as intended, and when she fell asleep in his arms, he kept his lips against her temple, his mind inside hers one last time, following the pleasant drift of her dreams.

Like most dreams, they were nothing cohesive. Snippets of this and that while she rocked along on the waves of sleep. He realized he was going to miss being in her mind. What if that connection had helped keep him more balanced and focused? Without it, he would feel even more isolated...than he'd always been.

Mariela was the only third marked servant he'd ever

had. Up until her, the bond had not fit with where his path had taken him. With Hugh's warning always in his head, he knew he couldn't afford to get overly dependent on someone else's companionship. His fate, his mission, had always required severe mental isolation. It was best to reinforce that with actual physical isolation. But as a Council vampire, the day-to-day demands, the need for an easy blood source, and then the availability of an Inherited Servant for that purpose, had made taking a third mark seem a functional convenience. An InhServ was a safe choice, more formal, controlled, detached. He could have simply second marked her, but no Council vampire was without a third mark servant, and he had always been conscious of the need to blend.

But was that the true reason he'd capitulated? He hadn't expected things to change so drastically in the past decade, such that the bond with Mariela had become a lifeline of sorts, a way to not feel so alone.

He wasn't alone. Had his faith faltered so much that he thought severing his bond with Mariela would abandon him to a hellish abyss, the void of his own mind? His gut cramped, realizing that was exactly what he feared. He'd fought on the side of armies who were vastly outnumbered, he'd been cornered by aggressive vampires, he'd been trapped in places where the sun would have reduced him to ash if he hadn't figured out how to escape in time. All this time, he'd feared nothing...except becoming the one thing he feared most.

Forgive me my weakness, oh Lord. I will not fail you. I am not alone as long as I walk Your path.

He fell into fitful dreams full of shadows. Demons reached out to him, their fingers like fat slugs impregnated with barbs that latched onto his skin. They dug in and drew him down into oblivion where he would know nothing, remember nothing. But as he thrashed, as he fought, a hand reached through that, clasped him, drew him free. He was back in that silver tower with the scent of magic, clean air and peace. Only he didn't see green and silver eyes in the face bending over his. Dark eyes watched him, sensual fingers sliding down his throat, opening his shirt. Keldwyn's mouth was on his chest, his long hair on Uthe's bare skin. The Fae moved his touch between Uthe's legs, cupping his balls, rubbing his cock. As Uthe arched into the stimulation, he realized his arms were bound above his head, his body a feast for the Fae's pleasure. It didn't inspire panic. Far from it. Here in his dreams, he could be safe.

There is a freedom of thought and feeling in the service of a Master.

Surrendering all to a Master...

It was as if he were in an elevator that dropped suddenly, jolting his eyes open. He knew it was broad daylight, early afternoon, a time he wouldn't normally wake unless something had disturbed him. Mariela's scent was upon him and his sheets, as well as that of the coupling they'd shared. A desolate emptiness swept through him. He pushed up, logy, his mind spinning. He couldn't figure out what was going on, where he was, what...why did things feel upside down?

"Easy." Keldwyn's voice was against his ear, part of his dream. "Lie back down, my lord. Your servant is with Lord Brian. I suspect the procedure is complete and that's why you are feeling so out of sorts."

"Brian said...easier for vampire. She should be disoriented. Not me. Why am I..."

"You know why. It's all right. I'm here. Just lie back down with me. We'll talk chess. I still think you cheated last time."

"We play chess."

"Of course, my lord. Several times a week." Keldwyn was somehow easing him back down onto the sheets. He had his arm over Uthe's chest, was coiled up behind him. He never slept naked, always in lounging pants and a shirt, with the candle burning on the dresser. A Templar slept in his breeches and shirt, and kept a light on through the night.

He'd fallen asleep in the dark, without clothing, for Mariela. The sheets were tangled over Uthe so he felt the press of the other male's thighs against the back of his own through the cloth, but the heat of his body came through the thin fabric. He wasn't alone. Even though something was missing in his mind, far too many things, he wasn't alone. That was the most important thing right now. Uthe wrapped his fingers over Keldwyn's forearm. He was wearing one of those laced shirts, and Uthe plucked at it, irritated at not being able to get past the cloth to the flesh. He tugged harder.

"Hold on. Don't rip it." Keldwyn lifted away from him, shifting in a way that told Uthe he was stripping off the offending garment. "Here, let's do this."

Uthe flinched as the shirt, folded into a thick strip, was wrapped around his eyes. He put up his hand to stop him, but Keldwyn tapped his knee against Uthe's tense ass. "It will help. Closes out a sense you don't need right now and reduces input."

Uthe thought he was wrong about that. Keldwyn's scent, captured in the fibers so close to Uthe's nose, increased other stimuli considerably. Somewhere in his fuzzy mind, he remembered not to pull Keldwyn's wrist to his mouth to bite the male, but it was a close thing. He gripped Keldwyn's forearm, banded across his chest once more. The straight lines of bone to the wrist were layered with prominent veins and sleek muscle, evidence of a male warrior who worked out with weapons. There was a light layer of hair over the firm flesh.

Keldwyn moved the sheets out of the way. Since he was wearing those tight, thin leggings he favored, when he brought his legs up to cradle Uthe's ass again, what pressed against his buttocks was unmistakably a generous-sized cock.

Though he'd had a strong sexual reaction to the male for

some time, the response Uthe had now was deeper and even more intense. Keldwyn's contact wasn't a message about sex alone. It was about want, connection. Impending possession.

It was best just to sleep. He took deep, slow breaths, because the act was rhythmic and helpful. He kept his fingers latched over Keldwyn's forearm, and the male stroked his hair, his shoulder, his side. He was curled up naked in the shelter of the Fae's body. Uthe recognized it as a vulnerable position, but he felt better, stronger, with Keldwyn's heat against his back. Reaching back and up, he found some of his hair. Since the Fae male had so much of it, it wasn't a difficult task. Uthe pulled some forward over his shoulder like a cloak, those few strands bringing him as much warmth as a blanket.

"Sleep, my lord," Keldwyn said, and this time Uthe heard sadness and regret. They all had those, though. It was impossible to live as long as they did without them. His own deepest regrets had happened within the first fifty years of his existence. Would regret disappear when awareness did? Why was Keldwyn sad?

With a sigh, Uthe let it go and allowed sleep to pull him down again.

Chapter Five

When he woke, he was alone. There was no lingering scent of Keldwyn, no evidence he'd been there. Just Mariela's scent, a couple long threads of her blond hair. So the Fae's presence had been part of the same unsettling dreams. Telling himself that was a good thing, Uthe put his feet on the floor. He still had that emptiness, the initial effect of no longer having a servant connected to him, but the heavy disorientation, if it had existed outside his dreams, was gone. He picked up the in-house phone, dialed. Debra picked up. "How is she?" he asked.

"Lord Uthe." Fortunately Lord Brian's servant recognized the location of his phone, since he'd neglected to identify himself, and his throat was still froggy from the twilight rising. "She is doing well," Debra said. "Better than usual. She said you fed her before the procedure?"

Had he? He must have. Yes. That was right, he'd said he was going to do that. "Yes, I did."

"Interesting. The few of these we've done so far have involved vampires and servants less kindly disposed toward one another, so we hadn't considered having the servant feed from the vampire before the procedure. That may make the transition even easier for others in the future."

"Good. Is she...is someone checking on her?"

"Yes, my lord. She left the infirmary about a half hour ago and returned to her quarters, where she's been ordered to rest for a few more hours. The InhServs and novices-in-training are handling her with great compassion and respect. Lord Brian made sure they knew your praise for her, as you requested. I expect you'll see her back at her normal duties within another day." Debra hesitated. "By that, I mean whatever work she's given while she's waiting to be assigned to another vampire. Did you need her?"

Probably more than he'd expected. The unusual progression of emotions he'd experienced only a few hours before swamped him again, but he cleared his throat. "No. I just wanted to check on her. Thank you, Debra."

He hung up before she could say more. He needed a shower to clear his head, and he needed to pack for his departure. He'd no idea if Keldwyn would obtain Rhoswen's permission to allow Uthe entry into the Fae world, but he had another task to complete before that could happen. He'd handle his own travel arrangements, because no one could be privy to his whereabouts once he left Savannah. Once he entered the Fae world, that wouldn't be a problem, due to the difference between the timelines and realities of the Fae world, but until then, he would take all necessary precautions to cover his tracks.

After showering, he donned casual clothes he rarely wore when at Council headquarters, an undyed cotton shirt over black jeans. After packing his few belongings in the chest, he sat down to finalize some correspondence. He didn't want to leave any Council business assigned to him incomplete, but for those things he couldn't finish himself he provided Lyssa enough information to assist whoever had to pick up the baton.

It took longer than expected, but his confidence came back to him as the pen flowed and he recalled without effort all the necessary details for each situation. As he made his notes, he accumulated a neat stack of directions and information at his elbow. Though he knew how to use a computer, he didn't trust their security. He'd often recommended that Council members hand write and code anything they didn't want to fall into the wrong hands. An encrypted hardcopy was the safest way to transmit information. It was how the Templars had protected the pilgrims' funds. Those coded and complicated systems still existed in some forms in the Swiss banking system. When the Order was destroyed in 1307, a contingent of Templars had made it over the Alps and helped the Swiss fight for their freedom. As a result, most of the funds he'd accumulated over the years were banked with the Swiss.

He couldn't observe the vow of poverty, because he had to fund the responsibilities under his guardianship, the things that were guiding his departure now. However, he adhered to its spirit as much as possible. He'd used the funds to help those who needed his help, and to take care of his basic needs, so he wouldn't be a burden on others. The Rule stated if a brother died with money upon him that was not in trust to him for Templar business, then he should not be buried in consecrated ground, that his brothers didn't have to pray for him. That his body could be treated as a slave's and thrown to the dogs. Forgotten.

"My lord? May I enter?"

Uthe looked up from his desk. Mariela was standing in his open doorway, her eyes on the travel chest, which he'd pulled to the center of the floor. It was still open, his small cluster of belongings from the closet stacked on the top.

"Of course." He rose, closed the chest and met her at the door. As he drew her over the threshold, he gave her an assessing look. She did look strong and healthy, if a little pale. "I hope Lord Brian's process didn't cause you excessive discomfort."

"No, my lord." She pressed her lips together before she could say *Not that kind*. He didn't have to hear it in her mind to read it from her face, but then he'd always been exceptionally good at reading body language and facial expressions. Since there was nothing he could do to ease that pain, he gestured her into a chair before taking a seat at his desk and waiting to hear what she needed. She would not have come to him without specific purpose.

She sat quietly, collecting her thoughts, then she lifted her head. "It is new, this separation of vampire and servant while they both still live. A few months ago, there was a servant who was in Lord Brian's facility for several days for the same thing. I tended her afterwards, because helping in the infirmary is something else the InhServs do. She was not at ease until her vampire had departed. Though the separation was something they both desired, she said the loss of his presence inside her was like a wound. She could not bear to see or speak to him knowing...he could no longer hear her or her him, inside. I understand what she meant now."

"I'm sorry, Mariela."

She looked startled. Absurdly enough, apologizing to a human was considered a breech in vampire etiquette, part of the rigid social structure they maintained. In times past, a vampire who desired to sever a third mark bond did so by killing the human. It was considered a regrettable but acceptable decision to protect the secrets of vampire kind.

He looked at Mariela's straight and strong posture, her serious brown eyes. Those surface features hid so much more that he knew about her. He could no more take Mariela's life than he could lift a hand to Lady Lyssa, or any other woman he valued.

She firmed her chin, lifted it. "I am at the service of the Council, and of you, my lord. Even if I am no longer your servant, you have never done anything that made me wish I was not yours. I do not want to take up your time when you are preparing to leave, but for some time, there has been something I wanted to give you. Or to do for you. I thought you might feel it was inappropriate."

"Mariela, I think I would do something inappropriate long before you did." When he reached out, touched her face, he was glad to see an easier look upon it. Mariela loved him, he knew that, but that love was inseparable from her InhServ training. It was why their bond had worked so well. She would love her next Master, as long as he was deserving of her service, and Lyssa would make sure of that.

"What is it you wish to do?"

She hesitated again. "It is very difficult to put into words, my lord." She left unsaid that she would normally have placed the image in his mind, making the communication easier for them both.

"Well then." He lifted a shoulder. "How about you do whatever it is you intended to do, and I will trust myself to your hands."

She flushed at that, a becoming reaction. She rose. "Um...I'd like to stand behind you."

When he nodded, she approached his chair, circled behind him and laid her hands on his shoulders. Realizing he'd never expected to feel her firm and female touch again increased its potency.

"If I can ask the gift of your trust, would you close your eyes, my lord? I know this is very unusual, but it is truly easier to do it than to explain it."

She'd certainly stirred his curiosity. Keldwyn might call him foolish, trusting a woman he'd essentially scorned, exposing chest and throat to her retribution. But while Mariela, like most InhServs, was trained in a variety of fighting techniques, she had no capability for such violence in her. Not against him. He did trust her.

He closed his eyes, and she moved her hands to the sides of his throat, behind his ears, fingers gliding along his close-cropped hair. Drawing a breath, she started to hum, working her hands slowly over his skull, to his nape, around to his shoulders, then back, a slow, rubbing cycle of comfort, more caress than massage, but equally soothing and pleasant.

It wasn't her skilled hands that stilled him, though. It

was that song, and her voice. It lulled him, wound around his heart, offering comfort and pain together. As that reaction swelled within him, he caught Mariela's wrist, his grip tight enough she flinched. He immediately eased his hold, but he brought her around to face him, still holding onto her. He didn't ask, though he knew the intensity of his gaze demanded the explanation.

She bowed her head. "I have come into your room just before you wake many nights, my lord. You have a dream, often enough I've noted it, especially of late. You hum this tune, and you are moving your hands..." She paused, kneeling between his spread knees. He let her go so that she could finish the motion, running her hands just above her own stomach in slow, methodic circles, as she'd done it to his head and shoulders.

"Like a pregnant woman." She gave him a searching glance. "It seems to soothe you, bring you peace. I deduced it was a memory from being in your mother's womb, so when I was stroking your head and shoulders, I was thinking of when she did it." She colored again, as if realizing anew how outrageous a conversation this was to be having with a Council member, and a vampire it was clear she still considered her Master.

"It was...unexpected, but welcome," he said gravely. "It is a lovely gift. Your singing voice has improved since the Christmas carols the servants performed for us last year."

She offered him a small smile. "I've been working with Lady Helga. She said a girl as pretty as I am shouldn't sing like a braying mule. She's been giving me voice lessons."

Uthe sighed. "Helga, the epitome of tact."

Mariela offered a diplomatically noncommittal noise, but fished a slim, digital recorder out of the neckline of her blouse. As she laid it in his hand, he absorbed the warmth of her body through it.

"I recorded the song, hummed it over and over. I didn't know if you remember it when you wake, but I thought it might bring you peace and memory during your waking hours. If you'll forgive my presumption, I thought it would also give you something of me to have with you, if that would be of value."

"Ah, Mariela." He set the recorder aside, and lifted her to her feet. He saw the lovely touch of surprise in her face again as he drew her close. Then he was holding her against him, her arms wrapped around his shoulders, head bent over his, her blonde hair curtaining him. He pressed a kiss between her breasts, inhaling that sweet heat. "You are a treasure, my dearest. Should I return and find anyone has undervalued you, I will rip his or her unworthy heart out, toss it before Council and demand they give you a proper vampire."

Mindful of the need not to make this more painful to either of them, he eased her back. As he looked away from her to give her a few seconds to compose herself, he discovered someone else in his doorway. Keldwyn leaned against the frame, waiting on them. Uthe wondered when the Fae had arrived and how much he'd heard. "I bring news from Queen Rhoswen," he said.

Mariela stepped back, her normal expression in place, his faithful InhServ. But no longer his, he reminded himself. "My lord, do you have further need of me?"

No was the right answer to the question. However, under the circumstances, it seemed harsh to say it that way. "Thank you, Mariela," he said instead, gesturing to the recorder. She offered him one more faint smile and a glimpse of her sad brown eyes before she turned.

He expected her to move past Keldwyn with her usual brief but respectful acknowledgment to the Fae. Instead she stopped and looked directly at him. She never met the Fae Lord's eyes, always deferring to him as she did other vampires. The expression on her face wasn't deference. It concerned Uthe enough he rose from the chair. "Mariela," he said, a low tone of warning.

Keldwyn had not moved, though a thrum of tension vibrated from him. It was what had brought Uthe out of the chair. She looked back at Uthe.

"My lord, what you said about being undervalued? Should I have the means and strength, I would do the same to any who treated you badly."

Keldwyn's brow lifted. The Fae and Uthe's former servant held locked gazes for a protracted blink, then Keldwyn spoke. "Close the door when you leave, Mariela," he said in an even tone.

It was a direct order. If Uthe didn't countermand it, she was required to obey. Her jaw firmed, but she looked Uthe's way. He nodded, not unkind, but firm.

She bowed to him as Keldwyn shifted away from the frame, taking several steps in the room. Mariela left them, the door closing silently behind her.

Queen Rhoswen and her party had departed after the ball and a short, private visit between the two queens, but tonight Keldwyn was dressed more as Uthe would have expected during the Queen's visit. His swallow-tailed coat was a deep green velvet, over another ruffled, laced shirt in the golds of summer. His hair had several slim braids overlaying the loose weight of the rest. The braids were woven with gold ribbon, and the shell of one of his pointed ears was lined with copper rings. A leaf pattern was imprinted on his right cheek and brow, a colorful tattoo that surrounded the right eye and made it somehow more piercing, looking at Uthe from among that camouflage.

"If that woman wasn't human, she might be mildly unsettling," Keldwyn said.

"I find most strong women to be unsettling, in a very stimulating way. And never to be underestimated. Our Lady Lyssa, for example, as well as your Queen Rhoswen." Uthe settled back in his chair. He wanted to ask if the Fae had been here earlier, if it hadn't been a dream. But he couldn't. His desire to ask the question was problematic enough. The answer would be even worse, whether it was yes or no.

Keldwyn lifted a shoulder. "On that note, Her Majesty

has granted you the right to enter the Fae world for the sole purpose of completing your mysterious quest. She also sent you a gift."

"Should I be worried?"

"Always, my lord." Keldwyn withdrew an amulet on a cord, tossed it to Uthe. It looked like a piece of ice, and was cold like one, but there was no melting against the fingers. Inside something shimmered, like captured energy.

"The cord is to help you hold onto it, but do not put it around your neck until you need it."

Uthe wondered if it was a noose that would strangle him, then dispelled the morbid thought. "What will it do?"

"Repeat these words." Keldwyn spoke a short sentence in the Fae language. Uthe repeated it, then the Fae Lord had him do it several more times, until he had the pronunciation correct.

"Roughly translated, it means: *Should all about to be lost, may those true of heart and of like mind come to aid my purpose, be it of the highest intent.*"

"Ah. And that means..."

"Your guess is as good as mine. Either it will help, or it will summon an army of blue Smurfs. They are very true of heart."

"You have been watching TV with Kane again."

"True enough." Keldwyn crossed his arms over his chest as Uthe tucked the amulet safely in a drawer. "It can only be used once, so save it for when the need is dire."

"Good to know. You told me to trust you, and you came through." The Fae preferred gifts to thanks, so Uthe usually worded praise accordingly.

Keldwyn swept a gaze over him. "She had a condition for your travel in the Fae world. In order to act 'freely' there, you must be bonded."

Uthe's brow creased. "Meaning?"

"Meaning you are the full responsibility of someone from the Fae world. She has an aversion to letting a vampire wander around the Fae world like an unsupervised child." Kel spread out his hands. Today he wore only the amber ring with the rose petal. "Her words, not mine."

"Though I'm sure you would have been capable of supplying her the phrase if she was at a loss to find it."

"I have never known Queen Rhoswen to be at a loss to find the right words."

Uthe studied the Fae. There was a curious expectancy to Keldwyn, an energy humming off of him that made Uthe want to shift restlessly in his chair. "Who has been assigned to babysit me?" he asked lightly. "Or am I not allowed the information until I have breached the gate to your world?"

"I am the obvious candidate, since there is no one else who knows you well enough in our world to vouch for you. Unless you have other relationships with Fae royalty I did not know about until now?"

The slight trace of sarcasm was unexpected. Keldwyn already knew Uthe hadn't fully recalled Reghan until contact with Rhoswen had brought those memories rushing back. But the Fae were easily irritated. Uthe chose not to remark upon it. He was digesting the idea of Keldwyn as his guide.

He genuinely hadn't expected it to be the Fae Lord. While the male might like toying with him in the Council setting, the Fae Lord had many responsibilities, to both Fae courts as well as to the Council. "My lord, I have no problem with you vouching for me to another, rather than tying yourself up with this matter. I have no intention of causing harm in your world, but I've also no idea how long my task will take."

"Accompanying you is my decision. I have conditions for that patronage, and I am your only option. While you are bound to me, it means you are subjugated to my will, Lord Uthe. My vassal, so to speak." Keldwyn took the guest chair across from Uthe, stretching out his legs and crossing his ankles to the right of Uthe's. "Are you aware the origin of the word of *vassal* is 'boy' or 'vessel'? So if I called you my vassal, you would be 'my boy' or," his gaze slid over Uthe, "my vessel."

Uthe didn't rise to the bait, burying the images Keldwyn was planting in his head under far bigger concerns. "What does subjugated to your will mean, Lord Keldwyn? I have a goal to accomplish. It does me no good to go to your world if that mission will be hampered by your demands."

"I will not get in the way of that, never fear. Her Majesty wants you out of the Fae world sooner rather than later, and on that we are in agreement. The Fae world is sensitive to incursion from other species, and imbalance is never a good thing there. Until your task in the Fae world is done, you will lie with me when I desire it."

For a moment, Uthe thought he'd misheard him. The request was so banal, at odds with the complexity that he normally associated with Keldwyn's motives. He blinked. "Your price for being my tour guide is that I be your whore?"

"I will not be paying for your services, my lord. Your payment to me, for my sponsorship, is your body." Keldwyn swept his gaze over it, lingering on the columns of Uthe's thighs, the way the cotton shirt stretched over his shoulders. Muscles tightened under his regard, and Uthe had to quell the desire to shift again. "You have compromised your chastity over the years to prove yourself vampire rather than Templar," the Fae said. "And to protect your mission and secrets. You deemed them far more vital to your charge than your personal pride in keeping your vows."

"You are not that privy to my thoughts, my lord. You are guessing."

"I am deducing, based on what I know of you." Keldwyn lifted a brow at Uthe's passive expression. "Maintain that sphinxlike look all you will. It is no less transparent to me. You have always compromised your oath with women, giving your vampire kind the impression that you enjoy them more than men. When you have had a servant, you choose females. Though you can be aroused by sexual interaction regardless of gender, male flesh is far more distracting to you.

"All of this is, I suspect, your way of honoring your Templar chastity code in the only possible way in the vampire world, whose politics are inseparable from their sexually-based power games. It's far less tempting to partake of the gender you don't prefer, isn't it? Then sex is simply sex, a necessity like eating or drinking. What would your Templars, so opposed to sodomy, have thought of that? Did any of them ever accuse you of being a sodomite? You know they were remarkably free of that taint, compared to other Orders. Or maybe they were more discreet."

Uthe templed his fingers. He would treat this as a debate, like the many topics they'd dissected and argued over chess. That would calm the nerves jumping in his belly, as ridiculous as those experienced by a virgin bride on her wedding night. "Or maybe they just subjugated their will to God, abandoning all desire in favor of serving Him, no matter what those desires were."

Keldwyn made a noncommittal hum. "I wonder how many of your Templars preserved their ideals as faithfully as you have. They had to do it only for a mortal life span, or until the Order ended. Whereas you have clung to them for centuries. Is it hubris, a fear of having no faith, or something else that makes you that stubborn?"

"To believe in nothing is no better than to believe in too much," Uthe said between his teeth.

"A sentiment on coffee mugs and T-shirts. It is cliché and old, unoriginal."

"Just as you putting a sexual price on your patronage is."

"Careful," Keldwyn said. Uthe felt that thrum of energy again as the Fae Lord's gaze flashed with heat. "I will have your oath on bended knee that you offer yourself to me

Night's Templar

willingly. If you do not, your mission cannot proceed, whatever it is."

Uthe met the onyx and moonstone gaze. "You weary me," he said. "Whatever it is you hope to gain with your torment, Lord Keldwyn, I wish you well of it. If it is my body you desire, it is yours. It is merely future ashes and dust."

He could defuse the intensity building behind this conversation by bringing up other topics. Like blood sources. If he was in the Fae world longer than a few days, he would need blood to fortify him. Since no Fae would feed a vampire, Uthe had to determine how he could stay nourished.

Keldwyn didn't give him a chance to bring it up. He straightened in the chair, uncrossing his ankles and planting his booted feet. His elegant hands dangled loosely on the end of either chair arm. "I would have your oath before we proceed with any other details, Lord Uthe. Trivial though you consider the matter, it has value to me."

Keldwyn looked pointedly at the floor between his braced feet. It drew Uthe's gaze to the columns of his thighs, the spread of his legs making it impossible not to note the impressive evidence of his virility under the molded fabric. He forced his gaze upward, but refused to look at Keldwyn's face to see if he'd noticed him looking.

"I am waiting, Lord Uthe. Unless you have decided your quest is not as important as your virtue."

"Perhaps your revulsion for sharing your blood is only matched by my distaste for sharing your bed."

"If that was the case, you would not be aroused now."

His shirt was loose over his jeans, but neither Fae nor vampire needed visual evidence to detect arousal. Rather than confirming or denying, Uthe bared his fangs in a dangerous smile. He'd hung his sword on the back of the chair. Rising, he drew the blade from the scabbard in one swift movement, a whisper of menace. Let the bastard think he might try to skewer him, regardless of the consequences.

Keldwyn did not move, though Uthe had the satisfaction of seeing the sensual mouth thin, the eyes rivet on him in that cool, watchful way that suggested he might be close to inciting the Fae's temper. He liked the idea too much. There was more at stake here than a pissing match, and he was channeling desire into aggression to deny his need. He ignored the faint tremor in his hands, the tightness in his chest as he teetered on the precipice of doing the unthinkable.

Planting the tip of the blade in a groove of the oak flooring, he dropped to one knee.

"Speak your oath, and I will repeat it in good faith, my lord," he said, a growl. "You have my promise to adhere to it, unless it countermands God's will."

"I have noticed you still speak like a Templar, vampire. After all these decades."

"In this modern world, promises are broken for convenience or comfort. I will not use casual words to speak a true oath."

"Very well." Keldwyn stood, moving the chair back and putting his hand on the pommel, curling his fingers over Uthe's. His touch was cool, his palm smooth against Uthe's knuckles. "Swear to be bound to me, offering your body willingly to my desires and demands, no reservations, until your quest is done. In God's name."

"I think God has little to do with this," Uthe said, but he repeated it, his gaze lifting to meet the Fae's. "I swear myself bound to you, the Fae Lord Keldwyn, liaison of the Unseelie and Seelie Courts, liaison for the Vampire Council. I will offer my body willingly to your desires and demands, until my quest is done."

"With no reservations," Keldwyn prompted. "You will not hold your mind apart from me, Lord Uthe. I will not consider the oath served if you lie like a board while I fuck you." He slid a curled hand along Uthe's cheek, so Uthe felt the rough edges of the ring resting above Keldwyn's knuckle. "Say it."

"With no reservations," Uthe said, hearing the harsh rasp of his voice, a reaction to Keldwyn speaking his intentions so baldly. His hand was clenched on the pommel, and Keldwyn's, still upon his, would feel it. "I swear."

Keldwyn removed his hand, giving him a speculative look. "Access to our world must mean a great deal to you, Lord Uthe. I did not expect to win your agreement so easily."

"Accomplishing my quest is all that matters. The rest does not." Though he had sworn the oath, Uthe wasn't going to count the edge in his voice an infraction of the "without reservations" part. He could still react to the Fae's irritating nature.

"Clever. You imply my demands do not matter, that they are as nothing to you. I am glad you are so unaffected. Because I require a demonstration of your oath, right now."

Uthe's gaze snapped up. Which was a mistake, since he could ignore the Fae's proximity only so long as his eyes remained focused on the floor. Now he was looking up the full length of Keldwyn's body, the temptation of it inches away from Uthe's fingers wrapped around the sword hilt. This close to him, he had an eyeful of just how well the leggings defined his lower body, the lines of muscle in haunch and thigh, the sizeable package of cock and testicles. If he inhaled too deeply, that autumn scent filled him. Keldwyn also smelled like a summer rain right now, the heat of thunder and the electrical spark of lightning.

"You have no mercy," Uthe said, keeping his voice even. He was thinking of the bed only a few feet away, of how Keldwyn would want the oath demonstrated, and trying to contain his body's far too enthusiastic response. On that, the monks of old had been right. Without the mind, the body had no interest in restraint. Its only intent was to satisfy whatever impulses seized it.

"Mercy is a boon only if it's the proper gift for what is needed," Keldwyn remarked. He reached down again, traced Uthe's temple, his cheek. Uthe steeled himself not to move, but when Keldwyn caressed his mouth with his thumb, it took all his effort not to part his lips.

"I was in the courtyard, watching you spar with Lord Daegan the other day."

He could be wherever he wanted to be, unseen. It was one of the things that Lyssa had warned them about. She'd had Keldwyn and Queen Rhoswen's agreement that he would not use the ability to spy on members of the Council in their private quarters, but the gardens and public spaces were apparently fair game.

"Something inside you opened up," Keldwyn mused. "It was like watching a confined animal suddenly freed. There is that moment when the creature realizes—truly realizes—he can now run. He bursts forth with such speed and enthusiasm, it's as if he never wants to stop. There are few things as beautiful as a muscled, well-formed male pushing himself in an extraordinary, deadly show of grace and power. Lord Daegan could only stop your headlong dash by disarming you. I wanted to follow you when you were done, take you right then, while you were still damp with sweat and your eyes were still flashing with the passion you show so rarely, but which is there in such glorious abundance."

Keldwyn brought his sharp eyes back to Uthe's face, pinning him in place. "I don't think you want my mercy at all, Lord Uthe. I think what you truly want is just the opposite. So stay on your knees and prove yourself to me."

Blood pounded through Uthe's heart, throbbed in his testicles. As Keldwyn held him in that pointed gaze, the Fae's lips curved. "Your clever mouth offers much wisdom to the Council. I'd like a memory of when your tongue was otherwise occupied. And hear me now," he added, "If you bite me, score me with your fangs, I will take my pound of a flesh in a way that will tear your soul wide open."

Devils came in many forms. The tremor in his fingers

Night's Templar

had increased. Uthe dispelled it with an act of will before he reached out, figured out the laces to the leggings. Keldwyn didn't help him, but Uthe stiffened when the Fae's fingers moved to Uthe's shoulder, tracing the breadth of him, coming back to curve over his skull.

The pants were a front flap style, laces on either side. Underneath was all Keldwyn. His cock stretched out, growing thicker and harder before Uthe's eyes. His pubic hair was smooth and trim, black silk framing his member and curling over the testicles beneath. His shaft was flushed to a darker flesh color, thanks to the blood filling it to such rigidity.

Uthe's heart was beating up into his throat. He was not a stripling lad, not a virgin by any means. It had just been so long, even before the Order. Had it truly been that long since he'd been intimate with a male?

"Your mouth, vampire," Keldwyn said in that same low tone. He slid his hand down to Uthe's wrist, resting on Keldwyn's upper thigh. Closing his grip around that, he guided Uthe's hand to his erection. Uthe watched the Fae curl his fingers over the base, making Uthe's thumb brush his balls. A different species, but still so much the same.

"It has been many years, my lord," he said, his voice strange to his ears. "Though I fear nothing so little as your retribution, if I score you, it will be by accident."

"Just imagine it's your own cock and you will take extra care. Unless you vampires get aroused by punctures in your genitalia."

"No, my lord." Uthe almost smiled at his tone. Keldwyn's wit was sharp and on the mark, often capable of amusing Uthe. This wasn't amusing, but the tease helped. Mixed feelings filled him. The practical part of his mind told him to just do it, get it over with. If touching Keldwyn this way was truly distasteful, he could have done that. It all would even be easier. But the problem was just the opposite. He was mesmerized, seeing his hand clasped around another male's cock, and not just any male. A male who had proven himself irresistible to Uthe. Even without the oath, Uthe had known it was just a matter of time before they ended up here. Keldwyn had merely tired of waiting and taken the advantage he'd been given. As a tactician himself, Uthe couldn't fault him. He might even be thankful for it.

Keldwyn increased his grip on Uthe. "You are shaking, my lord," he said. "Do not fear yourself in this. This is truth, for both of us."

Which was why it was so disturbing to him. Leaning forward, he put his mouth over the glans. The musky pre-come smell was clean, earthy, but with a heated flavor that tempted the tongue. He thought of spiced cider, or the tantalizing thick syrup formed by the sugar and juices of an apple pie. He traced the corona and teased the slit, collecting more of that taste.

Keldwyn drew in a breath, his body growing taut. Uthe curved a strong hand over his upper thigh, holding him, savoring the sudden tautness of the muscles under his palm. Knowing the Fae wasn't unaffected, and was less in control than he appeared, was useful. Needed. Uthe slid his whole mouth over the head, then down the shaft. By the Cross, it truly had been so very long since he'd done this, since he'd had someone he'd wanted like this. He couldn't help but take his time, reining back the wasteful urgency of lust. Keldwyn's hand moved to his nape, then cupped his skull, applying a firm pressure that told Uthe he was not the only one fighting that battle.

Uthe's fingers slid across the Fae's thigh and around, finding Keldwyn's buttock. It was tight as the iron the Fae preferred to avoid. His own cock was in a similar state, and every muscle was drawn and straining in anticipation. Desire was a sharp pain in his lower belly.

He took in more of Keldwyn's shaft, tasting the length of it. Now his hand was back alongside his testicles, petting the trim hair over the pubic mound, teasing the tight silken curls over the balls. Keldwyn had arrived at a Council

Night's Templar

meeting once with a fine down of a beard, like a man who'd not shaved in several days. When Lyssa had remarked upon it, Keldwyn said the Fae did not have to shave. They could choose to have facial hair or not, altering their appearance in various ways, like the tattoo that was on his face today, which might not be there tomorrow. The beard had defined his jaw even more, the short stubble on the upper lip drawing attention to the shape and firmness of his mouth.

Uthe slid down to the root, relishing Kel's indrawn breath as he took him deep into the tight clasp of his throat and wrapped his lips firmly around his base. He'd remembered how to relax his gag reflex and the Fae reaped the benefits. Keldwyn's hand flexed on his head, fingers pressing into Uthe's scalp. He ran his tongue along that pounding vein, the folds of flesh over his balls. A high Fae's sex organs had no apparent differences from human or vampire. Uthe wasn't surprised, since the way the male acted around him said sex worked in a similar way for them.

For the most part.

As Keldwyn trailed his fingers from his nape over his shoulders, under the collar of his shirt, Uthe jumped at the crackle of electricity teasing his flesh.

"Don't stop. Your mouth is skilled in far more than vampire politics." Keldwyn continued to draw that electric path along his skin, down his shirt collar, along the side of his working throat. A vampire's throat was sensitive to any type of touch, and so the feral sound Uthe made was almost involuntary. Keldwyn dug in his nails, which suddenly felt longer, sharper. As he descended to Uthe's nipple, that touch of electricity came again. Uthe shuddered at the feel of it.

"You should see what happens when I wrap this stimulation around your cock, Lord Uthe."

Uthe held onto that image and everything Keldwyn was giving him. Maybe the Fae Lord thought he'd resist this and had added the extra stimulus to help him get lost in it. That wasn't the problem for Uthe.

Keldwyn had been a temptation within touching distance for far too long. The difficulty for Uthe was not revealing how good this felt, how much the Fae was making him want even more. He should have put effort into being inept at this to frustrate Keldwyn. Since it had been so long for him, a lack of skill wouldn't necessarily be artifice. But that kind of calculation didn't honor the oath he'd taken. Keldwyn understood how seriously Uthe took a promise. However, oath or not, Uthe knew he was using it as an excuse to follow his own desires, tasting, sucking and stroking the other male with enthusiasm. Whether or not any skill was involved, the Fae Lord was responding to his fervor with some of his own, shoving into Uthe's mouth. It made Uthe's lips stretch in a primal grin around the male's cock.

That electrical sensation from Keldwyn's fingertips turned into a thrumming vibration, a surge of energy that wrapped Uthe up in a cocoon and made everything about giving and feeling pleasure. Keldwyn came, flooding his mouth with a release that tasted of honey, sunshine and smooth stone. Uthe's fingers curled into the Fae's quivering thigh, his other hand coiled around his cock and exploring the twitching testicles, the appealing softness of the skin covering the firm roundness of what lay beneath.

Keldwyn drew a deep breath. "Well done, my lord. Very well done."

He hadn't expected or required the praise. Though he expected his pride to be abraded by the whole situation, Uthe felt an odd peace at completing the task, doing it well. The only thing that wasn't peaceful was his own libido. He was painfully rigid, and Mariela was no longer his servant, to attend to him. Any second mark serving in a Council capacity could be called upon for that kind of service, but Uthe found the idea of exposing himself like that unappealing for reasons he didn't care to examine. He'd simply meditate himself back to a less aroused state once Keldwyn took his leave.

"Stay on your knees." Keldwyn bade him sit on his heels as he laced the leggings, covering himself. Uthe could tell him that serving his sexual desires was all he'd agreed to do. Sitting at his feet like a pet was not part of the requirements, but before he could make that justifiable argument, Keldwyn dropped to a squat before him and placed his palm on Uthe's chest. "Stand on your knees, Lord Uthe."

As he did, Keldwyn went to one knee, shifting closer. "Your hand on my shoulder. You will need the balance."

Uthe wasn't sure of his intent, but he complied. Keldwyn slid his hand down Uthe's front, deftly opened his jeans and pushed beneath his underwear, wrapping his fingers like snug vines around his cock. Then he began to stroke.

Uthe's grip convulsed on his shoulder and Keldwyn put his other hand around his waist, drawing him closer. "You may lean if you wish," he murmured, his hair brushing Uthe's cheek, his jaw. "You are beautifully formed, my lord. Not that I expected any differently. I like you in the jeans. Wear those more often. You too often hide your assets in the smooth lines of your slacks and loose trousers."

For his part, Keldwyn could have given hand jobs for a living. Uthe didn't often fall into the crudity of soldier talk anymore, even in his mind, but the alternative was letting himself react to the Fae Lord caring for his needs in such a decisive way, no asking for permission. When was the last time someone had touched him without permission? Uthe's breath caught in his throat as Keldwyn worked him.

I am in a box of steel. Suffocating. You put me there, and yet you are the one suffocating in your life for me. He will free you, and then I will be free.

The intrusion of that sibilant voice should have jarred him, knocked him out of the spiral of want building in his lower belly. But he was used to its interruptions, and the wants of his body were too strong. He ignored it. He kept pushing into Keldwyn's touch. Plus, if the voice was trying to make Uthe repel Keldwyn, it was a good reason to embrace the opposite course. Unless the serpent voice could predict that. His mind was whirling, his body tensing...

Somehow his hand was on Keldwyn's shoulder, then around it, fingers digging into the Fae Lord's back. He was leaning fully into Keldwyn's body. Uthe was not a massive male, though he was built strong and wide enough, but Keldwyn held him easily. He was speaking to him, a crooning language like music. When he tilted his head, Uthe's face was against the fall of dark hair, the gold ribbons and braids. He could sense the artery in Keldwyn's throat, pounding just beyond his reach. Since sexual release would bring forth his fangs, he turned his head away, pressing his jaw against the point of Keldwyn's shoulder.

Keldwyn adjusted without disrupting him. As his cock jumped in the Fae's sure grip, Uthe felt the press of cloth and knew the Fae had covered him with the tail of Uthe's shirt, containing the spray of seed that overflowed, thick and heated. Keldwyn's other hand dropped, slid into the back of Uthe's loosened jeans to squeeze his flexing buttocks, urging him on, increasing the intensity of the climax. When it was over, Keldwyn caressed those globes of pale flesh, then found his way up under Uthe's shirt to explore his back, hold him. He was holding him while Uthe was in his arms, leaning against him.

It wasn't sex. It was intimacy, succoring, something far too hazardous to him. Up until Mariela's peculiar request to stroke his head and hum to him, he'd rarely accepted such a thing from someone offering it sincerely, with no hidden motives. Which meant he couldn't afford it from a mysterious Fae whose intentions were entirely suspect.

He had a high regard for Keldwyn's intelligence, his abilities as a liaison. He enjoyed the intellectual challenge of him on a day-to-day basis, both in Council meetings and in their discussions and leisure strategy games. However, when it came to the personal, to friendship, a Fae was a Fae. They explained themselves to no one, and their motives could be detailed and pre-meditated, or capricious and whim-based. He'd seen all those things in Keldwyn.

He was attracted to Keldwyn, but who wouldn't be? Being alluring was part of his power, same as it was for vampires. Too many of the old stories suggested a Fae would extend something that looked shiny and appealing, but turned out to be an illusion, the quest for it destroying a person's whole world. A day in a Fae world could mean the loss of an entire lifetime in the person's actual one.

Fairy tales could exaggerate, but in the case of the Fae, the perils might well be understated. There was a reason the Fae and vampires had been enemies.

There was a wrongness to his thinking. Uthe knew he was denying his feelings for the male, and that denial could be fueled by his fear of making the wrong steps and jeopardizing the task he had to finish. It didn't make Uthe's musings untrue, however. It took him longer than it should have to draw out of the other male's embrace. But he did. That was all that mattered. He felt the Fae's gaze on him as he got to his feet, tucking himself back in and refastening his jeans. Stripping off the shirt, he took it to the bell elevator. Once a day, it was drawn up to the main floor, the clothes washed by the servants and then reappearing on the platform clean, ironed and hung on a rack.

"How long have you known you have Ennui, my lord?" Keldwyn asked.

He was in the process of pulling the elevator door back in place. His grip on the cable slipped and the door dropped onto his other hand with a bruising thud. Biting back an oath, he pulled it free.

"Good thing no other dangling appendages were close to that."

It might have been better if one had been, for an aching

dick might have lessened some of Keldwyn's effect on him. Though Uthe doubted it. He moved to the kitchenette and ran his hand under a soothing rush of water from the sink faucet. The edge of the bell elevator door had cut into the flesh, but it would heal quickly, gone in minutes, unlike the truth that had just been thrown out into the open between them. He watched the few drops of blood mingle with the swirl of water against the silver sink and disappear down the drain.

He kept his back to the Fae, turning over his words, trying to determine how best to handle them. Uthe had made the mistake he hadn't made in decades. He'd started spending his free hours with one person rather than keeping himself isolated, secluded, mysterious. To make it worse, the person with whom he'd been keeping company was his mirror image. Both of them skilled advisors, valued for their ability to notice the smallest details. To know every piece on the chess board as thoroughly as possible.

Had his judgment declined so much? He didn't like to think so, but the alternative was a big leap. Despite his concerns about Fae motives in general, his intuition had led him to one specific Fae whom he might be able to trust enough to let down his guard.

The struggle to find the right answers had turned him into a plank, the tension in his shoulders spreading to his whole body. He'd mastered a poker face long ago, yet there was no way to turn the current moment back to his advantage. On the surface, all he'd done was give oral sex to the Fae Lord. Beneath the surface, far more had happened. He'd left himself too open and had no defense that would be effective.

It didn't matter. He didn't want to discuss it, and there was nothing in their relationship that required it. Not yet.

When Keldwyn shifted, his footsteps indicating he was coming closer, Uthe stiffened further. "Please do not approach me right now," he said.

"I would respect that, except your words do not match

what I feel from you. Or for you." The Fae's fingertips whispered down Uthe's back. His nerve endings followed the touch like wheat bending to a calming breeze. When Keldwyn reached the waistband of his jeans, he hooked his fingers there, giving the fabric a tug that Uthe felt against his taut abdomen. The Fae kept his hand there, lightly stroking his lower back, the rise of his ass just below the denim. "I will not betray your trust in this."

"You compelling me to serve you sexually wasn't a betrayal?"

"A Fae does not offer assistance freely. An exchange must occur for balance. Sex is something we want from each other, but you would not accept that without compulsion. So it seemed the most reasonable price to put on my assistance, a benefit to us both."

Keldwyn's other hand slid down Uthe's arm, to the hand that he'd caught in the door. He exerted gentle pressure on the bruised area behind the knuckles, and Uthe realized he was ensuring Uthe hadn't broken anything. It wouldn't have mattered if he had. His bones could heal, in a way his mind no longer could. He shoved down the thought viciously.

"You have told me many times a Fae does not lie. I don't disagree with that, but you are excessively clever in how you say things, and what you don't say. This binding you impose is more than balance."

"Yes. It may be. But it is the best truth for now."

"Why?" Uthe turned then, faced him, making Keldwyn remove his touch. "Why can I trust you, my lord?"

That wasn't the real question. Behind it were far darker things. *Do you realize, if I do trust you, how far that trust might have to go?* Over the past year, as he'd become sure of what was creeping upon him, he'd vacillated endlessly between denial and desperation, praying and struggling to understand the divine purpose to this. He would have removed himself from the Council the moment he was sure his judgments were becoming unsound, but until the past few days, extra careful diligence and review of all his decisions and advice had assured him that time had not yet come. Now the missive on the postcard had come, at the same time it was clear the disease was starting to accelerate. It meant he had to leave his Council post, as well as address the one task that remained undone. He might have called that divine timing, but the hastening of the Ennui conflicted with that reassurance. He could only proceed, though, and hope he wasn't too late to do what he'd been charged to do.

That was duty, responsibility, his honor to his oath. Difficult but expected. Yet in the vulnerable and desolate dawn hour, or at the unguarded moment at twilight's first waking, the personal side of it often took him unaware and swamped him. He'd relied on his own judgment for over a thousand years, trusting only himself, and now...

He'd read all of Lord Brian's reports thoroughly. Ennui had a variety of symptoms. The milder form of it resulted in disorientation, loss of memory and self-control, a slow decomposition of the mind. Then there was the violent side of it. A total loss of impulse control, coupled to rage and overblown blood lust, manifesting in forms of sadism that even vampires would find horrifying. Each vampire experienced Ennui uniquely, some on the milder end of the spectrum, some on the bloodier side. But it all boiled down to loss of control.

All these centuries, he'd prayed as if he'd given up his will and destiny to the Lord. Yet every day, and in every prayer, it was a choice, and that choice meant everything. Losing that choice, having it taken away, there was nothing that could prepare him for that. Every time he saw evidence of the Ennui's advancement, he had to fight down the sense of panic clawing at his throat. He'd faced every type of danger imaginable without flinching, and this made him want to curl in his bed, pull his blankets over his head and cower like a child. Which enraged him, but he couldn't afford to let that rage take over. Control of baser emotions

Night's Templar

like anger, bloodlust and pride had been the core of the Rule, and he'd used those years of self-discipline to serve him well this past year. He would stake himself before he'd let that darker end of the disease have him.

When he focused on his duty, he could hold the despair at bay. But with Keldwyn offering the illusion of a safety net—for Uthe couldn't trust that it was more than a mirage in the desert—that desperate feeling threatened to take him over. He couldn't even reach for prayer right now. The only thing within reach seemed to be the male standing before him.

Keldwyn had remained silent. Or had he? *No. Don't do that to yourself.* He was not so advanced in the disease that he'd forgotten something someone said to him only a minute ago. If he was at that point, he would have excused himself from Council responsibilities months ago.

"Why can I trust you, my lord?" Uthe repeated. "I require an answer." He needed it, actually, and he needed it to be the right answer.

Keldwyn reclaimed Uthe's injured hand, inspected and then brushed his mouth over it. Uthe curled his fingers into a fist, fighting the feelings the oddly gentle gesture caused. "My lord, I am going to punch you in the face."

Keldwyn's lips quirked, but then his expression sobered and he met Uthe's gaze with dark eyes that held fires capable of warmth or burning. "Because you are bound to me by oath now, Lord Uthe. That means not only that I am responsible for your actions in the Fae world, but you are under my protection."

Releasing Uthe's hand, he moved back to the guest chair and dropped into it, one leg stretched out and one bent, his hand resting on a chair arm and his opposite shoulder hooked over the chair back. The casual pose, so like the one he took during their debates or chess matches, gave the moment a needed sense of normalcy. Uthe fished for another shirt in his closet, but Keldwyn shook his head. "Leave it off. I like the look of you this way."

Uthe paused. "Does this binding command me beyond my sexual service to you, my lord?"

"No. But it is up to me to determine what falls under that category, does it not?" Keldwyn swept him with an appraising look, unsettling Uthe. Ridiculous, really, but when was the last time he'd given any thought to how a lover looked at his body? He kept himself fit as most vampires did, ready to fight. His musculature was lean and layered versus bulky and thick, but he had a solid, large bone structure that provided a decently broad chest and shoulders. He saw Keldwyn eyeing and unmistakably enjoying all of that. It irritated him, which drove back less manageable feelings. He wondered if that was Keldwyn's intent, or if it was just a useful side effect.

"If you are worried others may have noticed the Ennui," Keldwyn said, "I do not believe anyone has. With the possible exception of Lady Lyssa, because her husband Rex had it."

That should have startled Uthe, but he thought of the way Lyssa had looked at him. Her intensity when she'd told him she would care for him however was needed—if he returned. The heavy weight on his chest was a mix of gratitude and mortification, and deeper emotions that made him glad he'd kissed the hem of her skirt.

"It is a gradual, insidious kind of condition, is it not?" Keldwyn continued. "Moments of perfect clarity, and then abrupt loss of time and memory. Surges of impulse control problems, blood and sex, violence."

"Yes." He'd read Brian's reports, then. Uthe took a seat in the chair across from him. He couldn't bring himself to look as relaxed as Keldwyn, but he did his best, trying to steady himself in all the ways he knew from other unsettling situations. There'd been many of those over the years. Being a vampire and a Council member made violence and crisis inevitable. Though when it came from within instead of without, it required an entirely different skill set to appear calm and unruffled about it.

Night's Templar

Keldwyn tilted his head, the lamplight glittering off the tattoo on his face. "I spoke to Lord Brian extensively about it, as part of my continuing education on the vampire world. He checked with Lady Lyssa to be certain how much he could say. Such caution speaks well of him."

"He is mature far beyond his years. He will serve on Council himself one day."

"He told me that the symptoms will present in different combinations and levels, depending on the vampire. Daegan Rei's mother was beset by apathy and lethargy, one of the most peaceful experiences of the disease documented. No bloodlust or impulse issues. She seemed touched by an almost divine calmness until the very end."

"Yes." Uthe had helped with her care and protection, as he was sure Keldwyn knew. She hadn't wanted Daegan to know her condition until it could no longer be concealed. Most vampire children did not stay in close contact with their parents after they matured, as demands and interests drew them apart, so it had not been difficult. Once Daegan had learned of it, though, he'd stayed close, sharing the responsibility for watching over her with Uthe as much as she'd allow. Unfortunately, he'd been away when she died, but it could not be helped.

The rumor on Council was that the confusion of the disease had probably made her think it was nightfall, and her servant had been unable to coax her in before the sun rose. Uthe thought it more likely that she had a moment of lucidity and ordered the servant to leave her be, to let her go. Or he'd had a moment of compassionate clarity and had known it was their time. She'd apparently lain down on a bed of flowers, her arms spread out like wings, because the ash had left an impression like an angel's against the delicate foliage. Since a third mark's life was linked to his vampire's, her servant's body was found curled at her feet.

"You loved her," Keldwyn observed.

"I did. She was a friend. There are those who thought there was more between us." Uthe lifted a shoulder.

"As I said, it has been easier for you to allow others to think a woman's flesh is your preference." Keldwyn shifted his leg so his ankle pressed against the side of Uthe's foot. "Your mouth dispels that impression rather quickly. Did I not have to honor your need to complete your quest in a timely manner, I would have you on your knees several times a day, Lord Uthe."

His loins tightened at the image, but Uthe said nothing. Keldwyn straightened and leaned forward, so his knees were within a few inches of Uthe's. The Fae's attention was on his face. "I would have you say it, Uthe. That you prefer a man's touch."

"Why?"

Keldwyn traced Uthe's collarbone, hooking the chain of the Templar pendant he often wore. The medallion, worn from constant wear and age, had the raised imprint of two knights riding one horse on one side; the Dome of the Rock was on the reverse. Around the knights was engraved *sigillum militum*, the military seal, and around the Dome was *Christi de Templo*.

Keldwyn passed his fingers over the raised image without comment, going from there down Uthe's chest, following his pectoral. Uthe drew in a breath as the Fae scraped a fingernail over his nipple, making Uthe want to shift in the chair. "Because I want to hear it from your lips while I am touching you. Because it makes me want you more."

When he'd agreed to Keldwyn's condition of sexual service, he'd known it would be a challenge to keep his reaction to such demands under his control, but he hadn't expected it to be impossible. Sex was a pleasant, manageable activity for him. He'd forgotten it could be like this. Or perhaps it wasn't a matter of forgetting. He'd never actually experienced anything as intense and strong as his reaction to the Fae's demands.

"I prefer a man's touch, my lord." His voice had a hoarse quality. Keldwyn's eyes darkened.

Night's Templar

"Good, Lord Uthe. Next time I ask you a question about your desires, do not make me pry it out of you." He sat back and picked up the thread of their conversation. The seesaw between emotional and physical turmoil was making it difficult for Uthe to find steady ground.

"There were those who thought Lady Lyssa's mother had Ennui, including Lyssa herself, but Brian is not so sure. After Lyssa was old enough to care for herself, Masako withdrew from the vampire world. He has collected data that suggests she started falling into melancholy. She also experienced episodes of violence where she had to be restrained to prevent indiscriminate harm to other vampires or humans. All indications of Ennui, but Brian postulated that the manner in which Lyssa's father died broke something within her, never repaired. Once she knew her daughter could handle life on her own, her emotions about that time of her life closed back in upon her and tore her to pieces. When she begged to embrace the sun, those caring for her permitted it. She did not go easily. She died weeping under its heat."

Uthe rose and moved back to his desk. "I need to finish packing."

Keldwyn's gaze went to the chest. "You must have been sure I would secure the Queen's permission."

"I was confident you would do all that could be done, but that's not why I'm packed. There is something I must do before I go to the Fae world. I can arrange to meet you back here when it is done."

"I will go with you. There is nothing to hold me here right now."

"That is not necessary, my lord."

"But is there anything to prohibit you from having company? Other than your wish to be rid of me?"

Whereas the Fae claimed never to lie, vampires had no problem with it, generally. Unfortunately, lying to Keldwyn and getting away with it was as difficult as getting a lie past Uthe himself. Plus, Uthe found he didn't want to lie to him about this.

"Nothing to prohibit you. But I see nothing to compel you. What you desire from me, you can get elsewhere easily enough during my absence and not have to endure this journey."

He'd said something that displeased the Fae, because Keldwyn got that tight look around his jaw. "Do not presume to know the shape of what I desire from you, my lord," he said. "But you are wrong. There is something to compel me. Your Lady Lyssa."

Uthe's gaze sharpened on him. "What do you mean?"

When Keldwyn turned his head, the leaf imprint on his cheek and temple enhanced the piercing quality of his expression. "Your Queen requested that I be with you throughout your charge, from beginning to end. She told me she would consider it a personal favor. It's a risky boon for a Queen to offer a Fae, though I'm sure she's well aware of the implications of it."

Uthe left the desk to stand before Keldwyn, his expression cold. "You will not obligate Lady Lyssa to anything. I will take on the burden. She should not be beholden to you. She is too important to risk such a favor."

"She is more important than your quest? You would risk owing me a favor rather than her, even if it jeopardizes what appears to be the reason for your existence?"

Uthe set his jaw. "Can a Fae have enough honor to tailor his favor so it does not risk something that could do great harm?"

Keldwyn's gaze narrowed. "A vampire, questioning a Fae's honor? Is that not like a sewer rat impugning the intentions of a—

"Pure bred poodle. With painted toenails and wearing a tiara?" Uthe swept his gaze over the Fae's finery, ignoring how appealing it looked on him.

Keldwyn came to his feet. As he did, a cold wind blasted through Uthe, sharp enough it stole his senses, blinded him, though for no more than a blink. When he focused

Night's Templar

again, Keldwyn stood before him in the far plainer but frustratingly no less tempting garb he'd worn to meet the Queen, the plain white tunic open at the throat, the snug trousers and laced boots. The tattooing was gone, leaving his face chiseled as smooth stone, his hair pulled back in a sleek tail to emphasize the harsh expression.

"Your anger is misplaced, my lord."

"Is it? How do you react to having your queen threatened?"

Keldwyn blinked. "I am no enemy to Lady Lyssa. I have never been her enemy. Favors form links, my lord. Those links often can be the only thing that keep us on the right path."

"Then consider the one she offered you another link in my chain to you, my lord. Release her from it. Whatever you need, I will give, as long as—"

"It does not countermand God's will. I know. I have an excellent memory."

Keldwyn tried to conceal it, but as soon as the words left the Fae Lord's mouth, Uthe caught his subtle flinch, the flash of regret. Despite the sudden tension between them and the uneasy quagmire within him, Uthe couldn't help smiling. "It's good that one of us does. That is the first time I've seen you put your foot in your mouth, my lord. Perhaps having your cock properly serviced diminishes your cleverness. I'll have to remember that."

Keldwyn harrumphed at that, took a seat again. "Those are the only symptoms you've yet experienced with any significance, correct? Disorientation and occasional lapses in memory?"

"And serious lapses in judgment in the company I keep," Uthe muttered. From the corner of his eye he saw the male's lips twitch. Uthe moved to the sink, stared down at the pink stain his blood had left. It was too much to hope that Keldwyn would let the subject go. "Were you here with me, the other night?" he asked before he could stop himself.

"I was."

Uthe nodded, eyes back on his muted reflection. The relief that it hadn't been a delusion wasn't all because of his fear of the disease's progress. It was just...relief. And he was far too content that Keldwyn was determined to accompany him on this first leg of his task. He had no reason to doubt that Keldwyn was serving Lyssa's interests, but that didn't mean he wouldn't be serving his own Queen's. He could have multiple reasons for staying so close to Uthe's side. But Keldwyn looking after the Queen's interests was honorable, what Uthe would expect of him. It was part of what he required of himself in his service to the Council and Lyssa, his own code of honor.

A Fae's capricious nature might seem incompatible with the vampire idea of honor, but Uthe knew it wasn't. He'd stepped on Kel's honor now, just to confirm it. It was something he respected, even as he knew Keldwyn was capable of straddling multiple roles—ally, enemy, impediment, danger, risk...or necessary friend.

God guide us both. This is too important for me to fail because of a weakness of the flesh. But it wasn't Keldwyn's flesh that compelled Uthe so much. If it was, this would be far easier.

"So, this task you must do first." Keldwyn spoke at last and nodded to the chest. "Where are we going, Lord Uthe?"

Though the Fae Lord remained in his chair, the way he met Uthe's gaze when Uthe turned to face him made him feel much closer. Uthe took a breath.

"Syria."

Chapter Six

A private plane was not a problem. Negotiating foreign air space and landing in the remote area that was their destination, even less so. Uthe had maintained the necessary contacts to open doors as needed.

He'd seen a couple of documentaries—what Lord Brian derisively called junk science—that speculated on the secrets the Templars might have kept to the present day. As with most conspiracy theories, the truth was further off the rails than they supposed, and far less dramatic than they hoped. While there were organizations like the Masons that publicly claimed ancestry with the Templars, those descended from the original Order led normal lives with no traceable connections to the Templars, in order to be useful when needed: an air traffic controller, a pilot. As well as a government official who, when the key phrase was used, would make the proper adjustments, no questions asked, to ensure Uthe could fly into the country unchallenged.

Once used, the phrase was changed for all. It was communicated to those who needed to know in a variety of ways. Carrier pigeon, coded correspondence, a cryptic telephone call couched as a wrong number. In the 1800s, Uthe had received such a code change from a young pickpocket with serious brown eyes and a face so burned he looked like he wore a mask. But his smile was happy and carefree, and he took the tip Uthe gave him with a grin before he disappeared into the crowd.

He suspected some of the descendants kept in closer contact with one another, working on more widespread efforts related to ancient Templar interests and influence, but he hadn't been part of any of that since the Battle of Hattin. He'd merely maintained the necessary connections to serve the singular charge he'd been assigned by Hugh. Early on, when he'd optimistically believed the charge would be accomplished sooner rather than later, he'd wondered what he would do after the task was done, how he could continue to serve his oath. Now he didn't have to worry about that, since his mind would not be reliable enough for anything by the time this was done. Well, amend that. God willing, it would wait until the task was done to become pea soup.

Not surprisingly, it was somewhat of a relief to have his second most closely guarded secret known by one other. It helped that Keldwyn had not remarked upon it further, nor treated Uthe any differently because of it. Rhoswen had only granted Uthe access to the Fae world for his official quest there, so he could not take advantage of the portals that Keldwyn could to make the trip from Savannah to Damascus. He and Keldwyn had parted ways at the Savannah portal, yet when Uthe stepped off the plane to make the connection to the private charter that would take them to their destination in Syria, Keldwyn was already waiting on him. Much like during Uthe's morning sun ritual, it was as if he'd always been there, a step ahead, waiting.

The oath Uthe had made to him seemed to be creating the biggest change between them. The Fae Lord had demanded nothing further of him yet. However, the warmth of Keldwyn's gaze upon their reunion showed he was enjoying the opportunity to look at Uthe as his sexual conquest. Even after they boarded the charter and took their seats across from one another, he felt the male's close regard. Uthe closed his eyes to meditate, then pray for guidance. When he at last opened his eyes, he bit back a chuckle. Keldwyn had opened a tattered copy of *The Fellowship of the Ring* and was reading it. "Is that from Jacob's personal library?"

"It is. He recommended I take the whole trilogy, since he indicated I would wish to know how the story turned out."

"You're so well read, I'm surprised you haven't read it."

"There are more stories to be read than days in an immortal lifespan." Keldwyn shifted, bracing his foot on the edge of Uthe's seat, between his spread knees. His attention followed a straight track from there to Uthe's groin. "You are wearing the jeans again today. A different pair, but still black." He slid his foot forward, braced the ball of it against Uthe's testicles, a teasing pressure he increased, eyes tracking Uthe's response to the discomfort. Uthe had to suppress the desire to push against him, rub, but he didn't conceal his reaction well enough.

Keldwyn's gaze increased its heat. "You enjoy some pain."

Imagining how much further Keldwyn could go, Uthe suspected he might enjoy a lot of pain, but he had no intention of revealing that. Keldwyn cocked his head. "Did you scourge yourself, my lord? Inflict penance on yourself in the service of your Lord as the monks do?"

"Most penances like that were forbidden to Templars because we had to stay battle ready."

"Interesting. Most would have said the Templars were exempt from the penances, not forbidden from indulging them. Did you crave the touch of the lash, Lord Uthe? The Lord's punishment? Or simply...a Master's punishment?"

Uthe ignored the electric sparks of sensation pinging his insides. The hardening of his cock was as much from Keldwyn's words as the teasing pressure of his foot. "You are a Dominant, my lord. As a vampire, I understand your desires. I can meet them in accordance with my oath to you."

Keldwyn's knowing expression obliterated the calming effect of the prayer on Uthe's mind. "A clever evasion. And I've no doubt you can."

Keldwyn had been right about Uthe's ability to control his response in the company of women. He enjoyed their bodies and the release, but being goaded by Keldwyn, kissed by him, produced an explosive sexual reaction impossible to conceal or contain. The secure walls around his mental celibacy hadn't been challenged so decisively in some time.

He'd initially attributed his attraction to Keldwyn to weakness. He'd told himself it wasn't Keldwyn specifically, but all the distractions and concerns he faced now that had made him vulnerable. Perhaps even the lowering of inhibitions that came with the Ennui were contributing to the problem. What worried him was not those theories, but how much he wanted them to be rationalizations, a lie he was telling himself. He wanted his absorption with Keldwyn to be unique to the Fae Lord and what temptations he offered Uthe.

Fortunately, the Fae wanted to change the subject. "In your story to Queen Rhoswen, it was Lord Reghan who saved you from the battlefield."

"Yes."

"What were your impressions of him? Did you spend much time in his company?"

"No. Only that meeting and one other, both necessarily brief. He was...charismatic. He said little, but what he did, had great import. Even with that brief exposure, I had the impression of many good things. Honesty, compassion, tolerance, a sense of vision that extended far beyond the world in which he lived. It was clear he was a formidable leader, but there was something...tragic about him."

Uthe's brow furrowed. Talking about it now, he'd

remembered more than he expected, but then, Lord Reghan had been almost as unforgettable as the male across from him. "Queen Rhoswen looked at him as if he were the rising sun, but he struck me more like a sunset. All the dusk colors, the painting the sun leaves behind so that we long for its return."

Looking up, he saw Keldwyn staring at him with a mostly incomprehensible expression, but Uthe registered one thing in it. Pain.

"You knew him." He paused. Despite the absurdity of it, the jagged feeling in his chest was jealousy. Now he understood why the name had caught Keldwyn's attention so effectively when Uthe met Rhoswen in the gardens. "You loved him."

"He was my best friend." Keldwyn's voice was carefully modulated, almost wooden. "Before Magwel, Rhoswen's mother, talked the Unseelie monarch at the time into having him killed."

"So is that why you and she don't get along?"

Keldwyn shook his head. "During one of our civil wars, Rhoswen herself killed Magwel."

He hadn't known that piece of the puzzle. Perhaps in deference to her sister, Lyssa had not shared that painful knowledge with the Council. Uthe thought of the Fae Queen's expression, so cold and remote. Yet when he'd been on his knees to her, his head forced to her thigh because of the physical attack of the flashback, he'd felt the touch of her hand on his shoulder, an almost gentle reassurance. When he'd looked in her eyes, he thought he'd seen something familiar, something that connected them beyond their initial meeting. Now he knew what it was.

"Reghan was all those things you said, and more."

The Fae spoke the words quietly, but they drew Uthe back to the present. Despite the curiosity such a loaded comment raised, Kel looked out the window, shutting down any further questions Uthe might have.

The pilot's voice broke in over the intercom. "Sir, we're

about to land. May I have your assistance?"

It was a small plane, but spacious enough that the pilot could give them privacy behind a closed door. Uthe rose as Keldwyn removed his foot, leaving the lingering sense of firm pressure. The Fae Lord's simmering glance said his mind wasn't entirely on the troubled shadows of his past.

They were landing in the dark, which was why the pilot required his assistance. Standing behind him, Uthe used his night vision to guide the plane down to a safe strip of ground. It was one the pilot had used before, for similar reasons, but Uthe's abilities verified nothing had wandered or fallen onto the faintly marked track of ground to cause the plane an issue. Once the plane bumped down and came to a halt, Uthe returned to the main cabin. Keldwyn was reading his book, or at least staring at the pages. Uthe left him to his thoughts, going to the partitioned area in the back to collect what he needed and change clothes. He wound a sash around the long, loose tunic, worn over light cotton pants, and tucked Rhoswen's amulet and his scabbarded dagger into the sash. The tingle of energy from wearing the dagger on his person reminded him of the advance of the sun. It was not long until daybreak.

As he emerged, Keldwyn rose. He was empty-handed, but Uthe rarely saw the Fae carrying anything. He suspected Keldwyn could call weapons or supplies to hand with his magic. Uthe shouldered his pack. "We'll help the pilot conceal the plane and then hike from here. He has a camouflage cover, but can you provide any additional warding to protect him and the plane?"

"Yes, I can do that."

Uthe paused. "Are you well, my lord?"

Keldwyn seemed surprised that he'd asked. Uthe lifted a shoulder. "We have lived long enough to lose those we love far more than once. Repetition does not lessen the blow. If anything, like a hammer, it just drives the nail in deeper."

The Fae Lord bowed, oddly formal. "I am well, Lord Uthe. I wish to leave this plane and the memories conjured here." He managed a faint smile. "They are thick as clouds."

He and Keldwyn helped the pilot pull the sand-colored plane in the shadow of an outcropping of rock. Any chrome on the plane had been painted, so it blended well. Keldwyn warded the plane and the pilot, despite the latter looking at the Fae like he'd cursed him to have ugly daughters and weak sons. But with those wards in place, hiding him and the plane from view, it was far less likely he would be at risk.

The pilot gave them a laconic farewell in Arabic and returned inside.

"How do we know he'll be there when we come back?" Keldwyn asked.

"Because he serves the Templars with his life," Uthe responded. "He has a week's worth of food and water, but if all goes as it should, we should be back to the plane in three days. It is an overnight trek there."

Keldwyn considered the rocky, barren terrain, dotted with scrub. In the pre-dawn hour, the hills were featureless craggy rises. "An overnight trip even at our usual speeds?"

"We must use a human pace. If I use vampire speed or you use your magic, we will arouse suspicion. We are being watched."

Keldwyn was only a moment behind Uthe in noting it, but vampires had a stronger sense of smell. The Fae's expression became cooler, more battle-ready. Uthe put a hand on his arm.

"Right now, it's just mountain people. They will do us no harm if we observe proper etiquette. Stay aware, but do not look around for them, my lord," he advised Keldwyn. "As long as we appear capable of defending ourselves and don't deviate from our intent, we will not see them. That is preferable."

"All right then." Keldwyn considered. "So we can only move at a human pace, and we've left the most immediate cover you have, less than an hour before sunrise. Where shall we take shelter, Lord Uthe?"

"It will not be necessary, as long as I wear this." Uthe put his hand on the dagger. "It allows me to be out in the sunlight like a human or Fae."

Kel's gaze lasered in on the object. "When you recounted your tale to Queen Rhoswen, I wondered if you still had it."

"I do not know why Lord Reghan recovered it from the battlefield, but when I woke in your world, it was by my bedside. I'm grateful he did."

"Let me see it, my lord. If I may."

At Uthe's look, Keldwyn snorted. "If I was going to kill you, I could think of other ways than holding your dagger away from you and watching you turn to ash."

Uthe grinned and unsheathed the blade, placing it in Keldwyn's palm. Keldwyn's expression turned inward. "Peculiar. The magic is...old. Yet I hesitate to call it magic. It is something else."

"Yes. Something else."

Purity of intent. A shining soul. So rare in this world, and therefore short-lived.

"Well, if we are going to walk, you may entertain me with stories. Like how you acquired your magical dagger."

"Anything to keep you from asking me 'are we there yet?' an endless number of times." Uthe smirked at Keldwyn's puzzled look. So there were some cultural references his companion did not know.

"Shall we go then?"

"In a moment." Uthe knelt, facing the east, and bent his head in prayer. It mattered not where he was. Whenever he could, he started or ended his day with paternosters and prayers. He felt Keldwyn shift, coming closer to him.

"You should have determined the location of a nearby cave, in case the magic is not as potent as it once was."

"There is one sixty yards to the northwest," Uthe said. "But this kind of magic doesn't dilute with time. Now hush, while I'm praying."

Night's Templar

He suppressed amusement at the Fae Lord's affront at being shushed, but Keldwyn did fall silent. He didn't move away, though, and Uthe sensed his readiness to help spirit him to the cave if needed. It touched him, though he could be giving it more weight than it was worth. The Fae enjoyed a good story, so Kel might save Uthe just for that potential. On another day, when there was no story to be told, he might not bother. There was never any telling what was going through his mind.

Yet at the tail end of his thirteen paternosters, he recalled a memory that had given him a different perspective on the Fae Lord. Keldwyn had arrived at a Council meeting fifteen minutes late one night. When Lyssa asked why he had been delayed, Keldwyn told her he was playing marbles with Kane, her young son. Most of the Council came to the conclusion he was being a wiseass, his way of saying his tardiness was no one's business but his own. But when Uthe spoke to John, Kane's older friend and second mark servant, John had confirmed it. The grandson of Elijah Ingram, Lyssa's majordomo, John was well-spoken, polite and serious.

"Yes, my lord. He was sitting nearby, watching Kane and me play marbles. We were rolling them down a hill in the driveway, trying to catch them in a cup at the bottom. Well, a few cups. You got more points depending on which cup... I'm sorry, my lord, I didn't mean to wander off topic. Anyhow, he got up and asked Kane if he could play." The young boy's eyes had widened. "Can you imagine, someone like him asking us that? Kane said yes, thank heavens. I'm not sure what would have happened if he'd said no, but you know how he can be."

Kane was a miniature version of his imperious mother. Uthe did indeed know what John meant, and amusedly wondered what Keldwyn would have done if Kane had told him he couldn't play. Probably turned Kane into a rabbit, put him a shoebox to deliver him safely to Lyssa, and taken the marbles, all to teach him a lesson in manners.

"Anyhow, he knelt right there on the path with us and played for fifteen minutes. Even showed us a couple other games he knew with marbles. Then he thanked us for letting him join us. He said he had to go to a meeting, but that had been far more fun and he wasn't sorry he'd be late."

Insights like that had enlightened him about the Fae Lord. Sometimes Uthe believed he really did know what Keldwyn was thinking. Depending on what he supposed those thoughts were, they by turns made him uncomfortable, pleased or disturbed. Keldwyn was savvy enough to make a vampire think he knew what he thought, which should warn Uthe never to relax around him. Yet, Uthe could and did relax around him more often than expected. Like now.

As he reminded himself he was supposed to be finishing up his prayers, he was aware of Keldwyn behind him. He'd shifted closer, his calf pressed to Uthe's hip, his body forming a shadow over him.

The first ray of the sun speared between the vee of two mountains. It touched Uthe's face, his lips. Adrenaline surged, that quick spurt of panic, but the same way he did during his normal morning ritual, he quelled it. Unlike then, he had no intention of fleeing the sun's touch. He had faith in the power behind the dagger. He kept his eyes closed, his head bowed, thanking the Lord for blessings and guidance, for His wisdom. Heat unfurled over his face and shoulders, warming him through the tunic.

Standing in the sun took him back to protection details with his Templar brethren. He recalled the sauntering movement of his powerful mount, Nexus, beneath him as they flanked a group of pilgrims along the road from Jerusalem to Jericho, the route to visit the river Jordan. Once they arrived at their destination, he'd let Nexus cavort in the lapping waters. It had been an infraction, but he'd stripped off his armor and ridden the horse barefoot, the water washing over his toes and legs, his knees pressed into Nexus's wet sides. The sun had glittered off the spray when Nexus tossed his massive head from side to side.

The heat penetrated his clothes quickly, and the exposed areas of his skin reacted with less fondness than his memories. It would take time for it to adjust to something it hadn't felt in a few centuries.

As he lifted his head, Keldwyn offered him a hand to his feet he didn't need, but he took it, enjoying the palm to palm contact. When the male registered it and began to draw Uthe closer, Uthe balked, a warning to them both. "It's best that we not act as we might...when alone. Those watching us are not friendly toward men who take pleasure with one another."

Keldwyn had his hair tied back, giving the sharp bones of his face a more severe look. He wore clothing like Uthe did now, and he'd used what he called glamor magic to conceal his ears, make them appear human to anyone watching. He was as prepared as Uthe for most contingencies, always thinking several steps ahead, and annoyed with himself when he didn't.

Which he demonstrated now with a frown. "We should have brought you sun screen, my lord."

Uthe smiled. "Even if I burn, I will heal, Lord Keldwyn. But your concern is appreciated." When he gestured in the direction they needed to go, Keldwyn fell into step with him. As they started to navigate the rocky terrain, Uthe calculated the number of steep inclines and steeper descents. The path to the sorceress's cave reminded Uthe of an exposed rabbit warren.

"You were going to tell me the story of the dagger," Keldwyn prompted. "Unless you feel you must keep that a secret."

"No." During their companionable silence on the plane, Uthe had thought it over, coming to the conclusion that certain things were going to have to be entrusted to someone, in case... Just in case. He'd accepted his reservations about Keldwyn were primarily rooted in a longstanding distrust of the Fae, not a distrust of the male himself. Keldwyn was clever and kept Uthe on his toes in Council meetings, ensuring vampire interests were not undermined by Fae ones, but representing Fae interests was Kel's job. He had no doubt Keldwyn would share information about Uthe's quest with Queen Rhoswen or King Tabor, but he didn't think Keldwyn would sabotage his efforts. Perhaps that was evidence of declining judgment, but his gut feelings were not connected to his mind, so he trusted them more. It was better for Keldwyn to understand some of this; otherwise, his ignorance could prove more detrimental than what information he could feed to Fae royals.

Besides, telling him the story would get Uthe's mind off the broiling sun. By the Virgin, he'd forgotten how hot it could be.

"I was born in Germany. The Holy Roman Empire, then. My father still referred to it as Germania. I left his care when I was close to fifty."

"Fifty?" Keldwyn glanced at him. "Weren't you still a fledgling? My understanding was born vampires are unable to control their bloodlust without guidance until they are well over fifty."

Uthe nodded. "I was also a target for other vampires who can be cruel to a born male fledgling. God blessed me with a cunning that helped me navigate those dangers, and a maturity to contain the bloodlust better than most vampires at the same age. Despite that, without an ally, I still might have been ended before I began. I met Rail in France. He was an old vampire, though I didn't know then how old. He let me stay in his home and asked nothing of me except my companionship. He treated me as a son and taught me how to protect myself."

Uthe paused. "He was different from any vampire I've known, then or since. You can detect the potential for bloodlust in any of us, even at our calmest. Not him. His peacefulness was like a lake, always. When we went out to find blood, he'd use compulsion to bring a human to him, share that human with me and then release the human after clearing his or her mind of the event. Throughout all of it, he'd show no urgency. He ate as a human breathes—naturally, without thought, without struggle."

Uthe placed his hand on the hilt of the dagger. "He had this in his possession. Since he always had it with him, I asked him about it."

He closed his eyes, remembering the other vampire. Rail had deep brown skin, dark as the earth and burned darker, for he'd been a made vampire, a human who'd once known the baking heat of the sun. His piercing brown eyes were laced with crimson, his voice rough like the warning rumble of an old dog...

§

"Why do you carry that dagger everywhere? What's so special about it?"

Rail didn't answer the question right away, his attention on the wooden horse he was carving. His vampire speed made him a prolific woodworker. He was the source of bowls, utensils, toys and tools for the nearest small villages. He lived on their outskirts, in a small hut with a cool, dark cellar dug into the floor, where he and Uthe slept during the daylight hours.

"I've been thinking." Rail ignored Uthe's question, or so he thought. "You should give yourself your own name. I named myself Rail, because of how thin I am. We live so many years, it doesn't much matter where we're from or what we were called as a babe, does it?"

Uthe thought about that, liked the idea. "We've been everywhere," Rail continued. "I've rarely met a vampire over five hundred who hasn't seen a lot of the world, because you can't stay one place too long with the same humans."

"You haven't thought of taking a servant?"

Rail shrugged. "I was born well before that started happening. I'm not even sure who did it first, who figured out the purpose of those marking serums hidden up behind our fangs. Maybe it's just instinct that guided us the right way, like the first person who figured out we live on human blood. But if you weren't born into that, and I wasn't, it seems strange, saddling yourself with a human, with all their weaknesses."

Uthe's father had felt the same way. He'd only taken a human servant to breed. Once he'd found one that could give him a son, he'd seen no further purpose to her save for one final, fatal meal. Their unwillingness to have a fully marked servant was the only similarity Uthe saw between his father and Rail. Thankfully.

"I hear the three marks make the servants stronger and faster," Rail said, "but we're still way stronger and faster, and so much of our lives are about survival. Can you imagine us ever being able to settle in one place and not worry about being noticed?"

Turning over the horse and clamping it in a vise, he started working on the hooves. "But I'll admit, our life can give a vampire male some low moments. Living on the edges of their world, seeing men settle in homes with wife and children, and them having a stable day-to-day routine. When the bloodlust and the need for violence comes upon us, as it always does, it might be a challenge to fit into that picture. But it's tempting."

Uthe took a seat at the table across from him. Rail was like that. First saying no to something, and then looking at it from different angles until he came to a wholly different conclusion.

"The ones of us that live like monsters, outside human law or vampire common sense, who see humans only as food and kill indiscriminately rather than just taking what they need—those vampires will get all of us hunted, you mark me." When Rail said that, he sent a shrewd glance toward Uthe. Uthe realized his fists had clenched, a response to uncomfortable memories. He forced himself to release that tension as Rail continued.

"Maybe having a human bound to us for blood would give us the chance to live our life in a halfway settled way. That might be something. The birds and beasts, they know how to live in the moment and make the most of it, not thinking behind or forward, but it's difficult for us vampires and humans to do that. We like to have a sense of marking a place as our own. Maybe having a servant's a way to do that..."

Uthe wondered if the old vampire had forgotten his original question. Now he looked tired and sad. "Are you well, Rail?" he ventured.

"Yes, son. Sometimes I'm haunted by ghosts. You've got them too, young as you are. Sometimes you worry that none of it is going to make sense, that *you're* not going to make sense. You feel despair, don't you? As if your crimes are already too great, and a million years won't make things better. Even if you live a million years, if we're dust at the end of it and all's forgotten, what did it really matter? What's the point?"

Uthe didn't reply, though he knew his hands had clenched again, and there was a sharp feeling in his gut, as if he'd swallowed a couple of knives whole and they'd cut their way down to his midsection.

"There was a time I felt that way. I'm nearly fifteen hundred years old." He chuckled at Uthe's shocked expression. "Yep. They say vampires that live past five hundred years are rare. Not sure if this has anything to do with it," he patted the dagger, "because that's about how old I was when it came into my hands. You thought I'd forgotten, didn't you?"

Uthe shook his head as Rail sat down in the opposite chair, drawing up one knee to clasp his arms around it. He balanced on one bony buttock. "I was traveling in Jerusalem. There was a good network of caves outside the city, and I'd holed up there for awhile. A man started coming out to that wild place. He'd pray a lot, then sit by himself, thinking. Though I kept myself hidden while I was watching him, and humans aren't supposed to detect us when we don't want to be seen, he knew I was there, every time."

Rail nodded at Uthe's surprised look. "But he never said a word to me. He had this feeling around him... Peaceful's a way to describe it, but even that doesn't quite catch it, because when we say peaceful, we think of it as a temporary thing, like being happy, sad, annoyed. Peace *was* him, who he was, through and through."

Rail offered a grim smile. "I was a discontent bastard at that point, so I thought of drinking from him, to see if his blood was as peaceful. Like a tonic. The night I had that thought, he turned around, looked right at me. "Will you sit with me?" he said. "I know you often sit with me while I'm here, but I would like you to come closer."

"I wondered if he was a sorcerer, something more than a man. But I came out of hiding and sat with him. First a few feet away and then on the rock next to him. I was like a wild dog, distrustful of a human offering his fire and meat to share. That night, he didn't want to talk. He didn't even start praying like he usually did. He just sat, studying the stars, the land around us, as if he was trying to memorize it. His eyes...they were brown as the deepest part of the earth, and you'd fall into them in a good way if you looked long enough. At last, he drew this dagger, cut his wrist and offered it to me."

Rail's expression grew distant. "You're young, and you'll think my mind is going, but when I tasted his blood, I tasted that peace. It was...there's been nothing like it ever since. You've wondered that I don't seem as ruled by my hunger as most, that I don't get angry or let the bloodlust take me. Some of that's age. You're at the age where everything is about the hunger. That dies back a bit as time goes on. But part of it was having the best meal of my life and knowing that there will never be any better. Doesn't mean you don't appreciate what others have to offer, but you just...the hunger goes away."

"So he *was* a sorcerer, of sorts."

"No. That's what was peculiar about it. His blood told me he was a man. A mortal man with sad eyes and a sad heart. It was near the time when he would die, you see. I didn't know that then, but he obviously did. I heard about it a short time later. That night, though, he smiled when I sealed the wound. Touched my brow and wished me peace and long life."

Rail pulled himself out of the memory. "You seek peace, young vampire? Go to Jerusalem, find your peace there like I did." He extended the knife, startling Uthe. "If you carry this, you can move freely in daylight. It won't take away your need for human blood, but you can walk among mortal men with less suspicion."

Uthe took the blade, examined it. "It will allow me to walk in sunlight?" he said dubiously.

"Yes. Don't share that information with any other vampire, ever. I shouldn't have to tell you something so obvious, but you're young yet. Your brain function's paralyzed by the stupidity of youth. This blade is meant to serve a purpose, and mine's almost done. Take it. It will guide you to yours. As long as you serve it well, it will serve you well."

Uthe handed it back. "It's yours. It serves you. I think the reason you're trying to give it to me and the reason you're sad are the same reason. What is it?" Though he already knew.

Rail's rueful look acknowledged it. "You're far too sharp to be pretending not to be, son. My time is coming to an end. Very soon. I can feel it. I'm sad because it's not easy to say good-bye to everything you've known. Not just turn toward the void, but step full out into it, not knowing if all your memories will go with you, if you'll remember the beauty of a full moon or the touch of woman's hand, or even what happened to me to have this knife fall into my hands. I want to hold onto that memory as I pass, take it with me wherever I go next."

He rose to come around the table and sit down next to Uthe, placing a hand on his shoulder. His brown eyes were kind and thoughtful. He was such a different vampire, the kind Uthe fervently wished he could be. The opposite of everything his sire was.

"Now that I look back," Rail said, "I know that's what that man was doing. He knew his time was coming and he was saying goodbye to this world and all it had to offer. Doesn't matter how good what comes after is. When you have to say good-bye to all you've ever known, and you don't know if you're going to remember it, facing that end is how a person grieves, on the front end, before you let go of this life. Whereas it's the job of those who remember him to grieve on the other side after he passes, and honor what he gave us. There's a balance to that too, I expect."

Grasping Uthe's wrist, he placed the dagger in his hand, closing his fingers over the hilt. "Take it. For whatever bit of foresight I've been given, I think the peace you need will be found in the Holy Land where I found it. Among humans, not vampires. You need to free yourself from the skin of your own maker, and that won't be found in your own world. Not yet."

§

After Uthe finished the story, Kel said nothing for quite some time about it, though Uthe could feel him turning it over in his mind. They roved over idle topics from there: Council issues, tidbits about the Fae world Uthe was curious about, and past debates they'd had. They also spent a good bit of time hiking in silence. It wasn't until the day moved toward twilight that Keldwyn returned to the dagger's origins.

They'd reached the summit of a rocky peak. A glance down said they'd be deep into another maze of them before long. Uthe stopped, propping a foot against a jutting stone, and tipped his head back, looking at clouds scudding across the darkening sky. He liked the way twilight turned the clouds into smoke against the firmament.

Keldwyn stood at his side. Uthe realized he was leaning against him as if he were dizzy and out of breath. He *was* dizzy. Must be the effect of the sun. Damn it, he'd forgotten. Yes, the dagger let him walk in sunlight, but it doubled or tripled his blood needs. He'd had to feed once a day when he was using it. Most vampires his age only had to feed once every several days. Sometimes he'd been able to go even longer, unless a stressor increased his metabolism. Well, he'd figure that out later. At sundown, it should be easy enough to steal through the night and take a meal from one of their invisible trackers, a sleepy goatherd or nomadic shepherd.

"So he was suggesting," Keldwyn said slowly, one hand steady on Uthe's back, his other curled loosely around his arm, "that Jesus of Nazarus gave him the dagger? And when he cut his wrist to feed Rail, it gave the blade the powers it carries today?"

"He said none of those things. But the timing and its properties suggest it's very possible. Or the knife may have already been carrying those gifts. There's a lot about the life of the Nazarene that's not known, particularly before he started preaching. There's speculation that he was engaged in more mystical studies before that time. But I've thought about what Rail said, about him being just a man. Maybe one man's extraordinary understanding of peace and love created a magic even stronger than a sorcerer's."

Keldwyn fished a band somewhere from within his clothing and lifted his arms to efficiently wrap it at the top of his thick braid. By doing so, he re-captured several of the shorter strands that had loosened from it and framed his face. "It is possible."

"Really?" Uthe watched Keldwyn's hands move over the task, the curving of his biceps. He imagined unbraiding the

Fae Lord's dark mane, letting the heat and weight of it spill over his hands, cover his face, slide along his chest. He wanted to touch Keldwyn's precise features, the lips that could be set in cruel, stern lines or a tempting, mocking smile. He thought of the way they'd feel, softening and curving under Uthe's fingertips. Clearing his throat, he turned his attention back to the sky. "It surprises me to hear you say that, my lord."

"The power of love is something no magic user can deny after seeing it in action. It is the most miraculous thing to witness when it succeeds. Just as it crushes the soul to see it fail." Keldwyn finished getting the hair out of his eyes, but he hadn't missed Uthe's absorption. "I think you like my hair, vampire."

"It is easy to enjoy beauty, my lord."

"That depends." Keldwyn swept a glance over him. "On how much it resists adoration. So you went to Jerusalem, then?"

Flummoxed by how the Fae Lord had thrown the compliment back over him, like a net of possibilities, Uthe took a second to recall the storyline. "I did. My first night in the area, I stumbled on a camp of soldiers, and shared a meal with them. Popular history tends to remember the Templars as an order that stretched through the Holy Lands and Europe, but in the beginning it was just nine men and their retainers. The men were mostly connected by family lineage to Hugh of Payns, the founder of the Order. It was those nine I met that night, and Hugh who invited me to share their meal. And that's a story for another time. I think it is your turn."

Uthe cocked his head. "This journey will be far more interesting if we trade stories along it. Perhaps for every story I offer, you offer one in return. The only parameter is that it must be a true one, and tell me something of yourself."

"But who better than a Fae to tell a fairy tale?"

Uthe chuckled. "These days, the lines of reality and

fantasy can blur for me. If I could rely upon your stories as truth, that would be a comfort. It shouldn't be too taxing for you. If the Ennui advances quickly enough, you can tell me the same story, and I will think it new."

Keldwyn didn't smile at the jest. He reached out and closed his fingers on Uthe's arm, but then, as if remembering what Uthe had said about the eyes focused on them, he dropped his hold. Instead, he asked a question as personal as the most intimate touch. "Your story about Rail suggests what I've always expected, that Uthe is not your given name. I want to know it. I've waited patiently for you to tell me."

"The word patience obviously means something different to the Fae."

Keldwyn merely gave him an expectant look. Uthe knew it should be of no consequence, but it had been years since he'd spoken it. He hadn't been able to bear hearing it in his head, and he'd been able to banish it, except in his nightmares. Yet it was simply a name. He shouldn't make Keldwyn think it had more significance than it did. He sighed. "Varick, my lord."

Keldwyn's eyes brightened, his lips curving in a way that made Uthe not displeased he'd told him, at least in this moment. "It means protector and ruler. Your parents had auspicious hopes for you."

"My father. I sincerely hope I disappointed him. I do not use my given name for that reason."

Keldwyn considered him. "A story for another time?"

"Or perhaps never. There are better stories to tell and hear. We should keep moving."

"Are you steadier now?"

"Well enough." Uthe lifted his head, inhaled. "Odd. A wolf, by itself. Loner."

Keldwyn didn't have a vampire's olfactory senses, though he could detect whatever life forms were in a certain range around him. His eye for terrain more than made up for his less acute sense of smell, since he'd already identified several better paths through the rocks. "Why is it odd? Syria has wolves, and a loner could be an injured or older animal."

"This one just smells...off." Uthe shrugged. "He's well ahead of us. If our paths cross, we'll see what's peculiar about him." He held still, reaching out with all his senses, nostrils flaring. "We also have a different form of watcher now. One far less benevolent than our mountain people. I don't detect anyone from the tribes, so they've backed off in the face of this new development, which suggests the new arrivals are a threat." Uthe frowned, brow creasing. "Their scent is...familiar, though I can't identify it."

"Should we try to circle around, flush them out?"

"I think it's best we continue onward," Uthe responded. "But when possible we should choose terrain where we have the tactical advantage. I'd dislike getting caught and surrounded in one of these gullies without knowing exactly what we are facing. It will be dark soon. My guess is they are waiting for us to reach our destination before they make their intent known."

"Is there any reason to conceal it from them?"

"No. Only I can obtain what is here and, once we reach that destination, we will be protected from the threat they pose. I detect about twenty of them. Human, mostly. Let's keep going, my lord, unless you object."

"I trust your judgment, Lord Uthe."

They started to descend the slope. Down into a crevice, then winding through flat lands flanked by rocks that jutted and curved over them like stone vultures with sharp beaks and pointed feathers. Another incline, back up and over more peaks. They repeated the up and down trek several times, sometimes the incline so steep they were climbing instead of hiking. Despite Uthe's weak jest about the Ennui, this didn't appear to be a path he had trouble remembering, for Keldwyn noted he never seemed to take his bearings.

However, though Keldwyn was not affected by the

climb, he noticed Uthe was slowing more with each incline. The vampire didn't need to feed daily but perhaps, dagger or no dagger, the sun took its toll. "There's a cave nested in those rocks over there." Keldwyn gestured in that direction. "Shall we take a short respite?"

Uthe nodded, but as they moved that way, he stopped, straightening up so abruptly Keldwyn heard his spine crack with the effort. When he did, a fitful breeze wafted toward them, bringing Keldwyn the same vibration, if not the scent.

Another vampire.

"What are the chances?" Uthe muttered. Any signs of tiredness vanished. He was alert, his gaze sharp, body loose with the expectation of violence, communicating his substantial ability to meet it with a greater show of force if necessary. The vampire world was so entrenched in power hierarchies, their protocols for dealing with them were as ingrained as their dominant instincts. This was one of the most important—establishing from the first instant who was the strongest vampire. Since it often saved the trouble of unnecessary violence, Keldwyn couldn't argue with its efficiency. Or how intriguing it was watching Uthe shrug into its mantle.

"Show yourself," Uthe said shortly, his voice ringing among the stones.

"I haven't had my coffee yet," came the reply. "And you're up awfully early for a bloodsucker."

"Uthe." Keldwyn said. "Downwind."

The vampire turned, following his gaze. On a ledge above them was the wolf Keldwyn was sure Uthe had scented earlier. In the deepening twilight, the creature was a menacing silhouette. It was an exceptionally large black wolf, with one blue eye and one gold. His expression was intent, a predator deciding whether or not to leap. Uthe showed his fangs and the wolf responded in kind, laying back his ears.

"It's definitely too early for that kind of shit. Ease up,

Rand." The vampire had emerged from the caves, but his attention was on the wolf, not Uthe and Keldwyn. The wolf's gaze flicked toward him and the vampire held the bi-colored eyes in a lock, his expression suddenly far more commanding, his voice sharp, not sardonic. "Ease. Up."

The air became saturated with tension, but then it sprung a leak. The wolf settled down on the ledge with a sound between a grumble and a snarl. If a wolf was capable of saying "Fuck you," Keldwyn was pretty sure he'd just heard it, but he'd complied grudgingly with the vampire's order.

Keldwyn, satisfied that the wolf was not an immediate threat, turned his attention back to the vampire along with Uthe. His black unruly hair fell to his shoulders and he possessed blue eyes clear as a daylight sky, a dark ring around the irises. He had the classic alpha male square jaw and sloped cheekbones. Shunning native garb, he instead wore faded jeans, heavy-tread shoes and a sleeveless T-shirt that showed the rippling layers of arm muscles. He was broad-shouldered, long-limbed and well made, as most vampires were, though Keldwyn expected this male had been striking, an athletic and impressive specimen, prior to his turning. He'd been around vampires long enough now to detect the slight differences between one born and one made, and this one was made. Probably about two hundred years old, so nowhere near a match for Uthe, though Keldwyn noted the younger vampire wasn't showing any apprehension on his own behalf.

The tension he'd exhibited when the wolf challenged Uthe had to do with the wolf itself. He probably was concerned about the wolf's well-being, knowing that Uthe could easily destroy the animal. Or perhaps not quite as easily as one might assume. Keldwyn saw Uthe studying the wolf, trying to place that "off" feeling, but now that Keldwyn was close enough, he identified it with no problem.

"Shifter," Keldwyn said.

Night's Templar

Uthe concealed his surprise. He'd never met a wolf shifter. He'd heard stories of them, but they were reclusive to the point they were considered myth—or extinct. He studied the wolf more closely, but the creature was ignoring him now, studying the darkness off somewhere to his right. He wasn't fooled, though. He expected the shifter was aware of every twitch either of them made, since he seemed to have the same protectiveness toward the vampire as the vampire did toward him.

"Want some coffee?" The vampire asked, lifting a cup. He'd emerged from the cave with it in hand. "I figured the smell of it was what drew you this way. Not many coffee shops in this part of the world. It's a good Columbian blend, not that chicory shit. Though if you can't hang around, that's fine. Just leave me and mine alone, and we'll be good. I've no quarrel with either of you." His blue eyes moved to Kel, lingered. "You're way too pretty, even by vampire standards. So you must not be vampire. Some kind of glamor? Fuck, you're one of those Fae bastards, aren't you? Hiding your pointy ears?"

Keldwyn said nothing, though the expression on his face had the vampire lifting a pacifying hand. "Don't get worked up. Manners out here can be rough. I'm not trying to be insulting."

"You did it without effort. Almost as little as it would take me to change you into a rat for your oversized dog to swallow."

The wolf let out a rumble, though Kel didn't remove his eyes from the vampire. "Him I can turn into nothing more than a stray wind that gathers desert sand. Keep that in mind, in case your appearance of affability is a farce and you intend either of us harm."

The vampire didn't seem concerned. When he blinked, one deliberate closing and opening of the lids, Uthe saw the dangerous soul lurking under the handsome charm. All vampires could be lethal when challenged. Whether this vampire posed an honorable form of hazard or not remained to be seen. "Is the wolf your servant?" Uthe asked.

"Depends. Is that against the rules of the mighty Vampire Council in their ivory tower?"

"Not to my knowledge." Uthe lifted a brow. "The Council meets on the ground level of a Georgia estate."

"Cushy digs all the same. Bet they serve great finger foods and Bloody Marys in crystal."

"Nothing better than this, though." Uthe looked around. "Endless scorpions and snakes and scant rainfall."

"True. Our little corner of paradise." The vampire took a step forward, held out a hand. "I'm Mordecai, go by Cai, rhymes with lie. That's Rand. Don't let him fool you. He may lick his own balls, but of the two of us, he's more civilized."

Uthe clasped his hand. "Uthe."

Mordecai glanced toward Keldwyn, who said nothing. Mordecai didn't offer his hand, which showed he possessed some common sense. "So, want that coffee? We don't get much company out here, except for the kind that's entirely disagreeable. Like the crew that's following you. I assume that's not your lot?"

"Not exactly. They are watching us, but they have not yet claimed to be allies or enemies. We suspect the latter."

"Hmm. Good guess." When Uthe accepted the invitation, Cai preceded them into a cave hidden among the rocks. It was deeper than the narrow opening suggested, providing a roomy space big enough to accommodate all of them. A scattering of camp supplies indicated he'd been here several days, his sizeable backpack positioned to provide a pillow to an unfurled bedroll. After Cai found two more cups and poured the coffee, he gestured to the ground on the other side of the pot, tossing Uthe a folded blanket as a cushion. Then he positioned himself so his back was propped against the pack, his long legs stretched out and crossed at the ankles. Uthe took the seat across from him, and passed Keldwyn his cup of coffee, since the Fae sat down on a rock a few feet away from them both, exhibiting his usual detachment from a conversation until he was inclined to participate.

"This doesn't seem a hospitable place for vampire or wolf," Uthe said.

Cai shrugged. "If you know the cave system in this area, you're fine enough. For blood, there's more than you think. Brigands, insurgents, the Russians who snuck through here with the WMDs from Iraq in the months before the 2003 war." He winked. "We had a nice little smorgasbord then. Fresh food every night. But the problem with bad men is they taste bad." The vampire spat. "So at least in this corner of Syria, Syrian food leaves much to be desired. However, the occasional shepherd...that's manna from heaven."

Rand slid into the cave, giving them all a warning look before he stalked over and took a seat on the other side of Cai, stretching out with front toes and ears pointed in their direction. Uthe noticed the wolf had a pronounced limp, and he lowered himself with effort.

"What does he eat?" Keldwyn asked.

"Whatever doesn't run away fast enough. He doesn't care too much for human flesh, though he's been known to share a brigand or two with me when his four-legged pickings are slim. And right now, while his leg is healing, he isn't as fast as usual." The vampire passed his hand over the wolf's fur and tossed him an enigmatic look when the creature curled a lip at him. "Fuck with me, and I'll rub your belly in front of company," Cai warned, then continued. ""Shifters don't heal as fast as vampires, but my blood helps. When he's on top of his game, even a vampire has a hard time outpacing him."

"What harmed him?"

"Someone who is now very dead." Heat flashed across Cai's gaze.

Uthe took a sip of the coffee, finding it excellent. He declined when Cai offered cream or sugar. He wondered if

Keldwyn found the sudden oasis of hospitality unexpected, but for Uthe it brought back good memories. The code of desert regions, where, as Cai had pointed out, company could be rare. Someone who didn't declare himself as an enemy was treated as a guest, as much for the news he brought as the companionship he provided. Plus, in this treacherous environment, a host might end up needing the same form of hospitality at some later date.

Cai looked toward Keldwyn. "Do you have a name, or should I just dub you Deathbringer, or some other moniker that goes with that forbidding expression?"

"*My lord* would be appropriate," Uthe interjected. Though Cai wasn't a fledgling, there was a restless, uncivilized character to him. The vampire demonstrated little understanding or regard for the dangers of offending higher ranking vampires or other powerful beings. "You've been here awhile, if you've been here since the Iraq War. What commends this isolation?"

"A lack of other vampires," Cai responded bluntly. "I'm no Trad, but I don't play well with others, nor do I care to learn. What's life without some risk? Still...I expect Rand might eventually enjoy a forest or two. We'll have to see if we end up back that way. Problem is there are overlords in more hospitable environments. No such oversight here." He glanced out of the cave. "Full moon tonight. If you wish to travel onward this evening you'll have good light for it, my lord."

When Uthe raised a brow at the title, Cai snorted. "It's obvious. You wouldn't know how to do commoner if your life depended on it." He dipped his head toward Kel. "He's another clue. His type doesn't waste time hanging with peasantry."

"You don't mince words, Mordecai."

"No point, really." Cai looked at the wolf. "Both of us came here to lick our wounds. He lost his pack, and I lost my family. And no, I don't care to talk about the hows or whys of that shit. But since I'm out here by my lonesome, it tends to consume my mind at times, so I can't stop myself from bringing it up. Self-flagellation and all that."

"I am sorry," Uthe said.

"It is what it is," Cai said shortly. "We love and we lose, because the gods are cruel. They like us to offer our hearts to one another, and then cut them out of our chests to show us how useless our love is before inevitable mortality, inevitable even for us. In the end, everything that matters is taken away." Cai made a dismissive gesture. "So, anyhow, I go where the majority of my food sources deserve to die and the loss of those lives won't be noticed, aka trigger the Council's worry meter about exposure to humans. We spare the shepherds, but everyone else... Well, let's just say the scavengers around here love us. Very few come out here except those up to no good, or up to something that they can't afford anyone else to see."

The charm had disappeared. Cai's cool tone and flat expression gave Uthe his true face. Unsmiling and savagely content to live in a place where he could kill his food, Cai was venting a rage that hadn't yet abated. Seeing the glowing eyes of the wolf, Uthe thought the two made a good match. Cai might be exceeding the Council's mandated human kill quota, but Uthe wasn't here to enforce Council policy. Plus, the vampire had a good grasp of the spirit of the policy, enough to avoid the wrong kind of human attention.

Cai took a swallow of coffee. "Since you don't fall into either category, I'm going to guess you're here for the sorceress. Which means you don't know."

"Know what?"

The younger vampire met his gaze. "She's dead."

Chapter Seven

It was like being punched in the chest. The ease of casual conversation disappeared in a blink. "What? How?"

"She was attacked while we were hunting, which we figured out too late was a distraction." The flash of anger in Cai's gaze told Uthe the truth, that Cai had been her ally. It saved the young vampire's life. "We would have helped her. She helped me fix Rand's leg."

She was in her eighties now, but she'd been descended from a line of strong, long-lived magic users. She could have prospered another twenty years before succumbing to Death's call. Uthe felt the loss of it, the waste. As well as anger that he hadn't been here to help protect her. She would have laughed at him, though, wouldn't she?

"I can destroy ten vampires without disturbing a hair on my head, my lord." She'd cackled, running a hand over her sparse, balding pate. *"You run and play your vampire games. Leave me be. I can take care of myself."*

"It happened a couple weeks ago. She was ready for it, though. She always seemed so ready for anything." Cai shook off the anger. "Soon as she died, I think it triggered some kind of protection spell on her place. Incinerated the bastards tossing the cave and blocked any more from going in. Been that way ever since. Neither Rand nor I can get in.

That's why these guys following you have been lingering. They're trying to see if it will wear off in time. They sneak up there to test it every other day or so. We took out a couple of them who did it after nightfall, but they've gotten smarter since then and now they only check it out during daylight. At least we make them sweat in the sun."

"So why aren't you concerned about our motives?" Keldwyn asked. He had one foot propped on the edge of the rock, his arm loosely wrapped around his shin to hold it, while his other arm was braced on the rock. With his head cocked, the dim light gleamed off his dark eyes.

"Christ, you can see why people wander off to your world and never want to come back," Cai said. "A coating of sweat and sand on you is like powdered sugar on a donut. You're a walking hard-on."

"Cai," Uthe said sharply, snapping the vampire's gaze back to him. "He is a Fae Lord."

"I understand, but isn't he your servant, my lord? Why else would a vampire and Fae be traveling together?"

Keldwyn's lip curled, his gaze glittering like embers. The wolf responded in kind, but Uthe suspected his reaction was as much his displeasure with Cai's appraisal of Keldwyn as defense of his Master. He couldn't say it thrilled him that much either—though it was an apt description of the Fae Lord's appeal—but he focused on more important matters. Like interceding before Keldwyn downgraded his sentence on the vampire from rodent to cockroach. Keldwyn was motionless on his rock, a bad omen.

Uthe wondered if the Fae could actually transform someone into something else, or if that was just a euphemism for hacking the offender into pieces.

"An instant and sincere apology would be wise, Cai," Uthe advised.

The boy wasn't actually as dense as he seemed. Cai blanched at the overload of tension. "Christ. I mean...I'm sorry."

The wolf rose, stalked over to the other side of Cai and sat down. Since he didn't lie down, his position impeded Cai's view of Keldwyn. Cai rose to his feet and gave Keldwyn a half-bow, including Uthe in the gesture. "My apologies to you both. It never occurred to me..." He cleared his throat. "I'm not all that familiar with the Fae, to tell the truth. I meant no offense."

"Most who do offend do not intend it. They just don't know how to guard their tongue." Yet Keldwyn's negative energy dissipated enough that the wolf's ears pricked back up and the pressure around Uthe eased so he could pursue the information he needed.

"So back to Lord Keldwyn's question. Why are you not concerned about our motives for seeking the sorceress?" Uthe asked again.

Cai sat back down, eying Keldwyn. "She told me a week before she died that she'd figured out something important, and a high-born vampire would be coming to get the information, to use it for good. She told me that Rand and I should help you if we could, because what you're going to do will be vital for all of us."

Cai gestured with the coffee cup. "I pay attention to words like vital. You're lucky, because if she'd said you all were here to serve the will of the gods, I would have said bollocks to helping you. Never helping them again, not in this life nor the next, even if they spend it roasting my nuts over hellfire. Piss on them."

The wolf dipped his head, brushing his ruff against the vampire's shoulder, before he took a light nip of his clothing. "Rand says I'm about to become morose, an odious trait for a campfire companion." He opened a flask, offered it to Uthe. "A touch of last night's meal with some chili pepper thrown in. It's good in the coffee."

Uthe refused politely. No vampire took blood from another without verifying the source.

"It's the hospitality law of the desert, my friend," the vampire said, serious now. "I intend you no harm, I swear it." He nodded to Keldwyn. "Plus, should I so much as stain your tunic, he's going to turn me into wolf food, so there's no point to me harming you, is there? Unless I have a death wish."

"You would wish for death before I was done with you," Keldwyn said passively.

"I've wished for death a long time," Cai said with disturbing cheerfulness. "Just can't seem to bring myself to it. That fucking sense of self-preservation, right? Makes you want to live through things no one should live through. I did mention the gods are bastards, right?"

Uthe's grip tightened on the cup. He had to remind himself to ease it before he crumpled the tin. Cai rose, tucking the blood flask back onto his belt.

"I'm going out to do nightly rounds. You're welcome to take your ease for a bit, my lords. My cave is well protected for such a rest. I'll be back in a while if you choose to stay for any length of time."

As he moved toward the cave mouth, Uthe caught his attention with a raised hand. "I don't expect the sorceress told you how I might get into her cave to find out what she left me?"

"No. I expect she thought you would know. I'll bring you back a piece of my hunt tonight if you want. Nothing so good as a juicy, blood-filled lung. It's like sponge cake. And you'll have one less enemy to face. Your hunch is right. This lot aren't your allies. Weirdly dressed, too."

"What do you mean?" Uthe asked.

"Like they're filming a movie about the Crusades. You'll see. Once you have what she left you, they'll close in and try to take it from you. I'll see what I can do about reducing the numbers this evening."

As Rand rose, Cai shook his head. "Not tonight. Your leg isn't up to this. We agreed. A few more nights."

Rand padded toward the cave opening, ignoring him. "Rand," Cai said sharply. "No."

Rand's response to that was to pin the ears fully back

and give him a full set of teeth this time, an impressive reaction coupled with a hair-raising growl.

"He always makes me pull out the rolled up newspaper." Sighing in resignation, Cai moved to join the wolf at the cave mouth. "Fine."

What happened next was almost too fast for Uthe to follow, even with his vampire senses. When he reached the wolf's side, Cai began to move past him, then pivoted instead. He seized the wolf around the middle. The shifter was so large, it wasn't an easy feat. Though a vampire was stronger than a wolf shifter, the wolf was as large as one of Lyssa's Irish wolfhounds, with three times the massive bulk in shoulders and chest. Rand's head whipped around, his teeth coming close to taking a chunk out of Cai's shoulder, but by then Cai had a steel collar latched around his throat, attached to a chain embedded in the stone floor. The wolf snarled, lunged, and this time made contact, sinking his teeth into Cai's arm.

Keldwyn was on his feet, as was Uthe, but Cai, instead of yanking away, banded both arms around the wolf's neck, pressing against him so his captured and bleeding arm put a strain on the hinge of the wolf's jaw. When the wolf began to struggle, Cai made a shushing noise. "Going to stop being an asshole about this? I'm not going to lose you to a couple jerks getting lucky, just because you don't think I should hunt without you at my back."

His blood was dripping on the floor before the wolf subsided, though the one eye Uthe could see was fiery blue. Cai had cut off enough of his wind that, when the vampire released his grip, he had to ease the wolf to a reclining position on the floor. "There you go. You don't have to make this a fight every damn night, you know. And lick that shit up. Blood's all over our floor."

The wolf's expression said exactly what he could do with his suggestions. Cai turned to Uthe. "I trust the sorceress's opinion of you, my lord. She said you were a Templar Knight. One of the true ones, who never abandoned your oath."

Hearing it was humbling. The sorceress had always treated him like something that crawled over her threshold with six legs, though in time he'd learned that was what passed for affection from her. Rising, Uthe gave the vampire a half bow. "I was and am a Templar Knight. It is not something one leaves behind. Though I have not been able to observe all the tenets of our Rule, I have never stopped honoring them however I can."

"I can vouch for that," Keldwyn spoke, surprising him. The Fae's tone was neutral, though Uthe detected the sardonic edge. "He is tedious about it."

"All right, then." Cai's mouth curved. "This wolf is my family. He can do you serious harm if you get close to him, but since I expect you would still prevail, I need your word you'll watch over him and do him no harm."

"For your hospitality and coffee, it is a small thing to ask," Uthe agreed. "He will come to no harm from us, and we will protect him from any harm that comes this way."

Cai gave him a searching look. "I wouldn't leave him at all, except we did promise to help you, and cutting those numbers is a way to do that."

"Then I will go with you and help you hunt them."

"No thanks. Like most of us, I hunt better alone." He flashed fangs. "I'd also prefer not leaving him bound like that without someone to watch over him. He won't be any trouble to you. I have a way of letting him shift back to human for short periods, but the sorceress gave him something that's keeping him a wolf pretty much full time until he heals. Which means you don't have to worry he'll shift and use thumbs to get out of the collar. You can sleep. Though if he does, best plug your ears. He snores like a freight train."

The wolf snapped, growling menacingly once more. Cai ignored him, though Uthe detected some effort in the indifference. When he left the cave, the wolf lunged against the chain, letting out a short, piercing howl. Up until now,

Uthe had detected human awareness in the wolf, but as his distress increased, the animal took over. Both eyes became gold, the blue disappearing.

"Here," Keldwyn said, in a commanding way that jerked the beast's attention to him. The Fae raised a hand. When the wolf's gaze followed the movement, his eyes glazed and his legs gave out beneath him, letting him sink to the floor. A moment later a rumbling snore filled the cave.

Keldwyn's magic always left a lingering heat and scent, like a blown out candle with a tart cranberry scent. Uthe resisted the urge to draw it deeply into his lungs. "He's protective of his vampire," he said.

"As are many servants, like your Mariela," Keldwyn noted. "He'll sleep until his Master's return. I am sorry about your sorceress. You were fond of her. It was in your face when he revealed her death so baldly."

Uthe grimaced. "She was the last of her line, unless she had time to train another. I have been in contact with the family as the magic was passed from woman to woman, all dedicated to this one task. She was the one to find the answer we sought. But beyond that...she was a unique soul."

"What was the task she solved?"

Uthe shook his head. "Not yet. Not until we're in her home." He glanced meaningfully toward the wolf. Even if the creature was unconscious, he was a fully marked servant and Cai could listen to their conversation through him. Understanding, Keldwyn nodded, though Uthe saw his frustration. Understandable, since Uthe didn't care for being outside an information loop either, but sometimes one had to be patient.

The bigger question was who were these men who sought what Uthe was after? Though even that question was less important than who was directing them. He'd know the answer when he confronted them. Like Cai, Uthe expected that to happen as soon as they approached their destination. While he appreciated Cai's help, it chafed to be here while another vampire handled the hunting. But he expected there would be plenty of bodies to go around before dawn came.

"He's a peculiar vampire," Keldwyn commented. "Do you have many like him that don't fall within the reach of an overlord?"

"A few, mostly in the mountain or desert regions like this. Lord Mason was outside the purview of the vampire world for the many years he spent in the Sahara, not that I think that would have made much difference to him. Especially with how powerful he is now. Our census of approximately five thousand vampires in the world assumes a certain percentage haven't been counted because they're loners, operating outside areas where we wouldn't cross paths with them. Like Cai, they also take precautions to ensure they are not noticed by humans, one of the biggest flags to put them on the Council's radar. As Cai said, he is not a Trad, but he exhibits some of their tendencies to protect his autonomy. We don't know how many Trads there are beyond those we've included in the five thousand, but their number unfortunately seems to be growing."

"You think the Council should be more concerned about them than they are," Keldwyn recalled the discussions. "Though some on the Council admire them, consider them purists."

"Because they've never met one," Uthe said flatly. "It makes it easy to romanticize them. We are much like animal predators in our instincts and impulses, my lord." He looked toward the wolf. "We have that in common with him. Yet we have a very distinctly humanoid trait. Our sadism. A Trad may consider himself a far more natural version of vampire, but their version is the monster depicted in human horror films. Conscienceless, driven by bloodlust and the pure pleasure of indulging it. The struggles of the victims only fuel the appetite."

Blood throbbed in his temples, his pulse beating

strongly in his throat. Damnation, he'd left this behind. That this damn disease would bring all of it back so clearly, so painfully... Truth, there was a cruelty in the design of the world that could stir hopelessness about what lay beyond its making. He understood Cai's feelings on that all too well.

"It sounds as if you will not run out of stories to tell me on our trek. But why don't you take your ease before we proceed to the sorceress's home?" Keldwyn slid down to the ground so his back was against the rock. He stretched his legs out in front of him. "Put your head in my lap. There are no eyes watching us here, and now that we know for sure those eyes are our foes, I could give a fuck about their opinion on man-love."

It was unexpected, Kel offering his lap for a pillow while he slept. When Uthe hesitated, Keldwyn lifted a brow. "Do I need to make it a condition of our agreement?"

Uthe snorted. "If I say yes, you will make everything part of it." What had him hesitating wasn't that, but how appealing it seemed. When Kel extended an imperious hand, his gaze fastening on Uthe's, he decided not to argue further. He lay down, stretching out so his head was propped on Kel's thigh. He emitted an uncertain sigh as Keldwyn's hand fell on his brow and began to soothe. Uthe inhaled the smells of the desert and the earth scent of the Fae Lord: a hint of cool stone, spring flowers waiting below the winter ground, and snow clinging to mountain tops.

"That's new," he observed. "I smell winter on you, my lord."

"The Fae have an affinity for a particular season, but there is some overlap, especially as one ages. I have a far greater connection to winter now than I did earlier in my life."

"Does that mean a miracle might eventually happen and your ice queen will discover the lighter touch of spring flowers?"

"Do not be disrespectful of her, vampire. She would say

that is my job."

Uthe smiled as Keldwyn flicked his ear. "Yes, she would." Then the humor died away as he thought of the sorceress once more. "God be with you, Fatima," he muttered. Closing his eyes, he began to say the paternosters that took the place of compline. He could say them on her behalf, and the rhythm of it would soothe him into a short sleep to replenish him. Keldwyn's fingers wrapped around his shoulder, a light hold. It occurred to Uthe that Keldwyn had stood as his protector before Cai, staying watchful of both strange vampire and wolf as Uthe questioned them and learned their mettle.

"You know, I can take care of myself," he said tiredly. *At least for now.*

"You are more than capable of it," Keldwyn agreed. "I never said you weren't, my lord. I simply have a vested interested in contributing to that intention."

"Hmm."

"Your father was a Trad, wasn't he?"

Uthe's fingers dug into Kel's leg, a jerk of reaction. "Don't."

Kel's hand paused on his shoulder. He'd been tracing the roundness of it, fingers slipping over the bunched curve of Uthe's biceps, testing their resilience with firm, caressing pressure. "You do not wish to speak of it."

"No. Not before sleep. It brings nightmares."

"Then we will speak no more of it. Will you tell me a story of your sorceress, though? It may help you sleep, and celebrate her life."

"You owe me a story before I give you another. I want more of your life, Keldwyn."

"Information is power. You intend to keep the playing field level between us."

A statement laden with meaning. The warning beneath it was a drawn sword, the slip of steel out of supple leather, an erotic threat. Keldwyn's touch had moved from his shoulder to the side of Uthe's throat. His fingers slid up

Uthe's carotid to the hinge of his jaw, and then back down, tracing the pulsing arteries and veins, moving around to the jugular. He slowly wrapped his hand over it, then released Uthe to start over. It wasn't an idle touch. Keldwyn was even now gathering knowledge, absorbing Uthe's reaction to the contact. Uthe put his hand up over Keldwyn's, curving his fingers into the spaces between the Fae's. It stilled the movement, holding pressure on his throat so he felt the beating of the blood beneath their combined touch. "And if I said yes to that?"

"When a chessboard is tipped over, all the pieces scattered, the game is over. All that is left are the two players, facing one another with nothing between them." Keldwyn bent so his breath slid along Uthe's temple. He didn't look up, but he knew if he did, the Fae's dark gaze would be close and large as a full moon at early twilight, tempting the viewer to think it could be touched. "I relish showing you how pleasurable a tipped playing field can be, my lord. I will give you a story eventually, on my own terms. But tonight let us honor the dead. Tell me of your sorceress."

Uthe suppressed a sigh. "To do that, I go back to the beginning. To Haris, Fatima's ancestor."

Haris had been built strong, with masculine features. She was quick, lissome as an eel with a blade. In hand to hand, she was almost a match for Uthe's vampire powers. He'd discovered that on their initial meeting, an ambush where Haris and her companions had been sent to assassinate King Louis III. It was during the Second Crusade, when the Templars had been charged with guarding the king and his army as they headed for Damascus. Louis's commanders had little knowledge of how best to navigate the Holy Land terrain or the dangers there.

It was one of their earliest encounters with the Saracen version of the Templars—the Assassins, a sect who served Allah and the Old Man of the Mountain. They would have succeeded, except for Uthe's vampire senses. He'd detected their infiltration into the camp, around the king's tent. He remembered the shadows against the fabric, the clash of steel as they'd engaged in that small area, the king's personal guard getting the monarch out of harm's way. Two of his brethren slew two of the assassins, and then the third had ducked free of the tent, cutting the cords as he rolled free.

Uthe was quick enough to slip out of the potential net. He'd pursued the assassin outside the camp, on foot, which meant he should have gained on him, but the short male stayed an impressive length ahead of him, until Uthe boxed him in among the more rocky terrain. Then the assassin turned, drew his curved blade, and waited for him.

That was when Uthe caught her full scent and knew he faced a woman. Then she was on him, her blade flashing like a serpent's tooth. When he finally made full contact with her weapon, the power that sang up through his arm, practically dislocating it from the shoulder, told him her already considerable abilities had been augmented by magic. He backed off and stared at her. She was doing the same, as if she'd expected the magic to end him.

"Vampire," she breathed, startling him.

He tipped his head to her, his sword still raised and ready. "Sorceress."

"Not a sorceress, no. Protected by one. As well as by my skill with a blade. Almost enough to take you out, vampire." She had a rough, masculine voice. She sheathed the blade, surprising him. "We will meet again. This is not our day to die."

She bolted, running lithely through the rocks like a wild cat. He could have continued to chase her, should have. But he had not.

"You recognized her as something more like yourself," Keldwyn mused.

"Yes. That was part of it. In war, strange bonds can form. You remain enemies on the battlefield, but sometimes a respect is born between those who fight." Uthe paused. "I told you why I went to Jerusalem. When I joined Hugh's company, I discovered hope and purpose in faith. Protecting pilgrims from raiders, protecting those who sought that same hope and purpose, was what drove us. We had no fight with Muslims or Jews. For a short time, despite what had happened in the First Crusade, we were able to find that balance with them that had existed before it, no matter how uneasy at times. It was only later, when the Templars began to be tangled up in the ambitions of kings and popes, that purpose was lost."

He closed his eyes, seeing printed script. 'Each should remain in the vocation to which he was called.' There was an anonymous letter written to the Order early in its life, as if the author knew what would happen to us. They discounted the idea that Hugh wrote it, but I think he may have done so. He was the type of man who realized an anonymous letter might be considered more for its content than the author, if they had no author whose motives they could dissect. It spoke with the voice of someone within our ranks, someone who had more foresight and divine guidance than those who eventually led us. He said the devil tries to persuade men to desert their true role to chase the 'phantom of the higher good'. 'This is a delusion, for God desires a patient acceptance of the gifts which one has received.' In hindsight, I think that letter may have also been Hugh's penance, for he started the Order on the road to material success and power, though with the best of intentions."

Uthe opened his eyes, though in his mind he still saw the complicated tapestry of battles, decisions and multiple paths that could have been, against those that had been chosen. "Bernard saw the same possibility: 'The temporal glory of the earthly city does not demolish its heavenly rewards, but demonstrates them—so long as we remember that the one is the figure of the other, and that it is the heavenly which is our mother.'"

Night's Templar

While he kept worn copies of the Rule and Bernard's *De Laude*, lately it was as if he was hearing them in his head as they'd first been spoken to him, rather than as an echo of what he'd read repeatedly and recently from his bedside. Since most Templars weren't able to read then, he'd sat in on oral readings of them often enough.

He brought himself back to the story at hand. "At the time I met Haris, we were starting to lose that vocation and our understanding of the gifts and the charge we were given. So I didn't kill her."

Collecting his thoughts, he returned the story back to the original point. "Haris was a male name. I never could get her to tell me what her birth circumstances were. Perhaps she'd been born to a family who'd wanted a boy or who'd had to conceal her gender and raise her as a male. Or she'd assumed the disguise herself because she wanted more freedom in a male-dominated society. Or, though she'd been born a woman, she felt more comfortable embracing a man's identity."

"We have those among the Fae. So you saw her again?"

"Yes. I often had separate tasks to handle alone, related to the quest we are on now. It was during one of those that she and I met again. We startled one another at an isolated oasis. Purely for form, we did our best to each kill the other. Then we sat down and spoke through most of the night. Her beliefs were strong and pure and, though she saw me as an infidel, she also had a touch of the Sight and the mystic influences of her aunt. Her aunt was the sorceress who'd given her the magical shield. When I met Shahnaz, she was quick to tell me that Haris's fighting skills were her own. The magic she'd bound to her simply kept her safe and augmented her strength when facing a preternatural threat like myself."

Uthe paused. "Shahnaz was as beautiful as Haris was plain, but a male relative had cut up her face when she refused to marry whom he demanded. She escaped to France with enough funds to set herself up as a reclusive widow of noble birth. She told me the lack of spouse suited her just fine, since it freed her up to pursue the study of magic. When I visited her there, a tanned skin was stretched over one wall, a beautiful piece of artwork, painted with magical symbols and elements of nature intertwined. To those who can detect such magics, like yourself, it formed a protection shield upon her and her home that was never challenged. Though her visitors assumed it was an heirloom of animal skin, it was human. From the way she touched the scars on her face when she was contemplating it, I knew it belonged to the man who'd injured her."

"One of the first complicated magics I learned was how to skin a man alive with one incantation," she'd mused. "Takes them a while to die that way. Horrible noise and quite messy. I wouldn't recommend doing it more than once and only when absolutely necessary."

"Not a woman to cross, obviously," Keldwyn said.

"Most of them aren't, my lord. At least the ones we know."

"So she was Fatima's ancestor."

"She was. The magic was passed on to the next female relative born with the gift, and so on and so forth. They compiled quite a body of arcane knowledge. Lines of dark and light magic can cross until they become so confusing..." Uthe trailed off.

When Keldwyn slid his hand over Uthe's short hair, Uthe sighed. "You are unexpected at times, my lord. I didn't expect you to be gentle."

"I am not." Keldwyn brushed his knuckles along Uthe's jaw. "Sleep. Think of things that bring pleasant dreams. Your Mariela's sweet lips, the comfort of your prayers, the things worth remembering."

Silken black hair sliding along his bare skin, Kel's serious profile as he contemplated one of Uthe's chess moves, the taste of a firm, heated mouth. Uthe turned over onto his back and lifted his hand, trailing his fingertips over that mouth, the fair brow. Keldwyn's arm circled him, bringing him up so their lips met. Uthe closed his eyes, muscles coiling like a snake writhing in the sun as Keldwyn found his way beneath the tunic, clasping Uthe's cock through the thin cotton pants. It was a leisurely exploration of what the Fae had claimed as part of the binding. It banished any shadows and replaced them with tight longing for a variety of things, the least of which was sex. Though that alone was a throbbing, constant undercurrent around the male.

With a vague embarrassment, Uthe realized Keldwyn had shifted him so Uthe's ass was planted between Keldwyn's spread thighs. The Fae was holding him in his lap. Uthe was of a similar length and breadth to Kel, so only by sitting on the ground like this would the position work, but there it was a secure embrace. Keldwyn's hand curved over his hip and buttock, the other arm wrapped around Uthe's back. His palm cupped Uthe's skull to deepen the kiss. Uthe curled his fingers in the front of Keldwyn's laced tunic, finding the lightly furred skin beneath. He savored the long columns of his thighs, one beneath Uthe's bent knees and the other against his lower back.

Keldwyn adjusted to a half reclined position against the rock, nudging Uthe into using the Fae's body as a mattress. His head was partly on Kel's shoulder, partly on his chest, his upper torso against the Fae's stomach and pelvis, the rest of him draped and tangled with his legs. His hand curved high over Keldwyn's thigh.

"Just rest, Varick," Kel said. "This is more comfortable."

It was. It was also the first time in his life that someone had held him while he slept. He'd held others, but he'd never been held. He should resist it, but his tiredness was not in the mood to play games he really didn't want to play anyhow.

He let sleep take him down, certain he was well-protected by the Fae Lord. Another first.

Keldwyn listened to Uthe's heartbeat even out. He stayed awake, watching over his vampire and the sleeping wolf. The creature's rumbling snore and Uthe's heartbeat filled the small, echoing space. He didn't listen for his own, though he was sure it thudded, sure and steady, an echo of Uthe's.

Keldwyn had never seen the vampire falter in his duty. All of those who had known him far longer showed him the great respect such responsibility warranted. He protected, advised and took whatever leadership or support role was needed to guide Lyssa, the Council and vampire kind. Though he'd not yet seen him in physical combat beyond the sparring with Daegan, Keldwyn did not doubt he was a fierce warrior who would not hesitate to sacrifice himself if the need came.

He recognized Uthe's capitulation to him, allowing him to watch over him as he slept, as the honor it was. Even if that honor was offered by a species that most of his kind, including himself, considered inferior. Inferior in strength and magic, perhaps, but not in character. Not this vampire.

His mixed feelings on that disturbed him. It had been some time since he'd felt such a strong need to bond with another. Having that feeling toward a vampire was problematic. Unprecedented, for him. Perhaps Uthe was not the only one losing his mind.

Keldwyn resisted the urge to increase his hold on the vampire, as if that would change his fate. Instead, he massaged the vampire's shoulder, resting his fingertips on the side of his throat, and half-smiled, a painful gesture, as Uthe murmured. His grip twitched on Keldwyn's thigh.

"You know my touch already, vampire," Keldwyn whispered. "Enough not to let it disturb your sleep. Take it into your dreams with you. Let me touch you there. Then you will know what I desire from you when you wake."

And maybe between now and that moment, Kel himself would figure that out.

§

When Uthe woke, Mordecai was back. He was at the other side of the cave, near the entrance, giving Uthe and Keldwyn whatever semblance of privacy the space afforded. The wolf was with him, splayed across his legs in a position similar to Uthe's with Keldwyn. Cai had left the steel collar on the wolf, but detached the chain. Moonlight filtering through the cave opening glinted off of the metal and the tips of Rand's fur. The lingering scent of fresh blood and human flesh told him that Cai had had good hunting. Both he and his wolf had fed their hungers, at least for food.

From beneath his shirt, Mordecai removed an amulet, the stone a swirl of deep turquoise. While Uthe watched, Cai attached it to the steel collar. A thrum of magical energy shuddered through it, and then rippled over the wolf's thick ebony pelt. Rand shifted into an upright position, then jerked back down as the magic took effect, his body twisting. Cai held him, moved with him, a dance it was clear they'd done together before. Three blinks later, Uthe saw the remarkable metamorphosis complete, from wolf to man.

Rand's shoulders lifted and fell, chest expanding from the exertion. He was curled on his side facing the vampire, head resting on Cai's knee. His taut buttocks were tucked under, his legs drawn up before him. Yet even naked and vulnerable, the human was as intimidating as the wolf. His broad shoulders and back, the bunched muscles, were a match for Niall. The big Scot had been servant to Evan, the vampire Uthe had sired, for nearly three hundred years, but now Niall was a vampire fledgling. Uthe expected Rand matched Niall in height, over six feet tall, his shoulder width at least half of that.

As the shifter pushed himself up on an elbow, Cai gripped the steel collar. It was loose now, so he could get his whole hand around it, clasp it in a sure hold that captured Rand's attention. Cai's sardonic personality and smart ass wit were absent. The unrelenting gaze he pinned on Rand was pure vampire master, taking control of his servant and leaving no doubt who was in charge. Rand shifted against his hold, lip curling in a remarkable similarity to his wolf persona, a show of teeth. Cai locked eyes with him, forcing him finally to drop his gaze, though it was a stimulating battle of wills to watch.

Cai leaned in, brushed his lips over his temple in reward for his servant's compliance, then followed a leisurely path with his mouth to below his servant's ear, nudging aside a thick, curly mane of shoulder-length brown hair. In human form, Rand's eyes weren't bi-colored like his wolf's. They were both blue, though Uthe thought he could see flecks of gold in them. Rand's head dropped back as Cai nuzzled his throat, then moved over to his shoulder. As Rand's hand curled into a fist on Cai's leg, Cai bit, the erotic act making Uthe's loins tighten in pleasurable reaction. Mordecai might feed on brigands, but like most vampires, he preferred the pure, sweet blood of his servant.

Keldwyn's hand slid along Uthe's throat, inside the tunic neckline to rest on his shoulder and bare skin. What thoughts were going through the Fae's mind? Despite his earlier reaction to Uthe trying to feed on him, Keldwyn didn't seem to view what they were watching as an abomination. Not if his slow, sensual pace along Uthe's skin was any indication.

The needs of the body were one thing. Like food or water, they had to be sated. Whether with decadence or sparse rations, it didn't matter. But the needs that rose in his heart and soul under Keldwyn's attentions, those were things far more specific and complex, responding only to certain stimuli. They were needs that had been dormant until now, roused by the touch of one enigmatic Fae Lord.

Though he knew he should get up and go seek blood, the rest had helped. His hunger would keep. He escaped the troubling thoughts by dozing off once more. When he next woke, it was a couple hours before dawn. Keldwyn had remained in the same position. Uthe pushed himself up off the cave floor. "You should have moved me," he said. "You have to be stiff."

At Keldwyn's grin, Uthe couldn't help a chuckle. "It has been a while since I've been subjected to soldier's humor, my lord. I am slow to protect myself from gutter wit."

"Well, you did just wake up. Otherwise, I expect you would have been more prepared." Keldwyn rose with no obvious signs of having been in the same position for hours. Uthe wondered how long he could stay motionless. Vampires were good at it for limited periods, but the way Keldwyn could blend into his environment suggested he could be a statue for as long as he wished.

"When did you last eat?" Uthe asked. Being in the company of vampires, and having a servant like Mariela who cared for her own needs within the ample provisions of Council headquarters, it had been a while since he'd traveled with a companion who might need regular meals. The last time he'd seen Keldwyn eat had been in Savannah.

"A couple days ago. I do not need to eat that often, though I do enjoy it. I can draw nourishment from the elements." Keldwyn placed a hand on the rock beside him. "There is an energy in everything of the earth, and I can draw in small samplings of those things to keep myself well-fortified. As well as use them for magic."

"Well that's awfully handy," Mordecai said, ducking into the cave. Back in wolf form, Rand trotted in to his left and stretched out on the far side of the cave, eying their guests. "I was going to ask if you wanted me to catch you a rat while I'm doing the same for Rand, my lord. They're tasty. The bones can be seasoned like crunchy noodles. I miss Chinese takeout, though Rand doesn't like the fortune cookies, not since he got one caught in the roof of his mouth." Cai shot the wolf a fond look. "He and I had to have a bloody wrestling match to get it out. When he's in this form, sometimes he can be more wolf than man."

"I appreciate you thinking of it," Uthe said gravely. "But we need to be on our way."

"So you're off to the sorceress's cave then? It's close to dawn. Not that that seems to bother you much, not from what Rand saw yesterday, you walking in the sunlight as you were like a human. Does Deathbringer here give you that ability? His lordship, I mean," Cai added at Keldwyn's narrow look, though his eyes sparked. The vampire enjoyed yanking chains. But he'd said death meant little to him.

Uthe was surprised Cai hadn't brought it up before now, since a vampire who could walk in sunlight would be a subject of great curiosity to most their kind. But it was clear the excess of solitude had made the vampire peculiar even beyond usual vampire eccentricities. "Something like that."

Cai shrugged. "I know the risk of death might be preferable to spending the daylight hours in my company, but if you wait until nightfall again, Rand and I can back you up."

"Our quest has some urgency to it. Once I'm inside the sorceress's cave, it may take me time to discover what I'm seeking. But we appreciate what you've already done for us."

"All right, then." Cai accepted his judgment without argument. "Once the sun goes down, we'll come check on you, see if you need help."

"Why would you help two strangers?" Kel asked.

Cai blinked. "Because you're here to do good. Fatima said so. Rand also has a nose for these things. Even I could tell you were honest and right when you came into range. I'm no slouch at character assessment myself. Plus, if I get a chance to kill every one of those fuckers, I'll be taking it. Whoever follows you to that cave had a hand in hurting Fatima. I enjoy my killing, but I like it to be righteous."

"'Truly a fearless knight and secure on every side is he whose soul is protected by the armor of faith just as his body is protected by the armor of steel... He need fear neither demons nor men.'" Uthe quoted St. Bernard. "I do take your meaning. Though righteousness is in the eye of the beholder."

"'Good... Bad... I'm the guy with the gun.' *Army of Darkness*, Bruce Campbell." Cai grinned. "And I'm officially designating myself beholden. She took care of my wolf, so I'll be happy to wreak vengeance on her killers."

§

Over the next hour, Uthe and Keldwyn moved swiftly toward the sorceress's home with minimal conversation. The closer they drew to their destination, the more their unseen followers closed the distance between them. They were both on alert for possible attack.

"I want to take out my sword," Uthe muttered. "Which doesn't make a lot of sense, since my strength and speed as a vampire are far more useful against the current weapons of men."

He knew why he was uneasy, however. The sibilant voice had been silent since they left Cai's cave. Over the years, Uthe had learned to muffle it like a distant conversation when he didn't want to hear its ruminations, but even then he always had a sense of it, like detecting the breath of someone else in a dark room.

The other voice, the rough one, spoke far less, but he usually had a humming awareness of its presence also. Nothing today. If he hadn't had the blood link with them, he would have thought they were entirely gone, but that at least was still there. He just didn't feel any stirrings on the other end of that connection.

The Fae Lord was studying their surroundings in a way Uthe recognized, a fellow soldier evaluating the terrain, the advantages and disadvantages. "What are you expecting here, my lord, so I shall be prepared for it?"

"In an ideal world, there would have been a woman wizened in face like a raisin, possessed of a tongue that could compete with a razor blade. She would have insulted us, then offered us her hospitality. She made an excellent tea with secret ingredients she would never divulge. The first time I drank it, she told me halfway through the cup that it would make my man parts fall off."

"I understand why she had your affection. In this not-so-ideal world?"

"We are about to find her body." Uthe sighed. "Since she enacted a protection spell at her death to protect the contents of her home, I believe that means she left me what I came here seeking. Those following us know it. Once we have it, they will attack. While they may be humans, I suspect what sent them is not. We need to stay alert."

Keldwyn put out a hand. "You promised me the rest of it today."

"Once we're in the cave."

"Understood. But I will know now what may have sent them. My magic can help you better if I know what I face."

That made logical sense. At this point, Uthe wasn't certain why he was withholding information from the Fae Lord, except old habits died hard. Like the desire to hold a sword in the face of an unknown threat.

"A demon," he said. "Powerful. Upper echelon."

Keldwyn's gaze widened enough to show his surprise. "Your not-so-ideal world is truly grim."

Uthe lifted a shoulder. "I did offer you the option of waiting upon my return, my lord."

Keldwyn's expression turned to one of mild offense. "I am merely annoyed that your sorceress isn't here to offer us her emasculating refreshment. I'm parched."

"You would have made a decent Templar, my lord, at least in your courage. I've yet to see your fighting skills."

"I expect that will change shortly."

Uthe nodded. "Be on guard."

The two males maneuvered up another steep incline. As they did, the opening to the cave Uthe sought became visible. It disappeared, then reappeared again. Like the entrance to Cai's chosen cave, it was narrow and, at most angles, difficult to see. It was a good spot for a sorceress to work unmolested.

"You face a demon, and you were going to come here alone, with no magical abilities of your own?" Keldwyn grunted. "You are not usually foolish, my lord."

"I wasn't this time. This demon and I have been connected for a very long time, my lord." Uthe didn't look for Kel's reaction to that. He had all his senses straining for evidence of ambush. The loosening of rock under a shifting foot, the scrape of a body against a stone wall, the scent of man or any other life form, a flutter of movement. Nothing. Which only made him more suspicious. At least some of the men should have been lying in wait here, so once Uthe bridged the protection on the cave, they could rush in, try to overpower them.

Keldwyn brought a hand up, pressing his knuckles to Uthe's chest. The Fae's gaze was intent. "There is not just one magic in use here. A second one. Very dark. Your demon, I expect?"

"Or whatever she found to fight him." Uthe met Keldwyn's gaze, wondering if the Fae remembered his comment earlier, about the sorceress being a magic user who crossed the boundaries between dark and light magic. She'd always known her forays into dark magic to find their answer carried the risk of overwhelming her, bringing her over to the demon's side. But Cai's assessment of her had assured Uthe that hadn't happened, as well as Uthe's belief in the will of the woman in question.

He smelled death, a few days old. Outside the cave, the odor came from the remains of those who'd tried to breach the sorceress's wards once they were activated. The stronger stench came from within, those trapped with her whom scavengers couldn't reach. He disliked thinking of her body sharing the same space as those rotting corpses, but he could hear her cackling response to that.

We're all meat in the end, my lord. A buffet for

scavengers. She'd say cold things like that when the darkness rose in her eyes. When she felt closer to the light, she'd speak a different truth. *The body's a home. One we should love and respect for its care of us. One day, probably sooner than we'd like, we'll all have to leave home.*

The entrance to her cave was flanked by layers of concealing rock, and the terrain leading up to it was steep, uneven. "If she didn't have time to craft an exception to my presence, I may be incinerated when I try to enter her cave, as the others were," Uthe said.

"When we get there, let me examine the shape of her protections. I may be able to keep you unsinged."

"That would be a kindness, my lord."

They moved forward together. One step, two steps. Uthe slid his pack off his shoulder, ready to drop it. A breath later, he felt the dark magic Kel had mentioned. It struck him deep in the bones, like a fever ache. He knew the touch of the demon intimately, but there was a distance to that touch. This was up close, a blast of power that speared terror through his soul.

Fuck that. He shook off the intimidation tactic and focused on the true threat. It came with the third step. The illusion of empty, rocky terrain vanished. A cloaking barrier. He ducked just in time as a blade whistled over his head.

He charged forward, ramming the solid body of a man swathed in Saracen garb. Like the Crusades, just as Cai had said. Turban, face scarf, and sashed tunic. A dozen more like him had been waiting, and now they spilled out, surrounding him. No, not all. Several were already gone, one of them leaving a brief impression of wide dark eyes, the whites rolling in terror as the man was yanked away from Uthe and disappeared into a blast of magic that sent a wave of heat rolling along the back of Uthe's neck.

Keldwyn had entered the fray.

Uthe slammed his elbow into the nose of one grappling

him from behind, and broke the wrist of another so his curved blade clattered to the stone. The weapon had been a poor choice in these close quarters, one surprise swing the most it could accomplish before the fight became grunting, ugly hand-to-hand. Elbows, knees and fists became the measures of survival. A dagger sliced Uthe's arm, but it brought his opponent close enough for a headlock, where he crushed the skull as efficiently as a nutcracker. Thank God, these were mere mortals, the only magical enhancement they'd possessed in the cloaking spell. Whoever had sent them had hoped the element of surprise would result in a lucky strike.

But they'd also moved too soon. Uthe and Keldwyn hadn't even breached the cave yet. Uthe detected an element of frustrated rage in the dark magic. Despite being immersed in blood and violence, he bared his teeth in savage satisfaction. *Not so easy to control your minions at this distance, is it?*

He caught a brief glimpse of Kel. The Fae Lord was using flashes of glamor to confuse his opponents, putting himself left when he was right, above when he was below. Yet when the time for contact came, Uthe wasn't surprised to see Keldwyn was accomplished in hand-to-hand fighting. The heel of his palm drove the nose of one attacker into his brain. A graceful pivot ducked him beneath the guard of another, putting him behind his opponent. Kel twisted the Saracen's head, a terrifyingly effortless snapping of the spine. It was like watching a cook take a chicken's head.

As another of his own assailants tried to rise, Uthe drove his fist into the man's rib cage and through the heart. The bloody heat of it, the violent disruption of its rhythmic beat, was something he hadn't experienced in some time. His own heart was pounding like thundering hooves. He rose to his feet, taking stock. Not that he was counting, but it looked like he'd taken down five and Kel took eight. Well, the Fae had the advantage of his magic.

Keldwyn came to him in a swift sinuous stride, assuming a back-to-back position with Uthe as they listened together for reinforcements. None were forthcoming. Not yet, at least.

Uthe dropped to his heels, giving the dead men a closer look. Head scarf, skirted tunic, boots, a belted jerkin over it. No evidence of the modern world. No watch, no T-shirt. He picked up the blade of the one who'd first attacked him. It was authentic, the same weapon the Saracens had used during the Crusades. Dipping his head, he inhaled deeply. People now had a different odor than they had during that time. Different food, less preservatives, different types of hygiene. Olfactory memory was strong for vampires. If he closed his eyes, this scent took him back hundreds of years.

"They don't belong here. This isn't a modern day sect." Uthe studied the dead men, eyes glazed, faces slack. "I think they've been brought here from the past. Saracens. Deserters, not part of the regular army or true believers, so at least not innocents."

"And from their mindless fervor, under a spell as well." Kneeling, Keldwyn tore a strip off a tunic and reached for Uthe's arm, gripping it above where the dagger had sliced him. "You'll need this to help the clotting. It's still bleeding heavily."

Uthe hadn't paid any attention to the wound, beyond positioning it so the blood dripped into the ground instead of on himself. Keldwyn did an efficient field dressing on the knife wound. His hands lingered on Uthe's arm, giving him a hard, quick squeeze. "You should be more careful, Varick. If you'd been a blink slower, that first human would have taken your head."

"If I'd been that slow, I'd have deserved it." Hearing his given name on Keldwyn's lips was unsettling. Uthe pushed away the feelings, as well as the kneejerk reaction to tell him not to use it. "Not all of us have glamor at our disposal, my lord."

"Hmm. Since you face possible incineration, I'll let the

insult to my fighting skills pass. Let's get into your sorceress's cave before more reinforcements are sent."

Keldwyn's expression said he wasn't going to wait much longer for that explanation Uthe had promised, especially since Uthe didn't seem overly surprised to have warriors from past history thrown in their path. However, he did understand the need to find a more defensible position first. Picking up the discarded pack, Uthe led the way up the incline.

He hadn't been certain how much of the terrain was actual and what had been manufactured by the cloaking spell, but the rock overhangs became even narrower, forming a useful choke point at the tapered entrance to the sorceress's lair.

The death smell increased exponentially, but he focused on the low hum of energy hovering around the opening. Mindful of Keldwyn's greater expertise in this field, he shifted enough to give the Fae a better view.

Keldwyn had closed his eyes, though, absorbing the magic through other senses. "An extremely complex protection spell, one with a variety of lethal snares to it," he said without opening them. "But there is a way past them, triggered by the right person. When you entered her home, were there traditional words of courtesy you offered?"

Understanding his intent, Uthe spoke clearly. "I come to your door in peace. In the name of the mission we share, may the Madman of the Wilderness forever be praised."

Silence, but the humming changed. His own senses weren't as keen, for vampires weren't magic users, but Keldwyn's gaze flickered in acknowledgement. "It responded to your voice." He looked thoughtful. "I believe she made provision for you to enter without harm."

"Are you certain?"

"No. But fairly so." The Fae looked annoyed. "I care little for you risking yourself, but see no way around it."

"Then no time like the present." He paused. From a sad spurt of tenderness, he finished the ritual greeting he'd used on his rare visits. "I enter as your guest, and will do you no harm."

"As long as you act like a guest, you'll be treated as one. If not, I'll feed you to my djinn."

He heard the echo of her tart voice in his head, saw the bright eyes and lips that rarely smiled, though she always seemed grimly amused with the world. He moved forward, eyes searching the darkness, all senses adjusted for anything amiss.

There was no threat, but as he moved through the narrow defile and into the main chamber, his heart constricted at the sight that awaited him. There were times he wished a vampire couldn't see in the dark so well. Cai's banked rage made even more sense now. While the younger vampire would not have been able to look into the cave and see the sorceress, a violent death had a particular scent to it that Rand's keen nose, as well as vampire senses, would have detected.

Her twisted limbs showed how valiantly she'd fought. What sickened him was seeing her torn clothing, the broken fingers, the ripped flesh. He studied the fanned out pattern and condition of the men's bodies that littered the cave floor. They reminded him of a group of wooden soldiers picked up and flung, then torched by fire.

How had they made it past her wards and protections? Her defenses would have been considerable, but the enemy she faced had found a way, and used weak men to do its bidding. As evil always did.

"She made a good accounting of herself," Keldwyn said.

Uthe looked up, surprised to find the Fae next to him. "How did you get through?"

"The shielding could not prevent a Fae magic-user of my level from entering, but it was clever enough I did not want to risk disrupting its nature and possibly destroying its recognition of you. It made more sense for you to go first."

"And if I was incinerated, there really wouldn't be anything left to do, right?"

"There was that, yes." Keldwyn didn't smile. He was looking at the ruins of Fatima's body. "So what happened here?" His voice was low and respectful.

"She used her magic to fight, until she realized the numbers would deplete her energy to the point she couldn't protect what they'd come to take. I think that's when she made the decision to sacrifice herself and put all her energy toward that protection." Kneeling by her body, Uthe put his hand over her mangled fingers, his throat thickening at the memory of how they'd once felt. Thin and cool, like gnarled sticks, but full of life.

"The explosion probably occurred when death was imminent. She knew the protection spell would be triggered by the release of her soul, but she wanted one more strike on her own terms. It burned the bodies." He imagined her summoning that last bit of defiance to blast them away from her and touched her face. "I'm sorry, Fatima. So sorry we did not come in time."

Bowing his head, he said a prayer for her soul to Allah, since that was the face of the Divine that Fatima had preferred. Then he rose. There were sconces on the wall, the torches burned out. But Uthe found more in a woven basket and replaced them. Fatima was a sorceress, so apparently she hadn't needed a lighter. As soon as he had the thought and glanced toward Keldwyn, he saw the Fae was already on it. Keldwyn moved to the first torch, touched it, and flame appeared.

"It looks far more impressive than it is," Kel said at his quizzical look. "More a conversation with the elements than actual magic."

A pragmatic explanation, yet Uthe couldn't look away as Kel moved to each of the four torches, bringing the flames to life seemingly from the touch of his fingers. Fire licked along Uthe's body as he thought of the way Keldwyn could do the same to him. He was standing amid rotting corpses and still affected by the Fae's mesmerizing qualities, not surprisingly. He'd spent a great deal of his life in violent circumstances, and other impulses and needs had learned to live and grow within their proximity.

Kel glanced over his shoulder. "I did not dismantle the spell, so nothing can get into this cave with us."

"But the longer we are here, the more time we give reinforcements to arrive." Uthe was sure reinforcements would be coming. They'd deal with that when necessary. As the light spread through the chamber, he saw the things he'd seen on past visits. A cot, some basic equipment for preparing and preserving food, a radio. Everything else was dedicated to Fatima's purpose. Containers for potions and ingredients, stacks of books. Hundreds of carved symbols on the walls, a language that stretched in every direction, like stars and planets crowding a universe.

He stood back, studied the symbols. There was something different. Colors. She'd used colors and dyes, so it seemed as if certain strings of symbols went together and intersected with others.

She couldn't make it simple, because she'd known other enemies would be sent to decipher it. The colors were for him. The colors of the chakras, which told him the order in which they should be studied, but that wouldn't make it an easier problem to solve. It just narrowed down the amount of data he would need to study. They wouldn't be leaving the cave anytime soon, which meant he had time to do something else first.

"There are several chambers beyond this main one," he said. "Including one with a water source. I'll clean and prepare the body there and form a cairn over her for burial. It won't be according to her faith, but she'll at least be laid to rest with respect and prayer. As for the rest of them..." His lip curled with distaste. "I'd like to burn them to ash, but the smoke would choke us.

"I'll take care of them," Keldwyn said. "But do we have time for any of that?"

"The answer is there," Uthe said, looking at the ceiling. "But I do not know how long it will take me to decipher it.

Hours at least."

Uthe went to his pack, removed a smaller bag. As Keldwyn watched him, he withdrew a generous length of shimmering silk, let it play over his hands. His fingers were too rough, snagging the delicate fabric. "I'd intended to give this to her as a gift. She loved beautiful fabrics."

Keldwyn gripped Uthe's shoulder. "I am sorry."

"She expected to die in the service of this quest, as do I. The manner of her death was undeserved for such a noble spirit, though. No matter how often that turns out to be the way of it."

His bitterness was the symptom of too many losses over the years, but as always, the sharpest bite came from the staring eyes of the long dead, on a battlefield where he had survived and they had not. It always went back to Hattin. He put the silk back in the pack. He would prepare her body, and figure out what he'd come here to find. He would honor her as well as those dead Templars by making sure her tireless work didn't go to waste.

He lifted his head at a waft of warm energy. Keldwyn stood at the apex of the corpses. He had his hands spread as a green glow left his fingertips and drifted down to the floor, settling over the dead like mist. A mist that started thickening, solidifying. Brown veins started to run through their flesh. Uthe inhaled the decay of the natural world. Dried leaves in damp earth, the bones of a mouse left by an owl, algae covering creek stone with slickness.

"We perhaps should have kept one alive," Keldwyn said absently. "Question them about who sent them."

Uthe shook his head. The bodies were starting to disintegrate, the odor of violent death replaced by something far less difficult to endure. "They are under compulsion, my lord, with souls already blackened. They are puppets of their master, with no true knowledge of him."

"Is that how you knew they were deserters and thieves from the Saracen army?"

Uthe nodded. "The demon possesses souls with capital crimes already marked upon them. It is how he is able to compel them from a great distance. Death brings them a chance to seek redemption in the afterlife, where they can cleanse their soul before they move on to another life and hopefully do better."

"A Christian who believes in reincarnation."

"I am not a Christian," Uthe said. "A religion isn't necessary to believe in God and obey His Will. Will you watch for our enemies while I take Fatima's body to the water?"

"I will. And since I will have time to kill…literally,"—a feral smile touched Keldwyn's mouth—"once you start your studying, I'll hunt in the immediate area. Dispatch any reinforcements who get close enough."

"Sounds like an efficient plan. Though Cai won't thank you if you don't leave him or Rand anyone to disembowel."

Uthe spoke in a casual tone, though he didn't like the idea of Keldwyn fighting by himself. Which was as absurd as his desire to pull out his sword earlier, since the Fae was capable of taking out a couple dozen humans on his own. But hadn't Keldwyn been the one that said even a human could get in a lucky strike?

"Cai should think about that next time he disrespects a high Fae," Keldwyn responded, unconcerned. "As his lupine companion would tell him, a bad dog gets no treats." The Fae positioned himself to watch the entrance, but he tilted his head toward Uthe. "Before you bury your sorceress, you will tell me what we face and why we face it. You may save the detailed explanation for later, but I will know the gist of it now."

His tone made it a clear command. Uthe would have taken exception to it, but in Keldwyn's position, he would have felt the same way. He met the Fae's dark gaze.

"The demon is an enemy that was imprisoned over a thousand years ago. We discovered him in the ruins of Solomon's Temple, and I was charged with his guardianship until a way to dispatch him back to his origins was discovered. That is the weapon Fatima has created. She sent me the message several ago that it was at last ready."

"So the demon knows the answer to his demise has been found."

"Yes, apparently." Uthe looked down at the twisted corpse, anger and pride surging through him. "Though it didn't come from her. The message to me may have been intercepted, or the demon was monitoring her progress another way. She would have killed herself before giving them anything. She was much like her ancestor, Haris."

"A demon at large is a concern to far more than the human race or even one vampire." Keldwyn shifted to glance out the entranceway, then brought his attention back to Uthe, his dark eyes intent. "Did you not think to seek other help?"

"All involved with it were sworn to secrecy, my lord. You know as I do what element is attracted to a power source like this. Containing the demon itself has often been an overwhelming effort. If news of it had gone beyond us..."

Keldwyn frowned. "Yet it can compel weaker minds. Why would it not have made itself known to those with evil intent that way?"

"As I said, it can only compel those minds, not identify itself to them. And even if it could, the demon does not reside in this realm. It is beyond the reach of those with malevolent purpose."

Awareness dawned on Keldwyn's face. "The Shattered World. That is what you have imprisoned in the Shattered World. And Reghan suggested this?"

"Reghan and Shahnaz."

The Fae Lord digested that. "It makes sense. Magwel was in line for the Unseelie throne, and had the ear of the Queen then. He could have asked her help to open a portal there. Since that was before he and Magwel dissolved their relationship, she would have agreed with little explanation."

"Yes."

"Why worry about a weapon to send it back to a place it escaped once before? Why not leave it in the Shattered World for all eternity?"

"Because there is more to it." Uthe held Keldwyn's gaze. "I would prefer to explain further after I attend to Fatima, my lord. Please."

"I tire of waiting for the full picture, Lord Uthe," the Fae said, an edge to his voice. "It feels like you are deliberately keeping me ignorant to serve other purposes."

"I swore a blood oath never to speak of this to anyone but those who had to know to achieve God's will." Uthe rose to his feet, faced him. "I have always had to weigh carefully who I tell of this, never blurt things out hastily that cannot be retrieved. Yet you now know more than anyone alive, except myself. Draw your own conclusions from that, my lord, when I ask you for patience."

"I've never known you to blurt out anything, my lord." Keldwyn's expression eased some. "I believe current circumstances suggest I am now part of those who need to know."

"Yes. I agree. It makes sense to me that someone with your intelligence and power would be sent my way now, when the integrity of my own mind is degrading." Uthe forced out the words, though the last one caught in his throat. "Yet I will be frank, my lord. I do not know your full motives for coming on this quest with me, but I know you serve both the Unseelie and Seelie Fae royalty. I have had one task to honor above all others. This noble woman died for it, and she was not the first. No matter how much my heart wants to trust you, the mind and heart are intertwined. If I cannot trust the integrity of my mind, I will not fail after all these years because your attentions make me wish for things I have set aside. I must be certain I can trust you, and for that I need your faith. I need *your* trust."

Uthe paused. He hadn't realized all those thoughts had been there, just waiting to be said, building up throughout their journey together, and that journey had only just begun. Keldwyn was staring at him with an unreadable expression. Uthe inclined his head and spoke stiffly. "I am going to prepare her body now. Do as you will."

Taking the blanket from her cot, which still smelled like her body despite the less pleasant scents saturating the chamber, he wrapped her up in it, and lifted her tenderly in his arms. So light and small. Humans seemed fragile as birds when they died. Even some of his fellow Templars in full mail had felt that way to him when he carried them from the field.

He left the chamber, moving back into the warren of tunnels. One led to the water source, a trickle through the rocks that splashed into a pool no bigger than a bucket. Laying her down on the floor of the cavern, he removed her torn and bloody clothes. She had a stack of wash cloths and towels back here, and he doused one in the water, using it to clean her. Then he wrapped her in the silk. Sitting back on his heels, he gazed at her once more, seeing the strength of her features despite the decomposition.

It was rare for a vampire to be known to one family through so many generations. He'd seen the physical and personality traits Haris and Shahnaz possessed resurface or meld with the features of each successor who took on the mantle of magic and the responsibility of adding to their knowledge. Whatever Fatima had discovered had been built on their dedication.

In her younger days, Fatima had been a nearly perfect physical replica of Shahnaz. It was as if, after a certain number of cycles, the genetics returned in full force. In Fatima's flawless features, he was able to see what Shahnaz's beauty would have been unmarred. It was not the only way the two women were similar. Shahnaz had made the first major breakthrough with the demon.

When they'd unearthed the demon's container under

Solomon's Temple, they'd found the binding on the vessel had an imminent expiration date. Up until then, Uthe had questioned the wisdom of removing the demon from where he'd been hidden, but that had suggested the discovery had God's favor.

Shahnaz had found a way to contain the spirit indefinitely. Relics had been useful to the binding, but finding a way to lock them to the demon and ensure the prison could not be breached as the years progressed had required magic of an extraordinary complexity. *"Binding something so a smart person can't figure out how to unlock it is difficult, but not impossible. Finding a way to protect something from random chance and dumb luck is the true challenge."*

He smiled. He'd heard computer experts say something similar about hacking. Appropriate, since technology had always seemed like magic to him. Shahnaz had at last found the right combination of spell craft, but it had nearly come too late. As the demon was breaking free from his older, weakened bindings, she'd shouted the right words and laid the architecture of his new prison. It pulled him back into captivity—barely.

He'd visited her shortly after it had happened. She'd looked as if she'd aged fifteen years, and he'd seen her only a year ago. Yet the close call with the demon didn't matter to her. She brushed aside his concern, having more important things to tell him. For years she'd lived with the demon's daily threats that it would break free and do unspeakable horrors to her, so Uthe guessed the threat nearly becoming reality hadn't been enough to rattle her. She only wanted to talk to him about one thing.

The angel who'd shown up on her doorstep right afterwards.

§

"You expect them to come down in a blaze of light and

clouds, with wings gilded by a heavenly glow." She unwrapped a sweetmeat and offered it to him. When he declined, she gave him a cup of tea instead and sat on a cushion, her feet drawn up as she rocked on the point of her buttocks. She preferred to wear loose cotton pants with a tunic over it, a man's clothes, and she kept her hair hacked short. Though her face was a tragedy, she had a curvaceous body any man might desire. She stayed cognizant of that, though her reputation as a witch woman kept most at bay except those who needed her healing tonics. She lived in France, in a stone cottage in the forest, near the village of La Couvertoirade.

"He showed up outside my door a day after it had happened. I thought a flock of birds had landed, and when I looked, his wings were folding up along his back. The eyes he turned upon me, they had no whites, my lord. His power was fearsome, overwhelming, but he was not unkind. He told me that he came to claim the demon, to destroy its container and send him back to Hell. Apparently when the binding faltered, enough energy from the demon had escaped to alert the heavens of the potential imbalance. Can you imagine? At first I got so excited, for all these years we thought we were facing this alone, but here was a potential ally of unspeakable power."

She rolled her eyes, looking so much like a fishwife at her wit's end with her husband that Uthe almost grinned, despite the seriousness of it all. "But I should have remembered that the gods, by whatever name we call Them, have their own agenda."

She pushed up the tunic, showed him an arm that had been burned to the bone. "I was still unsettled by this, else I would have known better. And the bastard gave me these white streaks of hair." She ran a hand through the short crop, ruffling it. "The demon, not the angel."

"You should have called me, Shahnaz."

"To what end?" She eyed him. "You are a powerful vampire, my lord, but you are no magic user. There is risk in what we do here, we know it."

"I meant to help with this decision, with the angel."

She shook her head. "The binding has been perfected, Lord Uthe. Thanks to your connection to Lord Reghan, we've secured a place to put the demon and the relics guarding it, far beyond the reach of man. Beyond the reach of any but yourself, really. Foolproof, since fools are the cleverest among us."

"You said the angel was going to take it."

"Yes. But I convinced him the sacrifice was too great." Shahnaz's eyes grew serious, and she closed both hands over one of Uthe's. "We cannot vanquish the demon at the expense of the others who share his prison. Giving him that victory would fuel evil in a way that would be worse than unleashing the demon upon the world. That was the argument I made with the angel."

Uthe imagined the sorceress standing toe-to-toe with a member of the heavenly host and making her point. It reminded him of Haris, the way the female Assassin had fought him that first time, so fearlessly. "I should have liked to see an angel, Shahnaz. Was he magnificent?"

"He was." A wistful look crossed her features. "He touched my face, and I felt beautiful. He told me if I let go of my anger, the scars would be only on my face, not my soul. As he departed, I saw several others with him. One of them winked at me, playful as a rogue, and then they were gone, following him back into the clouds."

§

Uthe came back to the present and the silk clad body at his feet. If the angel had destroyed the demon, what would Uthe's life have been? Possibly not much different from now, since he'd spent most of the past centuries waiting on the sorceresses to find the solution while he became involved in the politics and future of vampires. At first he'd steered clear of those things, thinking this might pull him away from the vampire world without notice, but he'd learned it made more sense to live his life fully. In a heartbeat, anything could end life as one knew it. Anticipating that was no way to make the most of the life the Lord had given him. His mission had not stopped him from joining his brethren at the tragedy of Hattin, and it was who he'd met as a result of that bloodbath that had given Shahnaz access to the Shattered World. There was no telling where life would take a man, but he had to live it to follow the path God gave him.

After dislodging enough rock to form a proper covering over Fatima, he knelt and said the necessary prayers for her soul and his grief. Rising, he placed a hand on one of the rocks.

"It won't be in vain," he promised her. "Unless my brain has gotten too stupid to figure out the clues you left me." Wouldn't that be a sad irony? Almost laughable, if he felt like laughing. Instead, he found himself wishing for Keldwyn's company. Good or bad, the male's presence steadied him, though he had no idea what the Fae was thinking after he'd made such a raw declaration about his feelings. But honesty was all he had now, and his only demand was for Keldwyn to give him the same. It was not the first time Uthe might have to accept painful truths, but he preferred them to sugar-coated lies.

Enough of that. He had more important things to address, a puzzle to solve. He headed back toward the main chamber where a ceiling full of ciphers awaited. It had taken generations of sorceresses nine hundred years to find the solution for sending a demon back to Hell. Hopefully, it would not take him that long to translate it from Fatima's walls.

Chapter Eight

When Uthe returned to the main chamber, Keldwyn didn't ask him further questions. The vampire looked somber from laying the sorceress to rest, so Kel let him begin his study of the ceiling and walls, and his examination of Fatima's books and notebooks, while Kel stood watch at the cave opening. He would go hunting once he sensed other demon pawns drawing closer. Until then, he refused to go so far out of range that he couldn't return to Uthe's side in a matter of moments.

While Keldwyn had been frustrated by Uthe's secretiveness, he knew Uthe was very much like himself. Dire consequences could result from a loose tongue: lives lost, secrets jeopardized. Withholding information was driven by those concerns, not a covetous need to keep everything to oneself, or an inability to extend trust when needed. Well, not entirely. Keldwyn was still reviewing Uthe's harsh words in his mind. On each replay, they roused a different reaction in him.

Uthe was an intellectually gifted male, one who rarely let himself act without thought. Though he'd frequently noted the fit hardness of Uthe's body, the battle readiness of it, Keldwyn had rarely seen the male use those assets. As a result, Keldwyn had begun to think of him more as a bookish scholar, a Machiavellian strategist, than a vampire ready to combat violence in any situation. The day he'd watched him spar with Daegan, he'd been mesmerized, as if he'd seen a harmless garden snake sleeping in the sun suddenly morph into a striking asp.

When they'd fought their way into the cave, Uthe's measured and thoughtful consideration to every matter of import had been replaced by quick, brutal decisiveness.

"Thus in an astounding and unique manner they appear gentler than lambs yet fiercer than lions." Keldwyn had read the three texts Uthe kept by his bed: St. Bernard's "In Praise of the New Knighthood," *The Rule of the Templars* and that anonymous letter addressed to the order around 1130. The quote came from St. Bernard's text, and Keldwyn had found it astounding in truth, the way Uthe unleashed an inner savagery for battle.

Now—that deadly warrior side put away—Uthe leaned forward, tracing one of those hundreds of symbols climbing up the walls. The motion made the tunic pull across his shoulders and buttocks. Uthe stretched upward as he followed a line of text with his fingertips along the arch of wall to ceiling. His dark brown eyes were flickering, his mouth moving silently, talking to himself.

Keldwyn's first direct exposure to vampires had been through Lyssa's father, Reghan. Keldwyn had been confounded by his best friend's inconceivable love for a female of the fanged species. He'd brutally rejected the idea, trying in every way to dissuade him. It was incomprehensible, that a Fae could truly love a creature so inferior to himself. Beyond race, there was class. Even among the high Fae, Lyssa's father was a cut far above, linked by blood to both the Unseelie and Seelie royal families.

Keldwyn had been several hundred years old then. He hadn't recognized his opposition to Reghan's relationship with a vampire was fueled by more than his fear of what would happen to Reghan if he pursued it. He had reacted to his own hurt at being rejected. Yes—trite as the saying was—love was indeed blind.

Until his death, Reghan had counted Keldwyn his closest and best friend. Never had one word had the potential to hurt so much, but Kel eventually understood the value and honor of being the male's friend. He hoped he'd honored what it had meant in his actions ever since, not only in doing his best to protect both of Reghan's daughters in the face of often violent politics, but in finally getting over his heartbreak enough to bring the two races closer together. It had taken him a few hundred years to give it his full energy, but the Fae were known to hold a grudge.

In his defense, during that time, he'd experienced vampires who were nowhere near as commendable members of their species as Uthe and Lyssa. More than once, he'd decided his initial impression of them as creatures limited in intelligence due to the inescapable hold of blood lust and an inability to overcome their predator instincts was correct, the exception far less common than the rule. But then he'd seen the formation of the Council. He'd watched while Lyssa and others like her had determined—since their nature could not be suppressed or changed—to guide and channel it with such concepts as the vampire-servant bond, and Council rules governing basic behavior to protect vampires from general human awareness of their existence.

Lyssa was half-Fae, though. He'd ultimately expected such sensible behavior from her. It was Uthe who'd taken Keldwyn's impression of full blooded vampires from benign disfavor and tolerance into a belief they could be something...more.

Lord Varick Uthe. Varick was a good name for him, far better than Uthe. Keldwyn's lips twisted. Perhaps it was no different from long ago. Then he'd used his belief in the inferiority of vampires to mask his resentment that Lyssa's father had chosen one over him. Now he used his revised opinion of their intelligence to avoid the truth. One particular vampire had caught his attention for far more personal reasons.

It had made sense to cultivate a good relationship with the right hand of the Council, but that had not included weekly chess matches, strolls through the gardens debating history, social inequity, or trading stories accumulated from their combined years and travels. After seeing Uthe spar with Daegan, Keldwyn would have added practice combat to their regular interactions, but this task had interfered with that pleasurable prospect.

Kel, you have become entangled with a vampire yourself. Wherever Reghan is, he is laughing at you. All the more because Reghan had set that situation up himself. What would Uthe think when Kel finally revealed that?

Before he was to be executed, Reghan had called Keldwyn to him. He remembered every word his friend had spoken to him, his facial expressions, the press of his strong hand, as vividly as if it had happened a moment ago. But the words that had meant the least to Keldwyn were what had resounded in his head the first time Lyssa had introduced him to her Council. "This is Lord Uthe, my right hand advisor on Council. Once upon a time, he was a Templar Knight, so he tends to be more honorable than the rest of us..."

Kel, there may come a time when a Templar Knight will make himself known to you. Help him however he needs help, for his cause is just and vital...

He'd assumed the plea was moot when the Templars were disbanded in the 1300s. Still, his curiosity about a vampire who had been a Templar had drawn him, whether or not it connected to Reghan's final words. And curiosity had become something more.

Despite his occupied thoughts, Kel continued to change vantage points at the cave point, watching for trouble. Still nothing. He glanced over his shoulder, checking on Uthe. Vampire males were handsome, but the wisdom and character in Uthe's dark eyes made him even more appealing to Keldwyn. Though he'd had male lovers who were far prettier, Uthe's body was a perfect sculpture of smooth muscle, long limbs, tight arse and impressive cock. He was a gift of mind and matter both.

Keldwyn stared back into the night. As he did, he recalled his first awareness of his attraction. Uthe had been waiting on his next chess move. The vampire had laid his head back on his chair, one hand loose on the arm, the other resting on his thigh as he closed his eyes. Keldwyn's gaze had been drawn to the exposed throat, the set of his mouth in repose, the way his fingers traced the carved arm of the chair without impatience. Kel could take a minute or an hour to decide his move, and Uthe would not demonstrate any urgency, not during leisure time like this.

They had both lived enough years, experienced the necessary trials. Neither of them were susceptible to excess drama. Every matter of significance was given careful consideration from many angles. Decisions were made in a timely but not rushed manner. Nothing was expedited by competition, pride or ego.

"You're settled in your head," Catriona, his ward, had once told him. "You understand so much, you don't even think about most of it anymore. But you don't really feel it, either, because you've felt it so much, you don't think about it as a new feeling. But every story can be told a different way, and you can fall in love with it all over again."

Thanks to her twenty years trapped in a tree in the human world, her way of communicating could be garbled like that, but when he was studying Uthe's face that night, he'd understood what she'd meant, enough to feel startled to the core by the truth of it. When the male's lips moved, a simple motion to moisten them, and his fingers on the chair moved to rest on his thigh, the muscles in Keldwyn's own leg bunched. He forgot to concentrate on his chess move. His whole focus was on what Uthe would do next.

At length, the dark eyes opened, a brow rising at

Keldwyn's regard, then his lashes swept down to examine Keldwyn's move. Seeing he hadn't made one, he looked up. Keldwyn said nothing, unsure of everything that was in his expression and lacking his usual compulsion to mask it. Uthe closed his eyes and tilted his head back again. "If you're considering how a mere vampire is beating you at chess, my lord, you will be chewing on that for some time. The only answer is the one you won't accept. I'm better than you at the game."

Something scraped against dirt and rock, and Keldwyn instantly returned to the present. Uthe's head turned like a raptor's, suggesting he wasn't as absorbed in his task as he'd indicated he would be.

"I will hail you if I need aid," Keldwyn said gruffly. "Though if I need it against a few humans, I deserve to be cut down."

"That may be true. But since I can't complete my task if you get cut down, avoid sacrificing yourself merely for pride. They may be augmented with more than human abilities. Be careful, my lord. I would not like to see your blood. Not for those reasons."

Keldwyn stiffened, shooting the vampire a glance. Uthe was staring at those symbols, but Keldwyn noticed his fingers uncurled and recurled at his side, something he did when emotion or arousal was affecting him. When he next spoke, his voice was somewhat thicker. "If you can toss one of them in here alive, I can feed."

"Kill your enemies and provide you dinner? I will expect sex."

Uthe chuckled. The way he moistened his lips sent Keldwyn's thoughts in a dark and pleasurable direction. "You would demand that if you did none of those things."

"Varick, look at me."

Hearing the raw command in Kel's voice, Uthe looked up, surprised. Keldwyn held his gaze. He knew fierceness and honesty was in his expression. He didn't fear that he would fall before the wrath of a few puny mortals, no matter how demon-enchanted they were. This wasn't a confession. It was something he simply wanted to say and had decided he wouldn't wait any longer to do so.

"What you asked me earlier, about motives? You are my only motive for being here, Varick. You can trust me on that."

He didn't wait for a reply. There was none he could accept, since the succinct admission made him think he'd lost his mind. A Fae didn't say things straight out like a school primer. A Fae used clever words to tangle meaning, leaving himself graceful retreats from the truth whenever necessary.

He'd given Uthe honesty, just as Uthe had demanded.

Thank the gods, there was finally enough happening outside the cave to keep him occupied. He detected three more of the Saracen raiders coming up the incline, with several more following behind, reinforcements. He could have handled all of the earlier attacks with magic, but he'd mixed it up with hand-to-hand because Uthe said he'd never seen Keldwyn fight. Apparently, whether fifteen or fifteen-hundred, he wasn't above wanting to show off for a paramour.

This time, though, he chose expediency and practicality. Suddenly they were pale-faced beneath their swarthy coloring, stumbling into retreat before the dragon they believed had appeared before them. A roar and a blast of heat had them spinning to face its twin. In the resulting confusion, he took them down in quick succession, though he knocked one insensible rather than taking his life. Carting him back up to the cave entrance, he tossed him inside with a quick incantation to keep him from being incinerated, then left Uthe to his meal.

He searched the other bodies for any useful clues about the demon who had sent them, but just as the vampire had indicated, there was nothing. They were merely pawns. As he'd done to the ones in the cave, he disintegrated them with earth magic. A quick perimeter check didn't result in any other incursions. This had been a test run, and his actions had told them they'd need to send greater numbers next time.

"The quantity will not matter," he muttered. "You will all die just the same."

He re-entered the cave. "Your demon did not expect you to have a Fae in your company, or his magical reach didn't give him that much influence. Else he would have prepared them for the glamor."

"Hopefully he doesn't have the energy or reach to do so," Uthe responded. "I am done with him if you want to handle the body as you did the others."

Keldwyn had been absent only a few moments, but he saw the unconscious male had two puncture wounds in his neck, tidily sealed so no blood was dripping from them. He also was no longer alive, the dead eyes staring. Uthe was back to studying his wall.

"Kill your enemies, provide you dinner *and* do the dishes," the Fae grumbled. "You are pushing it. I think you are forgetting who is in charge."

Uthe's lips tugged into a smile. "I'm sure you will find an opportunity to remind me of it, my lord."

"I will. Count on it."

That intriguing curl and uncurl of his hands again. It made Keldwyn want to take hold of one of them, press the roughened palm to his mouth and bite it, before he drew it behind Uthe's back, or above his head. The idea of the vampire bound and at his mercy was an intensely pleasurable one, and he embellished the image as he disposed of the other body.

Moving to Uthe's side, standing behind his left shoulder, Kel studied the symbols with him. Understanding Uthe had a complicated puzzle to solve, he knew he shouldn't disrupt the other male's flow of thought, but the vibration coming from Uthe suggested Keldwyn's compulsion now wasn't unwelcome. It had been a day full of unpleasantness, after all.

He laid his hand on Uthe's shoulder, fingertips sliding along the base of his neck. He could feel the strength of Uthe's feeding fueling him, and Kel wondered what it would be like, to be the one who nourished the vampire, helped keep him strong.

The thought was so unexpected he almost jerked his hand back. Instead he flexed it, strongly enough Uthe sent him a sidelong glance. "You are going to leave bruises, my lord."

"You say that only to tease me."

Keldwyn shifted his hand to the front of the tunic and leaned in toward Uthe's parted lips. He had a firm, pleasurable mouth to kiss, and Keldwyn enjoyed caressing the fangs with his tongue, knowing Uthe had to exercise particular restraint not to draw blood. That day on the stairs, Keldwyn had made it clear such behavior was unacceptable and would end a kiss. Since Uthe knew that, scoring Kel wouldn't honor the oath he'd made to willingly submit to him. Keldwyn fed off that sense of self-restraint. Behind that wall, Kel could feel the bloodlust rise in Uthe and his own body responded in kind.

Keldwyn drew back, brushed a thumb over Uthe's mouth. "I can taste his scent on your lips."

"Not the most pleasurable of meals. Not as sweet as Mariela, but enough to nourish. That's all that matters."

Keldwyn returned to the cave opening. Late afternoon was giving way to evening. "Next wave coming," he said absently. He touched his mouth, capturing Uthe's sensation in his fingertips. "I'll be back."

He slipped out before Uthe could suggest coming with him, which Keldwyn had already anticipated. The male chafed at not being able to be in both places at once, but Kel knew he needed to decipher those symbols. The quicker Keldwyn handled these threats, the less distracting they would be to the vampire.

This time, though, he set aside magic and indulged in some brutal hand-to-hand combat, no magic involved.

Duck, swing, kick, break, snap. Grunt, punch. The physical effort, minor though it was, helped ease the sexual energy building inside him. Yet when he was done, one thought of Uthe staring at those symbols with that intent, bookish look brought it back in full force. It would have amused Keldwyn if he hadn't also thought of the challenging way Uthe had looked at him as he suggested Keldwyn might leave bruises on his skin. He'd like to leave bruises on him. Teeth marks, a few stripes. He wanted to be rough with the vampire and give them both pleasure.

This time he didn't decay his victims back into the earth. As twilight closed in, he saw the slinking shadows of coyotes, the glint off their red eyes. He tossed a couple bodies down the slope, and offered them the benefit of his labors. The sounds of their snarls, whines and snapping as they began to feed was familiar. Nature was brutal, efficient and predictable. Beautiful in a savage way, demonstrating the root of all desires in its methods of survival and order.

Dominance, submission, need, want.

One of the coyotes left the feeding, coming up the incline toward Keldwyn. The Fae Lord frowned as the creature stumbled, saliva dripping in long strings from his mouth. While Keldwyn watched, he keeled over, the brown eyes starting to glaze over in death.

No. How foolish they had been, thinking a demon would be that simplistic in his attack. Sending a quick blast of sealing magic down to the bodies to drive off the coyotes and prevent further harm, Keldwyn pivoted and shot back up the incline. "*Uthe.*"

Bursting into the cave, he found Uthe sitting on one of Fatima's few chairs. He was bent over, rubbing his forehead. "The answer is there. It's just...elusive, hard to..." he tried to straighten, and Keldwyn saw his face had an unhealthy gray tinge. "Ah, bloody hell," the vampire snarled, recognizing the same thing Keldwyn had. "I'm an idiot."

Falling to his knees, he jammed his fingers down his throat, trying to expel the blood.

§

Heat. Unrelenting heat, the endless stretches of desert like the ripples of undyed sheets. The patterns were sculpted by the wind and limned by sparkling grains of sand. Uthe imagined those patterns as a writhing body with long fine limbs. Vulnerable, elegant fingers reached out to him. The sheets would be cool, whereas the folds of sand burned against flesh.

Flesh could burn against sheets, bringing release and relief in a way that the burn of hot sand could not.

Sand was always in everything. Heat, sand, desert. These were things one grew accustomed to enduring, accepting. That acceptance was proof of obedience to the Lord's Will. The discomfort was to be welcomed, a gift of the Lord, a way to prove devotion. Tangled sheets and burning flesh indulged the self, desires and longings. But each way brought a type of peace, so he wondered if they weren't both ways to God, in the end.

Uthe lifted his head. He was not alone. His sacred mission, the one that Hugh had given him, was attended in solitude. Understanding the wisdom of it, he'd obeyed. Which meant this being had to be a demon come to taunt him. No man was this beautiful and mortal. Not here in the stark desert, where fellow travelers almost always stank of perspiration and unwashed clothing.

"You say nothing?" the beautiful male asked.

"Idle words generate sin. You have asked no question, and you are too fair to be anything but temptation."

"But I am male. I thought only women could provide temptation in your Order." The voice of the beautiful creature changed, became smooth. Too smooth. "There is a reason your Rule requires you to leave a candle lit through the night, to stave off the temptations that a man sleeping nearby might provoke. Especially for one like you. Sodomite."

Uthe blinked. "Taunt me not, demon."

"But I must taunt you. Defeat you. It will not be as difficult now. Perhaps that is why my time has come at last." The beauty of that face disappeared. Instead Uthe stared into the face of a disembodied head floating in front of him. The skin was pale, the eyes staring, empty. "You are turning into a child again," the voice said. "You will be weak, easy to command. In the end, you will take my place in this prison, and I will be the free one, because you have lost the part of your mind that knew what to do, how to do it. You should have attended this a decade ago, when you had a chance. Now you have none."

He surged up to strike at the head with his mailed fist, but it jerked out of range like a balloon caught on a wind current, the mouth stretching outward in an obscene laugh. "Varick, you cur. You know now what true power is, and you lack the courage to capture it."

He fumbled for his sword, drew it, slashed at the head. "Yes, pierce me through. The innocent no longer matter. Only ending it does. It has gone on long enough, hasn't it? This prison, your life..."

He leaped, thrust. The head disappeared and became a beautiful black-haired child. Blood dripped from his throat, his sorrowful, accusing blue eyes on Uthe. "You are damned forever."

He struggled to reach out and help, to staunch the blood, but the child was gone. The world spun, rock and stone surrounding him, and suddenly he was on the floor of a cave, once again gasping for air he didn't need.

"It is all right, Varick. You're with me. You expelled the poison."

"Don't call me that. Not right now."

As Uthe's mind cleared, he realized his upper body was propped against Keldwyn, who sat behind him, holding him. But what made him wonder if he was still caught in illusion was he had Keldwyn's wrist grasped in both hands, the pulsing vein near his mouth. Keldwyn wasn't pulling away. He was stroking Uthe's hair.

"You have my permission to take the blood you need, my lord. I expect it is better than what you just had."

Uthe squeezed his eyes shut. Pushing away from Keldwyn, refusing that vein, was like removing one of his internal organs with a rusty knife, but he was no stranger to severe deprivation. He rolled to his hands and knees. He couldn't get to his feet, but snarled at Keldwyn when he tried to help. He accomplished it after two stumbles, and propped against a wall full of symbols. "Don't touch me. Stay away for a few moments." He had to get the bloodlust under control.

"I offered you nourishment, Lord Uthe. Is Fae blood not good enough for you now?" The expression on Keldwyn's face was ominous. In it he saw the formidable opponent Uthe had always known him to be.

"You consider a Fae feeding a vampire...like humans fucking animals," Uthe rasped. "I won't...I won't take your blood when you feel that way. Even if I have to starve."

To not take what was offered, even if to do so risked the success of his quest—that was nothing but pride. Which invited the taunt of that hated voice. *You are already halfway mine, Lord Uthe. Cling not to your illusion of God. For that was all it ever was. A way to save you from the darkness that is inevitable, because it was born inside you. You will never be rid of it, no matter how you deceive those around you.*

Shit. He'd fallen to one knee again. He should take it as a mandate to pray. To focus, to sacrifice his pride. No, not a sacrifice. It wasn't a sacrifice to give away something worthless, and his pride was certainly that. To decipher those symbols, he needed clarity of mind. That was far more important.

"Varick." Keldwyn's voice was quiet, firm. He was kneeling next to Uthe, his hand curved over his shoulder,

fingertips once again resting on the back of his neck.
"I told you not to call me that."
"You will have to become used to it. It fits you far better, and there is something in your eyes when I say it that makes me want to keep doing so. Your expression says you are listening to me, focusing on me, in a way I quite prefer. Look at me, Varick."
Uthe lifted his head. Keldwyn touched his face. "Find that calm you do so well. Shut out everything else." Drawing the dagger from Uthe's belt, Keldwyn lifted his arm before Uthe's face, showing his intent to open a vein.
Uthe seized his wrist, startling the Fae. "Not that dagger," he said hoarsely. "Except for that one time, to save my squire's life, I have never used it for harm. It seemed...a sacrilege."
Keldwyn's gaze flickered. "I understand. Be easy, my lord. I will honor that."
Uthe loosened his grip, dropping his hand back to the ground to support his swaying body. The Fae Lord slid the blade back in the sheath at Uthe's belt, fingers curving there for a brief tug. He extended his wrist to Uthe again. "Do it with your fangs, then." At Uthe's hesitation, Kel's mouth tightened. "I command you to feed, my lord. Our journey is long and important, you have told me so. I feel no revulsion at nourishing you. It is...a peculiar honor to me, to care for you thus."
Uthe raised his gaze from that tempting meal to Keldwyn's face, and saw the truth of it there. "Most Fae don't feel that way. You didn't feel that way, just a few days ago."
"Many things have changed. Are changing." Keldwyn stroked his head once more. "Take what I have offered, Varick. Take it as a gift, and do not offend me with your refusal."
Watching Uthe mull it over, Keldwyn restrained the urge to push, to command him more sternly than he already had. He was still concerned about the vampire's

pallor. More than that, there was a curious anticipation in him, now that the decision was made. He wanted Uthe to get on with it, before that feeling abated, before the mores of a lifetime kicked in and made Keldwyn rethink a decision that he was sure was going to change things irrevocably between them.

The vampire's eyes slowly focused on Keldwyn's wrist. Even more slowly, he lifted his hands, closed both over it. One over Keldwyn's hand, the other over his forearm, so Keldwyn could feel the beat of his own pulse against Uthe's strong grip. Then Uthe put his head down and bit.

It was painful, as was to be expected when a pair of fangs as sizeable as a wolf's penetrated flesh. Keldwyn could claim not to have anticipated anything beyond the pain, but the way he held his own breath right before Uthe did it, the tight coil of need in his lower belly that seemed to affect both heart and cock, belied that indifference.

He'd had a mix of feelings about offering Uthe his blood, the beliefs of his people conflicting with his own conscience and desires. That mix expanded into something different as Uthe drew on his vein, as his throat moved to swallow Keldwyn's blood. He still had his hand on the back of Uthe's head and used that contact to draw Uthe closer. The male was half reclined, one elbow hooked over Keldwyn's thigh, the other pressed close to his groin, his shoulder against Keldwyn's torso. Keldwyn dropped his touch, sliding it along Uthe's back, down to the curve of hip and buttock. He'd been able to sense the vampire's arousal from his most casual touch for some time. Right now it gave him a sense of power so heady, Keldwyn wanted to turn him as soon as he finished feeding and take him here, in a cave where death overshadowed everything.

This vampire filled his mind, was so large in his thoughts, Keldwyn realized the idea of possessing him, calling him his own, almost superseded the urgency of anything else, at least in this moment. Rhoswen had mocked Keldwyn's Dominant tendencies when she'd appointed him as liaison for the Vampire Council.

"Perhaps you will like being closer to your own kind, Lord Keldwyn. Those who enjoy overpowering the will of others for sexual pleasure."

It was an empty taunt, for she was well aware it wasn't about overpowering the will at all. Not exactly. He used his dominance to get other things out of the way so that the will could be freed. When that happened, a gift could occur. A male surrendering to his own desires, feeding on Keldwyn like this.

In the vampire world, Jacob was Lyssa's possession, to do with as she pleased. At least until the latest policy introduced by Lord Mason was passed. If it passed. But anyone with eyes knew the relationship between vampire queen and servant was far more complex than that. No matter the inequity of the relationship on the surface, it wasn't the surface that mattered. Unjustly treated servants like Alanna or Jessica needed the laws, the policies. Servants like Jacob never would.

In the eyes of his Council and the vampire world, and even himself, Lord Uthe was as Dominant as any other of his kind. He wouldn't have made it to the top ranks of that world without proving his ability to take the upper hand. When Uthe so desired, he could level an opponent with nothing more than a look. It wasn't the threat of violence simmering in his dark eyes that did that, though Uthe could certainly back it up with that if necessary. In most every race and species, there was an intuitive recognition of hierarchy, of dominance and submission.

Uthe's dominance wasn't a façade, which was probably why he intrigued Keldwyn so much. Tangled with that dominance was a complicated sense of service and duty, flavored with a heavily guarded vulnerability that suggested deeper needs, conceivably spawned by the burdens he carried. Those needs had been buried at such a deep level Keldwyn might not have ever detected them, if not for the male's struggle with Ennui. The only gift from the hated condition, though he'd much rather have figured it out without its influence.

With Uthe's mouth on Keldwyn's arm, his tongue sliding along his flesh and his teeth still embedded, holding Kel as he drank, Keldwyn saw that complicated mix of dominance and surrender. He slid his arm further around Uthe's back, holding him closer. From whatever well Uthe's tremendous sense of duty and service to the Lord had come, also came the capacity to submit to the right Master. The one deserving of his submission.

Up until this moment, Keldwyn expected only God had received that privilege.

As Uthe gave in to his hunger, Keldwyn felt like they'd slipped off the spinning wheel of time into its fulcrum, where matters of Fate were decided. Where things so precious existed, they had to be experienced in the space of a held breath. Any longer than that and the heart and soul would be immersed in something too overwhelming. They'd shatter into the stuff of the universe. Perhaps the ether into which they all returned in the end, to find bliss at last.

Uthe sealed the puncture wounds with the firm pressure of his tongue and a tingle of sensation Keldwyn expected was some kind of coagulant. When the vampire lifted his head, his face was suffused with want. Keldwyn was more than willing to provide him with what he needed. He captured the vampire's mouth, tasting his own blood. Clamping a hand behind his neck, he savored his lips fully, before becoming too impatient even for that. Keldwyn shoved Uthe onto his back and yanked at the loose cotton pants. He pushed at the edge of the tunic. "Off," he said shortly. "I want it all off of you. I want you naked."

Uthe's eyes sparked at the challenge, but he didn't fight him. His erection was already thick and tall, swaying with his movements as he arched his upper torso to pull off the tunic. Keldwyn dipped his head and attacked with teeth and mouth. The protrusion of rib cage, the taut nipple, the ripple of abdomen muscles. Uthe's fingers slid into his hair. It was bound in the braid, and Uthe tugged at it, freeing it and combing his fingers through the silken strands. Keldwyn let him do as he liked as he tasted every inch of him. Uthe's cock brushed against Kel's chest and his abdomen as he moved upward. He rose to stand over Uthe and stripped off his own tunic, but he waited no longer than it took to unlace his leggings before he knelt, hooked a hand under Uthe's thigh and lifted it. With the other hand, he milked Uthe's cock, bringing forth viscous pre-come he smeared on his own cock, also using the arousal coming from his own slit.

"I'd advise you to carry lubricant, Lord Uthe. There's no telling when I might wish to have you honor your oath. Or how often."

"You've complimented me on my ability to stay prepared before, my lord," Uthe said in a rough voice, staring up at him. "Perhaps you ought to check the pack before you waste your time on unnecessary instruction."

Keldwyn found the tube of lubricant there. When he turned his stare to Uthe, he was charmed and goaded by the slight flush of color that stained the vampire's jaw. Had he argued with himself, telling himself such preparedness might be less about his oath to Keldwyn and more about his own desires? Keldwyn suspected he had. He was going to drive such arguments out of the vampire's head, no matter how often he had to fuck the lesson into him.

"Your desires serve my desires, Varick," Keldwyn growled. He added the lubricant to his shaft, his lust building when Uthe couldn't keep his gaze off of the movement of his fingers. When he curved an arm under Uthe's thigh and lifted it once again, this time to press his cock against Uthe's tight opening, he realized he hadn't been so eager to take a male in some time.

He slid his other arm under Uthe's opposite thigh, lifted both so that he had the male's ass several inches off the ground. He pushed in an inch or two, making sure he was well seated.

"I am going to fuck you hard, vampire. It's the price of your meal. Would you like me to make it hurt?"

Uthe's facial muscles were taut with arousal. "You cannot make it hurt too much, my lord."

Keldwyn shoved in deep, violent. Uthe groaned, body lifting into the penetration, accepting the rough treatment. When Keldwyn started hammering him, Uthe's hands clasped over his on his legs, giving him additional momentum. He caught a glimpse of harsh, brutal bliss on Uthe's face. The vampire had denied his desires for so long, he'd perhaps forgotten how good it could be to embrace them. Keldwyn understood the feeling all too well, taken by surprise by how violent the storm was that rose up and took him, sweeping them both along in its track.

Uthe's fingers dug into his forearms, and Keldwyn put more weight on his legs, bending them so he was closer to the male, eyes locked together as he fucked him thoroughly and well. "I would call you mine, Varick. All of you."

Uthe's expression flickered in shock, but the climax was too close. "Kel..."

Keldwyn's eyes closed. He'd called him familiar. "Come for me, vampire," he whispered.

Uthe released, cock spurting ropes of thick semen over his abdomen and chest. Keldwyn inhaled the musk of it, and his own organ convulsed as Uthe's torso and thigh muscles firmed like steel, his lips parting to show his gleaming fangs. Keldwyn wanted him to feed from his throat one day. He didn't shy from the knowledge or judge it. Not right now.

Keldwyn came, breath rasping in his throat, buttocks flexing against the inside of Uthe's thighs. The male pushed against the hold of Kel's arms to lock his legs over Keldwyn's ass, drawing him even closer. Keldwyn braced his hands flat on either side of Uthe's shoulders, his hair falling down to brush his arms and Uthe's chest.

"Careful," Uthe said, gathering it up in one hand,

holding it loosely against Keldwyn's shoulder. "You'll get it in the mess I made."

When he'd first met Uthe, Keldwyn had thought the harsh lines cut into his face peculiar for a born vampire, since those lines usually were marks of sun and aging. They seemed to emphasize Uthe's ascetic lifestyle, the plain, earth-colored clothing he wore, his propensity to spend time reading, doing Council work and praying rather than pursuing more playful or hedonistic pursuits, like others of his kind. But now that Keldwyn understood the stories those lines told, the character they reflected, it made the male vampire irresistibly handsome to him.

Yes, Reghan was laughing his very fine ass off. But he would have understood Keldwyn's fascination, wouldn't he? For Reghan had had an understated but solid Dominant streak like Uthe did, with that same intriguing undercurrent. Kel and Reghan had only started to explore a physical relationship before Reghan met Lyssa's mother, the beautiful Masako. During those couplings, Kel had led Reghan to that place of inner surrender, and Reghan had trusted him enough to submit, lose himself in the pleasure Kel could give him. In those blissful moments, Kel had been suffused with anticipation, wanting to find the bottom of Reghan's soul, cradle, keep and cherish it.

He now knew those interludes had been far less significant for Reghan, merely a beginning exploration between two best friends. Kel had been one of the few Reghan could trust with his deepest needs and desires. As a result, Kel had opened the path for Reghan that helped him actualize and act upon his feelings for Lyssa's mother. Which had just made the heartbreak worse, hadn't it? Not only had Reghan rejected Keldwyn's desire for more than friendship, Kel had helped him along the path that eventually took Reghan from all of them.

Yes, that was bollocks. Kel recognized that for the self-pity it was. Reghan was a decisive and intelligent male. He'd embraced his love with Masako because that was whose heart he was ultimately meant to share. Kel understood that now. Truth didn't make such things any less painful.

Yet it had taught Keldwyn an invaluable lesson. Submission didn't automatically mean a lover handed over his heart and soul. It just felt like he did. A Master learned the truth otherwise when it was too late, when he'd already surrendered his own.

He didn't want to think about any of that right now. This was a different road. He slid back down Uthe's body to run his tongue over a track of Uthe's release. The male drew in a breath, held it. Delighting in the reaction, Keldwyn traced every one of the glistening trails. He tasted Uthe, took his seed inside him. There was the flavor of blood to it, and Uthe's own essence, that indefinable taste unique to him. Uthe's cock twitched on his belly, reminding Kel that vampire recovery time was almost as good as a Fae's. Convenient.

No, not convenient, unfortunately. They both knew they couldn't delay their task here much longer. Keldwyn tilted his head, studied the symbols. He was well aware he'd not yet drawn out of the vampire, but he was pleased with his present whereabouts and would take the time he desired there. He was glad for the strength of the protection spell on the cave opening. An army of Saracens might be gathering outside, but for the moment they were uninterrupted. "So are you closer to figuring it out?"

"I think so." Uthe released Keldwyn's hair, let it slide over his fingertips, then he dropped his hand back above his head, gazing up at Keldwyn under heavy lidded eyes. He was returning to the present moment, retreating into his reserve. While Keldwyn had many ways to thwart that, he wouldn't press them now. Too much had just happened between them and he respected Uthe's need to consider the ramifications. The words Keldwyn had spoken were in the vampire's eyes.

I would call you mine.

Would he think they were words spoken in the heat of lust? It wasn't an inaccurate conclusion. Not that Keldwyn hadn't meant them, but his timing could have been better. More road needed to be traveled before that statement could be tested in a useful way, yet he'd blurted it out like an impetuous youngling. But once, a long time ago, he'd waited. He'd let Reghan believe their intense couplings were a brothers-in-arms type of things, a pleasurable indulgence for best friends. Before he could speak his heart, the one he'd loved had chosen to love another.

Once again he chided himself for false thinking. Time had had naught to do with it. Love wasn't a footrace, and it cared nothing for timing. Kel's heart would have been broken all the more deeply if their relationship had time to become more and then Reghan chose Masako anyway.

He withdrew, sat back on his heels and found Uthe's pants, tossing them to him as he tucked himself back in and laced his own.

"Lord Reghan... He allowed Lyssa's mother to mark him as her servant, didn't he?"

Keldwyn lifted his head, surprised. The vampire male read others well; Keldwyn just hadn't recognized how much progress he was making on that with him specifically.

"It was more complicated than that." Keldwyn paused before Uthe's steady regard. Yes, it sounded like a deflection. His lips twisted wryly. "It was not known to many others. At that time, in that environment, it would have sealed his fate even more quickly than the knowledge of their love did. But yes. He told me it was inevitable, for a vampire can only bind souls with a servant. To his way of thinking, regardless of how it would be viewed, he could not bear to let any barrier stand between them being as close to one another as eternally possible. 'Eternally possible.' That was the term he used."

Keldwyn cleared his throat, turned away and began to re-braid his hair in quick, efficient movements. "Make no mistake, he was a powerful leader, a strong male. I would not have you hold the wrong impression of him."

"Yet you do not assure me that he was the Dominant in their relationship, as I would expect you to do, to defend his honor. He was a leader who craved surrender, in the right circumstances. That is why he caught your attention, because you need that from your lovers. Submission."

Uthe's tone was neutral, giving nothing away. Keldwyn turned to face him. Now dressed in the cotton pants, the vampire rose, pulling on his tunic. He was modest. Not from embarrassment, but because of the dictates of his Order. That was in the Rule, that a man slept in breeches and shirt, never standing about indolently half naked. Keldwyn liked the look of Varick in only the loose cotton pants, though. His color was better, he noted. Fae blood had served him well.

"He caught my attention for many reasons," Keldwyn said evenly. "That being just one of them."

Uthe bent, picked something up off the floor. Coming to Keldwyn, he reached over his shoulder and slid the braid forward to his chest. Keldwyn had only retrieved one tie for the braid, and had used it at the end of the heavy tail. Uthe wrapped the other around the braid at the widest part at the top and caressed Keldwyn's still bare shoulder, since he stood before Uthe in only the partially laced leggings still. Uthe's hand then fell on the loosened waistband, finger tips sliding in to play in the silky hair over the pubis. The casual need to touch sparked heat, not only in Kel's lower region.

"Varick." Kel locked gazes with him. "Take the tunic off. If you have to return to solving your puzzle, I would like to enjoy the view. Even more than I already do."

Uthe smiled faintly, his dark eyes showing a mix of responses to that. Desire, conflict, and then a simple acceptance that touched Keldwyn. He complied after a single heartbeat. It made Keldwyn want to take him all over again, but instead he restrained himself, letting his gaze travel over the tempting proximity of Uthe's impressive upper torso, the striations of muscle. The heat of him.

"I promised to tell you more details about the demon, my lord. I think it is time to do that. Recalling all of it may help me figure out the clues Fatima has left me."

Uthe moved away, back toward the section of wall with the thickest covering of symbols. Keldwyn wasn't sure if it was to study the wall or to establish some distance from the unspoken questions that would implicitly come on the heels of the others they'd just raised. He wasn't sure if he himself was ready for insights about that. In the heat of passion, feeding the vampire, sinking deep inside him, had felt like the still point of the universe where nothing else would matter, but recalling Reghan's life and tragic death had dispelled that fantasy, perhaps for both of them.

It gave him a sense of loss and regret. He wondered what it would be like to have a vampire's marking so he could be inside Uthe's mind, understand what the other male was thinking right now. Perhaps it was best not to have that intimacy.

"When Hugh of Payns and his brethren were charged by the Pope and the King of Jerusalem to protect pilgrims, they were given lodging in a portion of the Temple of Solomon, or rather the building built on top of the supposed ruins of the Temple of Solomon. The underground stables there could house over a thousand horses, and were a perfect place for a vampire to sleep." Uthe's expression was warm and slightly ironic, an acknowledgement of what was being unsaid. Keldwyn couldn't help but respond to it. He nodded, which eased some of the tension in the vampire's face, as well as that holding his own shoulders in a straight line.

Uthe turned back to the symbols, his voice relaxing into a normal storytelling cadence. "We protected pilgrims, yes, but the pope had another charge for us. He wanted us to explore those ruins deep in the earth and see if the gold the Jews had supposedly hidden after the Roman invasion in

70 A.D. was still there. A large effort would have caught attention, so the small order was the perfect detail to pursue such a charge. From the beginning, there was little hope that we would find what the Romans and Saracens would not have. The rumor of the gold had persisted since the invasion. But no one had a vampire who could search deeper levels, where space and air were far more questionable, and whose senses could see further, detect the hollowness of chambers behind rock."

Keldwyn sat down on a boulder Uthe had been using as a vantage point to study the wall earlier. Uthe was trailing his fingers absently along his chest and abdomen. Keldwyn had used his own lips and tongue to collect Uthe's release, but he expected the vampire could still feel the faint stickiness of the combined fluids of his own body and Keldwyn's mouth. Uthe was fastidiously clean, so Kel wondered if the vampire choosing to discuss more of what Keldwyn wanted to know, rather than first going to the water source to clean up, was an intentional delay, so he didn't yet have to wash away the feel of Keldwyn's mouth upon him. He knew how he felt. He needed to wash up as well, but wasn't yet inclined in that direction.

Catching his fingers in the waist band of the cotton pants, he tugged Uthe back a step. The vampire glanced over his shoulder. "What?"

"Sit." Keldwyn indicated his knee. Uthe looked amused.

"I'm a little big to be bounced on someone's knee."

"Yes, you are." Keldwyn still pulled at him. Uthe placed his ass on Kel's knee with a sigh, but continued to study the wall as Keldwyn ran a hand up and down the faint bumps of his spine, his other hand curving over Uthe's hip. "Tell me the rest."

"We did find gold. Some. The Jews were far too smart to leave it all in one place, but it was enough to make the Pope ecstatic. It earned the Order his endorsement and, through his encouragement, the endorsement of Bernard Clairvaux, who was considered one of the most devout of all those sworn to the Church. At that time, he was the touchstone of the faith. Those endorsements validated our purpose. It launched the Order like a rocket. Donations of money and property came pouring in. Hugh was truly pious, a true believer. It was the validation that fueled him, not the money and power. He envisioned the Templars as a pure army of God, that simple squadron of nine knights protecting the pilgrims symbolizing the Order's enduring meaning, our one inalterable goal. Yet we became an army of men, with their usual failings in power and politics."

Keldwyn wrapped his fingers around Uthe's shoulder and pulled him back further so he was leaning against Keldwyn's chest. He adjusted his upper body against Kel's shoulder so Keldwyn could see what Uthe was seeing. The position allowed Keldwyn to slide the hand that had been around his back down his front. His skin *was* still faintly sticky, pleasingly so. He enjoyed that and the defined ridges of Uthe's abdomen, descending into the loosely tied cotton pants to find his cock. Uthe was already semi-erect. Under Keldwyn's knowledgeable fingers, he grew stiffer.

"Didn't we just..."

"Yes." Uthe let out a harsh groan as Keldwyn dug his fingers into the rigid shaft, an admonition, and increased the firmness of his strokes. "You started to look sad, unhappy. This will help."

Uthe made a strangled half chuckle. "I think it helps you even more, my lord. You are selfishly insatiable."

"My selfishness will benefit you. Keep going. You found more than gold."

"Yes, we found more than the gold." Uthe got quiet then, and his hand curled over Keldwyn's wrist, a request the Fae honored by stilling his provocative touch, though he kept his hand loosely wrapped over Uthe's genitals, absorbing the heat. He pressed a kiss against Uthe's back. Uthe let out a quiet sigh, a resigned acceptance to its comfort.

"I wouldn't have found it without the dagger. Magic can be mindless, drawn to other magics like magnets. One night I was so far down I doubted any human could get that deep, but a thousand years can change the earth's layers, and rope could have been used to take things even lower than men could reach. It was just a tiny crevice, formed where water or fire might once have cut a path. The dagger at my hip, it...vibrated. I could feel the heat of its energy warming my flesh even through my clothing. I dug through, following its direction. That's when I found the head. The head of the Madman of the Wilderness. John the Baptist."

§

Keldwyn came to a full stop. Uthe, his mind obviously now back in those tunnels, leaned forward. He braced his hands on his knees, eyes fixed on the wall. Keldwyn spread his fingers out over his back, absorbing the beat of his heart. "The head that Herodias, wife of Herod, had cut off as a result of her hatred for him."

"The same," Uthe responded. "Many things back then were considered relics, believed to hold magical power because they were the remains of someone sainted or holy. Most were simply bones. But there were advisors in Herod's court who saw an opportunity to use John's fabled power. Thank God, the Jews who hid the head there left a scroll with it, telling us what had been done. Though they'd never intended it to be found, they made sure if it was, the finder would not unleash mayhem unwittingly. The scroll explained black arts had been used to bind a demon in the same skull, to hold John's soul there for all eternity. To do it, they used the soul of an unformed innocent. So there are two innocent souls captured in that one head with the demon."

Uthe paused. "There is no record of what mischief those who did the foul deed were able to wreak with the demon, but our guess is their foolishness got them killed. And the ignorance of evil men left John a test for his soul these ten centuries. The Baptist's soul can be released if the head is destroyed, but if destroyed without the proper preparations, the demon would be released. He belongs to the ranks of the Horseman known as Plague, and he would unleash disease upon the world that could cause immeasurable harm. As long as there was no way to send the demon back from whence he came, John the Baptist's soul was not free to ascend. As far as the other innocent soul, I have always prayed that it—male or female, I do not know—is insensible to all of this."

"The gods be willing," Keldwyn said in grim agreement.

"Long ago, Haris's aunt, Shahnaz, was visited by an angel who said he could destroy the head entirely, but he'd have to obliterate all who inhabited it," Uthe continued. "The sacrifice of the innocent and the Baptist was considered a deeply regrettable but necessary act for ensuring the demon was not freed. Yet Shahnaz showed the angel she'd found a way to increase the strength of the bindings upon the demon and prolong their effectiveness, using other relics we'd discovered during our excavations. Through my contact with Lord Reghan, she'd also secured permission to place the heads and relics in the Shattered World until a means to separate the souls could be found. That changed his course."

He recalled Shahnaz's words once more. *"I thought of the angel as our enemy as first, but he was like us, Lord Uthe. He understood sacrifice and loss, the difficult decisions that often have to be made. He had no more desire to see those innocent souls destroyed than we did. John began to argue, to propose alternatives that would sacrifice him but not the innocent, unnamed one. However, the angel quelled him. He said, 'You can yet serve the Lord's Will inside the gates of Heaven, Madman of the Wilderness. If we can get you there, then that is the ideal solution for us all. Can you accept the Lord's Will and stay trapped until some way is found to free you that will spare your soul and consign the demon back to Hell?'*

"John replied, 'I will ever serve the Lord's Will.' And that was that."

"Unfortunately, we have passed the second millennium, and we are once again facing a similar dilemma. The binding Shahnaz imposed has been weakening, which is what allowed the demon to influence and call the Saracens to his aid. But the relics' strength has never diminished, so he is limited to what he can accomplish from his current prison."

"Relics strong enough that time cannot diminish them," Keldwyn mused. "Are you going to enlighten me, my lord, or let me fester in curiosity?" He played his fingers over Uthe's ribs, and the vampire shifted.

"The head is guarded and bound by three objects of power. The Spear of Longinus, the Holy Grail and the True Cross."

Keldwyn blinked. "The Templars had a splinter of the True Cross until Hattin. They lost it there. How did you get it back? And wouldn't Shahnaz's death have predated Hattin?"

"Yes, it did. But I did not say a splinter. There were pieces chipped off of it after the Crucifixion, but the remainder was taken and hidden with other relics."

"So the whole Cross is binding the demon inside the head."

"Minus a few shavings. Yes."

"Uthe, these are objects of power that humans would fight wars to obtain. And you have guarded them since the turn of the first millennium, hiding their existence from…everyone."

Uthe lifted a shoulder as if it was of no consequence. "Humans have always fought over religion. They fight over Jerusalem still. If we could have looked into the future and seen that, I've often wondered if the Crusades would ever have happened. Though now we can look back in time and see the same folly and wisdom in hindsight, and it still doesn't seem to matter. The fighting continues. It's not much more than common sense, realizing the relics would only increase the conflict. It's best for them to remain legends."

He spoke matter-of-factly. Since magic was such an integral part of Fae life, Keldwyn would expect that type of pragmatism from one of his own. Hearing it from a former Templar, a devout one, and a vampire who had as much magical ability as any human, was unexpected. No. Extraordinary. Putting that aside, he returned to the main point. "So this is why you said you often had separate missions from the rest of your Templar brethren."

"It was the charge given to me above all others," Uthe agreed. "When we discovered the head and the relics, Hugh prayed about what we should do. As faithful as he was to the Pope, he revered God more. He was ahead of his time, understanding that no man's heart was above corruption. He spoke to a wise woman about it. She was a village peasant woman and, much like Joan of Arc, tapped into the mysteries of the divine through the simplicity of her faith. Her views on God, faith and love were similar to that of Marguerite Porete, who would not be born until over a century later. As a result of their discussion, he called me before him and told me the head and relics must remain hidden together until we found the means to release the spirit of the Baptist and the innocent. He left me with that charge, because he knew I would live for centuries and the answer might take that long to find. I was to hide all of them where no one else would know about them, even Hugh. We never spoke of it again, though I reported directly to him and he authorized all of my travels and need for resources when necessary.

"When the gold was delivered to the Pope, Hugh made no mention of these things. The Pope rewarded Hugh for the riches by supporting the Order fully at the Council of Troyes. The Templar order mushroomed from there, though Hugh died shortly thereafter. Thank God, so he never saw what the Templars later became."

"The Pope never knew you'd found something far more powerful and valuable than gold."

"Again, thank God." Uthe went silent. Keldwyn sensed he was studying the symbols again, for he shifted, then dropped his head back to follow a string of markings up along the ceiling. Keldwyn accommodated him, wrapping his arms around Uthe's lower abdomen and chest, tipping his head to look up with him at the maze of symbols whose meaning was incomprehensible to him, but not to Uthe. "The village woman...what she told Hugh... 'It begins and ends with the mind.' I wonder..."

Uthe straightened, nearly bumping Keldwyn's chin as his head snapped around so he could look at a blood-colored string of words on the left side of the chamber. Then to the right and back to the ceiling again. He clamped a hand on Keldwyn's leg. "There. There it is. Right there above me. Ah, dear God, Fatima. There it is."

He surged up abruptly, though Keldwyn was amused and touched that the vampire reached back to steady Keldwyn from the violent motion. His eyes never left the code Fatima had left him as he did it. Reaching up, he traced the crimson symbols. His face was drawn as he lowered his gaze to Keldwyn, though there was a grim humor there, too.

"It's in her head. *Actually* in her head. She placed the spell craft there with a trigger to unlock it when necessary. This is the animation spell we will need to use when we get to the other head, and from there it is a matter of contact and containment."

He rubbed a hand over his face. "So now she's probably laughing at me, for being in such a rush to build a cairn over her body. I've created extra work for myself."

"I will help you uncover her. And I will remove the head, if that is easier for you. She was your friend."

Uthe focused on him then. A muscle twitched in his jaw, and he inclined his head, not accepting or denying the offer, but acknowledging the kindness. "I will pray over her before we remove the head. Are there any magics you have that can help us transport her...discreetly?"

"If the magic is malleable, I have a containment spell that will allow us to compact and transfer the energy into another vessel." Reaching out, he grasped the Templar Seal Uthe wore. "I will place it in this, and it can be called forth with the same trigger. It should not impact the magic already there, but I will examine the head closely to be sure. If that decision exceeds my own knowledge, we can always take it to Queen Rhoswen."

"Is that wise? I do not mean offense." Uthe added. "I've guarded this secret for a long time, because there are many who would misuse it."

"Your relics are items of magical purpose, and those types of things are littered throughout the Fae world, though admittedly these sound like objects of exceptionally strong power. Yet...yes, my lord. I trust Queen Rhoswen. Her capriciousness usually has more to do with unresolved issues about family than the way she rules her kingdom. At one time that was not so, but..." Keldwyn nodded. "She is a good Queen, a fair female. You can trust her as you do me with the knowledge. If you do, in fact, trust me with the knowledge."

Uthe's gaze glinted in amusement. "You seem to have little interest in riches or stolen power, my lord. You have ever struck me as the type of male who will not allow attachment, loyalty or personal gain turn you away from what must needs be done. No matter how much you try to portray yourself as a selfish, overly fashion conscious Fae."

The compliment was sincerely meant, despite the jest. Keldwyn looked mollified, though he tossed Uthe a narrow expression for the clothing barb. "Does the head possess any unusual powers beyond what you've already identified?"

"The demon and the Baptist can speak, dispense wisdom or guidance, or deception and misdirection, depending on whose voice it is offering the counsel." Uthe paused. "The Baptist still has the power of foresight and the demon can manipulate and lead a weak soul astray, in the twisted way that demons have always possessed to secure souls. You've seen that in the demon's reach."

"Understood." Keldwyn frowned, already crafting the binding he'd use for the sorceress's weapon. "Let's examine the head and see what we can do to leave here under the cover of darkness."

§

Keldwyn verified the carefully wrought magic embedded in the sorceress's head would not be impacted by his ability to rearrange its matter. He had his hands cupped around her smashed and decomposing face as he made the determination, feeling, probing intently. When he was done, he gently slid his fingers from around her skull. "I will still need the head to be severed from the rest of the body. Would you like me to do it, Lord Uthe?" he asked again.

He could see that Uthe did, which was why the vampire of course didn't relinquish the responsibility. Keldwyn knew he would have done the same. Uthe removed the sword from his pack. He took a couple practice swings, and then decapitated the body in one brief stroke. The expression on his face, the flash of soul deep pain, made Keldwyn wish he'd done it before Uthe could tell him no. The vampire dropped to one knee beside her, hand clasped on the sword pommel, his other palm on her chest. As he offered a plea for her forgiveness and prayers to lay her to rest, Keldwyn knelt by her severed head and began to do his part, speaking the words of magic in a murmur so as not to disturb Uthe. When Uthe finished, Keldwyn didn't want him to have to see the head there, detached from her body.

He'd taken the disk Uthe wore around his neck and cradled it in his palm. The warmth of Uthe's body lingered in it. As the head dissolved into light, it streamed into that target. Keldwyn caught the bright flashes of the magic it contained and power vibrated through his arm. He hoped these were optimistic signs the sorceress's weapon would work. A freed demon could wreak havoc. He understood why, knowing he was being besieged with Ennui, Uthe had felt such urgency to resolve the matter. Which, regrettably, could bring more stress and increase the hold of the Ennui. But Uthe had Keldwyn with him. He was determined to help the vampire however possible.

The Fae Lord tugged the silk wrap up over the neck so the body was shrouded fully once more. When Uthe finished his prayers, Keldwyn put the disk around Uthe's neck, rather than handing it back to him. Kel rested his hands on the male's shoulders, gauging the tension there. "Let me help you rebuild the stones over her," he said.

The two of them worked in silence for a few moments. "Whenever I see you do magic, I wonder that you don't do everything that way," the vampire said. "Levitate rocks, or get dressed in a blink."

"All magic requires energy and forethought, and it is wise not to waste it on what your body and mind already give you the power to do. Then there are things like this, actions that *should* be done by the sweat of your brow."

"Yes."

Keldwyn let the silence draw out. "It must have been very isolating, being the only one who knew all you know," he said at last. "Working to protect...everyone."

"You make it sound very noble. I never thought of it that way. It was simply what I was charged to do, and I had allies like Haris, Shahnaz. At first, I was foolishly stubborn. Soon before his death, Hugh warned I would not be able to continue my association with the Templars if their responsibilities expanded into armed military campaigns. He said I couldn't take the risk of falling in battle, but I pointed out my life or death was God's will. He did not argue with that, but he did say that the Lord expected us to have common sense."

Uthe's lips curved. "The compromise was he allowed me to stay on the detail to guard pilgrims. But when Hugh died, the subsequent Grand Masters did not know my primary charge. Hugh had left specific instructions as to what freedoms I had to come and go, different from my brethren, and those remained unchallenged, but he'd left the decision about fighting to my judgment. As time stretched out past his demise, I was eventually treated as one of the others. Gerard paid no attention when I joined the battle for Hattin. I respected Hugh's wisdom, and had tried to abide by it mostly, but I could not allow my brethren to fight without me against such incredible odds. But it was also the battle that told me how foolish I'd been, the risk I'd taken, all for the pride of saying I'd stood with my brothers."

Uthe fingered the silver disk around his neck. "However, it was also the decision that brought me in contact with your world, and gave us the chance to place the head beyond human reach. Until that time, I'd left it back in the tunnels beneath the Temple, since I was the only one who could reach it there. But though we were far from modern day drilling equipment, I could foresee it might not be safe there indefinitely. Particularly since the Pope never revealed that the gold was found, so there were those who still sought it. Also, while the desert countries were not overrun with vampires, who was to say one would not eventually think to seek the gold in a place beyond where men could reach it?"

Uthe lifted a shoulder. "So it is hard to say which of my decisions was God's will and what was pride. We do the best we can, my lord, and hope we serve the highest good. And when we know we did not, we ask God's forgiveness 'in such a manner that the words reflect the heart'."

At Keldwyn's quizzical look, he offered a humorless smile. "If a Templar missed formal prayers, you would say your paternosters wherever you were and, if they were said in a manner that reflects the heart, it was considered sufficient. It brought focus and comfort both."

A vision rose in Keldwyn's mind, of Reghan's serious mouth and warm eyes. His laughter, his ferocity in battle, his gentleness to Rhoswen. The pain her suffering brought to him when Magwel turned her against him. His anger and sorrow with Keldwyn when Kel refused to accept his love for Masako. Those memories caused Kel pain, guilt and regret, but he'd learned to manage them with the truth Uthe had just spoken.

Sometimes asking forgiveness—in a manner that reflected the depth of feeling in the heart— was all that could be done.

Chapter Nine

On the way back to the plane, they stayed alert for ambushes. Instead, they found a trail of bodies. Cai still wasn't permitting Rand to hunt with him, for death had come from snapped necks and bashed skulls, not the rending of teeth. Since Cai and his wolf had fed on one of them the night before, the demon had apparently only had the reach to poison a select few of those dispatched directly against Uthe and Keldwyn at the sorceress's cave. To play it safe, though, they went by the vampire and wolf's cave to warn them, but found neither there.

They could hear Rand howling in the distance, and the tone of it was a farewell, not a distress call. Cai had decided his purpose had been served and wasn't big on goodbyes.

Given the urgency of their mission, Uthe knew he should castigate himself for that unexpected coupling with Keldwyn in Fatima's cave, yet the break had relaxed his mind enough he'd figured out the clues she'd left him. Uthe had solved countless puzzles. He knew the importance of diversions when the mind was overtaxed. He'd denied himself the opportunity because it served other, more personal pleasures. Keldwyn had taken the decision from him and hence here they were, closer to the overall goal.

Faith, the Fae unsettled and distracted him. He also

helped him. It was a curious conundrum between purpose and desire.

It concerned him that the demon had been able to use the Saracens to do his will, but it only confirmed they needed to get to the Shattered World as soon as possible. Was it the possibility of it drawing to an end giving the demon extra fuel? Had he been reserving his power, in anticipation of this day?

When they reached the plane, they found Keldwyn's protection spell on the plane and pilot had not been breached, though the pilot reported some Saracens had circled the area. Confused by the sense that something was there, but unable to detect anything, they'd eventually left, frustrated.

Tricky wind currents made the flight out of Syria bumpy and loud, discouraging conversation. Despite their immortality that made the likelihood of dying in a plane crash slim, Uthe thought Keldwyn looked as relieved as he did when they landed and made the transfer to the Council's larger charter jet which would take them back across the ocean to Savannah. Keldwyn had determined it was best to enter the Fae world at a portal there, because the magic they were carrying would be blocked elsewhere. Securing the proper permissions from the Fae Queen for a different portal might take as much time as the plane ride.

Uthe didn't question it, trusting his judgment. Dawn was coming, so he bade Keldwyn good morning and then closed himself away from the Fae's speculative look in one of the several compartments designed to allow a vampire to travel by air during daylight. He stripped, putting the dagger away in the folded clothing. He wouldn't deplete the richness of the blood he'd been given faster than necessary by taking advantage of its protections. He could handle this part without magical aid.

Behind the walls and ceiling and beneath the floor, rich earth was packed to form a cocoon around the cot and small space. It made the air stifling, but would cushion him from the rays beating on the plane's flanks. Uthe closed his eyes, willing himself to sleep, knowing that was the best way to make the time pass.

Think I don't see you, vampire? Think you can send me back to my Maker? The demon wasn't ready to let him sleep. Uthe grunted.

I do not understand your resistance. After all these years, you should be homesick.

I will not return from whence I came without dragging the prophet with me. Nothing you do can prevent it. It is inevitable. Either it will happen when you err, applying the sorceress's dubious wisdom, or you will have to leave things as is. After the loss of your mind and your inevitable death, I will be under no one's watchful eye. There is much that can be accomplished in the Shattered World. There is far more potential here. Chaos is possible in a world of Chaos.

It cackled, a decidedly unpleasant noise.

"I am sleeping, demon. Your words mean nothing."

They will not mean nothing when you face me after all these years. Your cowardice has kept you from fighting me as a true warrior would.

"A true warrior does not fight the walls of a fortress with his sword. He uses battering ram, fire, water. The right weapon is what is needed."

A man fights with sword and shield. The bow and trickery are dishonorable.

"You are a dishonorable enemy, requiring dishonorable tactics."

As his tormentor kept nattering on, Uthe sighed, dragged himself off the cot. He knelt in the narrow space next to it to pray. When the demon was in this mood, it was the only thing that silenced him. Uthe was grateful for the other voice in his head that joined him, strengthening the prayer, drowning out the nefarious beast. *Bless you, Madman.* John seemed fond of the moniker, as fond as he seemed of anything. He was a somber, complicated spirit, and had never encouraged idle chatting. Uthe did not fault him for it. He could only imagine what the Baptist had endured, sharing the same space with the demon all these years. The Lord willing, he could end his trials soon.

Uthe wouldn't face the crossover into the Fae world hungry. Keldwyn's blood had been strong and nourishing. While Uthe still had mixed feelings about taking it, knowing the Fae world's opinion of feeding a vampire, Keldwyn hadn't seemed to be holding his nose at the time. It shouldn't have mattered to Uthe either way. At any other time he'd have wielded his considerable self-discipline and dealt with those feelings, shut them down. The problem was the Ennui could play havoc with his self-discipline. Or was it Keldwyn himself? He had no way of knowing. Something else he could not control.

The Lord will often send us impossible obstacles as further proof that we must trust His Will. Trust in him, pray for comfort and strength from his mother, the blessed Virgin.

Uthe was devout in his faith but not mindless about religion. Most of them were just sale tactics for their brand of God. He knew that. It didn't make what lay behind them, what their illusions were built around, any less real and solid. He didn't care what God was called; he served that energy. The demon had been right about that much. Without that purpose, there was simply the abyss. Uthe had come to God from the abyss. His version of divinity might be an illusion, but it was an illusion he preferred to the chaotic darkness in his own soul.

"My lord? You are well?"

"I am."

"I will enter to see for myself."

Before Uthe could tell him no, Keldwyn slipped in, quickly closing the door behind him so that he felt only a brief flash of heat, the result of the sun engulfing the plane as it winged through the clouds. It put both of them in darkness, except for the small flashlight Uthe had on the side table, pointed toward the wall so the thin beam was dimmed further.

Keldwyn's hand fell on his shoulder. "You are at prayer."

"I was. I am done."

Keldwyn sat down on the cot next to where Uthe knelt on the floor. "Gods, it's horrid in here. Like a cold shoebox."

The air piped into these compartments at double strength counteracted the sun's effect. It was mildly helpful. "A shoebox surrounded by flame."

Keldwyn moved his hand along Uthe's shoulder, discovering he was stripped down to nothing, his skin dewed with perspiration. Though normally Uthe would remain dressed while sleeping, this was an exception, since he had no desire to soil his clothes with excessive sweat. "Your skin is hot as fire," the Fae Lord said. "You need the Queen's touch. She can turn almost anything to ice." Keldwyn nodded toward the flashlight. "That takes the place of your candles?"

"It does. Somewhat."

"But it adds heat."

"Yes. But it is fine. I will lie down now, my lord. You need not trouble yourself further."

"You're no trouble." Keldwyn paused. "The Rule required that a candle always be lit while sleeping, to stave off the temptations that come in the darkness?"

Uthe remembered the earlier fever dream with the bad blood, when the demon had taunted him about that. There was no taunt in Keldwyn's voice, just thoughtful observation.

"Yes. But over time, it becomes a useful focus. A reassurance that the Light of the Lord is with us, even in darkness."

Keldwyn reached over and switched off the light. "You are assured of that more than any male I've met, Lord Uthe." An irritable edge entered his tone. "There are times your faith gives me hives."

"If it was a blind faith, untested, I would understand that, because nothing is more grating than courage in a sunlit meadow. But it is not. Have you never believed in anything immutable, Kel? Never wanted to?'

"I have wanted to. And the depth and breadth of that want is why I have no faith now."

The sudden roughness of his voice kept Uthe silent a moment, but then he closed a hand over the Fae Lord's knee. "Kel. I do not believe that of you."

"There are other things that come out of the dark," Keldwyn said. "Truths too painful to speak in the light. The inexplicable, horrible things of this world make the existence of anything beyond it an illusion. A child's wish."

"The inexplicable, wonderful things in this world make the existence of what lies beyond it a certainty. A comfort for the child's soul in us all." Uthe paused. "I had a fellow Templar who used to say it like a child's nursery rhyme: 'There is so much that doesn't make sense if there is nothing there; there is so much that doesn't make sense if there is.'"

Uthe could see even in full darkness. One short slide forward, and he stood on his knees between Keldwyn's spread legs where the Fae Lord sat on the cot. He framed Kel's face with his hands. When Kel's dropped to Uthe's hips, he muttered something against Uthe's mouth, likely a dubious reverence in the Fae language.

Earlier, the Fae Lord had initiated sex to pursue passion, to help Uthe find his answers, and to steady him after the near miss with the poisoned blood. Though Uthe had wrestled with indulging his desire under those circumstances, when it was Keldwyn who needed such succor, he didn't hesitate to serve Kel's needs.

Uthe kissed him, fingers sliding into his hair, pulling the bindings loose. He liked when the Fae braided or bound his hair, so he could be the one to free it, let it spill over his fingers. Keldwyn's palms slid around to grip his ass, drawing him closer. Uthe shuddered with it, the feel of his body, all muscles rigid, pressed against the Fae's clothed form. Keldwyn moved his touch up and down Uthe's back, over his shoulders, coming back to his ass to knead as Uthe deepened the kiss.

"I don't want to be him," Uthe said in a fierce, low voice.

"I do not want you to be him. I want you to be what you are. Perfect. Mine."

He was stunned by the depth of emotion in Keldwyn's voice. Perhaps he was right about turning out that light. It wasn't the temptations of lust that posed such dangers in the black, but the needs of the heart.

"I want inside you, too," Uthe said. "I want to fall asleep that way." He wanted to hold the male close to him, all that power and lean beauty. He wanted to hold something when he slept, something that would cover his heart, press against its painful beating, tell it that someone was there. That neither of them had to be alone, at least for these few moments.

Would Kel agree to it? He could feel him thinking, so Uthe kept up his exploring, tracing the biceps through the cotton fabric of his shirt. Kel had cleaned up and changed so Uthe tasted the soap-scented heat of him as he pulled the neckline open to lick the hollow of his throat, scrape a fang over his pectoral. He wrapped his hand in Keldwyn's hair, tipped his head back and pressed him against the wall behind the bed as he clambered up onto it, bracing his knees on either side of the Fae's hips and grinding his cock against his abdomen. Keldwyn took a bruising grip on his ass as Uthe sucked on his throat. He didn't bite him, much as he wanted to. Feeling Keldwyn's trust that he wouldn't do that without his express permission had a crazy effect on his cock and everything above and below it.

Uthe ripped the shirt away from the Fae's upper body, not caring if Kel had brought a spare or not. He'd give him one of his. He moved down again, back to the floor so he could tease a nipple with his tongue. The Fae cupped the back of his head, tipping his own to the wall once more, arching into Uthe's seductions. Uthe gripped both his thighs and ran his hands along them, pressing his thumbs in the crease along either side of Keldwyn's groin. His cock was an iron bar, his testicles a perfect, heavy weight in Uthe's palm as he fondled, squeezed. At the same time, he tasted, nipped and flicked his tongue against the male's sensitive nipples.

Blessed Virgin, to take full pleasure in a male's body, and a male like this, with no reservations... Uthe wondered if he might be drunk on the pleasure of it, for he acknowledged no restraint on his behavior, except what Keldwyn himself imposed.

"You want to be inside me," Keldwyn growled, as if reading his mind. "But everything you're doing will get you fucked through this mattress, Varick. So I get my pleasure first."

Good. He wanted to challenge him, bring all that to the forefront to overpower and overwhelm. And not just because the idea of it speared Uthe with lust. He'd felt the Fae Lord's pain and bitterness when he spoke to the darkness, and he wanted to give him this to bring him back to the light.

My surrender will give you back your faith. I want it to do that.

He spoke in his mind as if Keldwyn could hear him, as if they shared a vampire-servant bond, for Reghan had spoken the truth to Keldwyn. There was no closer relationship in the vampire world, and Uthe found himself wishing for the impossible.

In one effortless move, Keldwyn flipped him over onto the bed. Uthe smelled the fragrant oil he'd shown Keldwyn earlier, felt the slippery heat of it injected in his ass only a blink before Keldwyn's cock shoved so deep into him he curled his hands around the frame of the cot to hold on. Keldwyn wasn't making an idle threat. He pounded into Uthe as if he would put him through the wall, and spoke Fae words that Uthe didn't understand. The savage passion of them had his own cock throbbing.

"Don't you dare come," Kel hissed against his ear, fingers wrapping around Uthe's dick and squeezing. "Not unless you want to lose your chance to be inside me."

He would hold out against any torment for that. Uthe gritted his teeth as the Fae realized his resolve and tortured him with it, working his cock in tune with his own thrusts. "Bastard," he choked out, and Kel let out a nasty chuckle against his ear.

He released him to grip Uthe's throat, jerking his face up for another kiss. Uthe felt overpowered in a way he hadn't ever experienced. By the Cross, the male could fuck. Uthe had watched a thousand vampire dinners where indescribable sexual games were played with servants, pushing them to torturous and tumultuous levels of desire before they were finally permitted to release. Kel needed no trappings, no elaborate games. He was covering Uthe, holding him, directing him, and Uthe was yearning for more, a complete takeover of mind and heart. He also wanted to challenge Kel, bring sword edge to sword edge, so when Uthe fell to his knees, it would be under the blow of a stronger opponent.

It was all a jumbled, disoriented reaction, but not the tricks of his mind he'd come to fear. Pure lust constricted him like rope, impossible to mistake for anything else. This kind of need could never be an illusion. It was stark, painful, blissful reality.

Keldwyn climaxed with a harsh series of grunts, the cot squeaking and in danger of giving way. He had one foot on the floor to give him more leverage for deeper penetration, and Uthe felt every flex of that taut thigh against his buttock. His ass was burning, might be bleeding, and he didn't really care. His cock was stiff against his belly, wanting only one thing. One destination.

Keldwyn slid slowly from him, making Uthe groan. "There you are, vampire." When Keldwyn grasped his cock again in a firm hand, Uthe bucked against his grip. "You have held nothing back from me. Almost. I grant your request to be inside me—if you call me Master."

Uthe stiffened. No matter the direction of his thoughts, validating it with that one significant word was a far-too-precarious road. "I only have one Master, my lord."

"I believe that is my point, Lord Uthe." Keldwyn's tone sent a ripple of heat through him, purring, seductive and implacable. His fingers slipped away and he rose. A rustling of clothing suggested he'd completely stripped off the leggings he'd unlaced to fuck Uthe. In his current state of pounding, throbbing need, just the idea he was standing naked so close to Uthe was enough to send him over. Kel squatted next to the cot, his touch on Uthe's brow, sliding along his jaw. "On your back, vampire. I would make sure you are well-oiled."

Another torment. As Uthe complied, Keldwyn applied lubricant to Uthe's cock with knowledgeable fingers. All the way to the root and back, around the balls. They didn't need the oil, but that slippery, heated, squeezing feeling made his cock convulse further. His breath clogged in his throat as he stared up at Keldwyn's silhouette, the hint of glittering eyes.

"If you come now, you will get nothing, won't you?" Keldwyn mused. "You must bear this as long as I wish. Or until you call me Master and ask me to cease so you can be inside me."

"You think blackmail will work? It won't...mean anything. It's a moment, that's all."

"Yes, rationalize it that way if you need to do so. We will both know better, will we not?"

"Islam...means to submit." Uthe gritted his teeth. "Trusting that something outside yourself will be—"

"—there when you most need it." Keldwyn rubbed a thumb under the corona, and Uthe let out another guttural sound as Keldwyn dropped to his knees by the cot and put his lips over Uthe's slit, clever tongue teasing, lips sucking pre-come from it.

"There are songs...Sufi poetry...that refer to that something outside yourself." Uthe grasped at the words with desperation, trying to hold onto some semblance of sanity. "*Yaar*...beloved. It can mean God. But also...friend...confidante... Everything you need and want. One to whom you desire to give your devotion and obedience... Ah, holy God...forgive me..."

"It is the same meaning then, is it not? Master and *Yaar*." Keldwyn bent over him, his breath on Uthe's face, hair falling along his brow and cheek. "Come inside me now, Lord Uthe. I will not force an answer to the question. I believe it's already there, and it will be all the sweeter to see you arrive there on your own. Move over."

Uthe put his back against the wall and Keldwyn gracefully settled before him. The cot was narrow, but when two were going to be pressed together as one, it worked well enough, especially when both of them had preternatural grace and balance. Uthe closed his eyes, no matter the darkness, wanting to fully savor the male's back against his chest, the muscular ass his thighs lifted up to cradle. Keldwyn didn't seem to mind that Uthe was slick with sweat from the effects of daylight. He'd pulled his hair over his shoulder so when Uthe wrapped an arm over his biceps and chest, he could put his mouth against Keldwyn's exposed nape.

Uthe remembered his fantasy of seeing Keldwyn on all fours, looking back at him over the incomparable view of a narrow, tight ass. He dropped his hand to slide a palm over Keldwyn's flank now, the upper thigh. He wanted to take his time, but he couldn't. Keldwyn had made sure need was raging through him like the sun's fire. Uthe gripped the male's buttock, using the hold to position himself at the tight opening. As he began to press inward, the slickness of the oil drew him forward. His control snapped.

Uthe pushed into the tight ring of muscles, moaning in agonized ecstasy as Keldwyn gripped him like a glove. He began to thrust immediately, the oil sinking in, wrapping itself around cock, balls and everything attached to them. The pleasure of it spiraled like a wild tornado. He'd have said the oil had some kind of aphrodisiac in it, but he'd had it in his ass, and it was no more than a good lubricant. It was him. He hadn't taken a male in so long, denying himself because he knew it was like a drug, the desire to bury himself inside, to hold that connection. With someone who mattered, who was already inside him in another kind of way... Insane pleasure surged through him at Keldwyn's grunt, registering the effort of taking him. He hadn't thought of such vanity in some time, but he was glad he was sufficiently endowed to impress a lover, to cause some pleasurable discomfort.

Kel reached back and put a hand over Uthe's hip, pressing him even deeper. Uthe was bucking and rocking against him, thrusting like he would die if he couldn't keep fucking him forever. The climax boiled in his balls, getting more intense by the second.

"Go now, Varick," Keldwyn demanded. "Let me hear you."

He strangled on his cries, they were that powerful, ripping from his throat and chest. Keldwyn had his other hand curled around the frame of the cot and Uthe found a way to snake his hand up under him and cover it, hold onto his fingers and the iron frame at once, the whole thing creaking at the force of their movements. But he wouldn't leave the Fae Lord without his own pleasure. As he was starting to finish, he lowered his other hand, gripped Keldwyn's cock. Keldwyn dropped his head back and fuck, his throat was right there, pulsing. Uthe's fangs brushed it. He tried to draw back, but Keldwyn spoke in a rasp.

"Can you bite me without drinking? Is your control that good?"

In answer, Uthe sank his fangs into his shoulder. Blood spurted from beneath his hold. It took an effort beyond description not to pull the blood into his mouth, to let it run wasted down Keldwyn's chest. But Keldwyn started to come, then. With stunned pleasure, Uthe realized it was his bite that had pushed him over the edge.

Even in climax, Keldwyn's movements had the primal grace of a sinuous, silk-skinned creature of myth. As he finished, Uthe slipped an arm fully around his chest and the other around his waist. Slowly, he retracted his fangs, wondering at the shudder that went through Kel's body at the retreat. "I'm not drinking, just making sure the punctures close up," he said, using the coagulants in his tongue to do just that.

Uthe wanted to push him to his back, lap the blood off his chest, but he didn't. It was as he'd thought. Keldwyn had fed him in the cave out of necessity, and had handled it respectfully, but that one time didn't eradicate his cultural revulsion to it. Even though the thought sacrificed some of Uthe's pleasure with the painful twist it caused inside him, Uthe wouldn't let it ruin the moment. Denying himself the taste of Keldwyn's blood was a trade-off for the other pleasures the Fae had just granted him.

He pressed his face into the back of the Fae Lord's neck. Keldwyn put his hand up over his forearm. They were silent, Keldwyn breathing, Uthe's heart thudding. In this contented position, the additional exertion and the sun's progress started to have their effect. All vampires, even the older ones like himself, experienced daylight lethargy, though normally he could stay up at least until noon. But they were far above the ground here. "I may drop off on you," Uthe said, hearing the telltale slur in his voice. "Apologies, my lord."

"No apologies necessary. You have more than earned the rest." Keldwyn's voice was neutral, which usually meant he was examining variables. He wouldn't reveal his thoughts until he had a firm grasp of the information he was sorting. Uthe respected and understood that, though he did wonder what the Fae was thinking about. Was he considering the condition he'd imposed on Uthe, what it was becoming? Did it matter? He was a vampire and Kel was a Fae Lord. In the end, this could be no more than what it had started out to be, a temporary alliance.

The strength of the feelings Uthe was having demonstrated how out of practice he was in a relationship like this. He wasn't going to make a fool of himself and cause embarrassment for either of them. They were both far too old for such misconceptions.

Why was he even debating it? One way or another, Uthe would not survive much beyond the quest, if at all. Either his mind or his body would be gone, or both. For a short time, he'd forgotten that, hadn't he? No, he hadn't, because he hadn't let go of the male. He had both arms wrapped around him, holding him so close. He'd never held someone like this. Someone he didn't want to relinquish.

"Uthe." Keldwyn gripped his forearm. The Fae paused as if he were going to say something significant, but in the end he went with the practical. "I assume you do not wish to go back to Council headquarters, but to the Fae portal, once we land outside Savannah?"

"Right," Uthe said drowsily. "I've already said my goodbyes there." There was no sense in going back, in feeling that pain again.

There would be plenty enough of that going forward.

§

Uthe slept deeply, but when he woke at twilight and found he was alone, a weight settled on his shoulders. He made himself sit up and used the adjacent water closet to wash up, get dressed. Turning on the overhead light, he studied the cot. There was blood on the sheets, and Keldwyn's ejaculate was an additional splatter across the floor. He used paper towels to wipe that off the tile. The staff of the jet were second marked, used to cleaning up after vampires, but for reasons he couldn't explain, he didn't want them handling the remains of Keldwyn's release. He passed his fingers over the bloodstains. Lifting his head, he saw a folded pile of clothing on the small chair in the corner. Keldwyn had left a note on top of it.

"*So you blend.*"

Unless Keldwyn could conjure textiles out of the air, and maybe he could, he assumed the Fae had brought the clothes on the plane. Uthe donned the brown leggings and a linen tunic with a belt and a small pouch. The supple skin boots were like those Keldwyn often wore. Helga had asked the Fae Lord once from what animal they came, because she couldn't identify the origin. Keldwyn had deflected the question with an enigmatic smile, so it must be a trade secret of the artisans who made them.

It was probably vampire skin.

Uthe snorted at the thought and finished his preparations. Kneeling, he began his twilight prayers. He started with meditation, progressed from there to reciting paternosters, and then submitted himself to God's will, praying to act in His Name in all ways. He paused then, holding off on the *Amen*.

"While I know our quest is of the highest importance, I pray that Keldwyn will not become a casualty in it. As your use of me draws to a close, I ask your protection for him, Great Lord, so he may continue to serve your purposes long after my departure from this life. A believer is not defined by his words or religion, but in his deeds. I believe his heart is firmly in Your camp. Amen."

Rising, he clasped his fingers around the Templar seal pendant containing the sorceress's magic. He'd considered putting it in the pouch, but he always wore it, finding comfort in passing his fingertips over the worn imprint of the two knights, and had decided it would remain safest on his neck. He also remembered Keldwyn's fingers sliding beneath the chain, tugging on it, and didn't wish to relinquish the sensory memory. He could always put it in the pouch later.

Pausing by the bed once more, he ripped a square of the sheet stained with the jeweled drops of Keldwyn's blood, and tucked it into the pouch. Ignoring the whys of the compulsion, he opened the door and entered the main cabin of the airplane. Keldwyn was in one of the comfortable reclining chairs and reading a newspaper, legs crossed. A mimosa was at his elbow. It was such an unexpected picture, Uthe paused to take it in. The stewardess, a second mark named Reena, dimpled at his appearance. "My lord, I hope you rested well. Can I bring you anything?"

"One of what he's having looks fine."

"Certainly."

Keldwyn creased the paper into a half fold and set it aside, giving Uthe a penetrating look from head to toe. "The clothes suit you."

"It was good that you had them on hand." It was ridiculous to feel awkward, wasn't it? By the Cross, they were both well over a thousand years old. He sat down across from Keldwyn, but when he met Kel's eyes, he flushed like a maid. As Kel smiled slowly, Uthe sighed. "Shut up," he said. "Not a word."

"I think it is charming that you can still be shy."

"If I throw you out of the plane at this altitude, I'll discover if your wings are vestigial."

Keldwyn leaned forward, clasping his hands between his knees. His outfit was similar to Uthe's, only embellished with embroidery around the loosely laced neckline. It drew the eye to the tanned skin beneath and the fine, silky chest hair. He was wearing his hair loose today, so it spilled forward over his shoulders and shorter wisps of it drifted along his strong jaw and teased his slash of a cheekbone.

"I find it...stimulating, that you've not had a male lover in so long."

"Stimulating? How should I interpret that?" Uthe asked warily.

"I feel an overwhelming need to possess you in ways that are against the laws of nature. And a few ways that are every bit about the laws of nature." No subtlety in his expression now. Keldwyn's dark eyes practically glowed like embers, so piercing and intent, Uthe felt pinned in the chair by them.

He wanted to tell Keldwyn he was not a good long term investment. He wanted to reach out and touch his face, trace the absurdly well-defined cheekbones. He wanted to thank him for the journey they'd taken together in the night. But he'd just vowed he wasn't going to make this embarrassing for either of them. "It is good you are finding pleasure in the arrangement you demanded."

In a blink, Keldwyn's face was devoid of any emotion. Uthe met his stare without flinching, though his own words left a burn inside his chest. He'd said the wrong thing. But damn it all, it couldn't be sound wisdom to treat this as more than it could be, no matter how much more it felt like it was. Could it?

"It is good we are both finding pleasure in it. I would dislike to think you are merely enduring my attentions." There was a faint trace of mockery to Keldwyn's voice, and Uthe flashed back to that moment in the dark when Keldwyn had spoken of losing his faith. Which was just another way of saying his heart had been broken beyond repair.

"Kel..."

"I have changed my mind about our arrangement." Keldwyn picked up the paper again. "You are released from it. I will not demand anything from you again, Varick." His eyes locked with Uthe's. "From here forward, if there is something you need or desire from me, you will have to ask for it."

Chapter Ten

Be without desires, serve only the Lord's Will. Those words had always been a comfort to him. Right now, they were anything but. He might be a novice in newfound infatuation, enough to make him blush, but he had a thousand years of experience in understanding people. Keldwyn had opened Uthe to the pleasures of that infatuation, and now held its benefits out of reach, demanding that if he wanted more, he had to ask.

He wanted Uthe to beg for his favor. Such was his power, and the depth of the connection that had lingered from their night together, that Uthe felt the allure of it as soon as the words left his mouth. A sexual Dominant could exert considerable strength of will. Uthe had been surrounded by vampires all his life, watched them explore the deepest realms of the soul that existed between Dominant vampire and submissive servant. But he'd stood apart from that.

Uthe had been solitary, his relationships to other vampires at arm's length except for a handful of those he counted as respected allies and sometimes friends. He'd become a Templar to resolve the nightmares of his past, pushing himself to serve as the others did and even further. Those nightmares had woken him with cold sweats for decades, and he still occasionally had them. Hell had set up a permanent room inside him and, if he opened it up, the tormented souls there could tear apart his insides with yearning claws, trying to get away from their torture.

A vampire's nature wasn't wired toward service, which was perhaps why the Templar Order had been enough of a compromise to work for him. Obedient to God and eschewing all trappings of wealth or prestige, they also trained to be the very best at what they did, assuming leadership roles in military efforts and as armed escorts. They were in command on the battle field, and committed to obedient service off of it.

The routine of life with the Order had quieted those howling souls for a time. He was content within that structure. But discovery of the head had changed everything.

Initially, the blood link with it had been very disruptive. At the time it had occurred, Uthe had never had a third or even a second mark servant. He'd had no experience with someone sharing his mind by choice, let alone when compelled. The demon had increased his nightmares until Uthe wished never to sleep again.

Over time, he'd figured out ways to block him while asleep. During waking hours, he'd learned how to turn the volume down, such that the demon had stopped trying to antagonize him with random conversation. Some of those dialogues had been as stimulating as those he had with Keldwyn, except Uthe had quickly realized the demon always had nefarious purposes for engaging him. Even knowing that, the demon's methods were disturbingly effective, the creature using charm, threats and manipulations to weaken Uthe's resolve and commitment.

John the Baptist had always spoken to him far less. Uthe had been awed by any contact, but over time he'd accepted the prophet was a man. An extraordinary, erratic man whose communications could often be so cryptic, Uthe suspected they were the ravings of a mind tenuously tethered to reality. Yet at other times, John was particularly insightful, and calm as a lake. He could still foretell things of import. He'd predicted the plague in Europe and World War II, but how could he not? He was trapped with a being fed off the evil spawned from the bowels of Hell or men's minds—if there was a difference.

So the discovery of the head and the mission he'd accepted had isolated him once again. But that road took him back to the vampire world. After the Territory Wars that ultimately led to the current Council formation, he'd been called to a leadership role where, once again, he led *and* served. And he found balance once more.

Service was not submission. Being submissive was also not the same as submitting to a greater force. The Dominant nature of vampires was far more like the dominance of the animal world than the known structure of a BDSM relationship. A vampire might submit to another vampire if one proved his psychological or physical strength over the other. The "something" inside that would relent to the proper pressure, did. An alpha pack member would become a beta, only to become alpha again if the leader faltered.

Uthe frowned, staring out the window into the darkness. He wasn't sure why he was cogitating so heavily about this when he had far more important things to resolve. Catching a movement out of the corner of his eye, he snagged the projectile before it bounced off his head. Opening his hand, he saw the maraschino cherry from Keldwyn's mimosa. "We're landing," the Fae said. "You were thinking so much, I thought you might not notice."

Uthe set the cherry on a napkin and used another to wipe the slight stickiness off his palm. "You could have stained my tunic."

"I put it in my mouth and sucked it clean before I tossed it," Keldwyn said casually. "But I've rarely seen a vampire caught off guard by a thrown object. You're like cats, the lot of you. The slightest movement draws your attention."

Keldwyn gestured to the window. "Looks like we have a storm brewing. It's not far to the nearest portal. There's one inside the forest around the airstrip, and it shares the energy line with the portal at Council headquarters. We can cross here instead."

"Sounds good," Uthe said.

"I took the liberty of going through the pack you brought," Keldwyn said brusquely. "While most things fashioned from this world won't pass through the portal into the Fae world, because the Queen does not permit it, the sword is acceptable. I spelled them, compacting their matter much as I did the sorceress's weapon. They're contained in the pouch at your waist. When we reach the other side, if you have need of them, think your intent, and they can be drawn out fully restored."

"Useful." And impressive, though Keldwyn didn't act as if it were of any more consequence than packing a suitcase. "So I won't find an empty Diet Coke can lying in the grass on the Fae side."

"Only the occasional stray golf ball. Sometimes the Veil can be thinner when it comes to innocuous inanimate objects. A slice at the right moment, on the right calendar day..." Keldwyn shrugged. "The small Fae enjoy playing with them."

Keldwyn returned to contemplating his newspaper. Or brooding. It was hard to tell. Uthe shifted.

"My lord Keldwyn."

The Fae Lord lifted his cool gaze to him again. Uthe met it without flinching. "It has been a long time since I've had an intimate connection with anyone. I spoke out of haste, and it was cruelly and awkwardly done. It was not meant as it sounded. I ask your forgiveness."

Keldwyn's mouth eased, his eyes warmed. Remarkably, Uthe's tension, held in his lower belly, relaxed almost instantly. A sincere apology was its own magic, though it took some effort to work up to it on the front end. "Well said, my lord," the Fae said. "But my condition still stands,

Night's Templar

if you thought diplomacy could get you out of it."

Uthe grinned. "I never contemplated otherwise, my lord. A Fae changing his mind based on a vampire's apology might be too much for the fabric of the universe to handle."

Keldwyn snorted, spoke a phrase that Uthe was fairly certain translated to "smartass" in the Fae tongue. Then he returned to his paper.

Uthe brought his attention back to the window. Soon he would be in the Fae world, the true start to his quest. He had little idea where he was going or what he was doing. He only knew the head was in the Shattered World and he had a weapon intended to destroy the demon. But that was more than most quests had at the beginning, with very little to accomplish them but faith. He had all that, plus a Fae Lord as a companion. While disquieting in many ways, Kel would have his back in case of a threat. No matter how surprising that was, Uthe didn't doubt it.

He picked up the cherry and tasted the sweetness of it, recalling the sweet heat of Keldwyn's mouth. When he glanced over, only thinking in hindsight how what he'd done must appear, putting the same cherry in his mouth that Keldwyn had tasted, the look in Keldwyn's gaze made it impossible for him to regret the impulse. The coolness caused by Uthe's earlier stumble had definitely thawed.

"I would ask a favor, Lord Uthe."

It was an unusual request coming from Keldwyn. "If it is mine to give, it is yours, my lord."

"Your courtesy is a genuine pleasure, Lord Uthe, probably because it is never artifice. I know your quest is urgent, but going into the Shattered World...it is typical for those who enter to never emerge again."

Uthe leaned forward, brow creasing in concern. "Then you will only accompany me to that threshold, my lord. If such loss is a certainty, I will not risk anyone's life other than my own."

"You misunderstand the favor, Lord Uthe. You will not

be rid of me. I fully intend to go with you, for I serve not only your interests, but that of two Queens, and I will not disappoint either of them."

Uthe didn't think Keldwyn could be inspired by regal authority to do anything he didn't want to do for his own reasons, but Kel pressed onward.

"If you feel we can sacrifice a few hours in our journey, I would spend it with my ward, Catriona. She knows we are coming and is waiting for us. She would like you to join us for the afternoon. If we cannot dally that long, I can make it a shorter visit, but I would like the opportunity to see her before we enter the Shattered World."

"Have you told her where you're going?"

"No. It is not the first hazardous trip I've made. Catriona is aware of the risks my role carries. It is senseless to overdramatize every perilous task I'm assigned."

Which meant this one was significantly more risky than others. Uthe nodded. "Of course we have time."

In truth, his urgency could have more to do with his uncertain state of mind than anything else. The head had been in its current state for centuries and, all things being equal, could remain that way centuries more. But the ability to release two innocent souls to the heavens was finally now possible. And it seemed the demon sensed things were about to change, and was coming up with unexpected ways to throw obstacles in their path. However, the possibilities Keldwyn spoke of were far more certain, and Uthe would not deny him the chance to see a family member.

"I'm grateful." Keldwyn settled back into a meditative silence. At least Uthe assumed he was meditating on other things, because the alternative was that he truly was reading about NFL draft picks. Uthe wondered if the Fae had sports. Most cultures did, but he couldn't imagine what that would look like in the Fae world. Dragon races? Whose magic could hurl a boulder the farthest? He supposed he was about to find out about that and many other things.

His most indelible memory of the Fae world had been waking in the silver tower with Lord Reghan. Any other impressions were overshadowed by the tragedy of losing his fellow Templars in battle, and wrestling with the guilt of not being with them.

Lyssa had spoken of some of the things she'd experienced during her time there, but like most things outside one's understanding, Uthe was sure it had to be seen firsthand for full appreciation. He discovered he was eager and curious to do so, especially now that he'd have an afternoon to simply absorb impressions of the Fae world. Another gift that Keldwyn's stipulations had given him, though this one had been couched as a favor instead of a demand.

He felt a tickle of amusement, thinking of Evan's reaction. Ever since the vampire Uthe had sired had found out that he and Keldwyn were spending more informal time together outside of Council, the young artist had been dropping not-so-subtle hints about getting into the Fae world for further inspiration. If Uthe returned, he'd be grilled endlessly for every detail.

It was a shame he'd likely never see Evan again, let alone be able to make that happen. But perhaps, if Keldwyn survived—and Uthe was going to do his best to make sure of that—Keldwyn would agree to give Evan a short tour as a last favor to Uthe.

The plane bounced down on the airstrip. The stewardess and pilot wished them good journey, and then they were off the plane, headed into the terminal. Keldwyn's glamor among humans was always a seamless transition. While Uthe could still see his exceptionally beautiful appearance, the pointed ears and Fae clothing, the humans passing them in the terminal didn't give either of them a second glance. He figured Keldwyn had cloaked them as nothing more than a pair of businessmen headed for the next meeting. Uthe was more fortunate than most vampires his age. Thanks to the permanent sun damage to his skin, and his dark eyes that masked the crimson flickers which could appear with blood lust, he didn't have the preternatural look far more difficult for older vampires to hide. Lord Mason's amber eyes were more tiger than human, and the aura of power around Lyssa couldn't be disguised by a tsunami.

Once in front of the airport, they headed into the parking lot. Keldwyn indicated the tree line beyond the air strip, separated from them by a series of fences. Though the area was well lit, there were enough shadows for a swiftly moving Fae and vampire. "I expect we can both make it there without being seen. Shall we?"

Uthe made a noise of assent, then Keldwyn was gone, nothing to note his passing but a slight ruffle of wind across Uthe's face. Uthe counted down like he did before his morning challenge to the sun, and then he, too, was gone. If any humans had been watching, which he'd made sure they hadn't been, it would seem as if he'd vanished, but he'd simply moved as a vampire moved, faster than they could follow.

He arrived inside the tree line not even winded, which was reassuring. Keldwyn was sitting on a rock, and Uthe caught an unexpected expression of relief on the Fae's face, as if he was drawing a breath of clean air after being in a cloud of smog. "It's not as difficult for a high Fae to endure being surrounded by man-made things, but it's still not comfortable, is it?" Uthe guessed. "It's why you rarely sleep in our world."

Keldwyn nodded. "I sleep, but it's not restful. It's like reposing on a bed of nails, surrounded by all the barriers you put between yourselves and nature. Your compartment was somewhat easier, with the cushion of earth, and our closeness." At Uthe's quizzical look, Keldwyn elaborated. "Nothing is closer to nature than life itself, Lord Uthe, so two beings twined together can also be a touchstone to the earth and the elements. Not that that was my only purpose for being there."

"I am not a maid who needs reassurances for why you sought my company, my lord," Uthe said. But, not wanting to commit the same casual cruelty he'd made earlier, he added, "I am glad I was able to bring you ease. Where is this portal?"

Keldwyn rose and stepped closer. He slid a hand over Uthe's back, a gesture of casual affection. "This way," he said.

He followed the Fae deeper into the woods. It was thick and tangled, wholly natural forest. Keldwyn found subtle trails through the undergrowth. At length, they were in a small clearing where a line of sapling trees followed a narrow strip of wet marsh. Uthe saw the clearing was a near perfect circle, and a ring of stones was arranged around it. Since some were half buried or set at angles, it looked random unless one examined them more closely.

"This portal hasn't been used in some time, but it is close enough to the other it should work, especially with the presence of Rhoswen's amulet. Pull it out now, my lord."

When Uthe flipped open the pouch and complied, Keldwyn extended his hand. "Clasp my wrist and do not let go until I say. It will be disorienting but not painful." He paused. "Have you been back since the Battle of Hattin?"

"Just the once when Shahnaz wanted Reghan to show me a glimpse of the Shattered World, but that isn't very clear in my head. The first time was equally as brief. I vaguely remember the tower, some of the grounds around it."

"Then it will be my pleasure to give you a better tour of my home this time."

Uthe had seen the Fae move through the portal at the Savannah estate. Without a Fae guide, crossing the barrier yielded nothing but walking a few steps across the ground, but Uthe was certain that would not be the outcome today. Keldwyn pointed to Uthe's dagger, scabbarded on his belt.

"In the Fae world, you won't need to draw on the dagger's power. The sunlight there does not burn a vampire's skin. The transition between worlds will be somewhat draining, though. You'll require nourishment fairly soon after crossing the portal. I've arranged a safe human source for your feeding."

That was a surprising revelation, and came with a stab of disappointment, since Keldwyn wouldn't be that source. Uthe refused to let himself resent that the Fae could fuck him senseless but reject the intimacy of feeding. Few vampire lovers fed off one another after all, though their reasons were political, rather than distaste.

"Shed the boots," Keldwyn directed. "Just drape them over your shoulders and they will go through, but the passage for a vampire is less jarring if your feet are in contact with the earth and water."

Uthe complied. At Keldwyn's gesture, he stepped into the wetter area of the marsh, taking a breath at the cold. Since only sparse sunlight filtered through during the daylight hours, once darkness fell, whatever heat was caught there dissipated quickly. Keldwyn gazed down at his curling toes. "You have exceptionally wide feet, my lord. Unexpected. You could use those as shovels."

"The sergeants used to threaten young Crusaders with them. 'If you don't listen, Brother Uthe will put his giant foot up your arse.'"

He'd not recalled that in some time. He could hear Manfred threatening it in his provincial French, amusement and true patience with those new soldiers hidden under the sarcasm. So many of them had known so little when they came to the Holy Lands.

"Sounds like a good threat." Keldwyn passed his hand before him, a smooth parting motion, as if he were lifting a curtain. Everything stilled. The bird song, the fluttering needles on the pines and leaves on the maples, the energy of the earth itself. Uthe realized he couldn't move. The water surrounding his feet and ankles seemed infused with more life, tingling and vibrant against his skin. The silence penetrated his mind and sank deep, a welcoming feel, not alarming. His eyelids were heavy as anvils. They fell shut, and then Keldwyn touched his arm. "We're here, my lord."

Uthe opened his eyes, his body relaxing into movement again. He was still standing in water, but it was no longer the marsh. The wide, free flowing stream meandered down a hill, turning toward the left to make a crescent, a natural bracket for a wide meadow and a stand of trees behind it. The forest climbed toward a castle that rose high above the tree tops, the earth-colored stone like the rocky slopes of a mountain.

The trees close to the meadow were laden with purple and pink blooms that glowed with a silver luminosity. Those same three colors floated through the air as motes, tiny specks like snowflakes. Others had more substance and more specific trajectories, which suggested the larger ones were insects or other beings adapting their appearance to the trees for camouflage. The meadow grass was the color of pale gold straw, tipped with fronds as delicate as swan feathers.

As remarkable a sight as all that was, when Uthe's attention slid back down toward the stream, he found something even more arresting on the bank a few hundred feet below them.

A female fairy and a snow white horse stood together there. The horse's golden tail was braided with the purple, pink and silver flowers. The colors were on the white flanks, small handprints, like a child had decorated the horse with ink made from the flowers' essence. The female Fae had long brown hair, caught in intricate coils and threaded with more of the flowers, the remaining fall of hair tumbling down her back between her wings, a green and gold color. She leaned against the horse's side, her shoulder pressed into the creature's shoulder.

In the water, another girl played. This one didn't have wings or pointed ears, but Uthe knew from Keldwyn that there were a remarkable number of Fae races, whose features and forms were similar to the diversity of the animal world he knew. A birdlike creature was flitting around her, dipping down to use its barbed tail and leathery wings to splash the girl as she retaliated, laughing. The bird made a piercing cry. As it twisted in the air and spouted a short gust of flame, Uthe realized it was a small dragon, with amber-colored scales and a tail whose tip was shaped like a pointed axe blade.

It was not the only wrong assumption he'd made. As the horse lifted her head from the water, a spiral golden horn on her forehead caught the sunlight. The unicorn's delicate nostrils flared and she snorted, drawing the Fae girl's attention to their arrival. Her eyes were large for her petite features, outlined by dark, thick lashes. She spoke to the girl playing in the water, then turned and moved toward them, so swiftly her wings lifted her off the ground, her bare feet teased by the tips of the meadow grass.

"Can you use your wings to fly like that?" Uthe asked Keldwyn, curious.

"Mine are more ornamental, though they can give me a lift advantage during fights. But like a cape, they can get in the way. Such as when my opponent tries to grab onto one." Kel tossed him a significant look, reminding Uthe of their fight on their stairs in Savannah.

"If I remember, you used that hold to electrocute me."

Keldwyn hmphed, but they left off the conversation as the fairy descended within a few feet of them, her soft smile dazzling. Her eyes were grey-green like smooth tree bark, her skin smooth as glass and the dusky color of the Oriental beauties Uthe had seen in his travels.

Her slender body and limbs reminded Uthe of a willow tree. The vivid green and gold of her wings were layered like its leaves. She wore an earth-colored pendant around her neck, framed by the neckline of a gossamer green tunic that clung to her supple body and separated into more layered leaf shapes around her slim thighs. Though her ears were pointed like Keldwyn's, they were longer and angled to mold close to the sides of her head.

While her expression indicated warm welcome, she said nothing right away, looking between Keldwyn and Uthe expectantly.

"This is Catriona," Keldwyn said. "She is a dryad. Catriona, this is Lord Uthe."

A dryad. That explained the impression of a tree. Uthe extended a hand. When she placed hers in it, curious, he bent over it courteously. Nothing about this place suggested a contemporary handshake would make sense. "My lady, it is a pleasure."

She surprised him by holding onto him as she turned to Kel. "How long can you spend with us today?" Her voice was breathy music like a gentle breeze, welcomed by the senses in whatever portion it was offered. Uthe realized she was older than she appeared. An immortal trait shared by vampire and Fae but, as Rhoswen had pointed out in her meeting with Uthe, it was the way one spoke, body language, or a certain look in the eyes that revealed maturity. While Uthe could not guess her actual age, she was an adult, though very young by Fae standards. Perhaps forty years.

"We can spend the afternoon," Keldwyn told her. "What would you like to do?"

Her gaze swept the meadow, the unicorn and her young friend. The girl had come out of the stream and drawn closer, taking a seat on a stump. The dragon curled in her lap like a kitten, but he was so large he hid most of her, the long tail wrapped around her calf. The dragon blinked at Uthe with gold eyes.

"I think we should play here," Catriona said. "You need to relax with your friend. I'll braid your hair. You don't usually leave it down like this when you travel. If you're going to fight monsters, you'll need it out of your way. It would be embarrassing to be dead because your long, flowing hair is in your eyes."

The girl behind the dragon giggled. Keldwyn cast her a mock intimidating look and she tried to subside, ducking behind her scaled friend, but she was obviously already familiar with the Fae Lord and had no fear of him. "This is Della," he told Uthe. "She is Catriona's human friend."

At Uthe's surprised look, Keldwyn explained. "We have blocked human passage into our world for some time, but Queen Rhoswen has always shown limited tolerance for special human youngsters, particularly if they are respectful believers in the Fae world. She creates crossing points in their gardens and natural play spaces. Della is one such special child. Though quite impudent," he added, raising his voice and tossing her that glare again. "I shall have to turn her into a bright blue frog to teach her manners."

"Ribbit, ribbit!" Della responded, dislodging the dragon so she could hop across the ground like an amphibian. Though she was somewhat chubby, she moved with great energy.

Uthe's brow creased. The same insight that told him Catriona was an adult told him that Della was less mature than her apparent age, around sixteen years old.

"She is what the humans would call slow, or mentally challenged," Keldwyn said low, reading his face. "An underdeveloped mind. But here, she is at ease."

"Will she not be missed?"

"She crosses over in her mother's garden." Catriona supplied that explanation. "She is out of view for less than a blink, even if she spends the whole day here. You are compassionate, my lord. It matches what Kel told me of you. Most of it."

She sidled closer to Keldwyn, sliding her fingers through his loose hair and tangling there, giving the freed strands a significant look that he answered with a narrow-eyed warning. Her lips quivered against another smile, though this one she suppressed. Uthe sensed she'd once laughed more freely, but the joy was still there, just exercised more cautiously than before.

"What did Kel tell you of me?" Uthe wanted to know.

"After Lady Lyssa, he respects you more than any other vampire. Maybe a little bit more than Lady Lyssa some days, but I think that's when he doesn't agree with her on something."

"What about the days he and I don't agree?"

Her eyes danced. "He says vampires were a mistake by Creation and will shortly be ended by their own stupidity. He also calls you names."

"Nothing I haven't called you to your face, Lord Uthe," Keldwyn said, unperturbed. "Stubborn ass. Brainless primordial ooze."

"I'm so relieved it was nothing truly derogatory."

"Maysie made some of her cakes for you." Catriona changed the subject, turning back to Keldwyn. "She didn't lace any with love potions. I checked. I'll get them and some mead and we'll have a picnic." She gave Uthe another studied look. "You are very handsome, in a different way from most vampires," she decided. "More lines on your face, but they make sense. I understand better now why he likes you."

As Catriona ran off hand-in-hand with Della, the unicorn and dragon in pursuit, Uthe was bemused by the declaration. Up until now, his understanding of Kel's regard for him had been clouded by the motives of their respective worlds. Catriona had no reason to tell him anything but the truth, did she?

Keldwyn didn't look discomfited by her revelation, which was even more unsettling. "Love potions?" Uthe questioned. Keldwyn winced.

"Maysie is quite lush and lovely, and as sturdy, stubborn and loyal as a brick wall. She has not taken the hint in several decades, sure that I will eventually tire of my travels and want to settle down in her cottage with her. When Catriona was much younger, she lost her mother and her father abandoned her. Maysie would care for her when

I had to be away. She seems to have no sense of the difference in our classes, or why that should matter."

"I expect you haven't been sufficiently cruel enough to make that clear. Or maybe she does know it and thinks you could be happy with a simpler life. It is usually true, but not always possible."

Keldwyn made a noncommittal noise. Wandering into the shade of the purple and pink trees, he dropped down onto the grass, leaning back on his elbows and stretching out his legs. His natural sensuality couldn't help but draw Uthe's close attention, unless he wanted to stab out his eyes to deprive himself of the pleasure. Keldwyn tipped his head up to look at him, his dark hair falling back and coiling on the grass. His lips curved.

"Come closer, vampire. I'm not the one who bites."

He could argue that point, but Uthe found no reason to resist sitting on the grass next to him. Keldwyn turned on his hip, his hand lying loosely along it.

"Is a simpler life what you discovered when you served with the Templars?"

"Yes. And no. I didn't come from excessive wealth, but there was no simplicity to the life I lived before I joined the Order. A very structured, predictable life proved...a way to peace. Later on, when they developed the Rule, with all its tenets for eating, sleeping, living, it almost eliminated the need for independent thought outside of battle. For a short time at least, that was easier. I embraced that."

Keldwyn remained silent, compelling Uthe to reach deeper. He wanted to say things to Kel he hadn't ever said to anyone, perhaps to reassure himself that his thoughts, the lessons he'd learned, would be remembered, even when he couldn't recall them. In that way, he would still somehow exist, even without an awareness of himself. "The things a soul actually needs is a short list. Yet the Rule stilled the clamor even for those. I centered my desires on God's Will and for a short time I found contentment. In that state, you believe the things you long to have will be answered in time, and that is enough."

The sound of wings and running footsteps told him Catriona was returning. He met Keldwyn's serious eyes but the Fae said nothing as Della knelt at Uthe's side and Catriona sat down in front of Keldwyn's thighs, using his body like the back of a chair as she spread out the cakes and the stoppered bottles of mead. Della pressed up against Uthe, peering into his face. "Your teeth are funny. Sharp. Like knives. Can I see them closer?"

Uthe obligingly bent. They shot forth, a quick snap that had Della jumping back and then giggling as he spread his lips in a comic snarl. Before he made them retract again, he let her draw closer and touch, but he clasped her wrist to control the movement so she didn't press against a tip and break her skin. Hearing the beat of her blood through her throat, hunger stirred. It reminded him of what Keldwyn had said about needing to feed soon after his arrival in the Fae world. Who had he arranged for a meal?

He wished he could regret Keldwyn letting Uthe feed off of him. But even if it dimmed the appeal of any other option, he couldn't. If he'd only been able to feed from the Fae Lord once, he would prize that memory. As for whoever the source was, it was just food. He would thank Keldwyn for the consideration.

The stubborn, intolerant, pointy-eared elitist. He'd called Keldwyn that once or twice in the heat of debate.

"Would you take a bite, Lord Uthe?" Catriona extended a small piece of the cake. "I remember Jacob said vampires can eat a little."

"I will. And if I end up taking Maysie as a result, it will be Keldwyn's loss."

"Like she would suffer a vampire." Keldwyn scoffed. "She'd make you her drudge, sweeping and scrubbing the floors."

"Nothing wrong with honest work." Uthe chewed. "These cakes might be worth an eternity as a drudge." He took a sip of the mead. "Though I'm now mindful of the fairy tales which say to eat or drink in the Fae world might keep you there forever. I may never be allowed to leave."

"That will be up to Kel, not what you consume," Catriona said. Keldwyn sent her a cryptic look which she returned with an innocent blink. She threaded her fingers through his loose dark hair once more, seeming to enjoy touching it as much as Uthe did. "Della, let's take care of my lord Keldwyn's hair. Shall we? Go collect some meadow grass for me. We must make it tight and fast, a warrior's style, for I fear he will be facing some formidable enemies on this trip."

Keldwyn touched her mouth, now in a somber moue. She was obviously under no illusions that his time with her today was not casual chance. She tilted her head into his hand, pressing her cheek against his palm. Uthe wanted to tell her that he would compel the Fae to stay if he could, but he didn't wish to patronize her. He knew little of the feelings of those left behind when a soldier went into battle. He'd always been the one going, never the one staying.

The moment passed. With a squeeze of Keldwyn's leg, she hopped nimbly over his hip and positioned herself behind him when he sat up to give her better access. Uthe stretched out on his hip to watch.

Even if he could compel the Fae to stay behind, there was no logic to that. The increasingly unpredictable state of his mind had been calmer for the past day, but if it flared, he'd need a companion whose steadiness he could trust. His mission was important enough to be worth both their lives. That didn't necessarily ease that decision for Uthe, but at least Keldwyn was a peer. He understood the risks and made his own choices.

Kel. That's what Catriona called him, and what Uthe was starting to call him more frequently in his own mind. He remembered the look on Keldwyn's face the one time it had slipped from his lips, his pleasure at Uthe calling him familiar.

Catriona had produced a comb from somewhere, and was working it through the Fae Lord's hair, the fine strands turning into flaxen silk under her ministrations. She was making idle conversation about what she and Della had been doing, things Maysie had said, and asking questions about the ball the vampires had held for Rhoswen. She asked how Jacob and Lady Lyssa were doing, particularly Jacob. The girl seemed very attached to Lyssa's servant, and Uthe wondered what experiences they'd shared together. However, females always gravitated toward Jacob as a general rule. Not for the reasons the camp followers used to trail the Crusader armies, but because the boy had a particular way about him. It told women he could be trusted with their wellbeing. Despite Lyssa's formidable nature, he expected that side of him called to her softer emotions as well.

Uthe tuned back in to find the Fae Lord watching him. Kel responded amicably to Catriona, but his eyes never left Uthe's. Uthe's gaze shifted, not because it bothered him to be caught in those onyx depths, but because he enjoyed watching how Catriona handled his hair. She'd woven four braids and twined the meadow grass in them to add to the binding. Two of the braids were slender ropes which followed his temples, behind the pointed ears and back, to be twisted and tied with the other two. She wrapped the full length in more meadow grass, forming a secure tail that kept every stray wisp from his face. When she finished, it was a very warrior-like look, enhancing the formidable edges of his features, lips, cheekbones and brow. Well, it was warrior-like, until Della stuck a few tiny yellow flowers here and there among the braids.

The Templar Code had forbidden long hair. Too many knights in the secular world had cultivated "flowing locks" to go with their ornately decorated horses and studded armor. St. Bernard had beseeched the Templars to eschew such trappings, only outfitting themselves as necessary to serve their fight in God's name. In their first few years, they wore only what was donated to them. Even the white mantle had remained unembellished for some time, no red cross until Pope Eugenius had authorized the cross of martyrdom for them.

Uthe's hair had been long when he'd joined, and Bernard's exhortation had not come for well over a decade after that. Yet, as if anticipating the nature of the role he was embracing, one of the first things he'd done was cut off his hair, and he kept it cut. The physical perfection of a born vampire was undeniable, but he'd done what he could to minimize it. Fortunately sweat and desert sand were good at concealing a fair countenance. Well, unless a male looked like Kel, as Cai had observed so brashly.

Uthe wanted to stroke the braids along Kel's temples, trace the outline of his ears. He hadn't done that yet, touched his ears. He'd intuited that was an exceptional intimacy, akin to a vampire placing his fangs against another vampire's throat. But he thought of doing it now. If they were alone, he would sit behind Keldwyn where Catriona was now, inhale the fresh scent of cut meadow grass and yellow flowers as he leaned close. He'd press his forehead against Keldwyn's back as he enjoyed a leisurely exploration of his ears, his shoulder, his biceps. He'd sit silently, so still in this meadow where he could be like Della, no fear for a lost or a poorly functioning mind.

He snapped himself away from that line of thinking. This was the temptation of leisure time, this meandering that could go to melancholy or self-indulgence. *"...all should take care of the sick, and he who is less ill should thank God and not be troubled; and let whoever is worse humble himself through his infirmity and not become proud through pity."*

So said the Rule. He was not a child, and Della's protection here was not effortless, no matter if it seemed like a magical world where nothing bad could happen. Protection always required vigilance from someone, somewhere. No world was without sin.

Della had sat back down in front of Uthe so she could lean against his bent knee, easy with physical contact with a total stranger. She had no reason to doubt her safety here, and he was glad of it. The dragon perched in the tree over him, his tail twitching not far above Uthe's head. He hoped dragons weren't like birds, with their profuse amount of droppings. Glancing up, he met slanted eyes that seemed amused, curious and highly aware. He expected the creature would be greatly offended by his concern, though not above acting exactly like a normal bird if Uthe annoyed him.

"I threatened to make Lord Uthe dance with me at the ball," Keldwyn was saying. "Though I decided I should show him some of our Beltane dances. The waltzes that night were far too gentle for a soldier like him."

Finished dressing his hair, Catriona slid her arms over Keldwyn's shoulders, her chin propped beside his jaw. "Be careful of his challenges, Lord Uthe," she said. "He has danced against other males on Beltane night in a grand competition. Long after they fall, overwhelmed, he dances on, even inside the fire itself, the flames twirling around his body."

"Have you seen this?" Uthe asked.

"No," she said gravely. "But I'm sure it's true, because he'd never exaggerate like a common boastful male. He's far above such ordinary behavior."

"I'm sure," Uthe responded, just as seriously. A dimple wreathed the corner of her bow-shaped mouth.

Keldwyn reached back and rumpled her dark hair. "Insolent creature. Go play in the stream with Della some more. I want to watch you enjoy yourself."

"You just want to finish the cakes." She snagged two, offering one to the unicorn and letting Della feed the dragon before they set forth down the hill again. The pink, purple and silver insects landed on their shoulders, heads and arms, coming back even when the girls' movements dislodged them. Looking up, Uthe saw more of them clinging to the tree providing them shade. Closer examination showed they weren't insects but Fae, with tiny bodies, antennae and wide, oblong eyes that studied him with as much interest as he was studying them. One drew what looked like a pair of tiny swords and brandished them. Obligingly, he showed his fangs. The whole flock dispersed with a whisper of sound like hissing.

"Did I just earn respect or a curse?" he asked.

"You'll find out in short order, I'm sure."

Uthe smiled, but studied the landscape around him, his gaze lifting to the stone castle behind the grove of trees. Though it was distant, he could tell some form of verdant green ivy climbed up the formidable walls. "It has been a long time since I have felt small in my world, my lord. And I suspect this is just a snapshot of everything that is here."

"Every world has its wonders. That is King Tabor's castle, Caislean Talamh, the Castle of Earth. Perhaps you will have the opportunity to meet him, once your quest is complete."

He hadn't thought about completing it. Uthe didn't see himself coming out of the other side of it alive…or aware. "I wish you did not feel compelled to do this with me, my lord." He set his jaw. "I wish I didn't need a companion for it whose value to his own world and my own is so great."

"Well, you do, so no sense wasting thought on that. I expect we'll both have plenty of room for regret before our journey is over. No reason to overload it on the front end. Tell me more about being a Templar. I was involved more in my own world during that time."

Uthe stretched out on his back to watch the insect Fae drift and buzz through the branches. He lifted his hand as if he could touch them. Caught by the motion, some descended, their weight like butterflies on his skin, the curve of a knuckle. Beautiful as they were, his vision swam before him and their presence was replaced by a stone wall, the one in his quarters in al-Asqa. He saw his fingers tracing the cross he'd carved there, like many of his brethren had. It had been a sign of devotion, proof that he was there to serve.

"In the beginning, it was very simple, like all good ideas are. Pilgrims on their way to the Holy Lands were being preyed upon by Seljuk raiders. The First Crusade had captured Jerusalem for the Christians, but then many of the Crusaders returned home. Because their salvation had been firmly secured by the Pope's decree, there was no need to stay in that hot, unfriendly part of the world. Which was just as well, since many of them were little better than thugs. When they took Jerusalem, the streets ran with blood. Men, women, children, Muslim, Jew, Christian."

"You were there for that?"

"No, thank God. Hugh told me of it. Under the Muslim rule that was there before the First Crusade, all three faiths had been allowed to visit and worship at the holy sites, though non-Muslims had to pay a fee. In the void that followed, Turkish raiders entrenched themselves on the popular routes to attack the Christians who then came to the Holy Lands in droves, thinking themselves safe because Jerusalem was now in Christian hands. Which is where the Templars came in. Hugh and his men were protecting the pilgrims. I was allowed to join their ranks after spending time with them and fighting their cause. I was no knight, but eventually Hugh knighted me. At that time, a knight could still bestow knighthood on another. I was content merely to fight with them, but he said knighting me would allow the Order to more fully utilize my leadership and fighting skills going forward. Though one of the Order's core tenets was 'deference to ability, not nobility,' he foresaw that might not always be the case."

"He was correct."

"Yes. As our numbers grew modestly, our skills came into demand. We knew how to fight against the raiders, protect trains of pilgrims and strategize to maximize our resources, all things that were useful to the men who brought armies to fight the Second Crusade. We were placed in charge to guide and protect them during marches, as they moved supply lines and men from place to place. We were drawn into their wars, becoming Crusaders instead of Templars." Uthe turned his hand to study a pink Fae who was rubbing her front arms together like a cricket, producing a thin flutelike music. Three others joined her, a small quartet.

"Yet though they were never intended to be that grand, they did in fact become that grand," Keldwyn noted. "Remembered to this day."

"Romanticized to this day," Uthe responded dryly. "In truth, we lost more battles than we won, though it was not for lack of courage or zeal. When we learned how to protect the pilgrims' financial resources through a credit system, we also became bankers, bankers who loaned money to kings. There are times I think Hugh's dream was co-opted from the very beginning, by a Pope who turned us into archaeologists to find a fortune in gold. The support we bought with that gold was the first step to turn the Templars into something they were never intended to be."

"An intriguing history lesson, my lord." Keldwyn had rolled onto his back, too, one knee bent, the other long leg stretched out. He lifted his hand, and the Fae on Uthe's arm took off like a flock, landing on Keldwyn's fingers and forearm. "Yet not entirely what I seek to know. You left Rail, came to Jerusalem and became a Templar, all for one painful reason. A reason that doesn't fit a lovely meadow, a unicorn and a picnic of mead and cakes."

"No, it doesn't." Uthe waited a few more heartbeats, thinking it through. Kel didn't say anything further, and Uthe suspected he wouldn't push, but Uthe was getting closer to the point he would tell him what he'd told no one. He didn't have to give him any explanation at all, but this inexplicable compulsion to leave his story in the mind of another was nudging him in that direction.

Base nature couldn't be dispelled by prayer. Sometimes

he'd wondered if the Templars had been an experiment to test that. Was it possible to combine higher spiritual aspirations with the human propensity for violence and come out with an outcome that served God? Warrior-monks. Killing in the name of God, but not like the First Crusaders. Those had been men in too much debt, those without enterprise, or felons escaping human justice under the Pope's auspices. Templars killed in the name of God, but supposedly without the avarice for blood, no pleasure taken in the deaths.

To God goes the glory. Back then, he'd needed that peace so desperately. Yet his life, before during and since had always been a river of blood. First with the Templars, then the various brutal struggles between vampire factions that had ultimately led to the establishment of the Council. He'd fought over a hundred battles for reasons that blurred in his mind and overlapped.

"When you cannot believe in a larger purpose, sometimes the best you can do is believe in its reflection. Hugh's piety fed my soul. There was something indescribable about his beliefs. They gave me a balance, a peace. I am vampire. I cannot be servile. I might die by the sword, but even violence can have a code, as the existence of the Vampire Council proves. He gave my savagery a nobility. In time, the service of it, the release of will to another that still allowed me to use my strength, my power, my bloodlust...it was freeing."

"I do not wish to disturb unpleasant memories, Uthe," Keldwyn said. Uthe heard nothing but sincere truth in the male's words. "But it is important for me to know the reasons for your path, to help you, as we go forward. Particularly if you get to a point you can no longer offer me information as freely."

He was right, it was logical. Yet it wasn't only logic. "I have already reached a point I must trust you far more than I expected to do, my lord. At times it is unpleasant and uncomfortable, for I still do not know you well enough.

An error could be easily made. Yet at no other point in my life has it been so important that I not err in the slightest."

"Which is why having someone you can trust completely is essential. And instead, you have me." Keldwyn's expression was blank, revealing nothing. "Either I have been sent as an answer to your prayers, or a way to foil them. You overlook a third possibility, however."

"What is that?"

"I could be neither agent of light nor darkness. I could just have nothing better to do with my time right now."

Uthe huffed a half chuckle, earning a curve of Keldwyn's distracting lips. "Not true, my lord. We have several debates pending on important Council policy changes. Endless hours in chambers, arguing minutiae with Helga and Carola. Thwarting Belizar and Stewart's every attempt to scuttle anything that hints of change."

"You make it sound so appealing. A missed opportunity. I'm sure the household staff would have served tasty snacks." Keldwyn sobered. "You know I speak the truth. If I am to be your proper ally in this, I need all the information I can."

"Perhaps it would be simpler if I thought that was the only reason you ask these things."

Keldwyn's expression was getting easier for him to read. There were small changes to the muscles around his eyes and along his jaw that intensified his expression, the potency of his gaze. What was also getting disturbingly predictable was Uthe's response to that particular reaction. His pulse accelerated and his fangs lengthened, as if to a threat or blood-based pleasure. Which made him want to move, fight or fuck. Touch, taste or bite.

"Give me another question for now, my lord," he said, more brusquely than intended, but it didn't seem to dissuade Keldwyn.

Keldwyn didn't speak immediately, his eyes fastened on Uthe's face, but then he relented. "The battle of Hattin. Why did the Templars blindly follow Gerard into such a fruitless battle? He was a vain man clearly not serving the will of God. Did you so need to emulate your relationship with God on an earthly plane that you abandoned your judgment, the judgment that Lyssa prizes so highly and with good reason?"

"No," Uthe said. "And yes. We were trained to trust the Grand Master unconditionally with our welfare, believing he would never act against God's will in favor of pride or ego."

"If you truly believed that, you were all suffering a fatal case of naivety."

"Soldiers have little choice but to follow orders. In time, we set that aside as a given. The ones in charge, even the ultimate purpose, become unimportant, because those are things we cannot control. We fought, because that was what we were charged to do. Our focus became loyalty to the code of battle and protecting the man at either side. That seems to be the way all wars go."

Uthe sat up, linking his hands around his knee. "For those of us who stayed in the Holy Lands for any length of time, it was clear the best way to praise Jerusalem and all the gifts there was for it belong to all three peoples to whom it was important: Jews, Muslims and Christians, not just one of them. It was those Crusaders who stayed and raised families who learned to co-exist with the Muslims and Jews in ways that ironically would have brought peace—if not for leaders who felt differently, who thought the only way to honor their understanding of faith was to let one religion try to crush another through bloodshed. Who kept bringing their armies out of Europe, Mongolia, Egypt, Turkey and God knows where else."

"You made your peace with it, yet there are still shadows in your eyes. There are demons you have not laid to rest."

"As I now know well, a demon cannot be laid to rest, my lord. It's not the nature of a demon. It can only be sent back to its cell to rage and plot its next escape." Uthe shook his head. "The wisdom I have gained helped me provide useful advice to the Council and know the best ways to make that advice heard, at least some of the time. You serve the same role yourself. After so many years, everything you know and understands crowds in on you. You know things without actively knowing, because only in a peaceful, still acceptance does it make any sense. You find the answers in the utter quiet, a lack of action. You're a vessel, but instead of moving in the ocean, it moves through you and you stay, if not still, without destination."

"A very peaceful outlook for a vampire."

Uthe touched the braid running from Keldwyn's temple, feeling the rough texture of the meadow grass amid the silk strands. "Whereas you question faith like the serpent in the desert."

Keldwyn's eyes morphed into a snake's, a slit pupil and vivid gold irises, the effect so real Uthe jerked back. The Fae blinked and the illusion disappeared. Keldwyn closed a hand on his wrist. "My apologies, Lord Uthe. It's a form of glamor that comes easily to me. I was teasing you, in perhaps a grim way, but teasing nonetheless."

Uthe nodded, but when he tried to ease himself out of Keldwyn's grip, the Fae turned Uthe's hand over to examine his palm. "How is it you have calluses?"

"The dagger, again. Because I practice with my sword regularly, then and now, the calluses remain." Uthe tugged on his hand, managing to free it this time. "Forgive me, my lord, but it is time for me to take some blood. You said there would be a source for my use?"

"Of course." Kel seemed to focus on something internally. A communication, for Della emerged from the wood, skipping along with the dragon floating above her.

"Della is of a sufficient size and age to give you nourishment. And yes, she is high functioning enough to make that decision. She donates her blood to the humans' Red Cross. When Catriona asked if she would give you a similar amount of blood, she was more than willing. She has a generous heart."

As she drew closer, Keldwyn waved a hand, drawing her attention the way he'd done to put Rand to sleep. When her eyes followed the graceful ripple of his fingertips, he spoke a word and the child came to a swaying stop, blinking dreamily. The dragon made a questioning noise, landing on a tree near her. "In this state, she will feel no pain," Keldwyn explained.

"I don't understand my lord." Though Keldwyn had made his intentions clear, the constriction in Uthe's gut refused to process it until Kel said it straight out.

"She will provide your meal, Lord Uthe."

Chapter Eleven

"She is a child," Uthe said woodenly.

"She is a teenager, and old enough to give you a cup of blood without it causing a problem."

Bring him to me, boy. Hold him down. Hate them grabbing onto me, their whiny little pleas. Shut him up. Now!

Uthe stood up and walked away. He faced a magnificent tree covered with purple blooms. While the trees in his world were alive, they didn't reach down with branches like questing fingers and brush them over his shoulders as this one did. Risking it taking offense, he moved closer and pressed his forehead against the rough bark. Sensation. In the end, it was best to focus on sensation alone. Thought was where true pain lay.

Keldwyn was behind him. "If you had specific menu requirements, it would have been good to know them ahead of time."

"She is a child. I cannot drink from a child."

"I told you, it will not—"

"You've been among us long enough to know this." Uthe turned on the Fae. "While sex is not required when taking blood, I cannot set my lips to her throat without getting sexually aroused. I can block that so she would be unaware of it, even if she were not enchanted, but it still feels unclean to me. Wrong."

"My lord." Keldwyn drew Uthe's attention to the empty mead goblet he held in one hand. Kel tapped the short dagger at his own belt with the other. "I am aware of that, which was why my intent was to do it this way, by drawing the blood and having you drink from the cup."

It made logical sense. It was all logical, but the things that had been loosed in Uthe were incapable of being called back to rationality.

"I will not touch a child's blood. You may make what you wish of that, play your mind games, but that is as it is, Lord Keldwyn. If you have nothing available, then I should be fine for the next couple days, or we can summon a second mark from the..."

Keldwyn reached toward him. "Varick, I—"

Uthe knocked his hand away. "How many fucking times must I tell you not to call me by that name? Do not speak it. Ever." No matter that it held no memory of Uthe's father when Keldwyn spoke it. Instead, the word possessed a seductive purr that made Uthe want him to say it over and over.

"There is more to this."

"This quest and the right to fuck me don't give you the right to every thought I have," Uthe snapped. "Let her go. Free her. I cannot look upon her until you do."

"All right. It is done. Will you look?"

"Not yet." Uthe turned away and stared into the forest again. "Leave me alone. I need several moments to myself." He should have said 'respectfully,' honoring the courtesies, but what had hold of him now was ugly, coarse. He prayed Keldwyn would heed him.

The Fae was a weighted force at his back, but at length, he withdrew. Uthe let out a breath as he heard him speak to Della in low tones. The girl giggled and chattered something at him. She ran off, her sneakered feet pattering over the grass. Uthe closed his eyes, seeing her precocious expression. But he couldn't hold onto it. He knelt, began the 23rd Psalm. It was an eternal comfort, though when he imagined lying down in green pastures, he saw bloody and torn sheep. Lambs. He'd wondered why they'd eventually called Jesus the Lamb of God, because nothing was as helpless as a lamb. But they'd crucified him, hadn't they? Sacrificed him, proving the fragility of the man.

His message had endured, no matter how much it had been warped and twisted. Kindness, compassion, justice, balance. Mercy. They were universal truths, spoken by myriad godheads and the enlightened. Noble ideals, worthy of protecting. Though sometimes how often they were violated could destroy the heart beyond repair.

He rose, turned. Keldwyn was sitting a few feet away. When he spoke, his tone was casual, as if there'd been no conflict between them.

"The vampire you sired, the artist. He is quite close to one of our portals right now. One of my favorites, in the Tennessee mountains. Would he lend you his third mark servant for a feeding?"

"Yes. That would be acceptable, if we can reach Evan without delay to our journey."

"It will cause no more delay than a feeding here, my lord. He is the one who hungers to visit the Fae world, is he not?"

"Yes. He has badgered me about my relationship with you, suggesting in not-so-subtle ways all the things I could do to get him a pass to see the Fae world. I told him it wasn't an amusement park."

Keldwyn's lips quirked. "Rhoswen does not yet see the benefit of vampire tourism."

Gratitude swept through Uthe at Kel's dry humor. He also felt shame at his anger. Della and Catriona were playing again, dancing in a clasped hand circle through the meadow grass. Della was visibly clear of any enchantment, beyond the natural magic spun by a child's happiness. The barbed feeling in his lower belly released, allowing him a deeper breath.

"I offended you, Lord Uthe," Keldwyn said quietly. "It was not my intent."

"I know. You are as clever as I am, my lord. There is no need to pretend ignorance out of courtesy. I struck out in anger at past demons. You have my apologies."

Keldwyn leaned back on his elbows once more, his attention returning to the two girls. They waded into the stream, the unicorn high stepping behind them, her tail trailing through the sparkling water. As she bent her head to drink, the dragon landed on her rump. The mare shot him a warning look, then returned to her drinking. Uthe propped against the tree a few feet behind Keldwyn, watching the wind ripple the grass around him.

During the time he'd been dealing with his reaction to Della providing his meal, Uthe realized Kel had changed what he was wearing. He remembered Keldwyn's reaction to seeing him in jeans, but Uthe couldn't imagine that he made the same impression in casual wear as Keldwyn did in a simple sleeveless jerkin, tight brown leggings and boots, a warrior's garb that matched his now plaited hair. The Fae Lord looked even more dangerously appealing, if that were possible. The jerkin drew the eye to the point of the Fae's shoulder, the smooth curve of his biceps. He tilted his head, the pointed ear dipping as he glanced back at Uthe, then he returned his dark gaze to the girls. Uthe swallowed.

"Do you have children of your own, my lord?" he ventured. This pregnant silence wasn't something he wanted to prolong. Large things waited in such a silence, truths best not faced.

"Catriona is my child. Not by blood, but her father has ever been disinterested in her wellbeing. Her mother loved her, but died too young, only a few years after her birth. Her father pushed her out of the nest as soon as he felt she could fly on her own, which was according to his convenience, not her needs."

Joey W. Hill

Uthe shifted his gaze to the Fae female. She was using her wings to lift herself over the water, flicking water at Della with her toes. Della was splashing back, calling "no fair." Catriona swooped, caught the teenager in her arms and spun the two of them in wild circles in the air. The dragon dove around them in excitement. The unicorn settled on the bank, legs folded beneath her, and dipped her head to scratch her horn on a rock.

Catriona was laughing, and there was a light in her face that Uthe thought should never be extinguished, that could never be extinguished.

"Her father does not realize what a gift he denied himself. Or gave to you."

"Yes. She had trouble readjusting after her ordeal in the human world. Della helped her find her way back." At Uthe's puzzled look, Keldwyn frowned. "Lyssa did not tell you of this?"

"You have come up in conversation, my lord. Never your ward. Lyssa and I...we are close, but not in the manner of casual conversation, like you and I share."

Keldwyn inclined his head. "I was not sure how much Lyssa told you. She gained entry to our world by rescuing Catriona from yours. She'd been trapped in a tree for twenty years, because she went too deeply into an urban area that saps a young Fae's strength, and she was being chased by criminals. She saved herself by locking herself into a tree, as a dryad can do, but she did not have the strength to free herself. Nor could any of us free her, until Lady Lyssa...the details are not important now. It is done and over, and she is back here."

Keldwyn glanced at Uthe. "Though passage is limited between our worlds, Catriona's mother was permitted occasional excursions there. She had a great fondness for your world, which she passed on to her daughter. She was killed by two vampires. I will not go into details here, but it was based in the long enmity between our species."

Uthe grimaced. "It surprises me that Catriona would be

so welcoming. Or interested enough in our world to go there at all."

"I think her mother's life, short though it was, made a stronger impression than the circumstances of her death. Catriona was very young then. However, she has not been as successful in overcoming the trials of the past twenty years." Keldwyn's voice held his concern for his ward. "Before she was imprisoned, Catriona would have given her heart wherever it is needed, and never think of any danger to herself. She is more cautious now, a little sadder and wiser than she once was. I am glad for the wisdom, not for the sadness. There are times I miss her carefree recklessness, though I know she is safer without its impulsiveness."

Uthe felt a surge of anger, thinking of the young Fae trapped as Keldwyn described. "Could no one do anything to rescue her before twenty years had passed?"

"I was magic-bound, specifically prohibited from helping or being anywhere near her, though I kept as close a watch on her as the field around her permitted. The Queen was teaching a lesson to our other young, and Catriona was the example. Though I do understand Rhoswen's motives and knew it was not a simple decision for her, it made for an uneasy twenty years between us. I think her willingness to give Catriona access to Della was a way of balancing the scales."

"Did it?"

"The scales between me and the Queen have gone up and down so often it wearies me to keep track of who is seated where, and whose turn it is to be on top and whose it is to hold anchor at the bottom. Catriona is back, she is safe, she is wiser and she is not irreparably broken. We live a long, long time, Lord Uthe. Often that is all that is necessary for things to be forgiven, if not forgotten. Life goes on, with all its priorities."

"Yes." Uthe cocked his head. "Do you have blood-related children?"

"I have had seven," Keldwyn said absently. "Four males, three females."

"Really?" Uthe was intrigued enough to leave the tree and sink cross-legged in the grass next to him. "Seven mothers? Wives?"

Keldwyn shot him an amused look. "While we don't suffer from fertility issues to the extent vampires do, high Fae do not reproduce frequently. Because of that, like vampires, we do not use birth control. Every child produced is a gift. If a parent like Catriona's father is not cognizant of that, there are plenty willing to step in to take in a babe. Maysie would have raised her in a heartbeat if I could not. In my case, the five women in question, for two bore twins, were not mated to me. They were affectionate yet casual couplings. And they were good mothers. They loved my children and I...loved them."

The truth of it jolted Uthe. "They're gone."

Keldwyn's expression emptied, the black gaze an abyss that Uthe thought might reflect the deepest well of the male's soul. "They did not have your longevity?" Uthe ventured, his voice low. He didn't want to ripple those depths if Kel didn't wish them disturbed.

"The twins might have lived to my age, because they were born of high Fae mothers. The others...they would not have lived as long, but they would have had a few hundred years. War took all of them. My first two sons died at my side in battle, one of the conflicts within factions of the Seelie Fae. Then there was the Great War between the Unseelie and Seelie, prompted by King Tabor's brother and Rhoswen's mother. That one took one daughter, one son. Graenad fought like a dancer, such grace and beauty in wielding sword and magic. But it could not save her."

Keldwyn kept his gaze on Catriona. "Like the humans and their WWI, we supposed that war would end all of them, because it was so horrific, but the one thing that links all humanoid species is our hunger for conflict. We had a usurper to the throne of the Seelie, and once again a civil war resulted that divided the Fae. I fought on the opposite side from my remaining three children. All three were killed, their cause defeated. I was able to see my last surviving daughter before she succumbed. She spat on me, cursed me as a traitor. And died."

His melodious voice didn't falter in the telling, yet when Keldwyn fell silent, Uthe could hear the discordant keys and notes of a broken song in the absence of words. He remembered the bitterness in Kel's voice on the plane. He'd attributed any dark corners in Kel's personality to the conflict and loss of Reghan, but that was far too narrow of a view. Tragedy and loss wasn't a singular occurrence in a mortal life, let alone an immortal one. And to lose seven children...

Uthe shifted, his side brushing the Fae Lord's tense shoulder. They sat that way for some time without speaking.

"Until this journey began, you did not ask me much about myself," Keldwyn said suddenly. "You asked me about my world, my relationship with the courts, all the things it is good and prudent for a Council member to know about the Fae liaison."

"You've placed a binding on me that's personal. Perhaps it's my way of evening the playing field."

"You told me I may have your body, that it is just ashes and dust. You deliberately indicated it wasn't personal."

"So I did."

"I could make you acknowledge differently."

"I think I just did that myself, my lord." Uthe met his gaze. Keldwyn's flickered, and then he sat up, propping himself on one arm. When he leaned toward Uthe, Uthe tensed. Keldwyn paused.

"A male brave enough to risk incineration to save a squire cannot fear a kiss made with open heart and clear eyes."

"Nothing is more personal or unpredictable as fear, my lord."

"Perhaps that is why I feel a need to challenge it now. To show you this is nothing to fear." But Keldwyn held still. "What is your greatest fear, Lord Uthe?"

"To not complete the task set before me." His gaze strayed over Keldwyn's mouth. "Everything that challenges that is something to be feared."

"Very well then." Keldwyn touched his jaw. "Should you falter in this quest—and I have no reason to think you will—I will bring it to fruition for you, using whatever resources I can compel or command to serve it. You have my promise and my oath."

Kel's eyes were so dark against that moonlit luminescence. How could one trust a being of light and shadow, one so ethereal and beautiful he seemed a walking fantasy? But the Fae had just spoken an oath that grounded him in Uthe's reality. It filled his heart with pain and need, and he wanted to reach out and touch. He didn't, his fingers curling into a prohibitive fist.

"You trust my oath to you, do you not?" Keldwyn asked.

"I do." Uthe said it without hesitation, which made the Fae's eyes warm, though his lips remained set in a thin line.

"But you do not trust me in other ways. You are wary of me having the upper hand." Keldwyn chuckled, sat back. "Nothing so suspicious as two males who have spent decades mired in politics.

"Sometimes warfare seems preferable, doesn't it?" Uthe mused. "The other can be wearying."

"It does. Until you're in the midst of bloodshed."

Studying the Fae's elegant profile, the resilient line of jaw and chiseled cheek bone, Uthe thought of what he'd learned about the Fae's manner of communicating. He was fluent in almost every language of diplomacy Uthe knew, plus some he'd taught Uthe since they'd become acquainted. He suspected he'd done the same for Kel, since Uthe had seen him use a few deft twists from Uthe's own arsenal. Lyssa had warned them the Fae were elusive in their motives, that they could turn a situation around and make you believe it was your idea. Or they could pull an unexpected outcome or direction from a carefully planned strategy. Probably because their strategy was more carefully planned, or had a wider view of the playing field and beyond.

Uthe remembered Kel's quick, raw declaration in the sorceress's cave, when he'd stated his reasons for accompanying Uthe were all his own. And now, he'd told him of his children. Uthe didn't think Kel had revealed those things as part of ulterior motives. The Fae had given him truth, opening his soul as Uthe had.

"I'm surprised you'd entrust me with such a personal recollection as your children, my lord," he said carefully, his mind spinning at the implications.

"You asked whether I had any."

"But you gave me more than I asked. You rarely do that."

"You told me yourself. You have Ennui. Rather than dealing with psychotic rages and impulse control crimes, it appears you have won the prize of rampant memory loss. Eventually you might forget all you are told." Keldwyn tilted his head back, his dark eyes mere slits, but Uthe read the acid humor there. "A bottomless wishing well to whom I can tell my secrets."

Uthe was amused. "Very insightful of you, my lord."

Before the battle of Hattin, he remembered his comrades in arms exchanging quips about the heat and dust... *"In five minutes, we'll be crossing Heaven's Gates, mes frères. No more sand in our arse cracks..."*

"Have you ever ridden a rollercoaster, Lord Keldwyn?"

"No." The Fae's brows arched. "Why would you ask?"

"I assume you have experienced a great many things. It intrigues me, what we have chosen *not* to experience."

"Hmm. Roller coasters are metal and electronics, and separate me from the earth. They are not the same pleasurable experience as they might be for others."

"There were wooden coasters before the metal ones."

"True enough. Perhaps because I have ridden dragons, I didn't see the appeal." Keldwyn gave him a considering look. "Would you like to ride a dragon sometime, Lord Uthe?"

"If the dragon has no objection."

Keldwyn smiled, but Uthe continued to study his profile when he went back to watching the girls. "You've been visiting the human world for some time. You can handle the energies that sap the younger Fae. You have served as regent for your queen when she was absent. King Tabor takes your advice. You are considerably powerful among your kind."

"More so than some, less than others."

"Modesty is not your natural state, my lord. Cunning, however, is more natural to you than breathing."

Keldwyn dropped his head back, studying the interlacing of tree branches above them. "What is your point, Lord Uthe?"

"Lady Lyssa told us she first met you in the forests when she was fugitive. I don't believe it was a chance meeting, and I suspect she no longer does either. When she was a child, Fae assassins were sent after her and her mother. She said that King Tabor brought that to a halt when he took the throne, but I suspect a different perspective influenced his thinking and that of those around him."

"The timing was right. Everyone was weary of killing," Keldwyn said. "I told them she would be more vampire than Fae, and likely have no power to wield."

"You were wrong." When Keldwyn offered him an enigmatic look, Uthe lifted a brow. "I stand corrected, my lord. You did say 'likely', did you not?"

"I knew her father. There was little chance she'd be born powerless. However, the political landscape in the Fae world changes quickly. By the time she embraced her power, if she had any, I knew she'd no longer be a target."

Those four words, "I knew her father" were filled with

things that would fill a thousand conversations...or were so precious they'd never be part of one. Uthe remembered the unexpected twist of jealousy he'd felt last time they spoke of Reghan. It was a pointless and unfounded emotion, yet the barb was still there when Keldwyn referred to him now. *You have rights to nothing but what he gives you now, and what little you can give to him, Varick.*

It startled him to hear him refer to himself by his given name. Fortunately, Keldwyn distracted him.

"My children were old enough to make their own decisions," the Fae Lord said. "I suffer painful regrets but not guilt. Aggression and conflict are innate to humanoid species. Just as there is no one way to most things worth embracing, there is no one way to maintain peace or restore it. One ruler requires a show of strength to respect borders, a threat of retaliation the only thing that will back him or her down. Another needs just the right amount of manipulation to feel it is his or her idea to not draw arms. And sometimes, regrettably, battle is the way to peace. Peace is never a permanent state. It requires constant vigilance for all involved."

"Peace is not very peaceful for those in charge of keeping it."

Keldwyn made a noise of agreement. "And the quality of peace itself must be considered. Things might be peaceful under a brutal dictator who will execute anyone who disagrees with him or her, but it is hardly conducive to happiness...or long term peace. Peace can be part of a benevolent tyranny, as it is under Lady Lyssa."

It was one of their typical discussions, a casual meandering through philosophy, theory and personal experience. But Uthe knew he'd made an important connection between Keldwyn's motives for being a liaison and the loss of his children. Maybe that was why his next question was one he had no right asking, unless he wanted to give the Fae Lord the right to dig just as deeply into his soul. Or maybe Kel was already so deep, Uthe was just trying to catch up.

"Was he the love of your life, then?"

He didn't say Lord Reghan. He knew he didn't need to do so. The mortal world might scoff at such a phrase, and the immortal world deem it endearingly childlike, but perhaps his heart had remained embedded in a time when such a declaration was a badge of honor, a favor to be worn in every endeavor.

If Keldwyn's decision to serve as a liaison, mediator, diplomat, devil's advocate or sacrificial lamb, depending on the situation, had been motivated by all those he'd loved and lost to war and conflict, especially Reghan, it would be the height of pettiness for Uthe to be jealous of that bond, seeing the good it had possibly done. It didn't abate his tension as he waited for the response.

"I do not believe the love of your life can be someone who doesn't love you the same way. No god is so cruel." Keldwyn pursed his lips. "Unless it's a form of atonement, for crimes from this or a previous life."

"I think I have been a good influence on you, my lord. You're pondering the wisdom of God's decisions and accepting His Judgment."

Keldwyn snorted and lay back fully on the grass, dropping a forearm over his eyes. "I am in no mood for debates today. I'm napping. Let me know if those silly children have need of us."

Uthe made an accepting grunt. He watched the slight rise and fall of Keldwyn's chest under the jerkin, the chest hair revealed at the vee neckline. The sunlight made the light mat of curling hair gleam. Uthe imagined unlacing the jerkin to trace all the layers of muscle with fingers or tongue. Yet as he thought about Kel and his children, he saw past the strength and thought of thick glass. Resilient, but not shatter proof.

"It does not matter how powerful a being thinks he is, Lord Uthe," Keldwyn said abruptly. "There is always someone else more powerful, who can take away what you value most. I learned that with Reghan. I thought I could save him with strength. I could not. I protected his daughter with cunning, which I learned was a far more powerful weapon, though it takes its cost, which at times is dearer than what the sword can take from you."

"What is that?"

Keldwyn didn't remove his arm, so his eyes remained hidden. "Trust. The freedom to love without cynicism, without calculation to maneuver things into the best position for yourself. Which is not love, of course. Cunning can become a permanent and irreversible state."

"I disagree. It is a language. Once understood, the true soul of the individual using it is revealed. And maybe once he knows that, he can stop using cunning all the time and trust someone with his true feelings."

"Your use of third person is clunky and transparent, Lord Uthe."

Uthe didn't disagree. Catriona was standing on the unicorn's back. She did a backward somersault, helped by her wings, and dove into the deeper end of the pond, to Della's delight.

"How are you doing on deciphering my language, Lord Uthe?" Keldwyn said after that pause.

"It's by turns a fascinating and puzzling endeavor, my lord. It tends to change quite rapidly, like an encrypted code. But it holds my attention sufficiently. It hasn't become tedious."

Keldwyn's lips curved, their appeal even more noticeable with his arm in place over the upper part of his face. "I am glad of it. Tell me what you have deciphered, that is uppermost in your mind right now."

"And why would I do that?"

"Because I might share the same, to balance the scales. I suspect our thoughts intersect and complement one another, my lord."

"Perhaps you should go first, then, since you brought up the subject."

The lips curved even more. Uthe suppressed a desire to lean forward, touch the Fae's mouth. He settled for plucking a piece of meadow grass and rolling it in his palms, inhaling the sweet scent of its core.

"Fine. But you have been reluctant to go down this path before. I will not stop this time, Varick. Should I proceed, or do you lack courage?"

Uthe chewed on the grass, found it as flavorful as its scent. "Do as you will, my lord." He was risking himself, he knew, but they were in more vulnerable territory right now, the both of them. The energy charging the air between them—despite the sunny day, their casual poses and the young ones playing nearby—told him so.

"You have been the right hand to two Council leaders and, while capable of leading, you have displayed no obvious desire to take over that leadership role," Keldwyn said. "That could be explained easily enough by your commitment to this quest. Yet during those social occasions where vampires orchestrate sexual play between their servants and often participate themselves in certain ways, you do not. You set the stage, you watch, you provide aftercare to your servant to tell her she has pleased you, but you do not actively participate in front of others. I suspect that has less to do with your celibacy vow and more to do with yourself. You are far more conservative than other vampires."

These were things a careful observer could deduce, though Uthe was impressed that Keldwyn had figured out he was genuinely conservative about open sexual displays. He made a quiet sound of acceptance and Keldwyn continued.

"You chose to take the Templar oath and serve them, not only for the duration of their recorded existence, but to the present day." Keldwyn shifted the arm enough that Uthe could see the fathomless pools of his eyes hidden in the shadows beneath it. "The most meaningful relationships in your life have been based in service. You are divided between nature and need, Lord Uthe. You cannot deny your Dominant vampire nature, and it shows itself in your leadership capabilities, your savage fighting skills. But you need service and—dare I say, in some very important, key way—the opportunity to submit to a lover. You need to let go of things so deeply buried inside you, it will take a very particular type of Dominant male lover to give you that opportunity."

Uthe wanted to shift his gaze, but he resisted the urge. He was remembering what Mariela had said. *Someone who is as much your Master as you are mine.* "An impressive sales pitch. Very compelling."

"You have perfected that poker face. But just as you are learning to read mine, I am learning to read yours." The arm shifted, Keldwyn's eyes disappearing again. "Your turn. Would you like to balance the scales?"

No, he wouldn't. Kel's words had sunk into him, holding him in place, weighing him down in a way that made his body heavy with anticipation, fueled by that very need he'd just mentioned. Offered. Uthe stared off into the forest, and felt rather than saw Keldwyn shift his arm again to stare at him. His skin felt hot, and there was an odd quiver in his chest, like a butterfly had been let loose there.

"I have a request, my lord," he said.

"If it is my inclination or in my power to give, it is yours."

Uthe smiled at the qualification, but his heartbeat remained erratic. "I would like you to reinstate the terms of your binding. You may demand of me what you wish, as part of the price of your assistance."

Keldwyn pushed himself up on his elbows and sat up. "Look at me, Varick."

Uthe turned his head, met him eye to eye. Keldwyn's mouth was close, too close. He couldn't take his eyes away from his lips, the slope of his jaw, the pulse beating in his elegant throat. That autumn scent was surrounding him. Apples and earth. It changed from day to day, but all within the same spectrum that let Uthe identify him by nose alone.

"If I do so, it will not be part of a barter," the Fae Lord said. "It will simply be what it is between us. Do you understand?"

The edge of command was in his voice, and raw need, volatile and strong. Yet he had it so controlled the demand of it felt like a fire pressing against Uthe's body. "Yes."

Keldwyn held his gaze. "Very well. But before I say yes or no, tell me what you know of me. I would hear you say it aloud."

Uthe didn't flinch, his voice coming out even and steady, no matter what was hammering inside him like a crazed lunatic. "When you have pursued a relationship with another, you are in control. Your preference for that is male. Your sexual liaisons with females still require elements of dominance, but you don't seek prolonged relationships with them, merely the enjoyment of coupling. Your deepest pleasure comes from holding the reins, exploring the lines of power and that give and take. It is why you are so effective in your politics, whether it is with the Vampire Council, Queen Rhoswen, or King Tabor and the powerful members of their courts. Yet behind closed doors, your craving is to exercise that desire on a male who is a Dominant...just not as Dominant as yourself."

"And how long have you realized this?"

"For almost as long as you've served as our liaison. Recognizing another Dominant is not a difficult thing for a vampire. Learning the shape of it is the challenge and the pleasure."

Pleasure was an understatement. In watching Keldwyn handle a volatile interaction with Belizar or Stewart, Uthe had occasionally realized mid-negotiation he wasn't calculating rebuttals to rescue his fellow Council members. He was doing nothing more than absorbing exactly how deftly Kel worked the conversation where he intended it to go, eliciting the response he wanted and gaining submission and acceptance to his direction. Most times they didn't even realize how effectively he'd done it. Lyssa usually did, if the gleam in her eye and set of her mouth were any indication. Her disagreements with Keldwyn mesmerized all of them, two Dominants fencing with words, body language. Uthe had never seen one get the upper hand on the other, but more than once watching the two of them had sent him to bed at dawn aching.

"You are a Master, Lord Keldwyn, in every sense of that word, in every aspect of your life. It defines your relationships at every level. Despite all his responsibility and leadership abilities, Reghan submitted to you sexually during the time you were lovers. He did not love you as you loved him, but that didn't matter. His loss, first to Lyssa's mother, and then to his execution, destroyed your desire to love, or to be anyone's Master, ever since."

Uthe didn't usually make the mistake of striking a nerve he hadn't intended to strike, but at Keldwyn's silence, the slight stiffening of his body, he wondered if that was what he'd done. Before he could offer an apology, Keldwyn touched his face, a bemused look crossing his face. "You have...stubble."

He put his hand up where Keldwyn was touching him to confirm it. "The dagger has that effect. Gives me body hair, facial hair. It disappears after I don't wear it for a few days. It helped me blend with the Templars, because they wore beards to increase their standing against the Saracens. They thought a man without a beard was little better than a boy."

"If they thought that, they've never sampled you up close." Keldwyn sat back. Despite the segue, Uthe could tell the Fae was turning over Uthe's words. It was in the set of his face, the look in his eyes. Uthe reached out and closed his hand on Keldwyn's shoulder.

"I apologize, my lord. I did not mean to open an old wound, asking about your children or Reghan."

"It was quid pro quo, for my misstep with Della. But it is

never an old wound, and it has never closed or healed. No apologies are necessary. I opened the line of questioning, dug into what you might perceive as your own weaknesses, so deserve the results of it."

"I wasn't striking back."

"I know that. You are a unique type of vampire, Lord Uthe. Dominant in all the necessary ways, and sincere about it. Yet you are more than that one thing. Your cunning and your strength defies a single definition. I seek to offer you a place to go where neither is necessary. A place where the relentless pace and restraint you have had to maintain on everything else is no longer necessary."

Uthe swallowed and looked toward Della and Catriona. "It is a kind offer, but I cannot embrace the desires of a child, my lord. Some things, if you let go even a moment, you lose for all time. I become prey, waiting for the right predator to notice. I will not be a burden, requiring protection from those I value."

Keldwyn nodded at Catriona. As if feeling his regard, she turned, waving in his direction. "She has some power," the Fae observed, "but it is like a drop of rain in a thunderstorm, and that thunderstorm represents the dangers that could take her from me. Protecting her is an honor, not a burden, because of the joy she can give the world. But that's not why I protect her. I protect her because of who she is in my heart. Because when I draw breath, I know she is in that breath. We are connected." Keldwyn brought his attention back to Uthe. "Love can often be a heavy burden, my lord. But without it, we are empty vessels, and the lightness of an empty vessel is a curse."

Uthe went still. To an outside observer it might look as if Keldwyn had cast a spell over him, and maybe he had. The bridge their words had built was overwhelming, the implications of it.

Go ahead, try to change the subject, the Fae's fixed expression told Uthe. *But I am holding your soul in my hands and we both know it.*

"I enjoy our conversations, my friend." Keldwyn spoke after a weighted pause, sliding a knuckle down the front of Uthe's tunic. "And you look more comfortable in Fae clothing. A tunic and leggings suits you better than your human wear."

"It is similar to what we wore at the turn of the millennium."

"That is my point." Uthe tried not to react as Keldwyn's hand dropped to his belt, tracing the bitter end of the strap to his upper thigh. In Uthe's cross-legged position, Keldwyn could slide his hand under the tunic to fondle Uthe's cock and testicles through the stretched, formfitting leggings, but the Fae only hinted at that with the direction of his hand. He slid his palm over Uthe's thigh, outlining the layers of muscle there.

"On a day as beautiful as this, one's impulses must be obeyed. Come down here, my lord. Stretch out with me."

Uthe glanced toward the stream. The girls were disappearing into the woods, the dragon and unicorn genially trailing behind.

"They are going exploring. They will not be back until I summon them. Come down here, Varick." Keldwyn's expression changed, that subtle shift that had Uthe's cock stiffening and his hands feeling too empty, his heart too full.

He stretched out next to him and then tensed, surprised, when Keldwyn pushed him to his back and shifted on top of him in one graceful movement, adjusting Uthe's thighs so he was pressed between them. For all his leanness, the Fae was more solid than one would expect, weighted with firm muscle.

"Yes, Lord Uthe. I will grant your request. The terms of the binding are restored. You will submit to my demands, as long as they do not conflict with your God's."

No caveats this time about those demands being sexual in nature, or about it being in force only until the quest was complete. Just as Kel had said—no bartering this time.

Chest to chest, groin to groin and Keldwyn's thighs spreading Uthe's open to pin him to the ground. Keldwyn was aroused already, but he didn't adjust any clothing. Instead, he filled Uthe's vision as he bent his head and began to nibble at Uthe's lips, his fingers sliding along Uthe's face and throat, caressing the line of jaw and carotid, the shape of his ears, his skull beneath his short hair. Uthe's lips parted as Keldwyn applied skillful short flicks of his tongue, a smooth tracing, then another short nip, continuing that torment until Uthe wanted his mouth fully on his, his tongue invading, capturing, a sucking, all-encompassing heat and strength.

Yet Keldwyn kept up the seductive tease with tip of tongue, light brushes of lips, a sharp press of his tooth. When he licked Uthe's fangs, Uthe bit back a groan. He realized his hands were on Keldwyn's hips, fingers digging into the upper rise of his narrow, tight ass.

"We are two immortals, at least by human terms," Keldwyn said thickly, his thumb stroking Uthe's jugular. "With all that time, the perfect day would be to lie here for hours, kissing you. Just your mouth, your face, your throat, in a million different ways, until you came simply from me rubbing my body against yours and kissing your hungry mouth."

He couldn't suppress the groan this time, for Keldwyn not only bit his lip, but pressed his groin more firmly against Uthe's. "Your cock is getting hard and thick, Lord Uthe. But I want to hear what you want me to do to your mouth. Beg me to kiss you, really kiss you."

Uthe vowed he wasn't going to do that. But Keldwyn knew he would, because he returned to kissing, nipping, licking and teasing until Uthe's body was shuddering beneath his. The friction between their bodies, the rub of cock against cock, contributed to Uthe's rising need, but even in his fevered mind, his focus was on that mouth. That hot, wet, firm, sensuous, full mouth, and all the things it was doing to his. Keldwyn moved to nip his jaw, tease his ear with heated breath and whisper things in his own language. Uthe didn't understand the words, but the intent was enough, especially when Kel's teeth grazed Uthe's throat.

His self-control snapped, but Keldwyn anticipated him. Before he could shove up from the ground, try to roll them and turn this into something Uthe could control better, the Fae Lord had shifted so his thigh was pushed between Uthe's legs, mashing his testicles into the base of his ass. His fingers were wrapped around Uthe's throat, holding him to the ground. Uthe knew Fae were stronger than vampires, but Keldwyn had rarely shown it so blatantly. He'd also done it without pause, warning or admonition. The Fae just kept kissing him. Sometimes his tongue would snake in a little deeper, but just as quickly retreat, teasing him with what he could offer him.

"Please..." Uthe growled it, desperate.

"Please what, my lord?" Keldwyn dipped his head to nuzzle his ear. "What do you need from me? What can I give you?"

Strength was not the only weapon a warrior had. Uthe shot a hand up to grab hold of Keldwyn's nape, determined he'd just slam his mouth onto the Fae's and be done with it. As fast as he was, Keldwyn was faster. He twisted away and manacled Uthe's hand in his own, shoving it to the ground next to him. Heat shimmered under Uthe's knuckles and he jerked, but the grasses were already wrapping around his wrist, forearms and biceps, holding his arm to the ground. Keldwyn forced his other arm down on the other side for the same treatment. They were the same meadow grasses Catriona had twined into Keldwyn's hair, but Keldwyn's magic reinforced their strength, held him fast. The edges cut into his arms, a sharp kiss of pain. Keldwyn's eyes were like heated coal as he bent to kiss Uthe again.

Uthe tried to snap at him. It had worked before, the threat of taking Kel's blood without his consent. Glancing up at the tree shading them, Keldwyn lifted one hand. A branch quivered, then snapped, dropping neatly into his hand. He forced it into Uthe's mouth like a bit, binding it around his head with more of those enchanted grasses. His expression unchanged, implacable, he bent to resume his torment of Uthe's mouth. With the stick gag in the way, everything was even more sensitive as he traced Uthe's stretched lips, nibbling on them with short, concise presses of his teeth, darting his tongue in above and below the stick, adding to the wood flavor with the heat of his mouth. He might look unperturbed by Uthe's resistance, but his exceptionally large, throbbing cock pushed against Uthe's suggested it was fueling his desire, as much as Keldwyn's mastery was provoking his.

Mastery. A word summoned by his lust, not logic. Lust was lust. Yes, it could spiral to a level where the mind ceased to function, but only if he allowed it, if he dropped his formidable discipline and self-control. He'd never been out of control with a lover. Nothing could override his discipline, the demands of his brain. Yet he was getting closer than he had in...ever. From nothing more than having the Fae stretched out on him for a slow, leisurely kissing where the Fae seemed to have nothing better to do.

"This is not your brain sickness," the Fae muttered, lifting his head and pinning Uthe with an expression that said he might be the one in control, but he was far from detached. "You will not escape the truth of what this is by lying to yourself."

He'd been about to summon that as his next internal defense, and it wasn't an illogical one. It could in fact be a symptom of the Ennui, his breakdown of self-discipline. But he didn't want it to be. God help him.

"Is it your pride that keeps you from begging for one simple kiss?" The Fae's eyes were obsidian fire.

Uthe shook his head. It was just too much. He was about to erupt like a volcano from a surfeit of pressure, and he didn't mean the seed boiling in his balls. The pressure came from the need for an emotional release, a storm roused by this devastating assault on his mouth. Vampires were masters at tormenting their servants sexually, bringing them to the brink of screaming orgasms, but they didn't usually use such intimate tactics as this unless...unless they had greater feelings for their servant than had heretofore been sanctioned in the vampire world. They did this kind of thing if they loved their servant, if they wanted to possess and cherish them, above and beyond all other relationships.

Keldwyn returned to his assault. Back to his throat, up to the jaw, and playing with his mouth around the gag again. Now Uthe regretted trying to bite him, because he would have liked to feel more of the press of his lips than this teasing play gave him. Keldwyn was a fascinating mix. Unquestionably male, but the long hair, the sensitive lips and sculpted cheekbones offered some of the erotic effects of the female form. He needed to stop. He was getting lost...

"You are not lost, Lord Uthe. I have you right here, and I am not letting you go. Now ask, damn you."

He'd only said it in a garbled way, through the gag, but the Fae had heard it. Just as he heard what Uthe said now. "Please. Kiss me."

Part demand and plea, but thank God, it was close enough. Keldwyn released the gag. It undid Uthe, how gently he dislodged it from behind Uthe's fangs before he returned to the violence of his passion, sealing his mouth over Uthe's lips, his tongue stabbing deep and thick into Uthe's mouth. Uthe yanked against the bindings holding his arms. But Keldwyn wouldn't give him that freedom, which only made the reward of his full kiss more potent.

He took his time, just as he'd warned. He captured Uthe's tongue, sucked on it, flicked it the way he'd tease his dick if he had his mouth on it. Then he bit Uthe's tongue, held it prisoner as he stroked Uthe's face and throat, squeezing the latter to stimulate that vampire erogenous zone. Once he released his tongue, it was so they could once again mate and part, an ongoing dance inside one another's mouths. Keldwyn had left his knee pressed into Uthe's crotch, an intentional discomfort that kept Uthe immobilized from the waist down, though Keldwyn's cock was firmly against his hip and upper thigh, a tantalizing promise. Keldwyn's mouth was his only avenue to bliss. But that pinioning knee, the pain of it combined with the torment of Kel's mouth, as well as the effect of being helpless like this to the other male's lust, was driving things to an unexpected summit.

Uthe realized he'd been moaning, a deep throated response to the Fae's demands. Keldwyn had been answering with savage whispers, sensual chuckles and rumbles of encouragement. When the Fae at last drew back, Uthe stared up at him with glassy eyes, mouth wet, chest heaving and loins drawn tight with an erection that had Keldwyn's full attention as he flipped up the front panel of the tunic and studied it, straining against the fabric of the leggings. His gaze slid upward, slow as a sword sliding along flesh and opening everything vital inside. He studied the tautness of Uthe's abdomen, every rigid muscle. Keldwyn loosened the laces of Uthe's tunic in the front, spreading it open so he could trace his chest with his fingertips.

"You are trembling, my lord." Keldwyn's voice was soft as a heated breeze. "You fight the restraint, but it allows you the freedom of your desires. I am tempted to keep you this way always. You are breathtaking. I want to fuck you into oblivion and yet, there is something about staying this way, on the edge of such anticipation…it is an enchantment whose power can only build and build until we would both gladly die of it, would we not?"

He didn't seem to expect an answer, but something cracked inside Uthe. He gasped as if he'd been stabbed. Keldwyn's eyes darkened, and then Uthe made a noise of pain as he bent, pressed his lip to Uthe's pectoral, over his heart.

Shifting next to Uthe, Keldwyn slid his arms under Uthe's back and thighs. The restraining grasses loosened and he turned Uthe over, a swift but controlled movement to ensure Uthe wasn't tumbled on his face, a contrast to when Kel had been rough and demanding in other ways. As soon as Uthe was lowered face down to the earth, the meadow grass reclaimed its hold on his arms.

Keldwyn straddled his back, putting his hands on Uthe's head to ensure his forehead was pressed into the soft earth, his chin tilted down to keep his mouth and nose free of it. Then he folded Uthe's tunic up until it was underneath his armpits, exposing his back, and unlaced the sides of the leggings so he could jerk them down to Uthe's thighs. To do that, he slid his hand under Uthe's abdomen to bring him briefly off the ground. But then he pushed him down again so his cock pressed into the grass, the blades an edgy, cool friction along his flesh.

Uthe didn't speak. Something was laboring inside his chest, his lower belly and clogging his throat. Keldwyn had effectively blindfolded him, forcing his face into the grass this way. His senses were still sharp enough that he smelled the fragrant lubricant. Keldwyn had implied magic was not to be squandered on the things a Fae could do himself, and Uthe recognized an unexpected benefit to that prudence. If Kel lubricated his cock at the blink of a thought, it might be more convenient, but the anticipation he built doing it this way was a different kind of magic. Uthe felt his small movements on top of him as the Fae worked the oil over his cock. Uthe imagined what it looked like, the long fingers curled over the glistening shaft, rubbing the flared head.

Just like with his kiss, Keldwyn was determined to tease Uthe into full madness. He worked the head of his cock into Uthe's rectum, rotating just inside the gate to stimulate before he pulled out slow. Then he did it again. The incredible friction was too brief to take Uthe to full climax, but it was something almost more intense. He'd done things to reduce Mariela to mindless gibberish, but pride and emotional abstinence had kept him from contemplating such a state for himself. Keldwyn was proving him wrong.

When Keldwyn finally let himself sink to the hilt, Uthe groaned, a near shout. Desire was a knife cutting open his insides, the blood in his stiff cock jamming him against the unyielding ground. The Fae made a grim sound of fierce pleasure.

"This is where I belong," the Fae said, his chest against Uthe's back as he bent, bit his ear. He was still fully clothed, except for what had been necessary to remove to fuck Uthe, another tease. "Your ass has needed filling for some time, my lord."

He withdrew again and went back to that shallow in-and-out movement, using the ridged corona to inflict mind-shattering sensation. Uthe's hips were rising, trying to take more, trying to give his aching cock relief.

"Ask for permission to come."

"No." Uthe strangled it out. "Not part of the deal."

"It is if you interpret it literally."

"Liberally, you mean... Oh, fuck..."

This time Keldwyn shoved in for full penetration, his testicles slapping against Uthe's scrotum, an admonishment and provocation. Uthe nearly bellowed a protest as Keldwyn pulled all the way out. He pressed a knee into the ground against one of Uthe's calves, so it was unmistakable what he was doing next. He leisurely began to masturbate, even humming a fucking tune as he did it, though he couldn't conceal the strain in the syllables. Uthe hadn't cursed this much in decades. He'd be doing penance for days. Fuck it, he would just press into the earth, hump the damn dirt and...

Uthe snarled as those twisted grasses twined around his dick, inflicting a series of sharp little cuts. More grasses did the same around his balls, cinching him tight.

"Cheating bastard," he said.

"Not cheating. Your climax belongs to me, and you will ask me for it. You understand the role between Master and subjugated, Lord Uthe, and you are bound to me." Keldwyn was suddenly fully against his back, cock pressed against Uthe's ass, his voice uttering a sexual threat up against his ear. "You asked for my binding, Varick. Asked for it. Deep inside, you knew that would result in me being even more demanding, crueler. Give me what I want, and I will give you something better than ecstasy."

When he wasn't keeping close company with vampires, Uthe had been able to observe celibacy for inordinately long stretches. Given a vampire's nature, it had been difficult beyond description, but he'd maintained. This was agony. Sheer, heated, blue balls agony, especially as Keldwyn resumed that rhythmic rock against his legs that said he was jacking off again. He wasn't even allowing Uthe to watch. By the Holy Relics, a blade of grass had an edge like paper, and he'd never been so cognizant of that as he was now.

Keldwyn released with a quiet groan, his hand gripping the back of Uthe's thigh. His heated seed splashed on Uthe's ass, his naked back. It should have been demeaning, humiliating, but that wasn't what Uthe felt. He was in pain, aroused to the point of ferocity, and the things hurting inside and through him were so agonizing the only answer was release. Meditation and prayer were beyond him right now.

"Please." He closed his eyes, pressed his face into the earth. "My lord, I would ask your permission to come."

The bindings around his cock released. A relieved breath shuddered out of him. Keldwyn's hands curved over his buttocks and parted them. "Whenever you so desire, my lord." The weight of his hands increased as he bent over Uthe, and then his mouth pressed against the crinkled ring of Uthe's anus. Keldwyn put his clever tongue to work there before Uthe could think of a way to stop him.

Another first for him, and oh...Mother of God, bless her and forgive his blasphemy, there was nothing he could do now except get swept away.

He came violently, hips jerking. Keldwyn's jaw worked against his buttocks, the slippery tease of his tongue deep in Uthe's channel, his hands bruising in their grip on his ass. Though Uthe was sure it was no more than the usual amount of time, it seemed he came and came, especially with Keldwyn's unrelenting tongue spurring him on.

When Keldwyn finally stopped, Uthe was spent and trembling like a baby, his hands in fists inside the grass net. Keldwyn stretched out beside him, his clothes adjusted as if he hadn't just fucked him to the point of begging. However, his expression was taut and glittering, the look of a male temporarily satisfied, only getting started with everything he wanted from his lover.

"Why are you doing this?" Uthe's voice was hoarse. "Is this simply pleasure, my lord? You haven't had a suitable playmate for awhile?"

"Is it easier if you can define it?" Keldwyn's tone was light, but Uthe caught the edge. They'd gone down this road before, and the Fae's tolerance of it had been short then. Uthe didn't feel up for a battle of wits. He asked a different question instead.

"What's better than ecstasy?"

"Peace."

The bindings on Uthe's arms loosened, freeing him, and the Fae lay back, stretching out and closing his eyes, as if giving Uthe privacy to pull himself together. Instead, Uthe rolled to his side and looked down at him. Keldwyn's eyes opened, mere slits. "You need something, my lord?"

"I would like..." Uthe realized a half smile was curving his lips, and he felt unaccountably shy. Seeing it, Kel's eyes opened fully and he pushed up to his elbows, curiosity on his face.

"What would you like?"

"I'd like to touch your ears. May I?"

He'd brushed them incidentally a couple times while enjoying Keldwyn's hair, but never a full exploration of the pointed tips. Keldwyn looked surprised, bemused but not displeased. "You may."

Sometimes the curves of his ears were pierced with tight rings. Sometimes they had intricate tattoos on the folds inside. Today they were free of any embellishments, so as Uthe's fingers slipped over them, it was just Keldwyn. They felt much like his own ears, merely a different shaping of the cartilage, but it seemed intimate to touch the most significant physical difference between their appearances. He wondered if that was why Keldwyn liked to play his tongue over Uthe's fangs so often. Uthe stroked the points of the ears lightly, the curve of the shell beneath and was intrigued when Kel's lids slid back down to half-mast. "It feels good when I do that?"

"It does. We do it often to soothe our children, but it has a similar effect on adults. Though if you ever offer to play with my ears when I'm in a temper, I will skewer you with a rusty blade."

Uthe smiled. When Kel shifted, Uthe knew the Fae Lord had reached his limit for the familiarity, but when he stopped doing it, Keldwyn didn't shift away. Instead he helped Uthe to his feet, and grunted at him to lift his arms so he could strip the unlaced tunic off him. Kel rested a brief hand on his chest. "We'll wash up in the stream," he said. "Take off the rest."

Since Keldwyn started to strip, Uthe complied, pushing the half removed leggings off with the boots. When he swayed, Kel's hand was on his hip, steadying him. The Fae's expression indicated it was a courtesy, but he didn't take the heat of his palm away as Uthe straightened.

"They say vampires are sometimes faster than Fae," Keldwyn noted. "But I have not found that to be true. You've never beaten me back to the estate during your morning sun ritual."

"I've never been racing against you."

"True enough. Let us race to the stream. We have both just climaxed, so that's an even handicap."

Given it didn't seem to have rocked Kel's world to its physical foundations, Uthe wouldn't agree, but he wouldn't argue that. He still hadn't had blood, so that was an acceptable reason for his knees to be shaky. He could level the playing field another way, though. In a flash, he'd knocked Keldwyn off his feet with a feint and side slam, and bolted for the pond.

He beat him by a stride. They splashed into the water, and Uthe was pleased to see the Fae Lord grinning. "A vampire must cheat to win."

"Leveling the playing field is not cheating. It's keeping your opponent honest. If such a thing is possible when talking about a Fae."

"Fanged barbarian."

"Pretentious fop."

Keldwyn's slim brows lifted nearly to his hairline. "An insult more appropriate to earlier time periods."

"I learn from all eras, my lord." The stream was waist deep in the middle, so Uthe could comfortably stand in it. Looking down, he saw brightly colored fish and a snakelike thing swimming around his feet. Like the insects, the fish were populated with similarly shaped Fae, who looked like tiny mermaids with whiskers and double-lidded eyes that studied him with interest.

Dropping to one knee in the shallow water, he spread his hands out so the tiny fish and Fae merfolk swam around them, investigating before drifting onward. He was of no consequence, just an obstacle. Feeling Keldwyn's gaze on him, he closed his eyes, thinking of all the things the Fae had opened up in him. All this time, he'd learned to contain his feelings with prayer and meditation. He'd learned the value of silence, and of knowing what to say, precisely as it should be said. All in the service of God.

But there were times when the need to communicate, to speak something aloud in the presence of one who could accept it, witness it, acknowledge the sheer weight it held on his soul and perhaps understand it, was needed. It was a type of spiritual nourishment too. He had struck at Keldwyn with words because he knew how to use them as weapons, but Uthe knew they should never be used as a shield to keep him from facing truth. He'd done that when he rejected Della as a blood source. Keldwyn had not pursued it, giving him space. Being a friend. As odd as it was to finally say that in his mind, it was the truth, too. The Fae Lord was a friend, a good one.

Uthe needed to make amends. He accepted the pain of saying his next words aloud as his penance.

"I will not drink from a child, because my father did," he said. "Because when I was a fledgling, he made me hold them down while he drank their blood and then killed them. He said I had a way of calming them. He liked their fear only at the beginning, not during the meal or the finish. I would hold their wrists pinned, and I would speak to them, tell them to look at me. I would tell them it was all right, that he was just going to drink from them until they fell asleep... Their small fingers would scrape at my closed hand, trying to hold onto me because I convinced them I could somehow make it all better."

When he felt Keldwyn draw close, he spoke through stiff lips.

"You gave me a gift just now, Kel, and my heart is so wide open I'm bleeding. So don't take this the wrong way, but I can't be touched when I'm talking about this. Especially by you, because I don't want to give the nightmares of my past a chance to taint the way I feel when you touch me. It's a treasure I can't bear to lose."

He moved toward the shore. "I need to feed. We should get to that portal you mentioned." Without a look back, he strode out of the water and back to his clothes.

Chapter Twelve

Keldwyn made his good-byes to Catriona. Uthe stood at a distance, watching as the young Fae wound her arms around him and held him tightly. When Kel tilted her head up with a hand on her face, speaking to her in a steady, quiet tone, Uthe was sure once more that Catriona was aware of the gravity of this particular departure, no matter that Keldwyn hadn't spoken of the details. She clung to him as he bent his head over hers again, kissed her crown, and then eased away from her, striding toward Uthe. Della ran to her side, wrapping her arms around the fairy, a fistful of flowers crushed against her hip. The unicorn nudged them back toward the water, the dragon making tight, protective circles around them.

Catriona let herself be led, but she looked over her shoulder, watching them until Keldwyn was out of her sight. Uthe noticed Keldwyn didn't look back, his shoulders set. He led Uthe down a trail into a forest filled with the iridescent light of small firefly Fae and flowers that bloomed in shade. While Uthe suspected they could only survive in the Fae world, he hoped Lyssa had had the opportunity to see these flowers, since anything that could blossom in the dark was of interest to her.

"She loves you deeply," he remarked.

Night's Templar

Keldwyn said nothing. Uthe sighed. "The Shattered World is an uncharted part of the Fae world, my lord. You have never been there. It therefore makes no sense for you to follow me into it. If no one can navigate it, then your guidance adds no value. You should leave me once we reach the gates."

"If that is the case, it is pointless for you to enter it, is it not? How will you find a detached head in a world that gives you no clear markers to follow?"

"Because I'm blood linked to it."

Keldwyn came to a stop and turned to face him. "What?"

"Shahnaz injected the head with my blood, and had me give it the first and second marks we give to servants. I also ingested some of its blood before she placed it in the Shattered World. Even from that dimension, I can hear the demon's voice, as well as John's, when he chooses to speak."

Keldwyn studied him. "So all this time," he said slowly, "you have had the demon's voice in your head. You have had to manage its manipulations while the Ennui has been advancing?"

Leave it to Keldwyn to zero right in on the main issue. "Yes. I've been able to control his influence in my mind, the same way I would a marked human. For the most part. The fortunate thing is that the voices in my head are distinct from my own consciousness. Otherwise, I'd be more muddled than I already am at times." He said it lightly, not expecting any humor in return. He wasn't disappointed. He could feel Keldwyn's incredulous stare burning into him, but Uthe shifted his gaze back to the path. "We should keep going."

Keldwyn put out a hand, stopping him. "There have been times I thought someone else was talking to you when we were together. At first I thought you shared a mind link with another vampire, like Lyssa or Evan, but I expected you would have made casual comments about such communications. There is usually a certain tension that radiates off you when it happens. That is the demon, is it not?"

"Yes, probably. He keeps me on my toes. At times, when he's gotten bored, he's even listened in on some Council meetings and offered his opinion on what we're debating." Uthe's lips twisted. "He's actually come up with the same solutions we have once or twice. He's clever as well as evil. Hence the need to always stay on guard when he's talking to me."

Keldwyn shook his head. "Remarkable."

"So you see," Uthe pressed his advantage, "I have a way to find him. There's no need for us both to risk ourselves."

Keldwyn began to move along the path again. "What if your mind's clarity deserts you, Lord Uthe? At such times you doubt the line between reality and fantasy. From the little we know of it, in the Shattered World it is almost impossible for a normal person to tell the difference, let alone a man fighting a brain illness that already clouds truth and illusion."

"Perhaps it will work to my advantage," Uthe said, pushing aside the apprehension Kel's words invoked. "I'll be clear, whereas those of you in your right minds will be the confused ones."

Keldwyn tossed him a deprecating look. "I am going with you, Lord Uthe. I am done having this argument."

"I cannot see your Queen being willing to risk your life for a confused old vampire on a quest that the Fae claim to care nothing about. Unless you misled me and she is actually interested in the demon's power."

Keldwyn turned on his heel so abruptly Uthe had to pull up short to avoid running straight into him. "Say the Queen was interested, my lord. What exactly could you do to stop her or me? We are in my world, and you cannot leave it without our assistance and permission. Beyond that, vampires cannot outmatch the Fae in magic or strength. But you know all that. You provoke me to no good purpose." Keldwyn's look was penetrating. "What is the answer you seek, my lord? What will bring your heart ease?"

"You not following me into certain death," Uthe snapped. "The knowledge that, whatever happens to me, you are safe. Knowing Catriona will not lose you. That your Queen and mine will always have your counsel."

Some of the anger drained out of Keldwyn's expression. "If you feel so strongly about me," he said slowly, "why do you find it so hard to comprehend why I refuse to let you go alone?"

He pivoted and continued to move through the forest, leaving Uthe standing there. Uthe shifted his glance toward a tree whose bark rearranged, revealing a pair of golden eyes that slowly blinked before the tree yawned, widely. A fairy the size of a hummingbird flew out of the mouth, flitted around and then zipped up into the tree canopy.

Uthe followed Kel. He wasn't sure why he had tried to pick a fight, except what had happened in the meadow, what he'd admitted in the stream, and watching Keldwyn have to say good-bye to Catriona had tangled themselves up inside him. The downside to denying himself excesses of emotion was that he was out of practice in managing them.

Keldwyn was setting a determined pace, suggesting he was still fueled by the argument. Uthe had seen a coldness come into Kel's eyes, or a certain tension in his body language, when he was offended or annoyed. This was different.

"Kel, hold up. My lord."

The Fae stopped, glancing over his shoulder. He had that neutral look, but Uthe wasn't fooled by it. Uthe put a hand on Keldwyn's chest, fingers sliding along the lacings in the jerkin. "I meant no offense. I am glad for your company, because your strengths are numerous, and I could hope for no better warrior to join me on this quest. But your welfare matters to me. It has been a very long time since I've been in a position to confuse my feelings for a lover with my responsibilities. I fear that I'm sacrificing you for my own comfort, not for any true need to accomplish my task. Do you understand?"

"I do. Which is why I would like you to rely on my own judgment in this and suffer no guilt at the outcome. If you can't do that, simply accept that I am stubborn, I am going with you, and there's nothing you can do about it. So that ends the discussion." Keldwyn glanced down. Uthe's fingers were beneath the lacing, lightly stroking his chest. Uthe wasn't sure when he'd started moving his fingers, but since it felt good and the Fae Lord wasn't objecting, he kept doing it. Keldwyn raised a brow. "Are you trying to seduce me into seeing things your way, my lord?"

It was such a surprising comment, Uthe pulled his hand back and scowled. "Of course not. I..."

Kel grinned, though there were deeper emotions in his eyes, in the oddly gentle note in his voice. "You think you have no power to seduce me, Varick?"

"It hadn't occurred to me, my lord, though I'm sure I do not. I was just enjoying...the feel of you. I thought I'd offended you, hurt your feelings. It bothered me."

It felt foolish to say something so sentimental, so he took another step back. Keldwyn reached out, squeezed Uthe's shoulder. "You need blood, my friend. Let us attend to it."

Keldwyn resumed course. This time, his pace was more relaxed, conveying that he was no longer angry. Uthe couldn't say he was any less concerned about the Fae going with him, but Kel was right. The time for discussion was over. They'd both made their feelings clear.

As they walked, Keldwyn pointed out features of the forest Uthe might have missed. He saw a tree with blue eyes and several teeth chewing meditatively on one of its own branch tips like a teenage girl chewing on her own hair. A two-headed serpent crossed their path, gazing at them briefly out of two sets of eyes. They passed a troop of small Fae riding a procession of woodland rodents: mice, rats, rabbits. Several rode on the back of a lumbering possum. Keldwyn nodded at them, and they bowed as he passed, their attention passing curiously over Uthe.

Uthe thought of Lord Reghan and his own father, and compared the respective hurts Keldwyn and he carried about the two males. The mercy of time was that it stretched out the pain, made it easier to bear, but there were vulnerable moments where it could hit as brutally as it had then. Forgiveness, guilt, service, vengeance, regret...it was difficult to know where one began and the other ended.

They moved into a grove of fruit trees where the fruits were dark shiny red ovals and bright orange orbs that could fit in Uthe's palm. Keldwyn pulled down one of the red ones. "Like your cherries, but different," he explained. He offered it to Uthe, bringing it to his mouth. Uthe took it that way, tasting his fingers. Keldwyn's eyes heated in sensual approval. He passed a thumb over Uthe's lips, gave his shoulder another reassuring squeeze, and they continued onward. Uthe found the fruit sweet and pleasurable, almost as much so as the brief sensation of Keldwyn's flesh.

Beware of a tongue so silver that evil can hide within its words. Terrible, terrible beauty... Monsters hide within that which shines...

The Baptist could rave with hysterical religious fervor or speak in the low, modulated tones of a college professor. Or offer insights with a warm certainty that filled the soul with hope. John had dedicated every aspect of his existence to God. His wanderings in the wilderness, his violent end and being a spirit in limbo, meant he often demonstrated erratic behavior, but it was always consistently in support of his faith. Sometimes it was expressed in a volatile way— like waking Uthe out of a sound sleep with righteous shouts of praise. Other times he mumbled hours of soothing devotionals. This was different from any of that, though.

The holy man sounded...scattered.

John, are you well? Uthe rarely questioned him. It could agitate the prophet. But something was amiss.

Bleeding...Varick...the lines are bleeding. He is aware, trying to...making us bleed...

A scream erupted in Uthe's head like a banshee shriek. He dropped to his knees, futilely covering his ears as the sound was captured inside his skull, illuminating every neural pathway with pain.

You will not win. You were impure from the beginning, never fit to take your oath. Did you confess to Hugh how you helped murder children, drank their blood?

I never drank from them. Never.

Yes, you did. You were so hungry, and he wouldn't let you leave until you did... You were a man, you could have fought, but you were afraid of him... A child in a man's body... You didn't tell your Fae lover that, did you? He would be disgusted by you.

Uthe was lost in the dark, unable to make sense of where he was. Was he blind? The insidious whispers were replaced by shrieks again, and they knocked him back to his knees once more. *You cannot fight me and win. Your mind is already half gone. You can focus on nothing but your Master's demands and your lust for him.*

Uthe was barely a match for the demon in full health. He couldn't beat him.

"'The victory of battle standeth not in the multitude of a host; but strength cometh from Heaven.'" Hugh's voice, reasonable and even, quoting Maccabees as they faced down a gang of brigands threatening a train of pilgrims. Outnumbered eight to one, four of them against thirty-two. They'd sent the living into retreat and the other twenty-four right to their Maker.

"The beauseant has not fallen, my lord."

A Templar did not retreat from the field unless the piebald beauseant fell, and even then he would flock to the banner of another Order if one was still standing. He'd fought under the banner of the Hospitallers more than once for that reason. Struggling to his feet, Uthe felt the grip of a strong hand, helping him. He knew that touch. He could rely on that strength and the mind behind it.

"The very noble armor of obedience..." Was he mixing up his quotes? It didn't matter. He remembered a few days ago when he'd knelt for the purpose of prayer, but he'd also been on his knees before Keldwyn. It wasn't the first time he'd been lost and the Fae had brought him back on course. It suggested that only by trusting the Fae would he have a chance of accomplishing what needed to be done. Had God sent Keldwyn for that purpose? Or was the demon right? Was he a serpent in the desert, a temptation and distraction?

No. Maybe. He wasn't inclined to tell himself lies. Since he'd had to observe the spirit of the Rule in a vampire environment for all these past centuries, he submitted himself to the harsh light of truth when making a decision, to be certain he didn't stray from the proper path.

But that same skill could be applied to softer truths.

He would always surrender to God's will, but now he required an earthly form of it, one that would quiet his soul of these longings for touch, for connection. In the past he'd seen it as weakness. In the face of the Ennui, he saw it as the path to stay strong.

"I have heard it said men may go to war for causes wide and varied, but they stay and fight for those they love. So perhaps whatever God is breaks off pieces of Itself in the souls of those we love so that we will never lose our compass to Him. Like breadcrumbs."

Uthe blinked. Who had said that? Bernard? Certainly not. He focused, and the light around him shifted, became less blurry. He was looking at trees with low hanging red fruit. Keldwyn was kneeling beside him. Uthe's forehead was pressed into his shoulder, palms flat on the ground as he tried to get bearings.

It is all right, for now. John's voice, calmer again. *He* has passed His Hand over the water, and all is calm.

The demon had tried one of his fits, a futile attempt to burst loose. It had been years since he'd had one, so Uthe had forgotten the feeling. At the beginning, he'd done it quite often, like an animal gone mad in confinement. During that time, Uthe had to shut out as much of it as possible, for the suffering the demon's histrionics caused the other two souls sharing the same space had been something he was helpless to prevent. It was John's prayers that had helped Uthe bear it. Not once had the Madman faltered, and Uthe could do no less.

"Until a way is found to send him back to Hell, you will not free us. I will not go to the Gates of Heaven knowing he is free to spread evil." How many times, and in how many ways, had the Baptist said that to him? But the demon's behavior this time was more savage. He knew they were getting close, and it would not be the last time he tried to throw Uthe off course. Maintaining his strength was essential.

"Varick." Keldwyn was touching his scalp gently. "You are all right."

"Yes." He cleared his throat, struggled to his feet. Keldwyn helped him, standing close as he swayed. "I need blood."

"You shall have it shortly. Walk with me and tell me what happened." Keldwyn looped his arm around his waist, keeping him steady as they moved forward.

"The demon is getting restless. Sometimes he gets…chaotic."

"It's a good sign." Keldwyn grunted. "If he thought you had no chance of succeeding, he would not torment you."

"I favor your optimism, my lord." Uthe stopped as they emerged from the forest. On the horizon, far in the distance, was a castle that looked as if it were made of ice, its blue, silver and white facets glistening in the sun. The land between them and it was a patchwork of beauty. Multi-colored flowers, trees with leaves of every kind of green, fields of lavender. He saw a herd of deer grazing, birds winging through the skies in as many colors as the flowers. Though he appreciated all of it, for some reason his mind clung to an image of the common wood dove, that simple lovely gray.

"That is Queen Rhoswen's castle," Keldwyn explained. "Should you ever dine there, she has the best chef."

"Good to know. Five-star rating on the Ice Castle menu." Moving in sync with Keldwyn, Uthe was getting uncomfortably aware of the pulse of blood in the Fae Lord's throat. He wasn't a fledgling who would give in to bloodlust from mere temptation, but he didn't want to test his resolve, when there were so many other things about Keldwyn he had difficulty resisting as it was.

"It is known as the Castle of Water, Caislean Uisce. What looks like ice at this distance is actually moving water, shaped and directed by the castle's exterior elements. It is a castle of waterfalls. However, with Rhoswen in residence, there is indeed much ice there, so your description is not inaccurate. Sit here." Keldwyn slid him onto the flat surface of a rounded stone, part of a grouping rising out of the ground like a cluster of dinosaur eggs. There were drawings on it. Uthe passed his fingers over the symbols.

"What do these mean?"

"Children's scrawlings. Things that mean something to them. All children have their secret languages. How old were you when your father made you drink from his victims?"

Uthe stiffened. He hadn't realized he'd spoken that part aloud, but he shouldn't be surprised. When the demon emerged like that, and John got involved, it was as real as being placed in a room with them. If he'd had any desire to hide the information from Keldwyn, as the demon had implied, he'd made that impossible. "It was only the one," he said, and despised himself for saying it, as if there was any defense for such a reprehensible act. "I was forty-eight."

"A vampire fledgling. Comparable to a human teenager. Usually unable to live on your own without a sire or mentor to protect you."

"Still capable of making moral choices," Uthe said. "Which I did. I killed my father right afterwards. I killed him, Kel, with that boy's blood still on my lips. I can still taste it..."

God in Heaven, why had he thought that? His stomach heaved and he was off the rock, bent behind it, expelling what meager contents his stomach contained. He'd told Keldwyn he never wanted to be touched when revisiting those memories, but it was no surprise the Fae didn't listen. When Uthe finished, he kept his head down, his fingers curled into the earth.

"Tell me," Kel said quietly. "Take the burden off your soul."

"No one can do that." But Uthe relented. "My father was a Trad. It's true that Trads have no regard for humans but, despite the scary bedtime stories about human massacres, only a few prefer to kill. Most Trads compel humans to them for food, wipe their memory and then release them. It's simple common sense, because we can't consume that much blood for a feeding, and we're all cognizant of the dangers of exposing ourselves to the human race."

He took a breath. "Some Trads are different. There's the human who sits down to a steak, never thinking of the animal's state of mind before death, and a true sadist, who feeds on the fear and pain as much as the blood. My father was the latter. And perhaps that was why, as he got older and Ennui set in, he turned into what he did."

As Keldwyn went still, Uthe nodded. "There is a very faint line between Ennui and the normal way a Trad thinks. I never noticed him crossing the line until he was there. We were solitary; he didn't associate with other vampires. I thought they were all like that. At first, I just thought he was growing lazier. He'd go out to hunt and decide to take a child instead of an adult, claiming it was easier. Then he started ranting about pure blood being best, and a child had pure blood. He'd say, 'Varick, what is the difference between the man who slaughters the calf and the vampire who kills a human infant? Both take the life of newborn food.'

"I was his son. It was how I was raised, yet his nurturing could not change my fundamental nature. Though I'd shared adult kills with him, I would not take a child. He saw how much it bothered me. That was when he started bringing them home. If I didn't help him hold them, he'd make it worse for them, make them more afraid. He was too strong...I couldn't stand against him, I didn't think I could leave, I was too young. Dear God, a dozen useless excuses. My father realized tormenting me was far more entertaining than tormenting the children. The only upside to that was as long as I tore my soul to shreds and soothed the children, held them down for him, he would be satisfied and make their end quick. That was because he knew I'd be the one tortured for days afterwards. Fifteen of them in all before I acted, before I realized no matter how young I was or how powerful he was, I couldn't bear it another day. I'd rather die."

He stopped, wiped his mouth with the back of his hand. A cup with sparkling water appeared by him, and when he lifted it to his lips and drank, it had a pleasing scent to it. He swished it around his mouth, and spit into the grass, wishing he could spit what had made him nauseous out also. "So there," he said with a hint of sarcasm. "My burden is all lifted now."

Keldwyn's hand rested on his back again. "I am honored you shared it with me. I like it when you call me Kel."

Uthe shifted back to his heels and looked up, surprised. He didn't see revulsion or condemnation in the Fae Lord's face, or even pity. His dark eyes held a steady flame.

"Even just out of boyhood by vampire standards, you were an honorable male. An impressively strong one."

Keldwyn clasped his arm, gave it a hard squeeze. "You did know right and wrong, and you stopped him, even though it cost you a piece of your soul to do it. It was long ago, and I suspect you made your peace with it somewhere along the way. The demon is goading your doubts and guilt back to life for his own purposes. Let us get you some blood and you will have the strength to fight him as you have always done."

"Sometimes I carry the burden of my task so close, it may seem that I don't trust those who offer me help." Uthe sank to one knee before Keldwyn and bowed his head. "If I forget that again during our journey together, I ask your forgiveness now, my lord."

Keldwyn's fingertips slid along his scalp, his nape, and he bent, pressing his lips to the crown of Uthe's head. "You are welcome in my heart and soul, Varick."

Gripping his wrist, Uthe pressed it against the side of his face, and nodded, holding that pose until he'd collected himself. "I fear age is making me mawkish, my lord."

"Eh." Keldwyn dismissed that. As Uthe let himself be helped to his feet, he was grateful that Keldwyn didn't say anything further on the matter. The Fae Lord gestured toward a shallow creek. "We'll go through this portal. It puts us close to where Evan is staying."

"How do you know that?"

"I am an ancient Fae Lord. I know everything of import."

"Except humility."

"You have enough for both of us, my lord. Though I have to say your arrogant side, when it shows itself, is extremely stimulating."

Uthe shot him a glance as they moved forward, which Keldwyn returned with an appraising look that stirred the blood. "I'll keep that in mind."

"Do. Remember, there is some disorientation..." Uthe stumbled, but Kel had him securely. When he straightened, they were no longer in the Fae world. They stood by a gurgling mountain creek, shadowed by a lacing of tall pines through which tiny shards of moonlight struck the water and glistened off the rocks embedded in the flow. A bird not yet fully roosted made questing chirps in the distance. The air was clean and tinged with fall coolness, the breeze sighing through the pine boughs.

"We're in Tennessee," Kel told him. "Evan's mountain retreat."

Uthe had never been there, though Evan had told him of it. As Kel and he navigated down a slope, the trees thinned and gave way to a cleared yard of grass and stone that overlooked a panorama of mountains, which at night presented in shades of gray outlined by the half-moon's light. The cleared area had a picnic table, a well, and a sturdy, battered Jeep.

Uthe inhaled all the scents of the forest and...cookies. A scraping noise of wood and metal came from below, and Alanna, Evan and Niall's servant, emerged seemingly from the hill beneath their feet. She moved several steps out of its shadow and turned to look up at them. A welcoming smile wreathed her lovely face, but Uthe saw concern behind the InhServ training. She was wondering at their sudden appearance here and what it might mean.

"My lord Uthe. You honor us with your presence." Shifting her gaze to Keldwyn, she dipped her head respectfully. "As do you, Lord Keldwyn. Evan asked me to come out and greet you. He's on his way down with Niall. He wanted to do his sketching at a spot higher up on the mountain today, something about the elevations giving him a different level of inspiration."

If Uthe wasn't Evan's sire, Evan would not have been able to recognize him at a distance. He'd have only sensed a vampire had come into his area. If that had been the case, Uthe was sure Evan's mental direction to Alanna would have been far different, a sharp order for her to remain inside and hidden until he and Niall arrived swiftly to determine what business brought another vampire up here. This was terrain through which a Trad might pass, since they avoided places of heavy human habitation. Trads didn't believe in taking human servants, except for temporary amusement or attempts to breed, as in the case of Uthe's father. Their respect for the third mark bonding between other vampires and their servants went only as far as that vampire's proximity when the Trad encountered the servant. If the vampire was not present, the servant's fate was far less certain.

Alanna was one of the most beautiful InhServs who'd ever been raised from childhood for vampire service. Dark red hair fell to her waist and framed a delicate face with doe-brown eyes. The lovely curves of her body were accentuated by a pale lavender tank top and dark blue jeans. She was a head-turner for anyone with a pulse. But an inanimate doll could be beautiful. What made her exceptional was the strength of character Uthe and the rest of the Council now knew lay beneath those delicate features.

Uthe remembered when she'd been brought before the Council. Lord Stephen had tortured her mind at length to avoid capture. She'd been so weak, she'd had to be carried to the Council chambers, but she'd knelt at Evan's feet and spoken her devotion for him as her Master, even knowing her Fate was not her own. While there was still some debate among the Council as to the wisdom of assigning an InhServ to a vampire who had no political aspirations at all, Uthe knew this was the right match. Vampires lived a long time. There was no telling in what manner Evan would end up serving vampire kind, but Uthe had always had a high regard for the younger vampire's strength of character and steady nature.

Alanna had since been restored to good health, though Uthe suspected her glow of contentment had as much to do with the two Masters she now served as the healing effect of time and Lord Brian's medical acumen.

"I just finished a batch of cookies and I have some fresh

Night's Templar

lemonade. Can I offer you something?" Color tinged her cheeks, her eyes twinkling as she realized how it sounded, offering a Council member and the powerful Fae Lord a cookie.

"Of course," Uthe said warmly. "Where did you come from?"

"Oh." She gestured in front of her. "The house is built into the earth, my lords. It's a cozy cabin but very rustic. If you'd like to come down here to the picnic table, you can see the door better. You're welcome to come inside, but it's such a beautiful night, it seems a waste of the moonlight to be indoors."

"I agree." The leap from the top of the hill to the lawn was fifteen feet, an easy thing for a vampire, like a leopard jumping out of a tree. Uthe hit the ground and one knee buckled. Keldwyn was at his side to keep him steady, a state of affairs that was beginning to irritate Uthe. Not the Fae's touch, but his need for assistance. "I'm fine," he said gruffly, shrugging away and moving to the picnic table. He refused to look and see if Alanna had noticed his clumsiness, though he hoped she'd gone back inside to get their refreshments. Pride was a useless emotion, yet he kept indulging it.

"My lord Uthe."

Uthe hid a tight smile. He'd expected Niall to arrive next. First, because it was difficult for Evan to pull out of the fog of inspiration, even for the demands of vampire etiquette. Second, Evan knew and trusted Uthe far more than Niall did. The big Scot hadn't wasted any time getting back down the mountain, and Uthe knew it had little to do with deference to Uthe's elevated status. His dark eyes flickered toward the house as Alanna emerged, confirming visually what he could verify in his mind—her wellbeing.

"We decided to wait and filet her when you arrived," Uthe said mildly.

Niall had the grace to flush. He gave Keldwyn a nod, though it was far less friendly, just within the boundaries of courtesy without extending clear welcome. He'd never been comfortable around the Fae male. Since Niall had been born in eighteenth century Scotland, where stories of the trickery of the Fae were rampant, his wariness was understandable.

Uthe had no objection to Niall's protectiveness, because it extended to both Evan and Alanna. A warrior by nature, he was far more likely to assess the potential threats of their surroundings than Evan. He'd had three hundred years as Evan's human servant to hone those skills, only recently having had his vampire transformation approved by Council. His Scottish practicality was a good balance for Evan's artistic nature, one of the main reasons his turning had been approved unanimously by the Council. Evan's art brought in considerable revenue to the Council. Beyond that, he represented a different path for vampires. Lord Brian, with his focus on science, was the closest thing to that course, both of them proving that vampires could pursue vocations that benefitted the vampire world without being mired in cutthroat politics.

Niall was a big male, broad and tall, with long brown hair he kept tied back off his shoulders. His tawny eyes were bronze in the moonlight. He bowed in acknowledgement to Uthe's jest. "My lord, I intended no offense."

"None was taken. Such a treasure requires constant vigilance." Uthe turned his attention to Alanna as she put a plate of cookies and two glasses of lemonade before him and Keldwyn, who'd taken the picnic table bench across from him. They were both tall enough men he felt Keldwyn's knee press on the inside of his, but the Fae didn't remove the contact. He took a cookie, his attention on Uthe as he bit into it, licked the crumbs from his lips.

Heaven help him, he was staring. Uthe pulled his gaze away. He really needed blood, but he wouldn't take it until Evan was present. "Have you three been here long?"

"Just these past few weeks. We were in France before

then." Every vivid expression of happiness turned Alanna's delicate features into a score of possible paintings. Uthe suspected Evan had endless photographs of her. Evan and Niall were two more vampires to add to the growing list of those who didn't conceal the depth of their feelings for their servant. Niall had no obvious interest in taking his own, the two of them sharing her for blood and whatever other needs they had. Theirs was a three-way relationship, since the two men were equally devoted to one another.

"Evan said you would have particularly liked one of the places we visited there," she continued. "La Couvertoirade, in Averyon. Do you know it? It was on the travel routes for the Templars to and from the Holy Lands, wasn't it?"

Pleasure and sadness swept through him as he recalled Shahnaz. "Yes, it was. We had a hospital there and a chapel. Martins nested in the eaves."

"They still do," Alanna said, pleased at the connection.

The town was peaceful, far more peaceful than the Holy Lands that had been the ultimate destination of many Templars who passed through it. "And what masterpiece did Evan create there?"

"Something with gravel and broken glass. I could have taken him out behind a Scottish pub tae find the same."

Alanna gave Niall an affectionate look of exasperation. "The picture features the different cross styles in the cemetery. He's changing the order of the crosses, making patterns of them. Patterns within patterns. It's a new technique he's doing, combining photography and paint, along with broken glass and rock gravel he picked up from the site itself."

"And you are serving him and Niall well?"

Her gaze swept down. "That is for my Masters to say, my lord. But I do my very best to care for them."

"I suspect that is far more than they deserve."

"No doubt, my lord," Niall said with amusement. "But best no' give her too many airs. She already thinks she runs things around here."

Uthe touched her face to draw her attention back up to him. Only a handful of months ago, Niall's joke would have discomfited her greatly, Alanna interpreting it literally as a black mark against her InhServ training. Now he saw humor dancing in her once far-too-serious eyes.

"If I was putting my money on which of them gets above their station," said a new voice, "it would be the newly turned vampire who likes to show off his fangs at every opportunity."

Evan was windblown enough to suggest he'd made haste, remedying any lack of perceived courtesy at his delay. The genuine pleasure in his face had a peculiar effect on Uthe. He'd always been very fond of the younger vampire, but Evan's obvious eagerness to see his sire flooded Uthe with sentiment. Vampires downplayed connections to other vampires; however, the young artist Uthe had turned on his deathbed was the closest thing Uthe had to a son. And this might be the last time he'd see him.

Even though he'd been frail as a human, Evan had been a handsome male, and the strong sculpted features of his Jewish heritage were only enhanced by his vampire conversion. He had thick dark hair he kept cut to his nape and gray deep set eyes that examined everything around him with an artist's eye. His shoulders were broad though he was rangy, muscles lean and knotted.

"Better one who likes tae show his fangs than one who's always showing his arse," Niall returned. At Evan's arched brow and what Uthe expected was a mind-to-mind reminder of the rank of their company, Niall cleared his throat. "My apologies again, my lords. 'Tis rough living out here."

"You had three hundred years to learn manners around vampires," Uthe said, rising to hold out a hand in greeting to Evan. "Though I expect you're less used to exercising them here, it's important to have them ready to hand. You don't want to offend the wrong vampire, Niall."

Night's Templar

Niall wasn't as bad as Gideon, but the reminder was needed, especially now that he was a vampire. A fledgling would be broken faster than even a servant if he got above himself.

"Thanks, my lord. He never listens to me."

Then, undermining the point irreparably, Evan bypassed Uthe's outstretched hand and gave him an exuberant hug. Uthe returned the gesture, though, keeping the admonishment to himself.

As Evan drew back, his eyes narrowed on Uthe's face. "You need to feed, my lord. You are exceptionally pale." His gaze shifted to Keldwyn, then back to Uthe. "What's going on? Why are you here?"

Uthe had somehow been maneuvered back down onto the bench. It was disconcerting to be handled, or maybe he'd sat back down himself. Cosseted or forgetful. He wasn't sure which explanation made him less comfortable. Evan sat down next to him. "What may I do for you, my lord? Anything I can provide is yours."

Uthe nodded. But rather than speaking immediately of his need for blood, he looked around at the house built into the hill, the beauty and solitude of the place. "You have my envy, Evan. This is a very good spot to create, and to love and live."

Evan was self-confident in ways that much more physically powerful vampires lacked, because he was exceptionally intelligent and used to relying on his wits instead of brawn. Uthe approved of that, for it boded well for his longevity. That, as well as the Scottish vampire who loved him and would in time be able to crush any physical force that could not be dissuaded by Evan's considerable intellect.

"Yes, it is." Evan swept a pleased gaze around them, but Uthe noted it lingered on Alanna and Niall, revealing they were the vital piece of wherever he called home. "I don't think I could live the life you live, my lord. I'm grateful you've given me the opportunity to live outside the structure of the vampire world."

Once Uthe was gone, that patronage might dry up. Why had he not asked Lyssa to watch after Evan? Because he needed to trust Evan was capable of his own care, he told himself. Niall was now a vampire, and Evan had an InhServ at the top of her class at his side. There were no better allies he could have, once Uthe was gone.

"What is going on, my lord?" Evan repeated. "What brings you here, with Lord Keldwyn?"

"Let him feed first," Keldwyn said firmly. "Then he will tell you what he wishes to share."

It was a clear command. Uthe registered Evan's curiosity about that, about his own passivity in the face of Keldwyn taking charge. He cleared his throat, straightened.

"I need a sustenance feeding. Where we are going, I may not have access to blood for several days. You may have heard I released Mariela from my service. I would prefer to draw blood from a servant rather than an unsuspecting human whose blood origins I do not know."

Though he certainly could have done that. It was Keldwyn who'd suggested Evan. He wondered now if the Fae had proposed it because it gave Uthe a chance to see Evan, Niall and Alanna once more before entering the Shattered World.

He kept assigning motives to Keldwyn that were entirely sentimental. Perhaps his judgment was already more impaired than he realized.

"Certainly, my lord," Alanna said immediately. Niall shot her a look.

"Might hold off offering what's your Masters' right tae give away, *muirnín*," he chided her. Alanna bit her lip, her gaze cutting to Evan. Evan rose and went to Niall, putting a hand on his suddenly stiff shoulder. "She didn't act inappropriately," he explained. "A Council member can demand blood from any vampire's servant, except one belonging to another Council member. It is his right."

"That is true," Uthe said. "But I am not demanding it,

Evan. I assume I do not need to do so, son of my blood."

It was an old term, not much in use any more. Evan looked toward him, his hand still on Niall. His gray eyes flickered and he inclined his head. "You are correct, my lord."

At Evan's gesture, Alanna came to Uthe and knelt in front of him. Her training reminded him so much of Mariela, his heart dipped in nostalgia, hoping she was doing well. He really was getting to be a sentimental old man. Until recently, he'd never felt old. Vampires didn't experience that. Physically, he didn't look older than a human in his thirties, and age only brought more strength and speed, unless a factor like the Ennui intervened. That was probably why he suddenly felt...ancient.

"I know you have resumed contact with other InhServs. Have you heard anything of Mariela recently?"

A shadow crossed Alanna's gaze, and he touched her chin. "Do not lie to me to spare my feelings," he said.

"She grieves, my lord. It is difficult for any of us to be reassigned, especially after serving a Master such as yourself, who is the epitome of what our service is about. But our purpose is to serve to the best of our ability, and she will. Mariela will never fail in her duty as an InhServ. Yet she has a high regard for you, my lord."

Her matter-of-fact praise of him was unexpected, though he hurt for Mariela. "I would consider it a special favor for you to convey that no matter her regard for me, mine is without limitations for her. I send prayers for her well-being daily."

"Consider it done, my lord."

He said nothing for a few moments, thinking. He wasn't even aware of the passage of time, or that his mind had wandered, until Keldwyn leaned forward and touched his shoulder. "My lord," he said. "It is time for you to feed."

He focused. Alanna's gaze was on him, open, caring, and probably all too understanding. He saw shadows in her lovely brown eyes, only now they were for him. There was little that InhServs missed.

"Your wrist, Alanna. That is my preference."

"Of course." Rising on her knees, moving between his, she lifted her right arm for him to grasp, her left hand resting on his knee. She had two rings on it, one a pewter band with Celtic-looking scrollwork, and the other antique gold. He expected both had inscriptions on the inside from the men who'd given them to her.

As he brought her wrist to his lips, he inhaled her lovely female fragrance, and nuzzled the silk of her flesh. As he'd told Kel, there was no way to separate a surge of sexual arousal from the feeding process, but he would channel it into the taking of her blood. The slight constriction of his fingers on her arm, a reminder of restraint, made her catch her breath. He was pleased to see her eyes getting that slightly unfocused look a submissive was powerless to suppress when the right triggers occurred. The charge of sexual energy was pleasant. Though it was a benign thing he had no intentions of pursuing, he was amused to see that, as gracefully as Evan had capitulated to his request, he was not entirely separate from Niall's feelings on the matter. His gaze was trained on her, his face a neutral mask, though his body was preternaturally still.

He was not concerned about Evan's reaction, though. His gaze shifted to Niall. Another reason Evan had been given permission to turn him was that deficit of strength and abilities a vampire Evan's age should have. Whereas, since his turning, Niall's strength had been gaining on his former Master in leaps and bounds, probably accelerated by his additional years as a servant. It would make for an interesting power exchange between them.

Yet as a fledgling, the Scot had less impulse control. He wasn't pleased Uthe was about to take blood from their servant. While it appeared Niall was doing his best to contain the reaction, Evan shifted to his side and spoke to him a low voice. Niall quivered as he put a hand on his shoulder. At another time, Uthe might reinforce that with a

Night's Templar

stern reminder to the young vampire he had every right to take blood from his servant, and back it up with a more physical response. However, he had no desire to go through the posturing and aggression vampires used to maintain pecking order.

He wondered what Niall's response would have been if Uthe had wanted to take blood from her throat. Though drinking from the femoral was more sexually blatant, with the head between the servant's legs and fangs sunk into the vein so close to the genitals, all vampires knew the throat had the most intimate implications. When a servant exposed his or her throat, the message was *I surrender. I am yours.*

He thought of sinking his fangs into Keldwyn's throat. There was also another message to it. *I nourish you. I care for you in a way no other can.*

Alanna was an InhServ, like Mariela, but Alanna would never be reassigned again. She would live and die with these two, her only heart's desire, and she'd more than earned it after her ordeal with Stephen. His gaze fell on those two rings, and he wondered what the inscriptions on them said.

"Can I give you nourishment, my lord?" Alanna made the formal request, prompting him.

He could hear and feel the pulsing of her veins, reminding him of his hunger. He unsheathed his fangs and Niall shifted. Evan shifted with him, but then a third factor intervened.

Keldwyn rose from the picnic table and moved so he was between Niall and Uthe. He was not blocking the vampires' view of their servant, which would have been a tactical error, but he made it clear Niall was not advancing further. Niall showed fangs, and Kel's expression transformed to the trademark cold look capable of raising the hairs even on Uthe's neck.

"He outranks both of you, and he is well within his rights. His actions deserve your deference and respect, and he is treating her kindly. You will stand down and ease back, and not present a threat to him while he is feeding. Or I can show you how easy it is for a Fae to put a vampire down."

Evan's grip on Niall's massive shoulder increased, a protection and steadying influence both. "He understands, Lord Keldwyn," he said. "It is an effort to control bloodlust at this age, and she is very precious to us." He pressed his body to Niall's, his mouth close to the male's ear. "She is fine, *neshama*. My sire has need of blood, and honors us by asking for it from our servant. He saved my life, nourished me through my change. She comes to no harm at his hands, and he has no designs upon her."

Protocol allowed Uthe to take whatever he wished from Alanna. He could have her body on the picnic table in front of them. According to the way the law currently stood, he could even kill her in front of them, though ironically he would answer to the Council and be required to make compensation to *them* for taking the life of an InhServ, a valuable Council asset. But Evan was expecting his sire not to point those things out. In certain circumstances, Uthe would have, since made vampires usually needed more reminders of the way things were in the vampire world. This was not one of those times it was necessary, even if he'd been willing or interested in doing so.

Niall relaxed somewhat, head jerking in a tense nod. Evan's calmness before Keldwyn's threat indicated he'd expected nothing less. Niall might soon outstrip Evan in strength, but those three hundred years as Evan's servant were still deeply ingrained in Niall.

Dominant, submissive, give, take, resistance, flow… There were so many ways it could go, and not just in the vampire world. Lifting Alanna's wrist to his mouth, Uthe sank his fangs into the tender skin. As the blood filled his mouth, his body's urgency began to ease, like a sigh of relief. Alanna kept her gaze lowered, her position one of obeisance as her training had taught her. He expected she was not so formal with her Masters. She was being so now to help Niall see the difference. She'd always been exceptional at the politics that commanded the vampire way of life.

As he drank, a hand clasped his shoulder, sliding over to the back of his head. He recognized Keldwyn's touch. But when he glanced upward, he saw something he didn't expect to see simmering in Keldwyn's dark eyes.

Keldwyn didn't like Alanna feeding him. Did the Fae realize he was having that reaction? Touching Uthe seemed to contain the reaction, but Uthe felt a weighted quality to that contact. Possessiveness.

He noticed Evan's speculative look. Whereas for most vampires, the idea of a closer relationship between a Fae and a vampire would be met with everything from puzzlement to revulsion, he suspected the boy was doing cartwheels in his mind, imagining his future visits to the Fae world. Uthe expected Rhoswen could freeze that idea right out of Evan's head, along with some other tender body parts.

He turned his attention back to the feeding. It took longer, because a sustenance feeding was three or four times as much blood as he would normally take from a servant. As he finished his meal, he pressed a chaste kiss to her wrist. "Thank you, my dear," he said. "I appreciate your generosity."

She nodded, a little wan from the blood loss. "It is what we are born to be, my lord."

"At one time, I might have agreed with you." He closed his hand over the rings on her fingers, squeezed gently. "Now I think what you are to Evan and Niall, *that* is what you were born to be."

Perhaps it was the ultimate intent for all of them. He thought of what he'd heard in his head about love and breadcrumbs, and wondered again whose thought that had been. His own? Or had Kel said such a remarkable thing?

As Uthe released her, Evan stepped forward and helped

her up, guiding her to Niall. She reached up to the Scot's face. He responded with a twist of his lips and a brush of his mouth over hers that Uthe suspected would become far more demanding, as soon as the appropriate moment presented itself.

Though Evan had handled the situation as expected, from the look he swept over both the Scot and Alanna, Uthe expected the older vampire would be part of that reclaiming. Vampires didn't quibble over issues of ownership, especially if heart and soul were involved.

Jacob had a T-shirt he wore occasionally when doing manual labor at the Savannah headquarters, or in the evening when relaxing with other servants. The words on it said: "If you love something, set it free. If it comes back, it was always yours. If it doesn't, hunt it down and kill it." Uthe had often wondered if it was a tongue-in-cheek comment about his lady, the indomitable Lyssa, and the nature of vampires in general. Uthe didn't disagree with it.

In the case of Evan, Alanna and Niall, whose balance of personalities and strengths could serve vampire kind as a whole, he fully supported their claim on one another. All three of them. Alanna was a submissive and a well-trained InhServ, but the way she touched Niall, how her eyes softened as she looked toward Evan, said she considered them hers also. As Keldwyn had said, servants could be just as protective of their vampires, and protectiveness went hand-in-hand with possessiveness, no matter how "inappropriate" that attitude might be.

"Why don't you take Alanna inside to rest?" Evan suggested to Niall, his expression making it not a suggestion at all. "If you will excuse them, my lord."

"Certainly."

Niall acknowledged Uthe's permission with a passable nod, and guided Alanna away from the table. When she swayed on her feet, he lifted her in his arms and took her inside, closing the door. She would rest and Niall would feed her to replenish herself. She would be all right.

Evan took a seat next to him. "You already are looking more restored, my lord. May I now ask what's happening here? We heard that you took a leave from the Council. Is everything all right?"

Uthe reached out and brushed Evan's thick hair back from his brow, an affectionate gesture that had the male's brows rising. "When you were a sick human, do you remember I asked you what you could do with your art, if you had forever to pursue it?"

"I do."

"When there is no time limit, miracles and marvels are possible. They're still possible with more limited time periods, but..." Uthe shook his head. "My time is dwindling, Evan. There is a vital task I must complete, if it is within my power to finish it."

"Then let us help you. Let us stay with you." The younger vampire's eyes turned to storm clouds. "You have watched over me for many years. It's only right you give me the same privilege."

"This is a task I must do alone." When Evan's gaze slid over to Keldwyn pointedly, Uthe knew that was too complicated to explain, so he went with the simplest version. "What I do, must be done in the Fae world, and I am required by the Queen to be bound to a guide."

"Can he be trusted?"

Evan could be as diplomatic as the flow of water, but when loyalty was involved, he wasn't much for pretenses. He sent Keldwyn a challenging look, but Uthe tapped his arm in admonishment.

"You will not disrespect the Council liaison, Evan. Should anything happen to me, I can assure you Lord Keldwyn will have done everything to prevent it that I allowed him to do. Do you trust me when I say this?"

Evan waited a long moment, sifting it, then he turned his attention back to Keldwyn. "My apologies, my lord. My sire is dear to me, and I do not know you."

"It only increases my regard for you. You also didn't

trade on your concern to curry my favor and gain access to my world."

A slow smile curled Evan's lips, answered by a glint in Keldwyn's eyes. "So you've shared that about me, have you?" Evan complained to Uthe.

"I figured it was best to give him a heads up before you did something foolish, like approach him on your own or send flattering letters, candy and flowers to Queen Rhoswen."

"He did think of it," Niall put in. He'd returned, and was standing a few feet from the table, arms crossed. Of course. While he would feed Alanna, their protection was his highest priority, and leaving Evan alone with another vampire and a Fae would take precedence now that Alanna was safely tucked away. "He just couldnae figure out the postal rate."

"I get no respect from him since he became a vampire," Evan said darkly. "I got precious little out of him when he wasn't."

"Perhaps if my lord Keldwyn is one day in a position to do me a favor, and his queen agrees, you will force him to follow you into the Fae world and it will make him more malleable," Uthe pointed out.

Evan grinned as the Scot's expression got predictably sour. "Your intuition is sound, my lord. I think Niall would rather face an army by himself than enter the Fae world. He's certain reality will shift and we'll never find our way back. Whereas I find that prospect not at all disconcerting."

"Which shocks none of us," Niall grumbled.

"One day you might go to the Fae world," Uthe said, sobering. "But I will tell you something, Evan. You could see every marvel there and here, but it is in the art inspired by your feelings for Niall and Alanna that you will learn the scope of the universe. No matter where you go together or what you do, your hearts contain infinite creation. Correct? I am telling you something you already know."

The sudden intensity of his words ended the jesting and

brought that resolute look back to Evan's countenance. He gripped Uthe's hand. "You are *mishpacha*. Family. Father of my blood, my lord. Hearing you may not grace me with your presence again breaks my heart. I would do anything to help you. Please, let me aid you in this."

"I cannot allow that, but your willingness to do so pleases me. You have surpassed my highest expectations, and I know you will continue to do so." Uthe rose, drawing the vampire with him. This time, he initiated the embrace, holding him close, feeling his heart ache against the beat of the other male's. "Know that I carry our bond with me wherever I go, and I am very proud of what you have made of yourself. Continue to explore your art, and wherever your interests take you. If the Lord has given you an immortal life, then honor me by taking full pleasure in it, and being the intelligent and compassionate man I know you to be. Who knows?" Uthe drew back. "You might yet one day sit on Council."

"You tell me you care for me and yet you curse me," Evan accused, a rueful smile tugging at his lips. But there were tears in his eyes. Jewish men were notoriously emotional. Being from German stock, Uthe shied away from open expressions of such things. But this time, he put his thumbs in the corners of Evan's eyes, framing his face with his large hands, and absorbed the tears into his flesh. "Go with God," Uthe murmured. "May His blessings always be upon you and those you love, so you will share eternity together."

Chapter Thirteen

They re-entered the Fae world at the same portal. Keldwyn told Uthe the Shattered World was less than a day's journey and that they would arrive there before nightfall. His mission was upon them at last, no further delays. Uthe had gone over all the possibilities he might face many times before this moment. Just like when he'd reviewed battle plans for Templars or vampires, there was a point at which further review was unnecessary. All that was left were prayer and meditation. Checking his horse, cleaning his weapons. Making casual conversation with his other brethren about simple things. There was no point in dwelling on what was ahead when all preparations had been made. The rest was in the hands of God, a matter of Fate or chance. Or capricious luck.

As they drew closer to their destination, the sun seemed to shift away from the horizon, as if it had slipped off a shelf and tumbled into a corner. The ground remained green but became more open, with less trees. Signs of animal, bird or Fae life dwindled. The sky turned light gray then darkened, like before a storm. But there was no texture to it, no clouds building against it to herald rain.

Then Uthe realized it wasn't a sky at all. As they topped another in a series of ever-steepening hills, suddenly there was nothing left to climb. Uthe came to a halt at the unexpected landscape before them. It was...nothing. Behind them, under their feet, was the green grass. Much further back were the woodlands, the mirror bright streams, ponds and lakes that embellished a panoramic view of the Fae world. Ahead of them was grayness. No ground, no sky. His brain struggled to make sense of it, to look for a solid reference point. The hill on which they stood simply stopped in mid-air, as if bisected. He extended his arm to test the substance in front of him, but Keldwyn caught his wrist.

"It is best not to touch the gateway until we are ready to pass through it."

"It looks like we're stepping into nothing."

"There is a reason the Shattered World is also called the Uncharted Plain. Nothing can be controlled or fathomed there. Throughout the years, Fae who believe they have figured it out go in, armed with their scrolls and their belief that they can make sense of it. None of those have ever returned. Yet."

"But others have emerged?"

"A few, to give us what little information they could, much of it with no clear interpretation. It is always those who stumbled across the threshold through accident. They either remember nothing, or it's a jumble of images and ideas. Some come out entirely mad, their minds destroyed. Reality and fantasy are defined by whatever magic rules the place."

"You have your theories." Uthe gave him a sidelong glance. "I expect you've studied everything you can find about it. It's a puzzle, and those bother you."

"Not bother. They challenge me." Keldwyn tossed him an arch look, though. "Yes. Whenever magic is used, I think there are residual energies—waste, if you will. Perhaps places like the Shattered World are a dumping ground for such magics, which is why it made a good hiding place for your relics. In the Shattered World, there is no authority to control what lies there, as far as we know."

Keldwyn considered him. "Which is why I find it remarkable that you can still feel the blood link with the demon and the Baptist, when even your bond with your servants has a limit of several thousand miles."

"Shahnaz thought it was because of the way the magic of the demon combines with the power of the prophet, fueled by the purity of the innocent. Regardless, it's allowed me to be sure the head has been unmolested all these years."

Keldwyn shifted his attention to the gate. "You took a tremendous risk when you ingested blood from the head. The demon could have infected you with darkness."

"The prayer and meditation have managed it over the years." At Keldwyn's surprised look, Uthe offered a faint smile. "What? You didn't make that connection? Do I really seem that devout without proper motivation? And you consider yourself so smart."

Keldwyn snorted. "You *are* devout, Lord Uthe. Do not try to 'snow' me, as Gideon might say."

You do not fear death, yet you will kill your Master. As soon as you cross this threshold, it is certain. I will make sure he dies an agonizing death. But that doesn't matter, does it? You won't even remember him, let alone his pain.

It wasn't the first time the demon had tried to ambush Uthe with violent, bloody images. He usually blocked them so that he barely felt the malevolence of the attempt, let alone saw the pictures, but the demon had hit him at a weak moment. As his mind filled with visions of Keldwyn being tortured in ways too horrific to even comprehend, his beautiful body torn apart, Uthe struggled to contain and vanquish the violent tornado of blood and screams.

"It is possible, once we pass through, that we will not end up in the same place," Kel was saying. "I will have your word that you will find me before you proceed."

"No. You shouldn't even be going with me. Completing the task is my charge, and if I can't—"

Keldwyn closed his hand on the pendant on Uthe's neck

and jerked it free, despite Uthe's swift attempt to block him. The metal disk disappeared into Keldwyn's clothing. "There. Since you need the sorceress's weapon, then you will find me, if not for my own sake or yours, for the sake of your quest."

He should wrestle the bastard to the ground, take it back. Only the knowledge that Keldwyn could probably glamor the thing into another galaxy stopped him, but he showed his fangs to prove his displeasure. Kel tossed him a kiss-my-oh-so-pretty-ass look in response.

"Damn it, Kel." Out of pure frustration, Uthe punched him in the side. It took the Fae by surprise, and knocked him several feet to the right. When he narrowed his gaze, Uthe braced himself, but Kel's mouth lost its tight look at whatever he saw in Uthe's face.

"The demon is speaking to you, isn't it?"

"Yes. Telling me you're dead as soon as you cross with me. In a hundred terrible ways." The demon had called Keldwyn Uthe's Master, and he hadn't denied it, had he? The thing was too connected to the deeper levels of his mind, to things even Uthe hadn't yet acknowledged.

"Is that all?" Keldwyn looked amused. "In well over a thousand years, how many times have your enemies threatened you with ostentatious declarations about your impending death, my lord? And how hideous and painful they plan to make it?"

At Kel's expectant expression, Uthe grimaced. "I once faced a Saracen who gave a five minute dissertation on how he'd tie me up in my intestines and feed my tongue to my mother before he fucked her to death. It made me glad I'd learned their language, just to hear how much thought he put into it."

Keldwyn chuckled. "Queen Rhoswen has threatened me with death in so many ways I could have them archived. My personal favorite was when she said she would hack my arms and legs from my torso with a dull-edged knife and pin them to each corner of her throne room. She would then cut off my manhood and give it to the household staff to beat rugs. My head would be delivered to the Queen's Guard and dumped in their latrine so they could shit on it until it decomposed. I told her I was honored that she considered my cock capable of maintaining enough size and rigidity after death that it would be of such use to the maids and, if that was the case, they might find other uses for it."

Uthe stared at him, then he let out a rich, full-bodied belly laugh as cleansing as a surge of God's pure light through his veins. Maybe that was what laughter was. "You're lucky she didn't do it."

Keldwyn's gaze had snapped to Uthe's face as he began to laugh, and dwelled there until he subsided and discovered how closely the Fae was looking at him.

"What?"

"'We altogether prohibit idle words and wicked bursts of laughter.' So says your Rule. That might not be a wicked burst of laughter, but it certainly gave me wicked thoughts."

Uthe blinked. "I will say a paternoster for us both, then, since I'm sure you will not." They stood in front of the Shattered World, facing all manner of serious challenges, and Keldwyn was dwelling on laughter and pleasures of the flesh. He wanted to give him an exasperated look, but instead Uthe touched Keldwyn's neck, following the line of it to his jaw, the side of his face, a drifting quest that had the Fae's eyes flickering.

"You had a tattoo here the other day."

"And I can have it again." The design reappeared. Uthe noticed Keldwyn's grimace, though.

"Does it hurt?"

"It has a momentary sting." Keldwyn captured Uthe's hand on his face. "I've never heard you laugh like that. You ease my heart, Varick. And lift it."

Before Uthe's surprised gaze, Kel pressed his lips to Uthe's palm. When the Fae raised his head, he didn't let go.

"You have wondered how much you can trust me, but you have known the answer to that for some time. It is only your mind you doubt, not your heart. But in case you harbor any further worries, I will say this to you. You said that the loss of Reghan destroyed my ability to love or be a Master to another. You were right. But you have resurrected the desire. Which is why I chose to take this journey with you, and why I intend to see it through with you to the end. If our fate is to wander the Shattered World forever afterward, then I shall have no discontent if we do so together. I am sure we can figure out how to have our chess games and argue Fae and vampire politics there as much as we have here."

Uthe had no words to answer such a declaration, no gift big enough to match the Fae's. He was a vampire beset with Ennui, charged with a quest that could cost both their lives. He should figure out a way to knock the Fae unconscious and go without him, but Kel would just follow him after he woke.

"As far as the politics," Uthe said, his voice unsteady, "we'll have just as much luck applying useful answers in the Shattered World as we do with the Vampire Council."

"True enough. Though the term 'shouting into a void' will be quite literal there, I expect."

"Agreed." Uthe paused. "I would ask a favor, my lord. And your trust. Give me back the medallion. If the Shattered World is what you say it is, and the demon is clever as only evil can be, then those two together might ensure we never find one another, since the magic can only be used by me, because of the blood link."

"So you think me having it might guarantee us being kept apart?"

"I do."

"A compelling argument." Keldwyn produced the medallion. He stepped closer, placing it back around Uthe's neck, fusing the link he'd broken. "Very well. But before we make this step, you will drink from me once more. I know you just drank from Alanna, but my blood seemed to energize you last time. In case we are separated for some length of time, I want to know you have that extra resource."

"Kel, there's a way we can make sure we find one another. Except..." In light of the other challenges they faced, it seemed ridiculous to be hesitant about such a thing, but Uthe was unsure of Keldwyn's reaction. He might not have brought up the topic at all, but Keldwyn's unprecedented words, and the freely given offer of blood, summoned it to his lips. "I can mark you. It worked on Lyssa, when Jacob was a vampire and she lost all but the abilities her Fae blood gave her. We could do only the first mark, the geographical locator, the most innocuous of the three. However, if the power in the Shattered World is as strong as you say, a second mark would be best, because then we can speak in one another's minds.

"You wouldn't be a servant," he hastened to say at Keldwyn's sudden blank expression. "It wouldn't be the third mark, which binds your mortality to mine. I could give you the blood mark the Region Masters and overlords give vampires in their territories, or the type given when we sire a vampire, but that may only work on other vampires, and it's not as strong as what we use for servants."

He stopped. He could tell nothing from Keldwyn's expression. "It is simply an idea," he said. "One that might not work. And if it did and we return, Brian could possibly reverse it. His experience with that thus far has been with vampires and human servants, though."

He shouldn't have brought it up. This was a high Fae Lord. It was a miracle he'd given Uthe blood once, let alone offered it twice. But damn it, he didn't want Kel to be where he couldn't aid him if needed. Uthe wasn't going to let pride, fear of rejection or the damn Fae's own ego stand in the way of protecting him however he could.

Keldwyn adjusted his stance so he was facing that gray

miasma. "What am I to you, Lord Uthe?"

"An ally. A friend." A friend he'd let deeper inside him than any other. "A warrior I'm honored to fight beside, on any field."

"Word games, Lord Uthe. The two of us excel at playing them." Keldwyn turned to face him fully, coming a step closer, the toes of one booted foot pressed against the side of Uthe's. Keldwyn curled his fingers in the belt of Uthe's tunic and held. "What am I to you, Lord Uthe?"

A miracle that had appeared when he needed it most, and not merely for the completion of this task. Someone willing to stand beside him as he faced the loss of his faculties, something he feared far worse than death, because of the decisions it would take out of his hands. Someone he could trust to make decisions for him when necessary, because Keldwyn understood his mind and needs as he understood his own.

He wished their minds were linked as a vampire's was to a second mark, so he could have shared that. Some things couldn't be spoken out loud in the same way they could be thought. Then Uthe thought of what the demon had said. He didn't like that the demon had spoken the truth first, but that was what made a demon so dangerous. He knew how to use the truth to drag down the soul. But Uthe had the will to take it back, elevate it by owning it fully.

"You're my lord Keldwyn. My lord." He swallowed, somewhat amused by his sudden nervousness. The thread of tension between them was wound tight as they stood on more than one kind of precipice. "My Master."

The reaction in Keldwyn's face was indescribable, so beautiful it sent a bolt of pain through Uthe. It was as if speaking that one word had staked him through the chest and destroyed him, but only so he could rise from his own ashes to this. Then the Fae's every facial muscle relaxed, Keldwyn's eyes glowing with heat and his sensual lips parted. His body thrummed with energy against Uthe's.

"I will take you here, Lord Uthe, on this threshold, in

case the powers beyond it do not give us that pleasure. You will give me your marks to safeguard, so I may hold onto your mind as you hold onto mine. And you will take my blood, now and whenever you have need of it, for as long as I have life to give you."

Keldwyn's hands were already on Uthe's belt, unbuckling it, nudging his hands out of the way as he stripped the tunic from him. It was good that he did so, for it took Uthe a few moments to recover from the import of Keldwyn's words and catch up. But then Uthe divested himself of the leggings and boots, everything except the medallion he wore, the heat of the medal burning into his tingling skin. Keldwyn pressed him down to his knees and made him stay that way as he stripped off his own clothes. He tapped his thigh next to his jutting cock. "Make your marks here, Varick. Take the blood you need, if you can do it at the same time. It would please me to see you nourish yourself off of me on your knees like this."

Uthe's own cock jumped at the heavy pleasure in the Fae's thick tone. Sliding his hands up the sleek muscular columns, he pressed his thumbs into Kel's inner thighs, a mute request for him to spread his legs even wider. He didn't deny himself a taste of that other hard column, though, licking a line up Keldwyn's cock, nipping at the corona and sipping the fluid collecting at the tip of the glans before taking the whole thing for one strong stroke in his mouth, savoring Keldwyn's taste. Keldwyn's hand fell on his head. "The marks and the blood first, Varick," he said, though his voice was rigid with desire.

Uthe moved to the pounding beat of the femoral, tracing it with his tongue. The skin was so smooth on the Fae's inner thigh.

He let his fangs unsheathe. The monumental meaning of what he was about to do, what it would mean to the two of them, overwhelmed him, even as his practical side suggested he not get too excited, since it might not take. Keldwyn wasn't Lyssa, half Fae and half vampire. His high

Fae blood might reject the mark, spit it out like chaff.

He didn't want to think of that possibility. It would either happen or not.

"Do it," Keldwyn said, his voice a harsh command. "Now."

He bit, sinking his fangs in as deep as they could go. The pain of that full penetration could be extreme, but he sensed Keldwyn would want to feel it. Kel drew in a breath, fingers clutching Uthe's nape and shoulder before he tugged him closer, holding him so tightly, Uthe's temple and jaw pressed against pulsing cock and heated testicles. His Master would take him once more before they faced what they faced. The thought made his ass contract and him pull on the punctures in Kel's thigh more strenuously, swallowing down the rich Fae blood.

It had a tingling magic to it, the tart metallic taste different from humans, like an exotic vintage never experienced before. The first time he'd been too disoriented to appreciate it fully. He didn't need much, not with what he'd had from Alanna so recently, but he took a couple extra swallows just for the pleasure of it. Not enough to deplete Kel, though. If blood loss could affect the Fae adversely, he didn't want to take away resources his lord would need.

His lord. He released the first mark, the geographical locater, and Kel's muscles tightened. The mark was like a form of GPS, making it possible to locate a servant anywhere within those few thousand miles. Humans described the injection of the mark as a sizzling sensation through the blood, not uncomfortable, but Uthe didn't know how a Fae would experience it.

On the other hand, doing two marks at the same time could be painful. To avoid as much of that possibility as limited time would give him, Uthe devoted his time to other pursuits. Sliding a hand up Kel's opposite thigh, he caressed and teased his balls, then curled his hand around the base of his cock.

Kel dug his fingers into Uthe's muscular shoulder. "Get it done, Varick," he rasped. "I want to fuck you *now*."

As Uthe released the serum of the second mark, he could almost feel it searing its way through Keldwyn, a shot of light and magic and chemical reaction through his circulatory and nervous systems. When Kel let out a shuddering breath, Uthe looked up, concerned. He had his head tipped back, his body rocking against Uthe's rhythmic hold on his cock, his hand still clamped on his shoulder. The tension in his face didn't look like excruciating pain, but there were a mélange of reactions to manage when the second mark connection activated. Would it work?

My lord? Are you in pain? He eased his fangs from Kel and licked the puncture wounds until they closed. Then he pressed his forehead to them, the way he might press his forehead to the ground right before prayer. Contact with the solidity of earth was a reminder of the miracles of creation. It was a comfort to feel that ultimate connection and gift, just as it was to feel it with Keldwyn now.

He shuddered at the jumble that dropped into his mind, like a child's spilled treasure chest of gold coins, creek stone, feathers and butterflies. He was familiar with the first disoriented spinnings of a human mind as it adjusted to the connection. Taking in the mind of a Fae Lord was like getting a whole amusement park, an explosion of color, sounds and images. Because he thought of Keldwyn as his Master, Uthe hadn't prepared himself the way he had with Mariela. With her he'd been ready to filter it down to a more manageable level.

The power of this mind, whirling like a tornado to form the connection with his, was astounding, mesmerizing, and he almost lost himself in it. Fortunately, his fear of what a wandering mind portended brought him back on track. Touching the edges of Keldwyn's thoughts, he made him aware of the connection and drew attention to the boundary edges between their two minds, so the Fae could find his own balance again.

No. I am not in pain. I am in a remarkable new world. Your mind is as amazing as your words have always made it seem. You are not just clever, Lord Uthe. You are astonishingly extraordinary. A world as complex as the Fae and vampire ones combined resides in you.

He realized then he had his mind wide open, something he would not have done for a human servant, either. Keldwyn caught that, his fingers touching Uthe's face so he would look up at him. Uthe thought he was looking into the sun, for Kel's gaze was so brilliant, full of emotion. "I expect it to remain that way, my lord," he said. "For I am no servant, am I?"

"No, my lord."

Keldwyn's expression became even more intent. He pressed Uthe down to the ground, onto his back, the Fae stretching out upon him. Keldwyn lifted one of Uthe's thighs over his arm, pressing the other into a bent position under his other arm as he probed Uthe's tight channel, ensuring it was still oiled from their earlier couplings. Too impatient to seek lubricant, Kel added some saliva to his palm and rubbed it on himself to ease his passage. Uthe coiled his leg around him, constricting the muscle, telling him his desire, his need, his want.

Kel slid into him, sinking all the way to Uthe's heart. "You fed as you should?" he asked, coming to a stop, holding there, eyes on Uthe's face.

"I did. Now let me give you pleasure, my lord. Though I fear there is no way to fill you as you have filled me."

The skin around Keldwyn's eyes crinkled. "I find your size more than adequate, Lord Uthe. No need to denigrate yourself because you lack a Fae's substantial girth."

Uthe shot him a droll look, despite the intensity of his own body's reaction. "Your glamor magic has infected your brain with the delusions it imposes on others, my lord. But don't fret. I've had difficulty of late separating fact from fantasy. It's what happens to us older folk."

Keldwyn bit Uthe's shoulder, a not-so-playful nip that

made Uthe's body rise against him, another groan slipping from his throat.

I will take you now, my lord, and you will have no say in it.

Kel's words branded themselves in his brain, the sensual threat sending electricity through the rest of Uthe's body. Keldwyn started to thrust in earnest, his eyes burning on Uthe's, his mouth set, fingers digging into his hips. Uthe's cock bounced rhythmically on his belly, a repetitive impact that branded him with pleasure, the shaft becoming stiffer with every thud. Keldwyn's gaze flickered to it, and he licked his lips. Uthe locked both legs around him, his arms sliding around the Fae Lord's shoulders, bringing his mouth down to him. Keldwyn gave him that, a deep, tongue-tangling kiss. He wished Kel's hair was loose to brush Uthe's face and shoulders, but he could settle for having the Fae's cock driving into him, the heated skin of his chest muscles rubbing against Uthe's.

"Now," Keldwyn demanded. "Come."

Uthe complied without thought, a response that grew even more intense as Keldwyn reached between them, wrapped his fingers around his cock and worked it relentlessly, milking every spasm out of Uthe until he was moved from groans to shouts. When Keldwyn's fingers convulsed and the Fae Lord began to release, ramming into him, harder, tighter, deeper, Uthe cried out with the further pleasure of it. They were under the open sky, under the grim shadow of the Shattered World, with the simmering thoughts of a demon growling in the base of his brain, but none of that mattered. Not right now.

Keldwyn slowed, putting his head down against Uthe's. "There. You will not be lost to me. I forbid it. You have marked me; I have marked you."

From his mouth to God's ear, and may God have mercy on them and not take the declaration as arrogance. Or perhaps God found Keldwyn's arrogance as appealing as Uthe did. They were all His creation, after all.

Pulling apart was a reluctant process, but both of them knew they could delay no longer. Still, as they cleaned up with the help of an anemic stream at the bottom of the hill and then donned their clothing, there were frequent touches, a stroke of a bare hip, a trailing of fingertips along a curved back. Uthe shook his head at the remarkable nature of the world. Now, when he stood at the end of his life, he was finally besotted, acting like a fledgling with his first love. Keldwyn's smile only made the feeling more poignant. When they were dressed, Keldwyn put his mouth back on Uthe's, and held them there until Uthe's knees started to weaken and his cock started to fill with blood again. Then the Fae pulled back.

"There. That should also help us find one another."

Uthe glanced down. "I'm not sure it works as a compass pointer, my lord, but it looks fully capable at the moment."

Keldwyn nudged him roughly, but his expression was warm. They went back up the hill and faced the gray void. "We simply walk forward?" Uthe said.

"There is naught to it but that. There are multiple safeguards on it now to prevent accidental entry like those earlier stumblings, but the Queen will have adjusted it for our passage, as she agreed. She will know when we have entered. She has worked out a complicated marking magic that may pull us out when it's done, but she warned nothing is certain because we know so little of this dimension."

"And she may decide she prefers to leave you there rather than deal with you anymore."

Kel's lips curved. "There is that."

"All right then," Uthe took a breath. "May God go with you, my lord. If He wills it, I'll see you on the other side."

Keldwyn reached out a hand. "As childlike as it might seem, we might as well attempt it."

"Sometimes the simplest gestures have the strongest magic of all." Uthe clasped it, feeling the strength of Kel's hold, and his gaze returned to the void. As he paused, Kel stilled beside him, sensing the direction of his thoughts. While he could read them from Uthe's head, Uthe chose to speak them aloud.

"I have sought a Master to ease my need for centuries, my lord. God gave me that succor, but I think He knew the time has come for an earthly balance to what he provides in a heavenly manner. As you said"—for he now knew the words had come from Keldwyn—"that may be the purpose of love in our world. To remind us it is the ultimate gift He provides, if our hearts are open to it. To give us breadcrumbs to show us His true face, and to guide us to one another."

Keldwyn's grip constricted in response, a mute agreement. Uthe began to move forward, drawing the Fae with him. Kel fell into step with him. One stride, they were still together. Two strides, Uthe felt Keldwyn's shoulder brush his. Three strides...

Nothingness closed in on him.

Chapter Fourteen

Something was crawling on him. Uthe started up, sending sand torqueing around him. As he blinked and focused, he saw the pair of scorpions scuttling away. His body felt unusually weighted. Glancing down, he discovered he was wearing his mail hauberk beneath a tunic with a red cross on the breast. The Crusader uniform. The white Templar mantle, with the cross on the left shoulder, fluttered over it. A sword was belted over the tunic. No helmet. He'd had one, but had hated the thing, the way it obstructed his sight. He'd usually made do with the mail coif of his hauberk instead. He pulled it off to rest on his shoulders and grimaced. The tightly knit links of mail were excellent at grasping and pulling out hairs. As he ran a hand over his scalp, he noticed carrying the dagger had accelerated his hair growth. It was a good half inch longer. Perhaps that was why Kel had been inclined to pet him so much these past couple days.

The dagger was in its scabbard and the pouch with Rhoswen's amulet was still firmly attached to his belt, thankfully. He felt around his neck to make sure the pendant with the sorceress's weapon was there. It suggested the outfit was an illusion, if the things he'd had with him on the other side were still in the same place, though the weight of the mail felt quite real. But that was the danger of illusions—they did feel real.

He focused on his surroundings. It was much like the part of Syria where they'd gone to claim Fatima's magic. Sand, rock and scrub. But he could be standing in the middle of a lush forest, by a babbling creek, with Keldwyn trying to return him to their reality. Waking up in clothing he wore a thousand years ago, in the middle of a desolate wasteland, that could be the illusion. How did he know the stress of crossing into this dimension hadn't catapulted his brain into one of the Ennui episodes?

The panic that gripped his bowels angered him and he shoved it away. The demon might fuck with his mind right along with the Ennui and the Shattered World. It mattered not. He knew what his task was, and he would accomplish it. So the Shattered World liked to play games with fantasy and reality? Uthe was uniquely prepared. He'd told Kel that, hadn't he? Time to live up to his bravado.

He took several deep breaths and closed his eyes. *Keldwyn.*

No response, but that wasn't the only way to find him. He turned his energy toward the blood link. Nothing. Pushing back a sense of foreboding, he reasoned it out. There was no way of knowing what fields of interference might exist, magical or otherwise. He could start walking. The sun was beating down like the fires of Hell and, while it was a Fae realm where the sun didn't have the draining properties it did in the mortal one, it was still uncomfortable. He could handle discomfort.

This was the worst case scenario, wasn't it? No connection to Keldwyn, no sense of which direction to go, no idea if what he was experiencing was the Shattered World's reality or his mind's dementia. He felt disconnected, adrift. Helpless. Rage, frustration and bloodlust started to stir and gather momentum. Lord Brian had postulated that the more volatile effects of Ennui were incited by a vampire's baser instincts. If Uthe had revealed his condition to the scientist, Brian might have concluded Uthe had experienced only memory loss and disorientation thus far because of prayer and meditation, keeping the more violent symptoms at bay. The same way he'd controlled the impact of having a demon in his head.

Of course. He shook his head at himself. A thousand years of routine, and he'd forgotten the most important part of it. Pushing away anxiety and the despised panic against a foe he couldn't fight, he put his trust in the Ally he understood the least but believed in the most. The One who had brought Keldwyn's faith, support and yes, love, to him in this final phase of his life.

Drawing the sword, Uthe drove it into the ground and knelt before the cross formed by the hilt. Bowing his head, he closed his eyes. "Lord give me the strength to do Your bidding, to fight Your enemies and be Thy servant in every way. I am armored in obedience to Thy Will. I will fear nothing but Your might. If it is Thy Will I die like this, then I submit to that decision. But if You desire me to complete my quest, then I ask Your help to see past what blinds my eyes. Help me serve You. I pray for Keldwyn's protection and a safe return to his own world."

Varick.

Uthe's lips curved as a breeze touched his face. *I should have known. All I had to do was start praying, and you would interrupt me. Heathen.*

He lifted his head, and the landscape around him had changed, to a surreal vision of color. He knelt in a meadow of long blue grass with tufted green crowns. The sky was orange, the trees red.

Kel. I've fallen into a melted box of crayons. He chuckled. As he rose, he saw he was still in the Templar mail and tunic, still armed with a sword, but he was heartened by the change of scenery, especially as he saw Keldwyn working his way across the blue field to him. He'd gotten used to having the Fae around, all in all. Was this dream or real?

Stop it. Keldwyn's voice. *You'll drive yourself into insanity with that nonsense. It's either real or not, but you have no control of knowing the difference, not here. You simply keep your intent before you and either you'll reach it or...* He reached Uthe then and spoke aloud. "You'll live out your life in a box of melted crayons."

He didn't give Uthe a chance to respond, instead grabbing a handful of the tunic and yanking him forward to plant a violent kiss on Uthe's mouth. It wasn't seductive or gentle, but a pure, rough branding, the reconnection a lover would crave after a prolonged absence. It had only seemed like a few minutes to Uthe, but it didn't make him any less receptive to the greeting. He gripped the Fae Lord's tunic as Keldwyn settled both hands on his face, holding him still to plunder his mouth, scraping Uthe's fangs with his teeth. His fingers pressed into the sides of Uthe's throat so he felt the beat of his own pulse.

Keldwyn's body leaned fully against his, so forcefully Uthe would have been pushed back a step except Kel snaked an arm around him. When he drew back, staring into Uthe's face, Uthe's still logy mind was unable to sort anything but the throbbing need in the Fae, which found an answer in his own body and heart. Since he wasn't one to speak his feelings when he could barely think a straight thought, he asked the first innocuous thing that came to mind.

"How do you know what crayons are?"

Keldwyn eased back, his expression becoming less feral and closer to the norm. "Humanoids have had the desire to create pictures for thousands of years," he said. "Plus, children are children, regardless of the world. We have crayons. We do not call them that, but they are the same thing. A mix of wax and dyes. After the last Council meeting, Kane found me and showed me a picture he'd colored. He wanted to know if I thought it was good. I said it was, but he was not satisfied. He knows when he's being patronized. He made me sit down with him and show him how to make it better."

Uthe visualized the Fae sitting next to the vampire child and coloring. It wasn't as unimaginable as it once had been, because he now knew his lord loved children. "Did you do that kind of thing with your sons and daughters?"

He wasn't sure why he was pursuing the subject right now, but his mind was still adapting to his environment. He felt like he was waiting for...something. Something that would be found right here. He sank to his knees in the long grass and came face to face with a purple spider perched on top of a feathery tuft of meadow grass. The legs were like long threads, the body the size of an unshelled peanut. It bounced at his appearance, like a daddy longlegs. Uthe glanced up at Keldwyn. "Sit with me a bit," he said. "I think we need to wait here for a while."

Keldwyn was studying him, but he dropped to a mirror position of Uthe's pose, bracing his hands on his knees. "Yes. Shelessia loved creating pictures. She could make them come to life for short periods of time. If she drew a dragon, it would leap off the page and play with her. It would retain all the characteristics of the drawing, the strokes of the crayon, the dark outline. The places where she'd gone outside the lines became jagged scales stuck out at odd places on the dragon's body. When she fell asleep in my arms for her nap, it melted back into the page, becoming two dimensional once more."

"Huh. I wonder if that's also what this place is. The inside of someone's mind, of many minds. A collection place for all our fantastic, unnatural and bizarre imaginings. Where the most random stray thoughts gather to play."

"Possible." Keldwyn leaned forward and clasped Uthe's hand, drawing his attention. "Varick. Are you with me? Wholly here?"

Uthe nodded. "I'm waiting," he said. "But I cannot tell for what. I know no one is playing a game with me right now. There's a particular feeling when it's the demon screwing with me, if that makes sense. How long did you look for me?"

"Time has very little meaning here," Kel said.

It wasn't a direct answer, which made Uthe pay closer attention to his companion. With his mind clearing, for the first time he noticed Keldwyn's face was more drawn than usual. Unlike Uthe, he wore the same clothing he had on the other side of the gray wall, but his jerkin had been torn, and a faded, rust-colored stain suggested blood. Since the Fae Lord always moved with lissome grace, Uthe should have noted that he was moving more stiffly, not only when he'd knelt just now, but as he came across the field. His hair was still braided, but they were no longer the smooth, silken ropes Catriona had created. They were snagged and knotted, long wisps of hair loose around his smudged face.

Uthe knew the look from extended campaigns. Keldwyn had been traveling, sweating and fighting for a few days at least. No wonder the Fae had asked him if he was in his right mind, if Uthe had not noticed such things right away, let alone remarked on them. Kel's fervent greeting made even more sense now.

"I just woke up," he said. "Kel, how long have you been here?"

"It matters naught. I have found you now."

The words yanked at him, a lifeline to pull him out of the dreamlike state trying to hold him like quicksand. "Yes, it matters. How long, my lord?" What was Kel trying to keep from him?

"If time could be measured here, perhaps a couple weeks." At his startled look, Kel made a placating gesture. "It is what the Shattered World does. You should not ascribe any significance to it."

Except it made Uthe feel as if he had lost more control of his mind than he'd expected, which he was sure was why Kel hadn't wanted to reveal it to him. Uthe ran his fingers over the blood on the jerkin, the rip that had torn it. The top lacings were shredded, so his touch grazed Kel's bare chest. "And who did this to you, my lord?" He knew his voice was hard, his eyes gone flat, because he saw the reflection in Kel's face as he closed his hand around Uthe's wrist.

"A few creatures who thought a new arrival in their world was fair game. They quickly learned otherwise. Fortunately it allowed me to acquire some weaponry, which is necessary here, because magic is unreliable." He touched a quiver of arrows he had strapped on his back with a bow, a brace of daggers at his belt. He'd unsheathed a sword before kneeling and it lay next to them. Uthe had assumed Keldwyn had woken up with the armaments like he had. He put his hand on the pommel of his own sword.

"Do I have weapons, Kel? A sword?"

"Yes, my lord." Keldwyn put his hand over Uthe's so they could grip the hilt together, confirming it. "You also have a long dagger at your hip, as well as the dagger you carry to ward you against sunlight. It seems the Shattered World wanted to gift you with weapons."

"Whereas it made you fight for them." Uthe already didn't like this place. He looked at the sword and weapons Kel was carrying. "They were heavily armed. You handled yourself well."

Kel shrugged. "My glamor did not work on them, but my time shift skills did."

"Time shift skills?"

"I can shift time for an opponent. Make his body blink out of this moment and reappear a moment later, perhaps only a few inches to the right or left of where he was. If I do it correctly, they phase into their future body. Most unpleasant and often fatal unless they have a way to counter it. I don't use it often, because it is draining and it can cause larger ripples, but in this case, it became necessary, since the initial numbers were too large for me to handle without such tactics."

During which, Uthe had been...what? Sleeping? Caught somehow in the limbo between the Fae world and this one?

Why had the Shattered World wanted them to have such a lag between their appearances in this world?

"You are trying to ascribe logic to how the Shattered World does things. Chaos is what holds sway here. I won't tolerate you castigating yourself. You will be the one who has to confront the demon directly. You needed your beauty sleep." Keldwyn swept a gaze over him. "I see it didn't do much good, but then vampires are not blessed with the natural beauty the Fae possess."

Uthe gripped Kel's tunic, drawing him forward. The Fae lifted a brow. "Do not get heavy-handed with me, vampire." But there was a smile on his mouth that Uthe couldn't resist touching with his own lips. He drew back after a light taste, but stayed close so he could lock gazes with the other male. He saw the relief in Kel's face, the weariness.

"I'm sorry I wasn't there." Kel fighting for his life while Uthe was taking some kind of nap, whether or not imposed by the Shattered World, rankled. But more than that, he remembered how he'd felt, thinking he'd never find Keldwyn. He'd experienced that for a few minutes only. The Fae had been wondering where he was, what had happened, and whether he and Uthe would ever find one another here, for a couple weeks.

Kel curled his fingers over Uthe's. "It is of no consequence now. I have found you." It was a reminder that Kel could hear all these things in Uthe's mind, because Uthe was not doing a thing to keep him out of it.

"If you wish to apologize for your tardiness, I can think of several ways for you to express your chagrin." Keldwyn leaned in, murmuring against Uthe's ear. "I can punish you to ease your guilt in ways that will have you begging, vampire. There are so many things we have not explored together. Your capacity to take pain for pleasure is something I ache to investigate. You called me Master before you stepped over the threshold to this world, and I will hold you to it."

Uthe's fingers convulsed on him, the wave of sensual

pleasure so strong he had to close his eyes. Since he'd only just begun to allow himself to respond to such things, the jolt of lust and need the threat incited was unexpected, part of the maze of surprising reactions he had to Kel exercising his Dominant nature around him. Over him.

"Your timing is appalling, my lord."

Kel chuckled darkly. "There is no better time than the present to plant such thoughts in your mind. It may give you even more incentive to survive this hellish place. I know it does for me. And truth,"—his eyes burned into Uthe's—"after the past few days, not knowing where you were, or if you had need of me at your side, I have a violent compulsion to impress things upon you far beyond the realm of appalling."

Uthe could see it in his expression, in the hum of energy coming off his body, a mix of magic and potent male need. Thanks to the vulnerabilities the Ennui created in him, Uthe now had a better understanding his own deepest, darkest needs. It wasn't an orientation like humans understood in their structured BDSM play; it was who vampires were at their core. No safe words or contracts. Apparently, his Fae had those same compulsions.

Which was why Uthe found himself relieved that Kel was much more powerful than him. He wanted that punishment, wanted to feel what it was to completely surrender to a Master, more than just the hints of what they'd experienced so far together. Was it this world that brought such longings out, so naked and raw? He thought of Keldwyn drawing the long dagger he carried, sliding it slowly along Uthe's flesh, leaving a thin rivulet of blood he would place his mouth over...

"By the gods, being in your head, seeing where you go with what I say to you, how I touch you... If we survive this, Varick, I will not permit you to leave my bed for a decade. I will chain you there, naked and beautiful, and savor you with all the decadence and cruelty the fairy tales tell you a Fae can possess." Kel moved his mouth to Uthe's throat, and Uthe tipped his head back as the Fae bit him there. Though it was just a light nip, he shuddered, a growl vibrating in his chest. Kel pressed his forehead hard against the column of Uthe's throat, his mouth on his shoulder. "I have lived long enough to know that two weeks is a blink, yet these were the longest two weeks of my life, thinking you were lost and wandering, under attack...needing my presence."

"Needing you." Uthe corrected him, making it more intimate. He stroked the back of Kel's head, slipped his fingers over the thick braid of dark hair. "Yet here you find I was just cheerfully napping, in no need of you at all. No wonder you want to take a strip off my ass."

Kel lifted his head, his expression showing the serious moment had passed. "More than a strip, I can promise you, my lord. Flaying comes to mind."

Uthe straightened abruptly. The wind had brought him a sound, the snorting of a horse. Keldwyn was on his feet next to him in the same blink. Shoulder to shoulder, they scanned the area around them for the threat.

The snort came again, and Uthe found the source. His eyes widened. "Nexus."

The destrier stood on the edge of the blue field of grass, just outside the line of red trees. He was a blood bay with heavy black mane and tail, and his dark eyes searched the meadow grass as he shifted restlessly left and right. Uthe gave a sharp whistle. The horse's head came back toward him like a rifle muzzle sighting its target, and then he burst into an artistic display of motion, a high stepping charge more like a dance than a run. His mane and tail streamed out, his powerful neck arched, and a series of piercing whinnies and snorts punctuated his short trip to Uthe.

"Show off," Uthe muttered, though he thought his heart might brim over with joy.

Nexus came to a halt before Uthe and shoved him backwards with his massive head. Uthe kept his balance thanks to his vampire strength, but he remembered how often Nexus enjoyed catching his squire by surprise with that move, sending Jacques ass over end into the dirt. When he thought Uthe was out of hearing range, the squire had often threatened to quarter the horse for stew, but Uthe knew Jacques loved the spirited creature almost as much as he did. Had.

Nexus had died at Hattin, just as Jacques had, despite Uthe's best efforts to save them both. Still, even if it was a trick of this world, he was going to call the horse's appearance a blessing. He petted the velvet soft nose and his muscular neck, pressing up against his shoulder as he did so. He ran his hands over the horse's back, sides and legs, a habit that came back to him as if he'd been doing the post-matins check of horse and equipment as recently as yesterday. "You are looking fine, old boy," he crooned. "Ready to take on Saladin's entire army, aren't you?"

A snort agreed with him. Keldwyn had drawn closer, so Uthe made the introductions. "This is Nexus. He was the mount I had the longest. Most horses fear vampires, but as long as I wore the dagger, they were fine. Though I think Nexus's courage overrode any concerns about me as a predator." He moved to the horse's flank, drawing Keldwyn's attention to the trio of scars. There was a matching set on the other side.

"We were chaperoning pilgrims to the River Jordan. When we made camp, after nightfall, we were attacked by a pair of lions. Leonard and I dispatched one of them, but the other got to Nexus. The lion had leaped and grabbed onto his flanks like this. Nexus spun around and around, screaming. He dislodged the lion, but he didn't run or retreat as most horses would when he got free. He went after him, and crushed the lion beneath his hooves."

Nexus had settled and was gazing at him with a satisfied look, as if knowing the story being told. Uthe remembered approaching the horse afterwards, speaking soothingly, touching him as he trembled. Nexus's eyes had flashed and he'd plunged forward, bringing his hooves down on the lion's inert body, stomping on him again and again, refusing to let Uthe pull him away. The pilgrims had crossed themselves at the horse's savage behavior. When Uthe had managed to coax him back at last, Nexus's hooves and forelegs were spattered with blood. Uthe had understood it, though. For certain warriors, a near fatal attack triggered a fury within them. They couldn't contain it in the aftermath, for that rage overcame any lingering fear of death. When he'd joined the Templars, he'd been driven by such a killing rage, though the fears he'd been exorcising were quite different in nature.

Keldwyn approached the horse's other side. After a weighted moment of eye contact, Nexus lowered his head, accepting the Fae's touch. "A remarkable earth spirit," Kel commented. "Is this what you were waiting for?"

"I think so, because now I feel like we can go." Uthe grimaced. "Apparently the Shattered World thought we needed a ride. We used to ride palfreys between battles. Nexus and the other destriers were only ridden to practice maneuvers and keep them in shape. But I expect he won't mind carrying us for something as mundane as a walk through the forest, will you, Sir Nexus?"

The horse shook out his mane and snorted, stomping his feet.

"I'll take that as a yes, though it's also a 'why are we just standing here' fidget. Jacques used to have to play a lyre to get him to sleep."

"You were fond of your squire."

Uthe chuckled. "The relationship between knight and squire was defined as Master and servant. Yet Jacques served for nothing more than food and shelter, and the Rule said, 'If that squire willingly serves charity, the brother should not beat him for any sin he commits.' He knew that, clever lad. Sometimes he let his smart mouth run away with him. One day after a skirmish, we were setting up camp for the night and I found a dropped coin from one of our fallen enemies. I tossed it to Jacques.

When he caught it, I informed him he'd accepted pay for his services and now I could take a sword blade to his arse. He led me a merry chase around the camp."

Keldwyn's smile brought Uthe more good feelings. Swinging up on the horse's back, he was delighted by how easily the memory came to him. All the memories of that time were flooding back into his head, more real and vivid than the vampire world he'd left behind only a couple days ago. It was reassuring, though he knew it could well be false confidence.

"The other knights used to wonder how I did that in full armor and mail. Manfred, my sergeant, would tell them it was the Lord's strength fueling me." He settled onto the horse's bare back. He would need no tack with Nexus, who could respond to the touch of his legs and hands alone. Uthe extended a hand to a bemused-looking Kel. "He can take both of us. Will you ride with me, my lord?"

Kel accepted his assistance and swung on behind him. Though Kel's own natural flexibility and strength got him there capably enough, Uthe embraced the firm grasp between their hands. He rested his palm on one of Kel's thighs as they framed Uthe's hips. Keldwyn's chest pressed against Uthe's back as he reached around him and withdrew the seal from beneath his tunic and mail, studying the emblem of the two knights riding one horse. Tucking it back under Uthe's clothing, he wrapped an arm around his waist, settling his groin firmly against Uthe's buttocks, making him wish he wasn't wearing a full mail shirt.

"Do you think it has significance, our current circumstances matching that symbol?" Uthe asked.

"I would neither assume nor discount anything in this world. Where are we going?"

"Hold on." Uthe fell silent, opening his mind. He'd learned his lesson in how Keldwyn had come to him. Instead of straining the limits of his senses, he used the meditation techniques of a lifetime to calm everything. No matter the obstacles in this world, he had to believe his blood link to the demon and two souls was something the Shattered World couldn't mask, because that link hadn't been blocked when he was in his own world. Plus, the mind link between him and Keldwyn had appeared quickly once he was able to focus on it through prayer.

There. At first, it was just a hint, but after hundreds of years, he recognized the connection, whether it was so slender it was a transparent thread, or a rope thick as his arm. He pressed his knees into Nexus's sides, and the horse moved forward at his direction. Keldwyn's arms tightened around him. They rode in silence for a time. Uthe figured Keldwyn was respecting his need to concentrate, which was why he was surprised when the Fae's weight against him grew heavier, his head dipping to touch Uthe's nape over the folded mail coif. A sigh, an adjustment, and his cheek was pillowed against Uthe's shoulder and the curve of his neck. Uthe covered one of the hands resting on his hip, drew it forward. Another adjustment, and the exhausted Fae clasped them around Uthe's waist fully. Kel grunted and subsided further into sleep.

Keldwyn had said he drew his food from the elements if needed, but was this the natural world? Did the Shattered World nourish him the way the Fae and mortal realms did? How often had he had to fight for his life over these past couple weeks?

He was afraid he had the answer to one of those questions. He'd never seen the Fae tired to the point of exhaustion, which suggested Keldwyn had not been able to find energy here to nourish him, at least not in the amounts he needed for full strength. His initial exuberance had been fueled by an adrenaline surge, caused by finding Uthe. But now that had ebbed.

A second mark could get nourishment from a vampire's blood. Not as much as they would if they were third marked, where their mortality was inescapably linked to the vampire's, but it could give them some energy, the way food might. Yet what were the chances that he could talk Kel into drinking *from* him? He'd just fantasized about Kel cutting him and the Fae tasting the blood from the cut. If Kel had seen that in his mind, he hadn't reacted in horror. But they'd had other priorities right then.

For now, Uthe let him rest. It was not unpleasant, to be walking through this endless collage of bright colors, Kel's arms wrapped around him, his body pressed to Uthe's. It was almost peaceful. In a misleading way, no doubt, but Uthe had learned not to waste the pleasure of small moments. He'd put his hand over Kel's clasped at his waist and held them firmly, stroking the long, elegant fingers. Sometimes the Fae Lord came to Council meetings wearing several heavy rings on them, the intricate settings sparkling with faceted gems. The Fae craftsmanship was remarkable enough to have Helga, typically standoffish when it came to Keldwyn, remarking on them. Once she'd even requested a closer look. Kel had indulged her, a flash of amusement on his face as she became enthusiastic enough in her perusal to unconsciously clasp his wrist. A blink later, she'd snatched her hand back as if ashamed at showing such a bald interest.

Uthe remembered Gideon joking to Jacob that the Fae Lord had the best fashion sense of anyone at the Council meetings. He was always superbly dressed and adorned. Uthe assumed it was something he could conjure, like the tattoos. No matter his lofty words about not using magic for mere convenience, the Fae didn't seem the type willing to spend time fussing over the lay of a ruffled collar, the shine of buttons on a long coat, or the suppleness of his boots. What Kel wore now looked distinctly battle worn.

Uthe remembered he'd once attended Council with a full complement of small rings lining the shell of one ear. The clasps looked like tiny bird claws. They'd distracted Uthe. He kept catching himself looking at them, wanting to reach out and trace their hold on Keldwyn's ear.

"I noticed," Kel mumbled against his back. "You

observed what I wear in a different way from Helga and the others. You were always very thorough in your perusal, even though you took pains to be sure no one noticed. You never remarked on any of it, yet when I wore something unexpected, like the earrings, you gave it special attention. I expect that's why I started doing more of that."

"You are a tease, my lord. I have always known it. And your ears are quite intriguing even without adornment."

Kel snorted. "Everyone always wants to touch the ears. Kane demanded it the first time he saw me."

"Did you permit it?"

"Not that time. I made it clear it was a highly impertinent thing to ask a Fae and cowed him into an apology."

"Miracles do happen."

"I threatened to tell his mother of his rudeness. He fears her, as does any vampire male with sense. But eventually, when he asked the right way, I allowed it. I expected to be merely tolerant when you wanted to do it, but I found your desire welcome, and your touch distinctly pleasurable."

Uthe tapped Kel's knuckles. "You need food, my friend. Don't you? Is there any to be had here?"

"No. Very little. Elemental sustenance is meager at best, though I did find some. Is it possible for the demon to interfere in that way?"

"Possibly. But though I don't detect magic the way you do, I think the magic here is like a capricious child. Cruel and random. Wanting to see how things play out if certain obstacles are put in our way. That would mesh with the demon's purpose, so either one could be at fault. Or both. How long can you go without?"

"For some time." Keldwyn shifted against him. "A nap will hold me for the time being."

"What about if you need to fight again?"

"I have you for that."

"A Fae deferring to a vampire for a fight. Now I'm certain your mind has been affected by your weakened condition." Uthe tilted his head back, brushing his jaw against Kel's, then straightened. "You can take some of my blood, my lord," he said with forced casualness. "That will help restore your strength. If we get out of this place, you can claim it was all illusion and I will not deny it."

Keldwyn's response was a long time in coming. Nexus maintained a comfortable walk, his normal prance toned down to a rocking gait, as if he knew one of his riders was resting. "It will deplete your strength," the Fae Lord said.

"No. Our blood regenerates at a rapid rate. It is part of why we heal so quickly." Uthe paused. "I would rather you be prepared for what we face, my lord."

"Afraid I will not have your back?"

"You are against it now," he responded mildly. "But yes, as a matter of fact. I do not wish you to suffer the ignominy of returning to the Fae world and admitting a vampire had to cover your ass because you were too weak to do it yourself."

"You have been spending far too much time around the Green brothers," Keldwyn said, referring to Jacob and Gideon. "Your usual diplomacy is absent. A blatant goad to make me act for my own benefit."

"Did it work?"

In answer, Keldwyn shifted. Uthe stilled as those long, elegant fingers wrapped around his throat from behind, nudging his chin up. He tilted his head back, resting it on Keldwyn's shoulder as he stared up at the orange sky. There were swirls of pink and red in it. He knew Keldwyn had canines sharper than a human's. He'd noticed them before, intrigued by that physical similarity to vampires. Though Keldwyn's didn't elongate like Uthe's did, the points would make the puncturing much easier. Kel wasn't asking for any guidance, which intrigued Uthe, but the Fae had seen vampires feed on their servants at the Savannah headquarters.

"You'll tell me when enough is taken," Kel said, his breath caressing Uthe's throat in a way that had his heart thudding. "Or I will be annoyed at you for allowing me to take too much."

Keldwyn slid a hand over his thigh and found his interested cock under the mail skirt of the hauberk. "This arouses you greatly, does it not?"

"Yes."

"Involuntary? Instinct? Or me drinking from you specifically?"

"Yes to all of it." Uthe closed his hand over Kel's, pressing the heel of his hand harder against his erection. Keldwyn overlapped their knuckles, forming a puzzle lock between their hands. Then he bit.

Uthe let out a primal groan of pleasure, buttocks clenching as Kel ground against him, responding to his own arousal. Mariela had fed upon him, but giving the Fae Lord sustenance was a different level of satisfaction. He wished he could feed him always, that Kel would need to look no further than Uthe's throat to sustain him. With a ripple of shock, he realized that was probably how a servant thought of his vampire. Mariela had certainly had such thoughts before. Uthe was no servant—the very thought only met puzzlement in his mind. But put it in the context of caring for Kel? It elicited a far different reaction.

Kel's touch left his cock, tunneling beneath his undershirt to stroke the muscles of Uthe's abdomen. The belt at his waist was loose enough he could trace Uthe's navel, sending a wave of response above and below it. He dipped under the waistband of the leggings, reached in to close his grip around Uthe's heated and stiff cock, flesh to flesh. Keldwyn's thumb rubbed over the damp tip, then probed the slit. His other fingers strummed the pulsing artery in the shaft. Uthe scented his blood filling Keldwyn's mouth, felt him swallow.

A second mark would need more to replenish strength, so Uthe gave him that. He would have given him as much as he wanted but, knowing Kel didn't know when he'd taken enough, Uthe turned his head toward him, a nudge.

"That should do it. If you don't mind, just keep your mouth pressed over it a few more seconds so I don't bleed on my tunic. My self-healing properties will close the puncture wounds in a matter of seconds."

Very well. Your blood tasted unexpectedly... pleasant. Keldwyn sounded surprised. He raised his head. "Bitter and rich at once, flavored by your personality. Well-seasoned oak sprinkled with spices and infused with the thick vitality of blood itself."

"I'm pleased to hear it," Uthe said. "Bottled for over a thousand years, it could have easily gone rancid, turned to piss and vinegar."

"There is some of that in there. I did say it reflects your personality." Keldwyn rested his chin on Uthe's shoulder. Uthe twisted around so he could see the Fae Lord in the corner of his eye.

"You honor me by taking my blood for your nourishment, my lord. I know it was necessity, and it's not considered an honor by your kind, but for me, it was."

"Hmm." Keldwyn put his temple against the side of Uthe's neck and jaw, then positioned his head on Uthe's shoulder in a resting position again. "I'll sleep now to complete the rejuvenation process. Perhaps your horse can keep to this pace to aid my repose until we come up against something that requires us both to be awake. Like an army of dragons. Any single beasts I'm sure you can handle yourself."

"Your confidence is fortifying, my lord."

Chapter Fifteen

Endless red trees. In time, they became purple like velvety pansies, then green, but not the green seen on trees in Uthe's world. This was the neon glow of the lime-flavored drinks Carola favored from the local Taco Bell in Savannah. Her servant brought one to her almost daily when she was there for meetings.

The wind, the birds, the breathing and rustlings of the earth so ever present that it was only by their absence that they could be noticed, didn't exist in the Shattered World. However, the hum of the blood link connection had strengthened, stabilized. In time, the demon decided it was in the mood for conversation. Because he thought it would aid in locating the head, Uthe did not mute or block the creature now, though he shortly debated the wisdom of that.

"You think using the sorceress's magic will resolve things," he spoke in Uthe's head. "Why do you care about the Baptist getting to Heaven? They could have helped him at any time and they didn't. They waited on a vampire and generations of sorceresses to find a way they already knew to attempt to send me to back. How would you know the difference between me being loosed on the world and the way the world is now?"

Blood flashed in Uthe's mind, the scream of a child. Uthe blocked it, but that snapshot had provoked the response the demon wanted, a wave of guilt and sorrow. "See? How could things be worse than that?"

That question is an invitation to discord and chaos, Uthe responded. *This world, for all the evil it has, also nurtures good, compassion and love.* He drew a deep breath, enjoying how it enhanced the weight and impression of Keldwyn sleeping against his back. Was there anything as humbling as a lover trusting him enough to sleep in his presence? *In your world, none of that would exist.*

"If you succeed in returning to your world, what you express for one another here will not exist." The demon scoffed, an ugly sound like a phlegm-filled cough. "Reghan paid for that transgression with his life. You truly think your pretty fairy would face those consequences for *you*? You are a curiosity to him. You have the intelligence to match a Fae, so his lust has confused you with one. But in the end, you are his inferior, and he knows it. His world would never tolerate your pairing. They have laws forbidding it. So there goes another thing that makes your life worth living. Except you're not going to remember your life for much longer, are you?"

No, I am not. Uthe made himself say it firmly, without trepidation. It was what it was, right? *So there is no harm in enjoying my time with him, no matter what he has to do to protect himself later. Why do you reject being sent back to your home, demon? If it is such a boon to serve the purposes of evil, why would you not want to be back at the source of all that vileness? We all gravitate toward home, if it's a home worth having.*

"Our mission is to spread chaos. My part of Hell is already chaos. I am redundant there. Who desires to be redundant?"

His cleverness was capable of making Uthe smile, as much as his crueler words could be painful to the heart and soul. As he tilted his head to brush it against Kel's in affection, he put a temporary mute on the demon's dialogue so it was a malevolent mumble. He had no choice but to enjoy each moment fully. Agonizing over the sands falling through that hourglass, not knowing when he'd lose awareness of the passage of time, let alone anything else, was pointless. Worlds like this, where time had such little meaning, made that even clearer.

He'd not yet experienced the surges of uncontrolled bloodlust and loss of impulse control that he'd seen in other Ennui victims, as if they'd been transformed into a different, more sociopathic version of their fledgling selves. However, in this world, channeling such violence might prove to be useful. Like perhaps now.

The world of crayons had come to an end. Ahead there was only billowing gray fog. Nexus shifted uneasily. "Kel," Uthe said, a warning. The Fae's head was already lifting.

"I see it."

"Anything?"

A pause, then Kel shook his head. "Forward or not?"

Uthe patted Nexus's muscled neck. "That's the direction I sense we need to go. So unless my mind is playing tricks on me or the Shattered World is, I think we must go through."

"Very well." Keldwyn drew his sword and slid to the ground, taking a firm hold of Uthe's boot. "You prepare to defend high, I will defend low, and Nexus will choose the elevation that best suits him."

"Agreed." Uthe pulled out his sword and held it at the ready against his thigh. Nexus snorted at the cue. His forward gait became more deliberate, his ears swept back, listening for Uthe's commands, the horse prepared for attack.

Immediately, the fog closed in. It was wet on the face, and blinded the eyes, so Uthe closed his, using the blood link and his awareness of Kel's hand on his foot to guide him. In this environment, a foe was better detected by hearing, scent and intuition. There was something in the fog. He could feel it pressing in on them. Sibilant whispers began like fitful breezes, becoming more noticeable, rising in volume. His skin crawled beneath the mail.

"Kel..."

With you still, my lord. And yes, I feel it all.

Kel had understood he needed the reinforcement, to know which was the illusion of this world and that of his own mind. Though illusion might be a misnomer, because an illusion in this world could become quite real and deadly. Like...

"*Gauche,*" he bellowed. Nexus jerked them left, Keldwyn moving with them. A serpent's head as large as Nexus's shot past on the right, its rotting stench a powerful rolling force that accompanied it on a hot wind. Water sprayed them, salty and rank. Keldwyn's blade flashed down, cutting into brown, spotted flesh. The being shrieked, whipping away into the fog. Nexus snorted, throwing up his head as his front legs plunged down and forward. Uthe kept his seat, but he reached down and caught Keldwyn's collar to hold onto him as the horse floundered. They were in water, water quickly drawing them into its current and spinning them. There was no backing out of it, because it was impossible to tell from which way they'd come. Nexus began to swim, legs powerfully pumping. Uthe gave the horse his head, because he would smell land faster than Uthe could find it.

"Damnation, it's coming back. Hold on." Keldwyn wrested free and dove, despite Uthe's sharp protest. He couldn't see through the Fae's eyes, but he could hear the thoughts whipping through Kel's mind.

Sea serpent. He's coming this way, beneath you. Get Nexus to swim faster.

He gave Nexus the command and the horse plunged forward, thrashing. The water around them illuminated and the charge of the magic electrified his own blood as Keldwyn unleashed it. The serpent reared out of the water over Uthe, raining water down on him. The fanged mouth gaped, eyes alight with crimson fire. Uthe made himself wait for the right moment, and he didn't have long to do so. The head shot down, teeth gleaming. He swung, his reflexes and timing sure.

No matter what else he forgot, *this* he would never forget how to do.

He sliced off a portion of the snout and knocked out a tooth as long as his forearm. The serpent screeched and splashed back into the water. Uthe threw himself off the horse's back and onto the serpent's neck, right behind the head. Clamping his thighs around the massive column, he spun the blade and drove it through the brain, skewering the creature before it could dive.

A shriek told him the serpent wasn't alone. He shoved backwards in the water, the ripples before him exploding into froth as another monster broke the surface. He saw the green scales and golden eyes, then crackling energy shot through its throat and body, x-raying the skeleton inside. It illuminated objects he didn't want to think looked like human remains. Kel was crouched on top of the waves, his sword thrust through the thing's body, the energy in the blade illuminating the serpent and holding him above the water in a shimmering field of fire.

"Another, Uthe. On your left." Keldwyn shouted it. Uthe yelled a warning in return, sending Keldwyn spinning around as a three-headed serpent exploded out of the water right behind the Fae Lord. The force of his appearance shot a wave over both of them. It tumbled Uthe through the churning liquid. Damn it. Vampires had no buoyancy. While he had the strength to keep himself aloft, even with the mail, it made more sense to let himself drop to the bottom and fight there. Except he had no idea how far the bottom was.

Before he could sink to any distance, a large body thudded against him, and it wasn't the serpent. Thanking God for Nexus, he grabbed the stallion's mane and pulled himself back upon him. Bless his indomitable soul, the horse was still swimming just as strongly, whinnying out a challenge.

The serpent broke the water to their left. The churning had apparently obscured its vision beneath and it was trying to locate them. It was as large as the first, with gnashing teeth and six sets of swirling eyes, venom dripping from a double row of fangs.

Being on Nexus's back gave Uthe a way to stay above water and strike at the creature. But his maneuvering ability was severely hampered in water, and the serpent knew it. He couldn't see any sign of Keldwyn or the other beast. Now his own enemy dove, and Uthe knew what was coming. He didn't take the time to imagine those gaping jaws coming up toward Nexus's vulnerable underside. Shoving off the horse's back once more, he let the mail take him down. He thudded to solid ground in a matter of several seconds. Seeing the serpent's body coiling around him, he'd never been more pleased to have his feet firmly on the bottom of an ocean floor, if that was what this was.

He could see the shadow of the serpent's head shooting through the water at him. A snake's primary weapon was its speed, and a sea serpent was no faster than a regular snake. A vampire could exceed that, making this a straightforward hand-to-hand combat, if one ignored the beast's enormous mass. He shoved off the ground and met the serpent's charge with a blow to the nose. As he came back to the sand, he had his sword ready. He shoved his blade into thick muscle, yanked it free and spun to face the retaliation that would come. The serpent's head hit him mid-body, and he jammed his long dagger tip into one of its eyes, rupturing it.

The fangs scraped against his mail as it tried to clamp its jaws on him, which provided him the time he needed to thrust the long dagger into the roof of the thing's mouth. The point emerged at the top of the head. The body thrashed, pummeling him. He fought to get clear of it, but this time he wasn't quick enough. The contact was as brutal and direct as a baseball bat hitting a ball, shooting him through the water. He couldn't see Nexus and still no Keldwyn, no telltale flashes of magical light. He couldn't hear the snarling expletives in his mind which would have told him Kel was still fighting, but he also saw no other serpents. He wasn't sure he'd delivered a killing blow, but his foe had not pursued him. If not mortally wounded, it had been discouraged from an immediate follow up.

A cadre of frogs swam past him as his forward momentum slowed. Their expressions were flat and disinterested, his altercation a minor annoyance.

He fought his lack of buoyancy and the weight of his mail to surface, to get his bearings. There was still fog, so he let himself sink to save his energy, and once again tried to tune into the demon's blood link. It made sense that the head would be on dry land.

Kel, can you follow me? I am trying to guide us to land, I think. Do you see Nexus?

His heart stopped beating in the silence, then began to thump again when he got an answer.

I am with your steed. We will follow you.

He was relieved that Kel had found Nexus, no matter the absurdity, since the horse was a figment of this world. It didn't matter though, did it? Reality was what you felt in your heart, and the way he'd responded to seeing the horse again, how the stallion had responded to him, was all that mattered. He was learning that from the Ennui. He wondered how many vampires denied the pleasurable things the hallucinations could bring them, until all that was left was the nightmarish ones.

He gave a prayer of thanks when the ocean floor beneath him began to go uphill, and he encountered more rocky surfaces, which he believed meant a shoreline. Once he was picking his way through a solid rock field, he changed his mind. The familiarity of it suggested where it was leading him, which he confirmed when he surfaced.

The fog was no longer a thick curtain. It hovered high enough above the ground to allow brief glimpses of what was ahead. The ruins of a castle, perched on a pile of rock. A zigzagging path worked its way up a steep hill toward it.

Uthe dropped to a knee onshore to regain his strength and get his bearings. He kept scanning the water, though fog still coated it fifty feet from shore. He tuned in with other senses. When he heard the lapping of water, the rhythmic churn of Nexus's legs, he whistled, in case they needed further bearings. The horse responded with a whinny. A few moments later, he saw the horse's nose break through the smoky mist. Another few blinks and he could see Keldwyn on his back, holding a handful of mane. He'd lost the jerkin, so he was only in the leggings wetly plastered to him. It wasn't an unfortunate occurrence.

"We are nearly eaten by snakes, and you are leering at my manly attributes," Keldwyn commented as they came to shore. "Good to know your priorities, my lord." Slipping off Nexus's back, he flopped down next to Uthe, panting.

Uthe didn't deny enjoying a leisurely perusal of the muscular terrain, the light layer of dark hair over the firm pectorals and sectioned stomach. The wet leggings, cut right below the hip bones and hugging the Fae Lord's groin, afforded him an equally stimulating view. Yet his scrutiny was primarily to be sure Kel had not sustained any serious injury. Like Uthe, he appeared to have suffered scratches and bruising alone.

Uthe nodded to the castle. "I think we just crossed a rather wide moat, my lord."

"Next time, let's look for a drawbridge. Vampires must do everything the hard way."

"The castle sits up too high for a drawbridge. I expect at one time it might have had a bridge, but the occupants have long ago left, and the Shattered World borrowed it for its purposes."

"You think this world takes things from other worlds?"

"Something does not come from nothing. I sense no

cohesive idea here. It's as we both surmised. Residual magic, collective nightmares, anxieties and random dreams, the absurd ones no one can explain, have all been thrown into one place by something that had no use for them."

"So the sorceress figured out the safest place for the head was a trash dump."

"It makes sense. Who would put something of value in a trash dump?" Uthe looked back toward the water. "Though those serpents felt fueled by the demon's power."

"It is probably too much to hope that's the worst he can do."

Uthe shook his head. "If allowed freedom, he can do far, far worse, but he shows his malice even while bound. This is his environment, the chaotic energy. He can do things here he could never do in your world or mine. I was glad for my mail. I'd been thinking of shedding it, but it kept those things' teeth from sinking into me."

"Indeed." Keldwyn's gaze moved to Uthe's shoulder where the links had fouled the serpent's teeth, which had broken and twisted the metal. The Fae grunted and sat up, surveying his bare upper body. "I would conjure another shirt, but it seems pointless. I should have tried to get a set of Fae-crafted mail through the door, though I doubt it would have passed. I cannot wear your mail without impeding my magic," he added, putting a hand on Uthe as he started to shift. "So don't even think it. I would not take it from you regardless."

He gave Uthe a hard look, but there was a set to his jaw that said it had moved him, Uthe's automatic reaction to offer it. "Your steed is a tremendous warrior," the Fae added. "One of the serpents had wrapped itself around him. I went after it with my sword and magic, but Nexus put his teeth to the creature's side and ripped out a good bit of what he found there, weakening it for me. He practically gnawed the beast into two pieces."

"He's fearless," Uthe said fondly, rising and putting a

hand on the horse's nose, the only soft place Nexus had. Then he turned and offered Keldwyn a hand. "Ready to continue, my lord?"

"I have nothing better to do." Kel clasped his hand, and Uthe pulled him to his feet. They both surveyed the ruins looming above them.

"Is that our ultimate destination?" the Fae asked.

"Yes."

"Then let's proceed."

Because of the uneven terrain, they chose to walk, Nexus picking his way behind him. Uthe suspected whatever castle this had been in another plane of existence was just as desolate when it wasn't in ruins. The air of despair and desolation upon it was heavy as the fog that had concealed it.

Many of the stones that had fallen from the walls had broken, showing dark brown innards the color of old blood. As they wound their way up the incline to the open gate, the grate rusted and off its track, he saw a trio of vultures sitting on it.

"They have a cleaning crew in place for our remains," Kel commented.

Uthe grunted in response. He stopped at the portcullis, looking around carefully. "Do you feel any magic, my lord?"

"No, but magic is a very malleable idea here. My glamor is one of my easier magics, but it didn't work. Whereas time shifting, one of the most complex, did. The Shattered World likes playing games."

Though the castle sat in the center of a body of water, there was a green field on one side, visible now that they'd reached a higher elevation. The field had perhaps once been used for tourneys and sword practice. Meadow grass rippled over it like a grimace.

"I wonder if the grass would feed him, since he's conjured out of this world?"

Keldwyn gave him a curious look and Uthe gestured to

the meadow. "Nexus. I know he's an echo, but I like to think he'll come to no harm here once our cause is served."

"He'll likely return to his soul, like a beam of light back to the sun." Kel shifted a step closer to Uthe. "Like his master, he doesn't look like he knows what 'at ease' is."

Uthe smiled absently. "We didn't have the term 'at ease' back then. Most commands I gave him in French, but I used 'compline' for off duty. He'd roll in the sand as if it was grass."

They were within the ruins of the castle now, and fell into the habit of fighting men, maintaining a three-dimensional alertness around them to protect one another's flank. Uthe kept a firm grip on his unsheathed sword. Though it had been years since he held such a weapon for actual battle, the constant practice with it had served its purpose. He felt like he'd never put it down.

Uthe guessed they were standing in the lower bailey. Nearly a dozen statues were arrayed like scattered trees in a dirt and rock field. As they circled them warily, Uthe saw they were fully armored knights wearing the Templar mantle. They were posed at ready, like before a battle charge, all facing the opposite archway to the upper bailey.

Keldwyn's gaze went there and his senses sharpened. "My lord, there is something of great power through that opening. Several somethings. Would that be what you seek?"

"We shall go and see. Do you feel anything here?" Uthe was still staring at the statues.

"No." As Keldwyn laid his hand on one, his brow creased. "Though it feels like there should be. The magic and its intent may be cloaked. Is it wise to put them at our backs?"

Uthe swept his gaze over them. Though the alabaster features were non-specific, he felt as if he knew each of them. "Yes."

He questioned his gut about that, however. What purpose did it serve, having these still figures of his past standing here? To plant the false, childish hope that they'd come to life and his aid?

"You yourself said the Shattered World seems to act like a capricious, cruel child," Keldwyn reminded him.

The stone archway appeared to be moving, but it was the vines upon it. The barbed tendrils pushed out of the cracks and crevices, creeping over the rock. As they moved toward the opening, the signature Keldwyn was detecting became powerful enough for Uthe to feel it. Identifying it was no trouble. It was one with which he was very familiar, though it had been a while since he'd come in direct contact with it outside his mind.

Uthe clasped the seal on his neck, thumb sweeping over the raised imprint of the two knights. The metal was humming, the sorceress's magic responding to what it had been created to destroy.

They passed under the archway with eyes trained on those animated vines. Once clear of the threshold, the dry rasp of their movement against rock stopped.

Keeping a peripheral watch on the sinister vegetation, they took in what lay before them. The vast courtyard had once been cobbled, though grass now grew up between the stones and piles of rock fallen from the surrounding walls littered them. The smell was of dry death, the life long ago sucked away and leaving only a skeleton. But pulsing, raw power sat on top of it, conjuring heat like a bonfire.

Sitting at the opposite end of the upper bailey was an altar, a T-shaped structure of wood planted over a narrow rectangular table. The table was a union of rotten timbers, and leafless, thick wooden vines tangled over the T, nearly obscuring its shape. Though these were signs of decay and neglect, Uthe could see and feel the magic pulsing from the altar. Red flame danced in the cracks between the timbers and flickered in the spaces of the woven vines. Sparks arced off the altar. Though there were no charred spots around it, a burning smell permeated the air.

On the altar was the head, mounted on a flat bottomed

spike. An old cup and a rusted spear sat next to it, like they'd left there by a warrior who'd sat down for an ale. Yet while the red flame surrounded and permeated the altar in continuous flow, the cup, spear and T were anchored, connected with silver-blue lines of energy that formed a spherical net around the head. That net was visible evidence of Shahnaz's binding that had kept the demon locked inside the head. The Grail, the Spear of Longinus and the True Cross had seen wear these many years, but that wear was an illusion. Their power remained just as true.

Uthe had inflicted decapitations, so he knew what a head looked like deprived of blood circulation, left to decompose in the sun and at the mercy of those whose business it was to clean up the dead, like the vultures outside. This head had never looked like that. But it didn't look alive either.

The thick brown hair was wild as a thicket. Dark, deep set eyes punched holes in a face weathered and taut. The eyes stared, empty and yet not. The flat bottomed spike kept the head upright, the mouth open and slack. The whole thing looked unnatural, eaten up by evil, and Uthe's first reaction to it, then and now, was to seek a way to destroy it. Fortunately, they'd come with one.

Uthe executed a deep bow, dropping to one knee. "I know you reject my devotion, John the Baptist, Madman, Prophet of the Wilderness, for you were ever a humble man, but I honor your courage and sacrifice these many years. If it is God's will, we will soon release you to the heavens you so richly deserve."

The eyes flickered. It was as if there were two or three interior lids, and they alternated between a serpent's gaze, feverish-looking brown eyes or wholly white orbs. In Keldwyn's mind, Uthe saw him realize why Uthe had been so discomfited by the Fae Lord's illusion of snake eyes.

"There is no God's will. There never was." The sibilant voice crawled like spiders into the ears, up the spine, across the palms of the hands, making them itch. "You will release him to dust, to nothingness. That is all. And I will be released, period."

"No, you won't," Another voice came from the head, this one rough like tree bark. "I would prefer God consign me to dust than endure another moment of your foul company, demon."

"It comes out of its shell to speak, thinking that somehow it is about to be saved." A harsh laugh. "I will destroy all your illusions and dreams. That will be my parting gift to you, Madman."

"I never asked to be saved. Only for your banishment. And I come out of my shell to feel your intent more clearly. Vampire, call for aid with the Fae Queen's power. It is time. He summons your enemies in force—"

A garbled scream, and the head vibrated with energy, as if two minds were doing battle within it. "*Now,*" the voice barked.

The transition was abrupt, but Uthe didn't question the Baptist's command. He yanked Rhoswen's amulet from the pouch at his waist even as Keldwyn turned toward him, the same order on his lips. Nexus trilled a challenge.

Pulling the amulet around his neck, Uthe clasped the shard of ice in his hand and chanted the words Keldwyn had taught him. Keldwyn's mind-voice echoed in his head so they spoke the words together, in both languages. "*Should all about to be lost, may those true of heart and of like mind come to aid my purpose, be it of the highest intent.*"

A rumbling began beneath their feet. Keldwyn yanked Uthe away from the archway, Nexus circling behind them. The stone crumbled, punctuated by a billowing wall of dust and flailing vines. Nexus skidded to a halt with a clatter of hooves and let out a piercing call Uthe remembered all too well. The horse's battle call had his heart thudding up into his throat.

Damn horse wants to give the call to charge, Sir

Leonard had grumbled good-naturedly.

The ground was vibrating. Uthe could hear distant yells. Something was coming up the rocky slopes around the castle. But those cries weren't close enough to be what was coming through the archway, climbing over the crumbled rock and materializing out of the billowing cloud of dust.

Uthe took a more secure hold on the sword, and Keldwyn unsheathed both long daggers at his belt, both of them prepared to face whatever came out of that churning dust. The Fae was fully in his mind, knowing this was the right time to move in sync with one another.

"Blessed Virgin..."

The first thing he saw was a black tunic with a bold red cross emblazoned across the front, and then the man inhabiting it came into focus. Manfred, his sergeant. Though he was as fierce a fighter as any knight, he'd come into the Order after the Rule had been written, and it required those wanting to take the white mantle to be knights before joining the Order. Jacques, Uthe's squire, was just behind him. He wore a studded jerkin and leggings, his dark hair just as messy and uncombed as it ever was. Uthe had doused him in a trough once to remind him to keep himself clean in the eyes of the Lord. Despite his stench, the boy had the courage of Nexus and a heart as innocent as a virgin's.

"Kel..."

"I see it, Varick. I see all of them. It is real."

Uthe's throat was too thick to say anything else. A wall of white mantles formed behind his sergeant and squire. Leonard, Carlos, Olivier, Jean-Claude, Barabbas... When the dust settled there was a line of thirteen of them, his closest brethren at the time of Hattin. They'd all died there, but today they'd come back from the dead to fight this fight with him. Not for the kings of Jerusalem, France or Constantinople. Not for the Pope. Today they fought for the cause of the Lord, not the men who claimed to act in His Name. And they were not Uthe's only reinforcements.

The residual power of the amulet was swirling around and through him. As it spiraled through his blood, he heard another message. The voice was indefinable, not Rhoswen nor any of the known voices in his head, but as soon as it spoke, Uthe knew its truth came straight from the magic itself.

"Their hearts must be like yours...warriors, reconciled to who and what they are, no fear of death, only of the triumph of evil and what that would mean to those they love. They fight for love. The only reason a fight must be fought."

Out of a narrow opening of what remained of the curtain wall, Daegan Rei stepped. He was not dressed in a Templar's garb, but in his usual dark clothing, the better to access the katana he had scabbarded on his back. He probably carried a dozen other weapons Uthe couldn't see. He gave Uthe a short nod, then adjusted to allow Gideon and Jacob room to step out with him.

Gideon was dressed as a traditional knight, in brown belted tunic over mail, armed with sword, axe and mace. A smile touched Uthe's lips. He'd always recognized the knight in Gideon, whether or not he'd actually been one in a past life, like his brother had been. Jacob stood at an alert resting state in the white tunic of the Crusader, marked with a red cross on the chest. His hair was longer, just past his shoulders, and he looked like every veteran Crusader Uthe had seen, limned with sand and sunburn. His blue eyes met Uthe's and he gave a short nod, much as Daegan had done.

"Your lady does me great honor," Uthe said, inclining his head in return. "She does not often spare you from her side."

"I'm not sure she's even aware I'm gone. I was there, now I'm here." Jacob offered a dry smile. "If this twisted world doesn't return me a blink later in the same condition, I have a feeling she'll make everyone involved feel her displeasure."

Uthe chuckled. "Do not give us reason to throw ourselves on the mercy of the devil." The intensity of the emotion he'd felt at their appearance had not vanished, but it was settling into something he knew like the sword in his grip. The calm before battle. It was what he and these others had been born to do.

They gathered around him now. They all had questions in their eyes, but whatever had prepared them to be here made their primary focus this battle, the foe they faced. It saved him unnecessary explanation. Nexus stood at his back, his breath short puffs of heat against Uthe's spine. Keldwyn was silent at his side, but Uthe felt the weight of Kel's mind linked with his like a chain they'd forged together, and perhaps they had, with every step they'd taken toward this moment. The shouts of whatever the demon had summoned were getting closer, the vibration beneath their feet increasing, but Uthe knew any distance was illusion. The moment he moved toward the head on the altar, the foe would appear.

"I must reach the relics behind me and banish the demon trapped in the head," he said. "Whoever the demon sends to prevent me from doing that, he controls their minds and souls, pulling them to him from some foul magic." He thought of the Saracens in the desert of Syria. "To kill them is to release their souls back to where they belong or let them meet redemption. Do not hesitate, for it is a mercy you do them."

He swept a gaze over all of them. "Fight until you know it is no longer necessary and then return from whence you came, with my thanks and the blessings of the Lord."

Manfred stepped forward, his green eyes sharp and flat. He had a handsomely trimmed dark beard and moustache they'd teased him about, suggesting a doe-eyed Saracen woman with generous thighs would eventually steal him away from the Order and have her way with him. "I have your flank as always, my lord. We made an oath. The sorceress called us back from the dead and gave us this choice, to remain frozen here until you had need of us."

Keldwyn touched his mind. *The statues, my lord. They're gone.*

Uthe looked beyond them. Now that the dust was not obscuring his view, he saw that the statues were gone from the lower bailey. His gaze snapped back to Manfred, Jacques, all of them.

"We could not enter Heaven after Hattin, my lord," Leonard said. "Not because the gate was closed to us, but because the gates in our hearts were. We lost our faith in our Grand Master and the Order. But our faith was never supposed to be in either of those things." He had a wicked scar across his face, and it pulled now as he gave Uthe an amused look and glanced at Jean-Claude. The two men had been so close, they'd often finished one another's thoughts, as Jean-Claude did now.

Jean-Claude was as pretty as only a Frenchman could be, and he spoke in the assertive, clipped tone that commanded attention on the battlefield as well as off. "We serve the Will of the Lord by serving the spirit of the Order. That spirit, it is beyond the Rule or anything else, *non*? Men and time, they confuse our minds, but hearts and souls, they are clear. Life, love and honor."

"We were not there when our Order was begun, my lord," Manfred added. "Not as you were, when the only charge was to protect God's faithful so they could visit the Holy Lands. By the end, the only thing I knew without question was I would protect the man fighting next to me to the death. That was how I served the Will of the Lord. I am glad He has given me that opportunity once more."

Life, love and honor. Uthe clasped the man's shoulder, hard. He felt Keldwyn's hand on his hip. He put his other hand over his forearm and gripped him, meeting the Fae's understanding gaze. Having him in his head fully, confirming everything he was feeling and seeing, provided a sense of ease and balance he hadn't had in some time.

His brethren saw the exchange, but Uthe wasn't going to

conceal his feelings. This moment was beyond all that. Manfred met the issue head on with a snort. His teeth flashed in a sharp grin. "Always knew you were looking at my beard with lust in your heart, my lord."

"No, it was my lovely French arse, you bearded curse of your father's loins," Jean-Claude rejoined.

"Least I knew my father."

Jacques snickered and Manfred cuffed him good-naturedly.

A menacing snarl vibrated through the chamber. It came from no creature of earth, snapping their attention back to more serious matters. The blood-curdling blast of cold energy told Uthe it was the demon itself. Manfred drew his sword as the others fanned out. "Reunion over. Time to do your task, my lord. We will make sure you can serve His Will, or die trying."

"When I reach those gates this time," Leonard told Jean-Claude, "I'm going in for a cup of wine."

"I'd settle for a few of those virgins the Assassins are supposed to get."

"I'll settle for an experienced wench who can ease the ache of a thousand years of chastity."

Uthe seized Nexus's mane and swung himself up. Daegan shifted to one side of the horse's head and Keldwyn to the other. At Uthe's look, Keldwyn shot him a no-argument look. "We are the best choice of an advance guard, to ensure you reach the demon."

Jacob and Gideon had moved up next to Daegan, the other soldiers arrayed in a line on either side of Uthe. Nexus threw back his head and gave a shrill screech, stomping his feet on the stone like a drum beat.

"Yeah. What he said," Gideon said. "Let's go kick some ass."

Uthe had been right. Though he'd known their time to dally was limited, the moment he set his heels to Nexus was the catalyst. All hell broke loose.

With a roar, the wall behind the altar shattered. Out of

that tornado of dirt and sand burst forth an army. As they streamed around the table, making the force field around it flicker with energy, Uthe glimpsed dark eyes and bearded faces, and rage stirred within him. He'd been wrong about the demon only calling marked men to his aid. These were the fighting elite, a unit of Assassins and Saracen fighters. Their faces were frozen in expressions of permanent aggression, the result of the demon's spell upon them. Uthe remembered them as his opponents in battles and skirmishes, honorable men fighting for a cause in which they had believed. *To kill them is to release their souls back to where they belong. Do not hesitate, for it is a mercy you do them.* He was glad he'd told his brethren that.

They were charging across the bailey, screaming their battle cries, metal clanking and feet pounding across the stone. Nexus leaped forward like a launched rocket. Even so, Daegan stayed ahead, the katana unsheathed, a dagger in the other hand. Jacob and Gideon had fanned out with Manfred, Leonard and Jean-Claude. As if they'd been comrades in arms all their lives, the men hit the wall of deadly Saracens without flinching. Daegan cut a swath before him that reminded Uthe of a bolt of red silk being cut in the air. His own blade found flesh, foes that grabbed at his legs, tried to unhorse him. The heat of Keldwyn's magic washed over him, and the reinforcements who flung themselves at him fell away. Uthe caught a quick glimpse of the Fae Lord, using the long daggers to channel and funnel his magic, energy to supplement his already formidable strength. Watching him and Daegan work on either side, just ahead of Nexus, was like watching the Hand of God part a sea.

The others were holding their own, pulling in their opponents as if they were magnets, drawing them away from Uthe. There was blood, screaming, noise. Steel clanging against steel, thuds, the splatter of blood. Noise on a battlefield was overwhelming. With a vampire's enhanced senses, it was an indescribable cacophony. It had been so many years since he'd experienced that, but he remembered it all so very vividly. The first time it had nearly drowned him, with his sensitive hearing, smell and vision. Now it was as familiar as sitting in Council meetings, and perhaps more welcome.

Plunging through the opening his brethren had provided, he thundered toward the table. The demon's dead eyes were fixed upon him. Was he afraid? Uthe surely hoped so.

He had a fleeting thought as to why the demon hadn't held back some of his army for his own protection, and then all of the red flame he'd assumed was part of Shahnaz's magic spiked like an eruption, spinning and tangling into a tight ball. He tried to change Nexus's path, but it was too late. The projectile of flame hit them in mid-charge, so swiftly it filled and obliterated his vision. The impact was like a cannonball. The horse screamed and went down beneath him. Uthe was flung free, back into the ranks of the fighting men. He felt hands upon him, thrusting him to his feet, shoving him forward, and then he was out of the fray again.

Nexus was still. He hoped the horse had been knocked senseless, not killed. Blocking out the noise behind him, trusting his allies to keep the area clear to do what needed to be done, he pulled the Templar seal from his neck and clasped its heat in one hand. As he stalked to the altar, he stayed wary for other magical traps, and hoped the humming energy that had built to a dull roar in his hand would provide some protection. Perhaps it already had. Perhaps the fire ball had been far more lethal.

Though from a distance their arrangement had seemed haphazard, the Grail and the Spear were placed so a line could have been drawn between them and the Cross to form an equilateral triangle. The Trinity, the most powerful number in the universe. The demon's serpent eyes were blood red, the slack mouth twisted in a sneer. "This will not be as easy as you think, Templar," he spat. "You will lose yourself. We will go to Hell together."

"So be it." The binding Shahnaz had originally imposed around the demon shouldn't hinder him as long as the sorceress's magic was in his hand, but he was prepared for anything when he extended it into that silver blue field. The power shuddered through him, the shape of it impressing him and giving him a sense of the woman who'd crafted it. Her small, secretive smile, the scent of French coffee that lingered on her hands.

He missed her, though he'd visited her less than a dozen times during her mortal life span. He missed all of them, from Haris at the beginning to Fatima at the end. A noble, worthy, female line.

His fingers trembled, the power countered by an energy surge from the head itself. When the red-flamed magic passed over his skin and burned, he fought the instinct to recoil. He dared the sun to burn him every dawn; he would not retreat from fire now. Seizing the jaw of the disembodied head, he thrust the Templar pendant between the lips. The skin was eerily supple and alive, yet cold as death. He shut the mouth and held it fast with both hands, one clamped under the chin and one on the bridge of the nose. The eyes flickered wildly, then rolled up to stare at him with the promise of Hell. A smell like hundreds of rotting bodies filled his nose, made his eyes water and his stomach heave. Blackness boiled from between the lips and out of the nose. When black tears started to pour from the eyes, he heard an earsplitting howl inside his own head, followed by pleading. John, begging for mercy.

No, stop...take it out...please, for the love of... Please...Uthe.

Every man had a line beyond which no more pain could be borne, but if whom Uthe was hearing was truly the Baptist, John would have said God's name. Instead, the plea trailed off like a frayed rope from a snapped tether. The blackness oozed over Uthe's hand, hot as boiling oil.

His flesh screamed, the agony insisting he let go. He refused, all his muscles taut, his chest squeezing in on itself in the effort to hold fast. The eyes were changing. Serpent, pure white, wild brown. And they kept changing, faster and faster, with a sound like a shuttle moving across a loom. It was like listening to the Fates accelerating their weaving, change happening so swiftly they were hastening to keep up. Else they'd all fall off the end of the earth, no tapestry to catch them all.

Hold…hold… The din behind him was receding. His knees were trembling. The jaw was straining against him, trying to open the mouth and rid it of the pendant. He wasn't a magic user, but he could detect the energy of the sorceress's magic oozing into the head and attaching like leeches to everything contained within the skull. As he felt that progress, his mind swam, and he could see the chambers inside the head, an endless maze. The demon's area was a pulsing, deep blood red. John's, the color of earth and gold. Then the final one, the innocent's. This was the soul he knew the least about, except that it had been the essential ingredient for the dark magic used to bind the demon and John in the same head.

The innocent's area of the maze was solid gray, like the Shattered World itself. He was being drawn deeper into that endless fog. He'd never find his way out. There'd be no Nexus or Keldwyn to help him, no spirits from the past. He would be truly alone, caught there forever. He tried to back pedal, to resist its pull. He could pull free, he could. He had the strength. Yet as he started to successfully back out of that trap, he felt a shift inside the head. The demon's anticipation was growing, John's silence a portent as loud as a shouted prophecy. He could feel the innocent soul, all the unrealized potential, yearning. Screaming without sound.

This was his Fate, what he'd been facing all along. He'd always known God's Will was mysterious but just. The Ennui was preparation to face his destiny. He would lose his mind here, wander in this amorphous gray world where he forgot who he was and those he cared about. He'd have no feeling for any of them; it didn't matter if he knew them or not. But with the Ennui, the violent need to destroy all he once cared about might possess him. There was no chance of that here. Here he would save an innocent. And this was all clouds. Gray storm clouds that stayed heavy with rain but never broke, never changed.

He turned. He had no sense of anything anymore. He wasn't standing before the head, holding its jaw clamped shut. He looked down at his arms. No boiling black liquid stained him or his tunic. He was naked, barefoot, in a foggy gray world, with no defenses of any kind. Helpless.

No, he wasn't helpless. As long as he had his mind, he had his greatest weapon with him.

But you don't have your mind, do you? It's floating away like a balloon, a child's toy.

Bastard. He knew that voice. It was... He paused, fought the panic. He should know that sibilant voice. Before he could identify it, he saw Keldwyn. The Fae was a few feet away, sitting at a chess board, facing a fully dressed Uthe. It was a memory. They were in Uthe's rooms in Savannah.

How many times had Keldwyn risen to take his leave near dawn? How often had he paused at the door, unfathomable things in his eyes? Uthe wondered what the Fae Lord would have done if Uthe had asked him to stay, to share his bed far sooner. Or what if Keldwyn himself had closed the door, latched them both in? What if he'd pushed Uthe against the wall, closing his hand over the front of his shirt to hold him still as he took his mouth, conveying his intention to take far more than that? How much more time would they have had to explore the feelings between them?

Back to the chess game. That particular night, they'd been discussing vengeance. Hate.

"Hate is a very insular, compartmentalized emotion," Uthe pointed out.

"Hate is different from anger," Keldwyn responded.

"Anger is often needed to serve the cause of justice. Righteous anger. Think of Jesus and the money changers in a house of prayer. He was ultimately enlightened, beyond ego, but he could feel anger, act upon it."

"Agreed."

The chessboard and Keldwyn vanished, and Uthe was alone in the fog again. Was there anything as disturbing as being cut adrift in a void, no one to call for help, no company to keep?

"Boy, come hold him for me. I hate it when they whine and squirm."

No. He'd endure an eternity of solitude before he'd long for the company of his sire. Yet here he was, standing at his father's side as blood ran off the table, as the child screamed and struggled. Uthe comforted him. "It's all right. Just lie still and it will feel better soon. I promise."

He was the liar of all liars. He'd wanted to believe in an afterlife, had needed to do so, because that meant the promise had not been entirely false.

Liar, liar, liar. You know nothing.

He focused on his hand. No calluses yet. The hand of a fledgling, not a mature vampire responsible for his own life. He groped for his sword and found none, but that didn't matter. He took his father to the floor in one swift move that had them crashing to the boards. Last time he'd done this by stealth, staked his father in the back when he was feeding, for he couldn't have stood against his strength then. He could now.

He had his hands on his sire's throat, was beating his head against the floor, cracking wood, cracking bone. He broke a chair, ripped it apart so the jagged remains of one leg was in his clenched fist. His father's eyes were enraged, frightened. Frightened, because some part of him was caught in the gray fog. He didn't know what he'd become, what the Ennui had made him.

The child was crying. Or was that his father? Uthe put a bloodstained, unsteady hand on his father's face. "It's all right. Just lie still and it will feel better soon. I promise. I should have done this for you long, long ago."

His father gripped his wrist, holding his gaze. Now his expression held a child's trust. Uthe could gain the trust of the innocent, of the fearful, of the lost, because he meant what he said and was sure of his faith when he said it. Or rather, he'd made himself sure of his faith, because to do otherwise was to be completely lost, and he couldn't handle being lost.

But that was what he faced. Being lost in that fog for the rest of his life, once it closed in and never let up again.

He shoved the wooden stake into his father's heart. His sire's hand clenched on his wrist, then slackened. His expression lost awareness, the soul slipping away. Everything slipping away.

Uthe was bent over, cut adrift in nothingness, floating in fog once again. The blood and his father were both gone, but the weeping continued.

Where was he? The innocent's mind. A blank slate. Was that why there was endless fog here? Like an empty vessel, yet something did exist. He could feel it, like the distant voice of a child. An uncharted soul. John would argue this one deserved to be freed even more than himself, for it was a story as yet unwritten. It had been trapped with him all this time, but if this was the world it had always known, had that made it less frightening? Would this be so bad, especially if he could relive memories like the one he'd just relived with Keldwyn? Keldwyn had teased Uthe about playing chess and debating philosophy in the Shattered World. Uthe could create any world he wished here, and eventually his mind might be so duped he would believe it was real, that he wasn't truly, forever alone.

The only way to release John was to release the innocent, but something had to be here to keep the demon pinned down until the two of them could get clear. He had to be willing to take the innocent's place, for it was the anchor. Then he and Fatima's magic would make sure the demon was banished. Uthe would be his personal escort.

It was what Templars had originally been trained to do, escorting pilgrims to their destination, protecting them. He'd be a prison guard instead of a pilgrim's guardian. A prison guard trapped in his own prison.

Looking down, he discovered he was in full Templar battle gear once again. It was the only answer he needed.

"You will play no more tricks, demon. We die together."

The sorceress had known Uthe would figure out. He removed the dagger from his belt. It wasn't wooden, but it was consecrated. In the cause of Christ, Uthe was certain it would do what it was intended to do.

"Whether we live or whether we die, we are the Lord's..." Should one of your number be killed, *"we know he has not perished, but has come safely home."*

Bernard again, whose words and wisdom had been the spiritual backbone of the Order.

Dropping to one knee and uttering a short prayer of thanks, Uthe closed his eyes, visualized Keldwyn one more time, and shoved the dagger into his chest.

Chapter Sixteen

Though they were merely humans summoned from beyond the grave, their foes were deft with their blades, quick on their feet, and savage. Still, Keldwyn and the others held formation, battling them away from the altar until their side formed a solid line in front of it, a crescent wall to give Uthe the protection he needed. Keldwyn and Daegan held the center, taking the heaviest crush. He and the vampire assassin fought only far enough apart to be outside the sweep of their respective blades. The Templars, Gideon and Jacob worked on decimating the numbers of those who tried to get past them on the ends.

Though there was always precious little time to notice such things, Kel had brief glimpses of clever, brutal maneuverings on the part of the Green brothers. They used grace and speed as easily as sheer toe-to-toe brute strength to put bodies on the ground. The Templars fought as fearlessly as their history had suggested, displaying no fear and giving not an inch a ground. The enemy fought just as courageously, though, the air punctuated with shouts, the clang of metal. Grunts of exertion. Wounds flavored the burning smell of the courtyard with the sharp tang of blood. Everything smelled of death and rage, and the intense heat of battle cloaked them all.

They were gaining ground. They'd started five to one, and they were facing a more even number now. The Templars, Jacob and Gideon showed no sign of flagging. Likewise for Daegan, whose blade and long dagger flashed like lightning, the strikes close together and lethal.

As before, some magic worked, some didn't. With split second decisions to make, Keldwyn fought mainly with fist and blade. Knowing he was risking having a vital appendage lopped off, he nevertheless kept an eye on Uthe, a mere twenty feet out of the fight, standing at the altar. But the Templars had thought of that. Jacques was positioned just behind the line, getting the least of the fighting, but it put him in a position to call out if the demon sent anything unexpected against Uthe. Like now.

The squire shouted. Kel glanced back in time to see a dragon thrust its large, horned head through an opening in the castle rubble, to the right of Uthe. Teeth bared, it raised its head, preparing to shoot flame upon the vampire. Uthe had both hands in that silver-blue net, his eyes unfocused. His sword was propped against the table, forgotten. He was defenseless, oblivious to anything happening outside that magical sphere.

"Re-form to the right," Keldwyn roared. Thanking the gods for experienced warriors, he saw his allies grasp the situation and adjust the line fast as a whip unfurling to strike. He and Daegan advanced, taking on the bulk of the remaining two-legged enemy with the Templars to the left, as the ones to the right closed into a tighter arc around Uthe and faced the dragon.

"Need a moment," Kel snapped to Daegan. The vampire assassin lunged forward to guard Kel's back as he spun. Magic might have a sporadic effect on the Saracens, but the demon had put effort toward warding them and his energy was limited, especially now that he was under direct attack from Uthe. Had he risked a bluff, hoping Kel would assume the dragon was warded like the soldiers, and wouldn't even test it? If so, he'd figured wrong. Charging one of his daggers, Keldwyn shot lightning-infused fire at the beast's open maw.

The dragon stumbled back, roaring, wings slapping against the walls. A Saracen sword whistled so close behind Kel, it shaved off a layer of skin. A shallow wound, a graze. He ignored it. Daegan's body brushed against his and Keldwyn vaguely registered a gurgled scream as the vampire took care of the distraction.

The beast was too big for single shots to be effective fast enough. Sheathing the daggers and raising both hands, Keldwyn shouted the incantation and flung the net he formed outward.

It caught the beast around the head. As it tossed its giant cranium forward and back, up and down, trying to rid itself of the impediment, Kel was grimly satisfied to see he didn't have to tell the Templars to take the advantage. Gideon ran forward, Manfred at his heels. The intrepid vampire hunter stepped onto the dragon's knee like a stair and flung himself upward, driving his sword into the scaled neck while Manfred stabbed at the underside. The throat wasn't an easy target since the scales could be like armor, but Gideon, clawing his way up the side of the beast like he was scaling a rock wall, twisted his blade to a different angle and shoved it through. The dragon collapsed with a shriek, making the ground shake.

Kel spun to help Daegan re-engage, and found there was no longer any need. The last of the foe dropped as the vampire finished a follow-through with that deadly katana. He and the other Templars stood over a pile of sprawled bodies. None were moving.

His attention snapped back to Uthe. His vampire was on his knees, a black oil boiling out of the head and crawling up Uthe's arms. Kel bolted away from the line and to his side.

It was a novice's mistake. The shielding on Uthe was so solid, it was like hitting a brick wall. It knocked Keldwyn on his ass, bloodied his nose. Sensing the others coming to his aid, Kel snarled to keep them back and reached into Uthe's mind with the second mark. He couldn't find any awareness in the vampire, couldn't latch onto a random thought. All of it was a maze of gray fog, so thick Keldwyn stood at the periphery with no point of reference.

Yet Keldwyn felt a sucking sensation, like something vital was about to be ripped out of Uthe's mind. Though he wasn't touching him, he could sense Uthe's body shuddering with the strain. The miasma of evil magic swirled around him, tighter and tighter, like a cocoon. Now Keldwyn heard voices, but they weren't Uthe's. A cacophony of chuckling, shrieking and keening, bone-chilling and repugnant.

"He might send me to Hell, Fae," the demon howled. "But I will not go alone. You are helpless. You do not have the strength to resist all the power I now have to defeat you."

Strength comes...from...God...

It wasn't the Baptist. It was Uthe. Uthe was still in there. Uthe lifted his head with painstaking effort, as if he was pushing against a great weight. His gaze locked with Keldwyn's. Kel saw the demon simmering in the brown irises, yes. But he also saw Varick. It filled him with a violent wave of pride and love, seeing the valiant struggle the vampire was making against the demon's hold. He was holding open a window, using his connection to Keldwyn to give him the strength to do it. Since Keldwyn was in his mind, and a magic user, he saw the soul slip through that narrow passage, out of the head and toward freedom at last. The Madman of the Wilderness.

The soul's essence swirled around Uthe, a gesture that was blessing and embrace. It would have been lost in the haze of dust left from the fight, except it shimmered. As it hovered between the detached head and Uthe, it formed a tight vortex, the center like a nest. A tiny spark of light emerged from the mouth of the head and dropped into that nest. The light of the Baptist closed over it, a safe cocoon,

Night's Templar

then both souls were drawn away, slowly moving upward.

As Keldwyn tilted his head up, he watched them rise, higher, higher. He wanted to keep watching Uthe, but Uthe's head was back down and Kel knew he'd want verification that the most important part of the task was done. As he followed the ascent of the two souls, a different wave of magic hit him. A flash in the smoke and dust gave him the brief impression of wings, a warrior's face and a drawn sword. An angel, now providing heavenly escort. Kel remembered Shahnaz's visit by one and wondered if it was the same being. A celestial being's help would have been advantageous in this fight, but no one told an angel what to do, did they? None except a Force beyond understanding.

It was done. He returned his attention to what was most important to him. The shield that prevented Kel from approaching wasn't giving way, which alarmed him. It meant the demon was not yet dispatched.

Varick, are you there? As he became more insistent, the shielding seemed to be thickening. Uthe's hands, still covered with the thick black oil, gripped the altar. When he wrenched one free, his face crumpled in agony from the effort. Kel could scent burnt flesh even through the shielding. Uthe's flesh. "Varick."

Uthe was beyond hearing him. He groped along the table, and clutched the Spear. The blackness on his hand began to coat it, the shaft pulsing with energy, the black oil catching fire and turning the weapon to flame from shaft to point. Uthe let out an animal noise of pain, but he held onto it, lifted it. He swayed on his knees. His eyes were still vacant, but now the expression was different.

Fear pierced Kel. It was the way he looked when the Ennui came upon him. Now he was not caught in a magical trance. He was drifting, the stress and strain of what he'd done catapulting him into the lost world in his mind.

"Uthe. Varick!"

Kel tried everything he could to breach the shield around him. The demon's laughter grew louder. "We're off to Hell, my lord," he spat from the head, a nightmarish effect since the lips stretched in an unnatural way, grimacing over the words. "Hooray to the victorious warrior. He has done the Lord's Will, and now it is my Will he will serve..."

"No," Kel roared. "My lord. The beauseant has not fallen. *It has not fallen.* Take him. Now. Your Master commands it."

Uthe paused, head tilted. But then Keldwyn saw it. It was the briefest of flashes, but in it Uthe clasped the one thing he knew better than anything else. Obedience to God's will, now reinforced by obedience to the Master who loved him.

By some miracle, Uthe made it to his feet. Kel could see the pain that racked the vampire, the effort it took to focus past the tricks of his mind and do what needed to be done. He tried not to think of what such a monumental strain could do to the mind. To Uthe's heart and body. The vampire's eyes were unfocused, lips peeled back in an agonized grimace, but he still had the Spear in his grasp. The demon shrieked.

"Now, Varick. *Do it.*"

Flame roared out from the altar, over Uthe, over Keldwyn, over the courtyard. But it was not enough to blind Keldwyn. In one violent move, Uthe shoved the metal point through the eye socket of the skull.

The bone shattered. Uthe jerked the weapon free and did it again, until instead of stabbing, he was hacking the skull into pieces.

When it was nothing more than shards and mangled flesh on the altar, he fell to his knees, staring at his hands. Kel pushed against the shielding, and it still refused to give way, though he could tell the demon's magic was churning, shifting. Uthe's mind was back to that gray nothingness again, no different from the wall of the Shattered World. He had no strength, no vigor left to look toward Keldwyn again. Only one word got through.

Goodbye.

"No," Kel snarled.

Energy was swirling around all of them. It was wild, unfocused, the death throes of a demon leaving the earthly realm. But the beast had had time to throw one more distraction their way as he sought his victory.

Daegan seized Kel's arm, yanking his attention out of Uthe's head and to the present. More Saracens were charging through the archway behind them. Screaming their war cry, some of them mounted, others on foot brandishing their swords, all coming at a full run. The line around Kel was regrouping at Jacob's shout, the men ready to start the fight anew.

Kel didn't care. Uthe was slipping away from him. Had that been part of the price of Fatima's magic, a bribe to get the demon to go on his way? He'd lost the Baptist, but would be given a faithful Templar to accompany him into a hellish eternity instead?

He didn't accept that. He wouldn't accept it. Turning away from the fight, Kel threw himself against that barrier, calling on all his skill as a magic user, all his physical strength as a fighter. He would figure out the shape of it, he would get him back.

Then he felt a pulling sensation. The floor was becoming unstable, the air around him shifting. His heart leaped in his throat, his stomach thudding to his knees as he realized what was happening. The souls were freed, the demon on its way back to Hell. The task was done.

"No," he shouted. "Don't..."

Sand, blood and screams vanished.

§

He emerged from the nightmare, sweating, bloody, on his hands and knees, one long dagger still clasped in his hand. He was on sleek translucent tile, gazing through the thick wavering ice at a school of fish below. They were being herded playfully by a team of water Fae with feathery tails and high jewel-toned crests instead of hair. One twisted in the water, saw him and squeaked. Fish and Fae alike darted away.

He was looking at the moat that ran beneath Caislean Uisce, the Castle of Water. What Uthe had called the Ice Castle. He was in the Queen's large throne room. Keldwyn pushed himself up to his heels, his blood-soaked blade scraping against the ice blue marble tile that outlined the translucent ones. The blood left a smear. Other drops fell as he lifted his hand to his brow to wipe it across his sand-gritted eyes. Now that he was out of the fray of battle, he noticed his arm had been cut. It would heal, like the mass of bruises and cuts he could feel over his body.

He shook off the disorientation and took an accounting of who was with him. Daegan and Gideon were a few feet away, both in similar condition with wounds that would need blood nourishment, but which would heal. Jacob was speaking to them.

Keldwyn looked around the room. His gaze passed over a small group of Fae nobles, but they were blurred images to him, of no consequence. Uthe. Where was Varick?

He struggled to his feet and spun around to be sure of it. Jacob was at his side. "He is not here, my lord."

He remembered now. Uthe on his knees, the demon trying to drag him down to Hell. If the demon hadn't succeeded, it still left Uthe in the Shattered World, facing the last desperate wave of the demon's army. The Templars weren't here, but had they vanished at the same time? Was Uthe facing them alone? Was he still lost in that gray void in his head, so the Saracens could cut the warrior down with no resistance at all, like a defenseless child? The idea enraged him. If the Queen had summoned them back, why were all of them here and Uthe wasn't? Had the demon's hold kept him from going through?

"Lord Keldwyn." Queen Rhoswen's imperious tone penetrated. Perhaps she'd been speaking for several moments, because Jacob touched his arm to command his attention. Yes, he needed to pay attention. There was nothing else more important than Varick, but only the Queen could permit him back through the gateway of the Shattered World. He'd have to find his vampire again. How long could he last, if he survived the Saracens, the demon? Keldwyn didn't want to think about Uthe wandering in that lost mind state for more than a second, let alone the two weeks Keldwyn had been there on his own.

"Your Majesty, you must send me back. Something happened. It is not finished. I don't know why I'm here..."

He registered that Rhoswen had a handful of her most powerful advisors in attendance, along with several of the Queen's Guard. Cayden, their captain, was here. He stood at her back, studying all with his usual singular focus. He'd assess threats to his Queen before assigning priority to any other matters requiring attention, like the new arrivals bleeding all over her floor.

"You completed the task, Lord Keldwyn," Rhoswen said, drawing closer. Her gaze was sliding over him, assessing his injuries. She made a motion to one of her attendants and the young woman disappeared. Probably to get him first aid he wouldn't be here long enough to need.

"Yes. And no. The souls are released, and the demon has been dispatched back to its proper place. The Shattered World is in no danger from it being released there. But Lord Uthe—"

"Good. The relics remain there."

He had a momentary image of Uthe lifting the Spear and driving it through the skull. The Grail had been knocked across the altar, but he expected it was still lying there. "Yes. The Cross was on fire, burning, but...it may have survived. I need to return immediately."

"Not according to your presence here. I set the spell to hold you in the world until the task is completed, and we were more than fortunate it worked to pull you out." Rhoswen spoke patiently. "And I wasn't asking you to confirm the relics are there. I was telling you they are. I could not bring them out, but they are safe there for the moment."

Keldwyn blinked. "Your Majesty, Lord Uthe is still there. Why was he not drawn back with myself and these others?"

"I do not know." She shrugged. She had her hair swept up and captured with an array of tiny icicle clips. The soft white strands fell over her pale arms and the silver gossamer dress she wore. Today she had scrolled tattoos on her arms like an ice skater's pattern in winter.

"Perhaps it was the Shattered World's price for your being there," she said. "It had to keep one of you. Perhaps he was too entangled with the magic he wielded to dispatch the demon. Perhaps because he was bound to the skull by blood, he is now destined to stay with what remains of it. Or he has been consigned to the same fate as the demon, a truly noble sacrifice for us all. But ultimately, it is no longer our concern."

He hated her then. Truly hated her, in a way he hadn't allowed himself to feel in a very long time. Sometimes there was just too much of her mother in her. That compartmentalization of empathy in a damn box, hoarded like a scarce commodity she refused to waste on anything that truly mattered. When that quality surfaced as it did now, he saw Reghan's executioner, rather than Reghan's daughter.

"Is that the royal 'our', Your Majesty? Because it is very much *my* concern."

"And ours," Gideon said, stepping forward.

Keldwyn saw Jacob give him a warning gesture. Though Jacob himself wasn't always known for showing the proper obedience to a queen, one didn't speak in the presence of the Fae Queen until spoken to, a matter of intelligence as much as obeisance. If she was annoyed, she would simply turn him into an ice sculpture or a fish in the moat beneath her feet until she was ready to hear him talk. Recuperating

Night's Templar

from being turned into ice could take a mortal weeks.

Keldwyn shifted between her and Gideon, drawing her sharp attention back to him. "It is not simply a matter of him being adrift in the Shattered World, Your Majesty. Lord Uthe has Ennui."

He was aware of Gideon and Daegan's surprised reaction to that, as much as Jacob's lack of expression. It was as he'd expected. Lyssa had known. "His mind comes and goes, so it will hamper his survival chances if I am not there."

"From what I understand of Ennui, it might be best if the Shattered World finishes him off. You should not prolong his suffering. There is nothing you can do to reverse it."

"That remains to be seen." Keldwyn met her gaze. For all that he had thought about the repercussions these past few months as his feelings for Uthe grew, now he spoke without hesitation, sealing his fate once and for all in his own world. "He has given me two of their marks. I am his blood source now. My blood seems to rejuvenate him. It may reduce the effects of the disease."

He didn't startle her often, not deeply enough for it to be reflected in her face. He saw shock, which was echoed by the advisors around her. Cayden's normally impassive expression was twisted in an expression that showed he thought Keldwyn deranged. Or guilty of incomprehensible stupidity.

None of that mattered now. Only one thing did.

"If you feed him, if you are marked as his servant, you are no longer of the high Fae," she said stiffly. "It is a sentence even Tabor will have to accept, because it is in our laws. You know this. You had to know it when you let him mark you."

Her tone was accusatory, and he stood impassive before it, neither acknowledging nor denying. A flush suffused her pale cheeks.

"You will be stripped of everything. The Seelie and

Unseelie courts, as well as the vampire Council, will no longer have your skills as advisor or liaison. You will be denied entry to the Fae world and you will never be allowed to return. In time, without a connection to the life force here, you will die."

"Given my strength...that gives me at least another hundred years. I am already over fifteen hundred years old, Your Majesty. I can end my life with his. It is a fair exchange."

Rhoswen stared at him. "I will not permit it, any of it. You may not return to the Shattered World. Once he is dead, it will break that bond. You are too valuable an advisor for us to accept your banishment. You will instead be punished by this court for your infraction of the law, and continue your service once you complete it."

"No."

Cayden shifted to a more offensive position, registering the change in mood between him and the Queen. Daegan, Gideon and Jacob, all fighting men, picked up the same vibes and moved closer, but Kel knew they needed to stay back. They all did.

As he looked at her proud, beautiful face, the deep anger in her blue gaze, he knew what the rage she was experiencing felt like. The right trigger could always bring it to life, no matter how deeply he'd buried it, and he expected it was the same for her. No one had ever had the misfortune of being this close to both of them when that ignition point happened at the same time.

His lover, his best friend, her father. Until now, nothing had ever hurt like having Reghan taken from him in a way he could have prevented. Reghan had forbidden it. Keldwyn had thought about killing himself when Reghan had been transformed into a rose bush and placed in a desert world, an ancient and enchanted Fae prison, to suffer and die. How long had it taken? For years Keldwyn had dreamed he'd been standing over Reghan, watching him slowly die, knowing his suffering but helpless to stop it.

Uthe had felt the demon through his blood link, even in the Shattered World. Ah, gods. Had Masako felt Reghan's actual suffering, his dying? If so, her strength to survive long enough to see Lyssa raised to adulthood had to be commended, for Keldwyn had been overcome simply from imagining it.

It was a feeling that made one want to tear down the world, incinerate it whole to escape that pain. It was the feeling gnawing at him now like a vulture ripping out his intestines, as he thought of Uthe in the Shattered World. How much time had already passed there?

Rhoswen knew that pain, in a different way. She'd lost Reghan before he ever died, her mind poisoned against him by her bitch mother. He wondered if Rhoswen killing Magwel years later had helped assuage that pain in any way. Given the way she was looking at him now, he would say no.

They claimed themselves superior to vampires, and perhaps they were, but one thing was a leveler between all humanoid species. They fucked up their heads and hearts over one another in ways beyond comprehension. He wondered if their destructiveness was a mystery even to whatever Creator had made the whole sad lot of them.

"This doesn't involve any of you. It's between me and her," he said. It wouldn't stop Cayden, but it would safeguard the vampire and mortals at his back. "What is it you seek here, Your Majesty?" Keldwyn said stiffly.

Her lip curled. "I want to know you can learn humility, Lord Keldwyn."

"You first, Your Majesty."

One quick step and she was close enough to slap him, nails raking his face. He caught her wrist. He had her easily on weight and height, but that meant nothing in a fight between two Fae. Cayden started forward, sword sliding from his scabbard, and Keldwyn proved the point. A lift of his hand, and the captain was trapped in place, caught in a force field spun by summer winds. Rhoswen countered with ice that flowed up Keldwyn's arm to his shoulder. He showed no reaction to it beyond a muscle twitching in his jaw.

"You have been guilty of a thousand insults to my person," Rhoswen said through gritted teeth. Her fingers curled in his grasp as they stared at one another, inches between his sparking dark eyes and her cold blue ones. "This will be the one that gives me what I've always desired—a reason sanctioned by law to strip your powers from you. I will keep them as long as I wish, and you will beg me to give them back. On your knees, a hundred years from now."

Kel thought of the section in the Templar Rule about penances, where a Templar was stripped of his mantle and required to eat off the floor for a year. Every action had consequences.

"I will meet that price. Debase me, make yourself feel better about the past that we cannot change. But you will do it *after* you give me access to the Shattered World to find him, to help him."

"You claimed to love my father, yet you stood by and did nothing. *Nothing.* You let him die, and now, you want to give all for this...vampire." She was spitting at him. The ice was petrifying the bones of his arm, making it numb and excruciatingly painful at the same time. He channeled it into his savage response.

"Because Reghan told me not to stop it," he snarled back. "Because he loved her more than anything. Because apparently love means standing back and letting your heart be ripped from your chest without lifting a finger to stop the one ripping it out. I swore I'd never do it again, and I won't. Even if it makes me the most selfish bastard who has ever lived, I will not let the noble, fucking, self-sacrificing nature of someone else I love take him from me."

Her expression was as frozen as his hand manacling her

wrist, but he didn't stop. "Years ago, I stood before your mother when she passed sentence on your father, for no other reason than she hated him for not loving her more. Your father told me to let him go, to let things unfold as they should. I should have stood against the Fae court then. I should have stood against what was nothing more than a woman scorned, who knew nothing of what being a queen truly meant."

The energy building between them was so intense it had pressed everyone against the walls of the chamber. It overwhelmed Keldwyn's initial restraint on Cayden, such that the captain was there with the others, no way to get to his queen's side. Since sometimes those walls were conjured to be sheets of moving water that disappeared into a knee level mist, it was good that today they were simply walls hung with tapestries. Their audience would have been soaked, though Keldwyn reflected the water would have absorbed blood spatter better.

"If you want my head, Your Majesty, it is yours," he said between his teeth. "You do with it as you will. But I will not see history repeat itself. Not for something as trite as your feelings."

It was the final trigger. A burst of ice and cold met fire and earth. The reverberation that shook the room blinded and deafened their audience, knocking them to the ground. Cracks ran across the floor and glass rained from the ceiling. The Fae advisors fled out the side doors. Without glancing that way, Keldwyn shot a burst of energy toward Jacob, shoving him from one of the larger cracks before he fell through and was trapped in the moat. Daegan yanked Gideon into an alcove to protect him from the shards of glass which rained down on his own shoulders. Kel was sure the vampire hunter would give his Master hell over that move. But protecting the one you loved was second nature, wasn't it?

Then it was over. He and Rhoswen stood a few feet apart, staring at one another, the residual magic drifting around them like smoke from fired pistols.

"Fine. Go then," she said through stiff lips. "Go to your vampire lover. Perhaps I will leave you both in the Shattered World and you can wither and die there. All that awaits you here is banishment. Forever."

His laugh was contemptuous. "You have not been listening if you think there is anything you can do to me that would hurt worse than what I have endured. When will you ever grow up and decide the past is the past, and had nothing to do with you? *Nothing.*" She flinched as he fired the words at her. "The things that hurt the worst are inflicted by those who do not intend you harm at all. Because you are not the center of their world. We never were."

He stepped back up to her, toe to toe, but this time there was no anger left in him. It was that way with loving someone, that vacillation of passion. Now he could see the traces of vulnerability beneath her strength, the fragility in the tight set of her jaw. All of those qualities came from Reghan. It was just her curse that his stubbornness tangled with Magwel's bitterness in her genes.

"But when you find someone to whom you *are* that important, it heals some very deep wounds, Your Majesty. You will do anything to claim that love." His gaze shifted to Cayden, then back to her. The gravity that had kept the others away was gone. As soon as the captain had realized it, he was back at her side. He stood only a stride away, his gaze pinned on Keldwyn, though he did not interfere, sensing the change of mood.

"How long will you let the love you feel for him burn inside your ice heart before you let it melt and heal your soul?" Keldwyn said quietly.

Cayden was almost as good as his Queen at concealing his thoughts, but Kel saw the brief slip. He would always stand at her side, protect her, love her, care for her. Yet if Rhoswen allowed that love to become an open thing, growing without restrictions, it could change everything inside her soul. Cayden knew it, hoped it, wished for it. Keldwyn knew it would, because it had for him.

Rhoswen was now looking into the space beyond Keldwyn's shoulder, away from everyone. She was barely breathing, it seemed, her energy glowing blue around her. Keldwyn passed his fingers through that aura, making it curl around his fingers and dissipate. He'd done that when she was younger, making her laugh, snapping her out of a tantrum.

"Most of my life, I've watched over amazing, powerful and supremely frustrating children. Uthe is no child. He is my equal." He met her gaze when it shifted to his. "Just as you know that Lyssa is yours, with or without Fae blood. He is balance and intelligence, steady as the earth itself, and I have ever been a creature of earth. For me, he is the fire in the center of it."

She turned away from him. The unbroken tiles beneath her feet changed to cracked ice as she stepped upon them. A blast of cold air whistled through the chamber, rustling the tapestries on the wall and frosting the skin of those left in the chamber. Stopping in front of her throne, she tipped her head back. A ripple went through her body, a hard shudder. Cayden moved to her side, closer this time. Once there, he stopped, paused. After a long moment, he dropped to a knee and bowed his head, but he put his hand at her waist, long fingers wrapping around her hip. It was an intriguing mix of messages. She tilted her head away from him, but her fingers touched his, curved into them and held. She said something too low to be heard, and Cayden rose to his feet. As she turned and faced him, the two of them exchanged a long look. Then she brought her attention back to Keldwyn.

"Lord Keldwyn, you have ever been a thorn in my side. I have imagined many ways to destroy you, yet I am not so caught up in the pleasure of such visions that I overlook a crucial truth. I rely on your counsel, your arguments and your clever insults that veil wise advice."

"Though you are a pain in my ass, Your Majesty, I would not offer counsel unless I thought you were a monarch worthy of my time."

"Proof that your arrogance is one of the least charming things about you, my lord. But..." She took a step toward him. She seemed to be struggling with something. Cayden moved a step closer again, and his proximity steadied her. She straightened, met Keldwyn's gaze. He caught a breath, for in the pain, resolve and raw honesty he saw there now, he remembered Reghan's face in their last days together, when so much had been about baring the soul, and saying their good-byes. He also thought about Uthe, calling him Master as they stood outside the Shattered World, admitting his desire to be Keldwyn's.

By the gods, he needed to go, now. He was quivering inside like a wolf in desperate need to go on the hunt. But she was his only gateway back to him.

"You have been the constant in my life since my father's passing. You loved him." Rhoswen's lips tightened. "I knew that. Countless times, when I felt the pain of his loss touch me from some passing memory, I saw it had touched you also. Since you hold so much away from the rest of us, I could only imagine how deeply that emotion ran. It changed, hurt and remade us all, didn't it, my lord?"

Her voice had become soft, her eyes weary. He nodded, not trusting himself to speak. He thought of Uthe, asking, *"Was he the love of your life?"*

"You have stayed by my side to help me learn to be a better queen," she said. "You have counseled me in ways large and small to keep my baser emotions from dictating my rule. Mostly. I think there were times you deliberately made yourself a target so I could channel my anger toward you rather than toward the responsibilities of my throne."

He didn't deny it, and her lips twitched, though there was no humor in her face. Pain was still a living thing in her eyes. "You watched over his other daughter as much as you were able, cared for her interests and brought us together. You suffered guilt over her mother choosing to meet the sun, because you felt you owed that to him as well, to protect the happiness of the woman you despised for taking him from you. But you figured that out, too, didn't you? He loved us. Just never as much as he loved her."

"Yes." Keldwyn spoke through stiff lips. "We cannot help whom we love, my lady."

"Nor whom we don't." She sighed. "That's the dark side the poems do not address. You have now given your heart to a vampire, and you are willing to let that love take you from my side. Forgive my reaction to that, but it opens old wounds."

"You are true Unseelie Fae, my lady," Keldwyn said slowly. "You have trouble understanding that the confession of love for one is not a denial of any love for another. You do not have to be the center of my existence to have my love, my regard, and my care for your wellbeing." Her gaze lifted to him, and he nodded, meaning every word. "If it must be done from the human realm, it will be no less strong or steadfast."

"I do not want to lose your counsel," she said after a moment. "But our rules on this are very clear. I am not of a mind to try and change them yet. Too much has changed, too quickly, between our world and the human one, the vampire one. There must be boundaries."

"There must." He dropped to one knee and bowed his head. If this was the last counsel he would ever give her, he knew what needed to be said. What Reghan would want him to say. "You are a fair Queen, my lady. The past is relinquishing its hold on you, the present moment notwithstanding. With every step you take away from it, you become an even better ruler. I wish you success and joy."

He lifted his head, met her ice-blue eyes. "Now send me back to Varick, damn it, before I lose my mind."

High spots of color appeared in her pale cheeks, but her

countenance held something other than anger.

"One day you will learn you do not order a queen to do anything. Goodbye, Lord Keldwyn."

§

He only had time to bow his head in acknowledgment. He experienced the familiar disorientation of a portal transition, and then he was in the castle ruins once more, surrounded by bodies, blood and a scattering of weapons. He scrambled to his feet.

The Templars and Saracens were dead. As he moved among them, Kel saw they'd either been taken by the fight or, once the fight was over, their purpose done, the Shattered World had no more claim on them. Curled up on his side, Jacques looked as if he were in his bed. He held his sword, his lips pressed to the blade.

Keldwyn squatted next to Nexus. The stallion lay where he'd fallen when the shielding around the demon had hit him. Had Uthe not had the sorceress's weapon protecting him, Kel expected it would have done far more damage to the vampire. It had broken the horse's neck. It would help Uthe to know the noble creature hadn't suffered more than a moment, illusion or not.

The only one missing from the courtyard was Uthe.

Varick? He spoke in his mind, hoping, but he heard nothing. It didn't mean anything, he told himself. He could be sleeping, unconscious. Kel didn't know if body decomposition was the same here or not, but those in the courtyard did not look long dead. So perhaps he'd only been gone a few hours.

Scanning the altar, he saw the pieces of the head had dissolved to ash. The Grail was still there, knocked on its side as before, the Cross standing silent above it. The traces of the demon's power, that insidious red, were gone, as was the silver-blue of the binding. With those two influences gone, Kel could feel the drumbeat pulse of the power innate to the Cross and Grail, a golden heat like the sun, constant, steady. Beneath that was the power of the earth, fueled by that light, as well as by blood. The vines were gone from the Cross, and the goblet no longer looked like an artifact recently dug from the ground. The wood of the Cross gleamed and the Grail's clay bowl had a luster.

He didn't see the Spear. Perhaps it had dissolved to ash with the head.

Kel moved away from the altar and began to search the crevices around the main courtyard. A handful of shallow, shaded alcoves seemed to be former entry points into the keep. Even though the sun wouldn't cook Uthe here as it would in the earthly realm, instinct might send him to a cool, dark place to recoup his strength.

Keldwyn discovered a hallway that had deteriorated into a cave, which became a tunnel leading downward, perhaps once a hidden passageway out of the keep. He saw a blood trail and, as he traversed the tunnel, skidding a little from the steep incline, he saw signs of a scuffle against the rock walls. When he had to step over two more bodies, he knew Uthe had been required to finish off his attackers. The demon's last defiance. Yet it meant he hadn't succeeded in taking Uthe's soul with him. Kel curled a lip in savage satisfaction. His heart was too pure, his faith too devout. Hell would have no space for Varick Uthe.

That part was good news, but Keldwyn couldn't dispel the image of Uthe fighting on his own while he and Rhoswen wrangled in her throne room over the mistakes of a time so far past it shouldn't matter anymore.

Cursing, Keldwyn quickened his pace. He hadn't yet found Uthe's collapsed body, something he wanted to feel hopeful about. The blood trail continued and, since he didn't find any other Saracens, the blood had to be all Uthe's. Blood loss might not kill a vampire, but it would have severely weakened him.

The tunnel opened back up into a cave, which led out into the grassy area Uthe had thought might be a former tourney field. It was at the mouth of that cave that Keldwyn found him. His heart froze. The Spear was thrust through Uthe's chest, and the vampire lay motionless on his side.

Keldwyn skidded down to him, kneeling by his side. He was dead. He must be dead. Uthe's eyes were open and unblinking, his face in the rigor of death. *No.*

He didn't care how selfish it was, he wanted to rage at Uthe's God, at any god that was listening. He'd let Reghan go, because Reghan belonged to another, and Fate had been too strong for him to fight its course, but Uthe was his. *His.* He'd given his heart to Keldwyn—at least he'd started to do so. They were going to belong to one another. He'd known it down to his soul.

He couldn't bear to see the Spear there, so Kel maneuvered Uthe gently forward, clasped the shaft behind the tip and pulled it free, setting it aside. If the trail of bodies hadn't told him vengeance was already served, he would have hunted down those who'd done this to Uthe, charting every corner of the Shattered World necessary to make it happen. He didn't care if Rhoswen brought him back. He'd rather stay lost here, never having to go through the painful farce of facing others in his life, forced to cope with yet another loss he couldn't bear. It would end here.

He was cunning as needed without ever telling a direct lie, the epitome of legendary Fae cleverness. He always presented the face he intended to present. It had been many years since someone had looked beyond that to see the soul beneath. That spoke to how good he was at the tasks he'd set himself over the years. Yet the perverse hypocrisy of being so good at such dissembling lay in the soul deep longing to find someone with the intelligence and strength to see that and far more. To accept Keldwyn as…Keldwyn. Someone who would look at him like Uthe had, with no mask or artifice between them. No separation between their souls.

Catriona loved him, and he treasured that, but a child's love was different. Uthe had looked into his soul and understood in a single quiet moment how much Keldwyn grieved for his children and for Reghan. He'd seen how important peace between their worlds was to Keldwyn, how Keldwyn did so much of what he did as a memorial to those he'd lost.

The gods thought a soul was supposed to have a limitless endurance against grief and loss. It didn't. He was done.

Keldwyn placed his hand on Uthe's chest, sliding his other arm around him to pull his body halfway into his lap. Wrapping both arms around him, he rested his forehead on the top of his head. A thought crossed his mind and he reached up, unraveled the braids Catriona had made. His time in the Shattered World had knotted them, but he yanked the strands free with impatient fingers. His hair tumbled down to brush Uthe's face and neck.

Beauty didn't mean much, except as a strategic advantage or as something that just *was*. But it became something different when offered as a gift to one specific person, one of many gifts he'd wanted to offer. The vampire liked his hair, liked feeling it on his face, and on his body. It had pleased Keldwyn so deeply, so absurdly. He'd liked how the vampire touched his ears, wondering at their shape and feel.

When he gripped Uthe's limp hand, he found there was still warmth in it. The discovery twisted the knife deeper in his gut. He could not have been gone long. Not long at all...What if the thrust of the Spear had happened a blink before Kel arrived, the last body thumping to the ground and Uthe stumbling or rolling to the bottom of the tunnel, coming to a stop here only moments ago? The quest was done, the relics now all that was left of his task.

The thought drew his mind back to the altar. Kel lifted his head, staring into Uthe's face. What if there was a way to restore life to him?

Keldwyn knew how magic did and didn't work. The idea that the Grail could bestow immortality was a legend born of men's perpetual fear of death. Yet there might be some truth in the embellishment. The Grail had power; he'd felt it. What if it had regenerative powers?

He left Uthe for only as long as it took him to run back through the tunnel, faster than he'd ever moved before. If he'd been matching himself against Uthe in one of his sun rituals, Kel would have left him far behind. But he had no intention of leaving the vampire behind, or being left behind himself.

The Grail was still on the table, an unadorned goblet lying on its side. Some of the inert black ooze that had come from the head was still pooled on the table, but it had cut a deliberate swath around the sacred cup, such that the Grail lay in a cleanly marked circle. Proof of its properties of Light gave Keldwyn hope.

As he headed back down through the tunnels, he was suddenly seized with a fear that the Shattered World would play tricks on him, change the track back to Uthe and keep him away from the vampire forever. But Uthe was still there. He also still had the dagger that Rail had given him. Keldwyn was going to use every possible advantage he had. When he pulled it from the scabbard, the blood on it made him pause, because Uthe had said he'd never used it to take a life, except for the one time with his squire.

It didn't matter. Keldwyn wiped it off on his clothes, then drew the blade across his wrist, a deep cut that brought forth a swift gush of blood. Holding his arm over the Grail, he filled it halfway. He hoped it was enough. He didn't dare wait any longer. Shifting Uthe back across his lap, he held the Grail to Uthe's lips, cradling his jaw. It took some awkward maneuvering, but though Uthe couldn't swallow, blood was draining down his throat.

"Live," Kel muttered. He'd gone numb. There were things too large to be felt, so painful that they shut down everything else just so a person could keep breathing. But Kel knew firsthand it would be far more merciful if such a loss killed him outright, so he didn't have to feel it when the numbness wore off. Because it would. It always did.

He kept the blood going down Uthe's throat, putting aside the Grail when it was empty and bringing his arm directly to Uthe's lips. He cut himself again to keep the flow going. The world started to swim, but he didn't stop. It was the Shattered World, anything was possible. Maybe Uthe's brain fever would infect him, and Kel could wander in an illusion where Uthe was still alive, and they were together. They'd exist forever in this hellish fantasy.

If they were together, it wouldn't matter. There would be no Hell.

§

Being dead wasn't so bad. After impaling himself with the dagger, proving his willingness to take the innocent's place, he'd swum out of the grayness to find himself by the altar. The Spear was in his hand and Keldwyn's thunderous voice rocketed through him, bringing him back to what needed to be done. The Fae Lord would make a good battle commander, for his bellow could have carried over the clamor of two armies.

That was when Uthe realized he wasn't dead. The dagger was metal, not wood, so he could feel the pain of the wound but it wasn't mortal. Stabbing himself to prove he was a willing sacrifice, apparently that had been the important part. It had dislodged the innocent, snapping that tether so it could go free. Uthe could take care of other things now.

Things long overdue.

When Uthe shattered the skull with the spear, he watched the demon turn to smoke and get sucked through the floor. It was as if the Devil drew a deep breath and pulled him in. Uthe's attention returned to the fight still in progress, and he plunged into the battle, joy surging through him at the chance to stand with his fellow Templars one more time.

He didn't see Kel, Jacob or Gideon, but Jean-Claude shouted at him between thrusts of his sword and the clang of answering metal on his shield. "They disappeared—poof—in thin air."

That meant they were no longer needed. The quest was done, and Rhoswen had likely pulled Keldwyn out of here. Good. The Fae Lord was safe. All was as it was meant to be, though a fierce ache gripped him as Uthe longed for that most precious commodity of all, the one so intimately connected to love—more time.

It was what it was. The Lord's Will must be followed, and he'd been given more gifts than most, including love at the end of his life. He threw his strength and speed behind those still standing, and they fought and fought and fought. They battled as they'd done at Hattin, knowing the end would come here and, when it did, they would meet it with courage.

Jean-Claude, the strongest fighter of them all, was the last to fall. Though Uthe did his best to dispatch as many as he could, the Frenchman was at last overpowered, and Uthe faced a half-dozen Saracens alone.

He took down four. The other two maneuvered him out of the courtyard and into a tunnel where they thought they had the advantage. One had seized the Spear during their fighting in the bailey, and found the opportunity to stick the relic through him. He paid for it with his life, Uthe jamming his sword into the Saracen's chest.

The Spear hadn't gone through his heart, but the organ beat right up against it, a painful thudding. Then the last of the intrepid bastards grabbed the Spear and twisted it. The twisting ruptured the organ. Uthe decapitated the man in the same moment.

He supposed having his heart rupture from the force of the wood was as fatal to a vampire as a stake, because his vision grayed and he tumbled the rest of the way down the tunnel, ending up on the grass field next to the castle.

Being impaled on the Spear of Longinus has to carry

Night's Templar

some weight in Heaven, *non*? As Jean-Claude might say. Bernard had talked about being welcomed to the Virgin Mary's arms in the afterlife. Uthe thought of his mother. He'd like to put his arms around her, hold her, thank her. She could have found ways to kill herself if she'd truly despaired. He was sure she'd known his father was going to kill her. He'd probably told her that himself, repeatedly. She must have known Uthe's life would be difficult with such a sire, but maybe she thought he might have a chance at something better eventually. Which suggested she knew all vampires weren't monsters like his father.

She'd given him a chance at life. He didn't know if what awaited him was the Heaven Bernard envisioned or not, but if there could be a quiet meadow like where he and Kel had spent the day with Catriona and Della, and he could sit with his mother for a little while, that would be nice. Then he would stretch out in the meadow and think of Keldwyn. He'd let oblivion take him as he imagined the Fae against him, his arm around his waist and chest, holding him close. He could almost feel him doing it, his breath and heartbeat as close as a wish.

Everything after that, except for that brief thought of his mother, was quiet and dark, as if he were waiting. Perhaps that was how it went. You waited to see what your fate would be in this featureless stasis.

After a time, things started to feel different. He was more aware of his body, of his surroundings. Intriguingly, he still sensed someone holding him tightly, thanking all the gods that ever were for their mercy. Warm liquid splashed upon him, like a tear. Then things started to spin, get fuzzy, and he was drifting once more.

When he came back to awareness again, it was still dark, but that was because his eyes were closed. It took a while, but eventually he opened them to see what the afterlife looked like.

A blue sky and green trees. It looked much like the Fae world, everything far brighter and more vibrant than earth.

The Fae didn't spread out and change the face of things the way humans did with their technology. Despite that, Uthe had to admit he had the oddest desire for a soda. One Mariela had given him. What had she called it? Cheerwine. He thought of her curled up in the servants' common area, watching the shows she liked. She didn't know he occasionally tuned in to her mind, sitting unnoticed inside it to absorb the tranquility she had, at peace with herself, him and the world as it was.

Heaven had even more to offer him than he'd expected. His gaze slid left and he found Keldwyn. Unlike the last time he'd seen him, when they'd both been blood smeared and travel worn, the Fae was clean and as impeccably groomed as he normally was. His long, rippling hair was loose, and he wore one of his ruffled shirts unlaced in the front over those snug breeches that were so temptingly immodest. Perhaps Heaven had allowed Uthe to sleep until the end of Keldwyn's life so they could be together. A fanciful thought. Their relationship in some ways had only just begun when Uthe had died. Yet seeing him now, he felt as bonded to Keldwyn as if they'd been intended for one another since the first skeins of time had been woven.

Keldwyn was tying ribbons on his wrists and arms. Tiny fairies fluttered in and out of Uthe's field of vision like moths, bringing Kel strands of different colors and thicknesses. Uthe imagined all the places they'd found them: out of the shining hair of little girls, from rose-laden arbors at weddings, from cheerful gift packages and whimsical shoes.

What are you doing?

The Fae Lord's gaze rose, and never had darkness held so much light. His lips curved, and he touched Uthe's face before lifting his limp hand to press his lips to Uthe's knuckles. Uthe couldn't parse out the Fae Lord's thoughts, but his expression said as much or more. There was a sheen to the dark eyes that Uthe realized with a shock might be tears.

"It is an old ritual," Kel said, clearing his throat and blinking that sheen away. "There is a clan of the Fae who create tapestries of ribbons over and around the body of a loved one."

What does it mean? He didn't have the strength to speak aloud yet, but he was glad Kel did. He liked hearing the male's voice.

Kel's lips quirked. "It is a sacred ritual to one of our clans, with much ceremony and structure to it. However, years ago, the original idea came about like a single flower, simple and spontaneous. It started with a human child. When her grandmother died, the little girl tied several ribbons from her hair to the body. She said she would hold onto one end so that she'd always be able to stay connected to her grandmother. In her mind, it was a real idea. To the Fae of that clan who witnessed it, it made an impression. A symbolic tether. When his mate passed, far before her time, he did it to give himself comfort. Then someone else did it, and it became part of their customs, the weavings and ribbons becoming ever more elaborate. Someone made up some spiritual reason for it, but all it means is the living need rituals to hold onto a loved one, even when death separates us."

"Am I dead?"

"No. But I have waited some time for you to wake. Nearly all morning. An eternity to me."

Uthe's fingers curved around Keldwyn's. "I'm sorry I kept you waiting."

"You should be. I am a high Fae lord, not used to waiting on a lowly vampire."

Uthe smiled, but he would not give himself to the moment yet. "The relics?"

"They are safe. We did remove them from the Shattered World, but they remain in the Fae world, out of reach of those who would use them for wrong purpose. You are considered their guardian still, Lord Uthe, and we will follow your guidance if you are dissatisfied with their placement."

Trusting Kel, he accepted that they were secure for the time being. Uthe glanced down at the ribbons tied to his legs and arms. "You have spoken of wanting to bind me. I didn't expect you to turn me into a Maypole." He was lying on soft grass, wearing a loose robe that Keldwyn had opened to place the ribbons upon him. Uthe was naked beneath the robe. But Uthe was even more naked in his thoughts. While Keldwyn was speaking of seemingly simple things, there was an intense restraint to his touch, like he wasn't certain he could keep his touch gentle if he let loose his hold on those emotions. Uthe could feel the shape of them, like a dam set to overflow. It made him incapable of guarding his tongue.

"My episodes of Ennui, the forgetfulness... I think at times they are triggered by my fear of it happening at the wrong time, wrong moment. I do not fear that when you are by my side."

"Well then, that is where I shall stay. For I would not want your reputation of astounding courage to be tarnished."

"It could be awhile. I am immortal."

Keldwyn scoffed, though his eyes remained steady and focused on Uthe. "A vampire's immortality is but a child's life span next to a Fae's. Spending that time with you will be like taking a vacation, give or take a century. But I will make a demand of you."

"Only one? It must be a slow day for you."

"You goad my temper only because you think yourself spent," Keldwyn said mildly. "Else you would not risk it."

"You assume I've ever been intimidated by Fae arrogance," Uthe informed him. "Power is in the hands of the Lord. You may decimate me, my lord, but I was ever only dust."

"Not to me." Keldwyn closed his hand over Uthe's, and the strength of his grip brought Uthe's eyes back to him. "Though if you know anything of me, you know how highly

Night's Templar

I prize the earth. But I would ask that you attend to my words seriously, as they are meant."

"Of course." Uthe sobered. "I did not mean to hurt you, Kel."

"You have the ability to do that, vampire," Keldwyn said after a weighted moment. "My soul is in your hands, and I demand you not take it anywhere I cannot be with you. Varick... I want you to give me your third mark. Bind us permanently, in the way of your kind."

Uthe stared at him. "The Ennui is affecting my brain, my lord. I thought you just asked to be third-marked."

"Your mind is sharp as necessary, and you heard me correctly."

"Ennui is degenerative. If it accelerates to violent mood swings, savage acts of sadism and total apathy to a moral code, I was relying on you to take my life, if I did not have the clarity to do it myself."

Kel's expression darkened, but he inclined his head. "You may still rely on me for that."

"Kel, with the third mark, if I die, you die. That's the way it works. I'm not sure even a powerful Fae would be exempt from the pull of that bond."

"I'm fifteen hundred years old, Lord Uthe. Do you think I have not lived long enough?"

"Perhaps I don't want to be stuck with you for all eternity," Uthe retorted, "especially if it's true that the mark is not severable, even after death." But his hand constricted on the Fae's. "You could never live long enough, my lord."

Kel's eyes gleamed. "Perhaps it is no request, but a demand I make of you. Though it may not be a problem, regardless. You drank from the Grail and the power of it gave you back to me. Perhaps the Ennui was eliminated with it, or its acceleration arrested for a time."

All attempt at humor disappeared. "You had me drink from the Grail?" Uthe tried to struggle up, but found he was still terribly weak. Even the ribbons impeded him. He shoved Kel's hands away from him, though, managing to sit up on his own. "What if it only has a limited amount of magic to give? *Not for me, but to God goes all the glory.* I would not have taken from it. You know that."

"No, you wouldn't have. But I would. I put my blood in the Grail." Keldwyn leaned forward. "I did not care if you were already bathed in the light of Heaven, lolling in eternal bliss with a hundred handsome male virgins. I was not giving you up without a fight, without trying every means at my disposal. I had to let Reghan go because his heart was not mine. Yours is. I will not share it with anyone or release it before I am damned ready, even to your God. You are bound to me, and that is how it will stay, unless you convince me that you do not care to be mine."

Pissed off, Keldwyn was impressive and intimidating. And beautiful. Uthe was overwhelmed by him, by the rage and determination he felt emanating from the Fae Lord. He was the epitome of every temptation the Templars had been exhorted to avoid, reject or deny themselves, but that wasn't what held Uthe spellbound. He truly was handing Uthe his soul.

"So you love me then," Uthe said slowly.

Keldwyn had risen to his feet. His brow creased, his eyes narrowing. Then he crossed his arms, shifting to one hip, which merely drew Uthe's eyes to the way the tight leggings outlined his buttock and cradled his sex. Blessed Christ, the male was a feast for an insatiable vampire appetite. Any type of celibacy, emotional or otherwise, would be impossible around him. "As discomfiting as it may be for both of us, it seems it is so," the Fae Lord said darkly.

Uthe lifted a hand. "Please let me stand on my feet before you, my lord."

"You are still weak. I will come to you." Keldwyn knelt in front of Uthe so they faced one another. "You did not answer me. Do you not care to belong to me?"

"You know the answer to that." Uthe reached out and threaded his fingers through the male's hair. "I called you

Master," he said, low. "And I meant it. But I will not join you to my fate, my lord. Over time, as the Ennui takes more and more of the mind, there is evidence it begins to affect a servant. Not only would it be unconscionable of me to give you the third mark knowing that, it would be a hazard to both our worlds. We are powerful members of our respective species. You could kill me to stop any unforgivable transgressions. In the vampire world, I do not know who could stop you and your magic."

"Life and love have a great deal to do with risks," Keldwyn said. "You are an intelligent male, my lord. I believe when you take my blood, your mind is sharper than it is when you take a human servant's blood. When you fed from Alanna, she sustained your energy but not your mind. I think the magical properties of my blood might reduce or delay the impact of the Ennui upon you."

Uthe considered it, hope kindling a small light inside him. Keldwyn didn't make wild or unfounded hypotheses. "The theory in your world is that Ennui is an affliction of time, the torpor that can descend upon a soul at the endless cycles of life," the Fae Lord continued. "What if it is also chemical, certain vampires more disposed to it than others? Look at Lady Lyssa. She has had no effects from it, but Rex, who was younger than her, was heavily afflicted. From the stories I've heard, he was well in the grip of those sadistic urges of madness within a short time of being affected. You have been dealing with it far longer."

"You have no proof of any of this. Just some random observations. Lord Brian would say that is not enough."

"I can give Queen Rhoswen the ability to end my life. As Unseelie Queen, as long as she has my oath of fealty, I am bound to allow her to strip me of my powers whenever she deems it suitable. She threatens it often enough."

"But you have to allow it. What if you are so far gone that you will not allow it?"

"There are bindings I can let her place on me now, or at the first hints of these things, to ensure she can force it to happen if need be." Keldwyn set his jaw. "I am already cut off from the Fae world, Uthe, as long as I am marked by a vampire. I will not be serving as the Fae court liaison for the immediate future. I am officially removed as the Vampire Council liaison, though I expect Lyssa will still want my guidance for Fae matters."

Uthe grimaced. "You told Queen Rhoswen."

"There have been many things happening since you have been taking a nap."

Uthe curled his fingers around Keldwyn's wrist, never mind that his grip was as much to keep him from falling over, even in his seated position, as it was to make his point. "You may command some things of me, my lord, but this will be my decision. I will not make it until I am sure I can protect you from both my deteriorating mind and the repercussions of your Queen. She is lovely and powerful, but she is not kind."

"Neither am I." Kel shrugged. He put his hand on Uthe's shoulder to steady him. "We are Fae, after all. You're vampires. You should understand the scintillating appeal of sadism."

"I will not see you suffer on my account," Uthe said firmly. "And I won't make this decision in this weakened state, bound in your ribbons."

"Very well." Keldwyn toppled them with one graceful move, so they were stretched out on the grass together. Sliding an arm under Uthe's shoulders, he turned him toward him, tilting his head back so the artery in his throat pulsed close to Uthe's lips. "Strengthen yourself, my lord, and then notice how much clearer your mind becomes. Regain your strength so you can see things my way."

Uthe chuckled at that, exasperated, but as Kel's arms circled him, palms heated against his back, he inhaled the scent of him. He remembered the last scent he'd had of Keldwyn in the Shattered World. Dust, sweat and blood. Now it was sunshine and warm earth.

In this position, he discovered the patch of grass on

which they were lying was just inside the entrance to a cave. The ceiling of the cave was covered with color, crystals and pieces of stained glass, pressed in different patterns into the arched ceiling. Red, blue, purple, green, yellow... The rush of a waterfall had him tipping his head back further, his hand going to Keldwyn's hair as the Fae Lord's mouth slid along his own bared throat. There was a waterfall in the cave, a deep pool. "So why are we still here? You said you were banished..."

"It's like your TV westerns. The sheriff, my Queen, gave us one full day to depart once you woke."

Uthe studied the cave ceiling. "Evan would donate a limb to see this. How was it created?"

"When the Fae moved more freely in your world, there were a group of them attracted to stained glass. Many Fae are like birds. We like shiny things." Keldwyn smiled against his throat, and Uthe's body yearned toward him as Kel scraped him with his teeth. The Fae Lord dropped his touch to grip Uthe's buttock and bring him closer. "As wars and violence destroyed your churches, they would collect pieces of it and bring them here. I suspect there are bits from the Holy Land and Templar churches, places you've visited. Which is why I thought you might enjoy it. There are also crystals, collected from secret, magical places in the earth that human development was getting too close to disrupting. So this is a holy place in many ways, a place of memory and preservation. Of what beauty undisturbed can be."

Keldwyn cupped the back of his head, bringing Uthe's gaze back to him. "I would like to see your hair long, Varick. Will your Rule allow you to grow it out for me?"

"No. But I think it is all right now to put my mantle aside and please my earthly Master, embrace the gift the Lord has given me. As long as..."

"As long as it doesn't conflict with God's will."

Uthe thought of what Jean-Claude had said. "As long as the spirit of being a Templar is always honored and served."

He'd accomplished his mission. He'd served the will of God. Now he could serve the will of his Master with a clear conscience. Uthe let Keldwyn see it in his face, his touch, and was rewarded by what he saw in return.

"I do not foresee you having any trouble with that, my lord," Kel said. "You are one of the most honorable and devout males I've ever met. Tediously so. I think I've mentioned that several times."

"You said my faith gave you hives."

"I've learned to adapt." As they'd been speaking, Kel was plucking the ribbons from him, as if Uthe was a package he was unwrapping. Tossing them aside, Kel stroked Uthe's nape and then turned his attention toward the stained glass, exposing his own throat once more. "Sink your fangs into me, vampire. I want to feed you, because once you regain your strength, I am going to fuck you into oblivion in this magical, holy place."

A matter-of-fact statement laced with an implacable demand, sending a surge of reaction through Uthe. When Keldwyn swept another unsmiling glance over him, a trace of impatience in his gaze, Uthe was fairly sure if he didn't feed, Kel would still fuck him senseless. He was giving him a few moments of courtesy, but he wasn't going to wait.

"Is that why I'm naked?"

"I washed you, in the pool. You had wounds that took longer to heal, even with my blood. Particularly this one." He put his hand over Uthe's heart, drawing his gaze to the place the dagger and Spear had both pierced. "I kept you naked because your body was warm to the touch. I also kept you that way for my own pleasure, so I could touch you as I desired, see your reactions to my caresses."

Uthe had been caught in the languor of near death, but now his Master was calling him back to life, offering him the sustenance he needed before he took what he wanted from him. His gut and heart leaped in anticipation of it like a dog on his Master's leash.

Keldwyn's gaze intensified at that imagery, his fingers sliding around Uthe's throat. "I really must learn to stay in your head as often as possible," he murmured. "But as intriguing as that is, I don't need such bindings between us, do I? I will not tell you again. Feed."

Uthe pushed up onto an elbow. The male's arm tightened around his back, his hand once again taking a firm grip on Uthe's ass. It steadied and unbalanced him at once. Uthe slid his mouth over the pulsing artery, the autumn scent of Kel's flesh, and bit. Deep, no holding back. He growled in response as Kel pressed him harder against the Fae's long, strong body, wearing too many clothes.

God in Heaven, his blood was sweet, vital. Uthe was gulping like a fledgling, as if he'd been starved for days. Fortunately long habit had him easing up when needed. But as he fed, his hands had been sweeping over Kel, fingers curling in his shirt, his thighs pressing against the Fae's. When he decided to drop his hands to grip Kel's fine, narrow ass, the Fae rolled them so he was on top of Uthe. Uthe retracted his fangs and Keldwyn dipped his head to take over his mouth with a demanding kiss while he reached down to capture his cock and work it in his strong grasp. Uthe pressed into his touch, and Kel tore his mouth away, proceeding to devour Uthe one inch of flesh at a time.

Uthe writhed against the pleasure of it, shocked by the sudden ferocity of the Fae's demands. Kel bit his nipple hard enough to have him arching and jerking, and then moved down to replace the grip of his hand with the heated cavern of his mouth. Kel's hands slid under him, opening his thighs, cradling his buttocks. He paused long enough to put two of his fingers in his own mouth, making them slick enough to ease them into Uthe's backside and play. He bucked even more, groaning with pleasure. Kel's blood was tingling through every limb, through his torso and rushing into head and cock, pushing his mind past thought and into sheer pleasure.

Despite Uthe's best attempts to hold him, Keldwyn drew back and turned Uthe over. He continued his sensual attack, setting his teeth to Uthe's throat and shoulder as he pushed his cock against Uthe's ass, a promise and a threat. His knee pressed against his testicles, a mute command to bring him up on his knees, but Kel kept his hand on his nape as he rose above him.

"Stay on your elbows, Varick. I like you in this position."

Uthe groaned again as Kel parted his cheeks, putting his mouth there to lube Uthe up with his own saliva, preparing him for being taken. When he heard Kel shifting to take off his shirt and unlace his leggings, he shuddered. He was fucking trembling. The significance of all of it was crashing down on him. Kel had allowed a vampire to feed from him, and would continue to do so for the foreseeable future, at least until the dubious wisdom of it hit him and he wisely changed his mind about that. Uthe was his, but both of them would be completely outside the bounds and rules of their respective worlds.

They'd just survived the Shattered World and sent a demon back to Hell. Really, how scary could any of the rest of it be?

Kel dropped down over him, chest pressing into his back. His chest hair teased Uthe's skin. "I can be quite scary, Lord Uthe," he said pleasantly. "You haven't seen even a shadow of what I can be. Keep thinking that I'll back away from what I feel for you because of the differences in our species, and you will see that side of me sooner rather than later."

He guided himself into Uthe's backside and, as the muscles released, he shoved in, wresting a grunt of pleasure and discomfort from Uthe. He held there, deep and tight, and wound an arm over Uthe's chest, an iron bar that made it clear just how strong he was.

Now listen and listen well. I will speak it in your mind so you can brand it on your heart and soul. I am fifteen fucking hundred years old. I have been in love, I've had my heart broken. I've lost children. I know what I am and what I want. I want your third mark. I want you, Lord Uthe, as long as the powers greater than both our worlds permit it. Yet should they or anyone else ever try to take you away from me, either in mind or body, they will see just how truly powerful and capable of destruction I am.

"Do you understand?"

He punctuated that with a thrust that was intended to hurt, and a curse escaped Uthe's lips. "Understood, my lord. No offense intended."

"Oh, I want you to offend me, Varick. Believe me, I relish the opportunities that your offenses will provide the both of us." He eased up then, though, dropping a kiss on Uthe's nape. He still had on his leggings and boots, and Uthe wished he was equally naked, so he could feel every inch of his flesh against his own. Keldwyn withdrew from him, touched his back.

"Then come attend to that."

Uthe straightened. His ass was smarting, his cock was throbbing, but he was far steadier now with the Fae's blood in him. Kel's own organ sat up thick and mouthwatering between his thighs, the leggings open and framing the thickness of it. Uthe was still trembling. He couldn't get over that, but he'd never seen Kel quite like this, so unleashed and demanding, his eyes burning. Magic sparked off his skin, making it obvious how easily he could overwhelm and overpower Uthe. Uthe's response, rather than wariness or a need to counter such strength with whatever wits he could summon, was to surrender to it, revel in it. Enjoy it fully for once. To trust another with all that he was.

Perhaps it was the Ennui that made him that foolish. Maybe he was just tired of always having to be on his guard. Or perhaps it was something else.

He was in love.

He'd always viewed that idea with a certain detachment, his intellectual grasp of immortality saying such feelings would run their course. He now knew that wasn't the case.

Submitting to another's dominance was not even the most startling part of it, because if he examined his life with a brutal honesty—and he always did—he'd sought the Templar Order as an attempt to escape the squeezing torment upon his soul from his life with his father. The children, patricide. He'd surrendered what he was to find a way out of that turmoil. He'd desperately sought a sense of purpose for fear he'd be sucked into the blood and death of that time and never escape, becoming like his father. With the Ennui, he faced that possibility. Except he knew he wouldn't reach the same lows as his father had, because Keldwyn wouldn't permit it. He could trust Kel to do what needed to be done.

The thought had more than one aspect to it, though. Kel wasn't simply the object of his desire and love. He was Kel's, and that gave the thought a problematic dimension. One that transformed this moment into something different as he turned on his knees and faced the Fae Lord. Keldwyn had stood up, but Uthe stayed on his knees, relishing the reactive spark in Kel's eyes, the set of his jaw that enhanced the thin, precise slash of his mouth, the column of his throat. Uthe tugged the leggings down his thighs, bent to remove his boots. Kel's fingertips whispered over the curve of his spine as he adjusted his stance.

Then Uthe slid his hands up the outside of his thighs, thumbs on the smoother terrain of his inner thighs. Uthe wanted to lean in and press his mouth against his testicles, the base of his cock. Kel hadn't given him leave to go down on him, but it wasn't exactly about that. He wanted to pay homage, try to touch Kel's soul through a worshipping of his flesh. Try to tell him...

I accept your care of me, even as I want you to know I understand what it has cost you. And what it may cost you in the end. It is that which breaks my heart, even as it overwhelms me.

Kel's hand fell on the crown of his head. A tremor went

through his upper thigh where Uthe's palm still lay upon the Fae Lord.
Be easy on all of it, Varick. This moment is just us. Do as I bid you. Remove my clothes.
Uthe finished that, then rose. As he moved around Kel, Uthe laid his hands on his Master's hair. He spread the strands like an ebony cloak over Kel's shoulders. Sliding his arms under the other male's, Uthe pressed against his back, heart to heart. His cock pulsed against Kel's firm ass as Kel closed his hand over Uthe's clenched fingers.

"Varick, you steal my breath," he said in a thick voice. "Get back down on your knees for me."

Uthe placed a kiss on his nape, his shoulder, sliding the hair out of the way to do the same to the pulse in his throat, his heart thudding as Kel tilted his head to the right, giving him more access. "What are you doing?"

"Being offensive, my lord." Uthe smiled against his flesh. "I respect your rule, but you are far too appealing. Your body and all that you are, it's impossible not to touch, to kiss, to steal every possible moment to give pleasure and derive joy from it."

Kel closed his eyes, the thick, dark lashes fanning his high cheekbones. "I am ever glad your courtly language was not leeched away by your years in the modern world. When you speak to me this way, time stops where things are as they should be. It does not have to start again until we wish it."

"And we can have that back during any moment we make into this."

Kel's fingers slipped up to Uthe's wrist, his answer. He squeezed hard. Uthe was expecting the counter, but it was still breathtaking, how quickly the Fae could move. A twist and slip, and Uthe was on his knees beneath him, Kel leaning over him, pressing Uthe's wrist against the small of his back, Kel's knee pressed against Uthe's buttocks. "On your elbows, vampire. As before."

This time, Keldwyn added some lubricant to ease his

passage, yet Uthe still felt the demand of it. The stretch made him groan, his lips stretched in a grimace of need and desire as the Fae pushed in to the hilt. "You will hold out for me," Kel said. "First your Master takes his pleasure."

Uthe had distanced himself from it, the games between vampires and servants. Intense games, yes, ones that could have serious political underpinnings, yet games all the same. Though when he'd seen the devotion in Mariela's eyes, had watched the whole, vibrant language between Jacob and Lyssa spoken without any words, he'd known there was a deeper level to all of it that superseded whatever base machinations came from it at vampire gatherings, or the structured roles of vampire and servant. He felt it now, as Keldwyn spoke the words.

In his breast, a desire rose, strong and irresistible, to pleasure the Fae Lord in ways Keldwyn might never have experienced before Uthe. He didn't mean some type of carnal acrobatics or skills learned through sexual experience. He meant whatever would match the ecstasy of surrender Uthe felt under Keldwyn's touch. A way to slip away from all the grief and pain, to find the wonder in all of it again, through love. Through this give and take, through offering all he was to the Fae Lord.

"Varick..." Keldwyn was in his head, could hear any of that he chose. Kneeling over Uthe, he banded his arm around his chest to the point it was good that Uthe didn't need to breathe, though the integrity of his ribs might be compromised. *You overwhelm me as well.*

His hips rose and fell, offering Uthe a sweet, prolonged promise that built into a churning in his testicles, a painful rigidity in his cock. Yet when Keldwyn covered him again, pressing mouth and teeth to his nape and the taut skin between his shoulders, Uthe embraced the agony of denial.

In his pretty clothes, with his ethereal masculine beauty and the magical power that emanated from him, Kel had seemed reassuringly unattainable. Then had come the casual interactions that turned into chess games, debates over morals and history over wine. At some point, the Fae Lord had become part of his daily schedule, in ways large and small. Yet it was now, feeling the press of his damp skin, the heat of his breath on his shoulder, the passion and urgency of his lust pounding into Uthe, that he was blissfully real, as much in need and in love as Uthe himself.

He moved his body in rhythm with Keldwyn's, lifting his hips to give him a deeper penetration, though it tested his own restraint unmercifully. Kel plunged and thrust; Uthe grunted and made feral noises of encouragement. When he started constricting all his muscles on that thick shaft invading him again and again, Kel's breath left him in a ragged moan. He climaxed, flooding Uthe with his heated response, a charge that Uthe felt from brain to genitals, that surged through his chest, his loins, even the palms of his hand upon the earth.

"Now, Varick," Kel demanded. Uthe's hips jerked, convulsed, and his come spewed forth into the grass beneath him, drops splashing against the blades. They splattered against his wrists, his belly. Kel's hold around his chest was still there, secure, holding him together. When Uthe finished, his cheek was pressed to the ground between his elbows. Kel adjusted him so they were both on their right sides. He was still inside Uthe and they were spooned together on the soft ground. A firefly Fae landed on Uthe's limp hand. Several more landed on his thigh.

The one on his hand crawled up his arm to the bend of his elbow, sat down and started to chirp on a tiny lute.

"They have no manners at all," Keldwyn said, his voice hoarse. "They tempt one to get a flyswatter."

Uthe chuckled. Closing his fingers around the Fae's on his chest, Uthe dipped his head to press his lips against his knuckles. Kel let out an incoherent but pleased sound, shifting his hips to shoot a tingling aftershock through Uthe's testicles and spent cock.

They dozed for a time together. Nothing to do, no

battles left to fight. It was a unique feeling. Uthe opened his eyes at times to watch the firefly Fae, who had congregated around his elbow and had turned it into a stage, all of them playing wind instruments. It was a quiet, soothing noise, like distant birds. He didn't want to disturb it in any way, but there was something he needed to say. He said it in his head so if Keldwyn was asleep, he could practice it a few times. If he wasn't, well...it needed to be said.

Kel, I cannot third mark you. And I need your promise that, if the Ennui gets too advanced, you will take my life before I become a burden.

No. Because there is no scenario in which you would ever become a burden, Lord Uthe. To me or any who care for you.

Keldwyn gripped Uthe's wrist, manacling it against his chest, against his thudding heart. Uthe closed his eyes, sighed.

"If it was just pride, my lord, I could bear it. Becoming no better than a child, with no sense of who I am or how to care for my own needs or how to protect myself, is terrible enough to me. But if the aggression takes me, where I would hurt another, an innocent..." Uthe pressed his body into the curve of Keldwyn's. "I will not take my life preemptively, before God has done with it, but if I reach the point that I might harm another vampire if they tried to do the task...that I could not bear. You have the ability to destroy me without even touching me. You are the only one I trust for it, Kel. Please. If you care for me, swear you will do as I ask."

Kel let out a quiet curse, but then he nodded against the back of Uthe's neck, one quick jerk. "You have my word. But it changes nothing about my demand that you make me your third mark."

"Nor will it change my refusal. I will not bind my life to yours if it could mean the certain end of it. I will do anything else."

"Hush. I will not speak further about this right now. You are ruining it. Enjoy the afterglow of a good fucking and we will fight about this later. At which time, I will win."

Uthe closed his eyes with a light smile on his lips, though a weight on his heart. But he agreed with Kel, that he didn't want to lose the pleasure of this moment. Like it or not, the subject would come up again. They would deal with it then.

"*Anything* else? Including grow out your hair?" Kel scraped his teeth against the back of Uthe's neck and then bit his shoulder, which sent a jolt straight to Uthe's cock. The Fae was getting too good at playing Uthe's body to his desires. His smile deepened.

"It could never compete with yours, my lord. There are female vampires who want to chop yours off while you sleep and weave it into theirs."

"I've seen Helga eying it covetously. I will stay on guard." He stroked long fingers over Uthe's scalp, sending a pleasurable ripple through him. "I merely want yours long enough I can tug on it when I'm inside you, remind you of my claim."

"That might be sufficient incentive."

"Might?" Keldwyn's voice was sleepy again, but with a touch of affront. "Do you need more?"

I have lived an ascetic's life, my lord. It has brought me comfort and guidance. But it doesn't seem to apply to this. Whenever I think of you, all I want is more.

"Your way of speaking from the heart is more potent than any level of charm, Varick." Keldwyn pressed closer to him, releasing Uthe's wrist to wrap his arm around his chest once more. The Fae spoke against his ear.

"Before we leave my world, would you like to ride a dragon?"

"I'd love it."

Then they slept some more, letting the world's machinations turn without them. For once.

Chapter Seventeen

"Kel... *Kel*... Help!"

Keldwyn came out of the sound sleep with the alertness of long training. Uthe was a little slower to rise. He was still feeling the effects of his near-death experience. Kel's assessing look seemed to be considering the same thing, but Uthe waved off his concerns. The owner of the voice was getting closer, coming swiftly. It was Della.

Using Fae swiftness, Kel was quickly dressed. Since Uthe only had the thin robe, crumpled and discarded inside the cave, Kel conjured him a suitable tunic and leggings in a blink. *An easy enough magic to do with cotton fibers,* the Fae told him. When Della reached the clearing where they were, they were dressed. While modesty wasn't a big issue for either of their species, Della might have been startled to confront two adult naked men.

"Della, calm down." Kel came to her. "What is it?"

The girl's face was tracked with tears. Her jeans and pink T-shirt were dirt-stained, as if she'd tripped and fallen several times on her way to find them. "I didn't know where you were, but the trees told me where to go. They said you would help."

"I will. What's happened?"

"Cat...she said the Queen is going to send you away.

Everyone is talking about it. She went to yell at the Queen."

"Ah, bollocks," Keldwyn muttered. He lifted a hand to the sky and spoke a sharp word, punctuating it with a shrill whistle between his teeth. Energy vibrated off him like a shock wave.

"This wasn't the way I intended to do this," Kel said shortly to Uthe. "You don't get air sick, do you?"

"You really think that matters right now?" Uthe asked dryly.

A shriek cut off anything else he might have said. The sight that accompanied the sound took his words away, anyhow. He'd seen the smaller dragon playing with Della, and he had a vague recollection of one in the Shattered World—he needed to have Kel verify that at some point—but this was the first time since he'd been in the Fae world he'd had the chance to see one up close. While the sea serpents might be a related family, the circumstances of their encounter hadn't given Uthe time to appreciate them.

Purple gleaming scales, lavender eyes, green and purple wings. The creature was as large as a private charter plane, and Uthe assumed he was intended to serve the same purpose now.

"Yes and no," Kel corrected him. "They don't lend themselves out for transportation unless they owe a favor, or they're particularly fond of you."

Stepping onto the creature's front leg, Kel used the rough staggering of the scales and a firm grip on the curved wing to swing up on his back. He offered Uthe a hand. "Come. Quickly."

Uthe followed his lead, sliding on behind him. He was sitting on a dragon. Despite the seriousness of the situation, it flooded him with an unexpected sense of optimism about everything. He gripped Kel's hips as the Fae Lord spoke to Della. "Go back to your mother's garden, Della. I'll take care of Catriona. I promise."

"Okay." Della looked at him hopefully. Only then did Uthe notice she was clutching a brown lunch bag bulging with its contents. "I brought her tomatoes from Momma's garden. I thought she'd like them."

"Why don't you hold onto them until tomorrow, and then you can give them to her yourself. All right? She'll like them even better that way."

"Okay. I'll come back tomorrow."

Kel afforded her a short nod, then said a quick word to the dragon. "Hold fast to me," he told Uthe. "We will be making haste."

Uthe complied, wrapping both arms around Kel's chest. Looking down, he saw straps winding around him and Kel, holding him even tighter. "Just in case," Kel said.

The dragon launched itself like a rocket. They shot up into the air like a space shuttle leaving earth. Gravity pushed Keldwyn against him, and Uthe hung on even tighter, glad the Fae Lord had taken the precautions he had. It was exhilarating, the world rushing by beneath them, a landscape of vibrant color. From this height, he had a view of all the castles, though savoring the experience was hampered by the speed they were going. It underscored the urgency the Fae Lord was feeling.

Catriona had been locked in a tree for twenty years for defying the Queen. What would she do to her for challenging her on Keldwyn's behalf?

The Fae have as many rules about defying authority as the vampires do, Kel said grimly in his head. Only they can be far less merciful. Particularly the Unseelie side.

§

"You never learn," Rhoswen said icily. "Is that what you want, dryad? Do you miss your tree prison? Do you want to stay there a century this time? Is that what it takes for you to learn your lesson?"

Catriona was shaking, and the Queen's threat only made it worse. Her chin was firm though, her gray-green eyes bright with unshed tears. "I will do it if you will let him stay here. You can't banish him. No one deserves that. Have you ever felt it, Queen Rhoswen? Have you ever suffered the fate you find it so easy to inflict on others? I hate you. I don't care what you do to me. I'd rather tell you that you're wrong, and mean and evil, than to cower and pretend all those things aren't true just because I'm afraid. I'm sick of being afraid of you."

Rhoswen lifted a hand and Keldwyn skidded to a halt in front of his ward, sword drawn and charged with enough energy to cut a swath of orange and red light before both of them. "No," he said. "Whatever punishment she has incurred, I will take it."

Rhoswen glanced toward the throne room entrance. The two guards there were no longer upright. Uthe stood in the doorway over them. He sketched a bow her way and her lips thinned. Sighing, she continued the motion she'd started, pushing a lock of her pale white hair back up beneath the intricate comb that looked like a bouquet of snowflakes. Glittering frost highlighted the strands.

"They will wish they were dead instead of merely unconscious when Cayden gets hold of them." Turning her back on the three of them, she moved to her throne. "My lord Keldwyn, if you would sheathe your sword, you might greet Tabor and Lady Lyssa. We were discussing the upcoming Yule festivities when Catriona flitted over the heads of two armed guards like a deranged butterfly and interrupted our discussion."

Kel's gaze snapped left. King Tabor stood at a sidebar of prepared foods, pouring himself a glass of wine. Lyssa sat in a nearby chair, nibbling what looked like a sugar frosted flower petal. While there was some amusement in the Seelie King's leonine face, suggesting the tone of this confrontation was less dire than Kel feared, there was an underlying tension there, too. He knew Rhoswen as Kel did, and knew her mood could turn on a dime. He saw it in Lyssa's watchful expression also, even as she licked the sugar off her fingers delicately.

"*Dayel coeurose...*" Catriona beseeched him.

It was the Fae phrase for father of my heart. It made him think of Evan, calling Uthe something similar in the language of love they shared. Sheathing his sword, Kel turned and put his hands on Catriona's shoulders. "I cherish you in more ways than I can express," he said. "Your foolish championing of me only makes me love you more. But—"

"No." She wrapped her arms around him, burying her face in his chest. "I won't lose you like everyone else. I don't care. I'll go to the human world with you. I'll die there. I'd rather die there tomorrow than stay here a thousand years, where everything is perfect and beautiful, but so heartless. So intolerant of everything that's not Fae..."

"Ssshh..." Keldwyn laid his head on top of hers. "It's all right. You should have spoken to me first. It's all right."

Still standing by the inert guards, Uthe watched Keldwyn comfort the nearly hysterical young woman. He was sure the Fae Lord hadn't forgotten they stood before a royal audience, but the look exchanged between Lyssa and Tabor, and Rhoswen's unexpectedly patient expression, said they understood the dryad was having an emotional breakdown that couldn't be stemmed by threats or royal wrath, at least not until she calmed down.

Even the day in the meadow, for all her joy and exuberance, Uthe had sensed a fragility to her. She'd been locked in isolation for so long, and the trauma of that was still healing. As they waited on Kel, he glanced toward Lyssa and offered her a deep bow. He saw her assessing his physical and emotional wellbeing, and a faint smile touched her lips, revealing her pleasure at seeing him. The feeling was mutual. He didn't see Jacob, so he assumed this was a royals-only audience, which suggested more than a simple Christmas party was being discussed. How had Jacob explained his absence? Lyssa didn't seem out of sorts, so her servant had been returned to her in acceptable condition. Thank God. One angry queen was enough to handle.

Kel rubbed Catriona's shoulders, then glanced at Uthe. *Would you come stand with her, Varick? Reassure her.*

Anything, my lord. As Uthe drew closer, Kel eased back, gripping Catriona's shoulder and tipping up her chin to make her look at him. He took away her tears with gentle fingers, but his voice was firm, brooking no more histrionics.

"You will stand with Lord Uthe while I discuss this with Her Majesty. And you will be thinking of the apology you owe her, as well as King Tabor and Lady Lyssa."

He met her pleading expression with a kind but implacable one, a clear order. Uthe closed a hand on her arm and drew her to the side, though how long she held onto the Fae Lord's arm and shirt front, until she couldn't any longer, twisted Uthe's heart.

"It's all right," he said, low. "Let him do what he does so well."

Catriona cast a look at him full of worry but the humor he'd injected into the words summoned a look of hope. He squeezed her arm, kept her close. When she leaned on him, drawing strength from his steadiness, her trust humbled him. It also gave him an inkling of why Keldwyn loved her so well.

Technically the Fae Queen hadn't been directly responsible for the incarceration; the girl's youthful impulsiveness had been. Yet the twenty years she'd been left in the tree without any one being allowed to retrieve her was Rhoswen's decision, the spell unbreakable by any other Fae. The Queen had taught the Fae girl and others in her world an indelible lesson about the detrimental effects of the human world on Fae energy, particularly young Fae.

Uthe understood the difficulty of such decisions, making an example of one to dissuade many others from far worse decisions. It didn't make it easier for the recipient, or the recipient's family. Kel had been in the difficult position of having to do even more than bear the decision. He'd had to honor the ruling and still serve as an advisor to the monarch responsible for the sentence.

In another audience in this room, I observed that I've always watched over supremely frustrating children. I expect you've done the same, my lord.

Uthe managed not to look toward Lyssa, but felt Kel smirk. *I will use that against you later, my lord.* Uthe wanted Kel's humor to reassure him as much as his own had Catriona, but he knew such sardonic comments were merely Kel's way of sharpening the blade of his tongue before entering the fray of a political battle. In this case, the fate of someone he loved might hang in the balance.

"Let me bring my guests up to speed, and perhaps Catriona herself, since I don't know how accurate the rumors are that brought her here so inadvisably." Rhoswen spoke tartly, standing before her throne. "Lord Keldwyn has been feeding Lord Uthe blood to lessen the effects of his Ennui. He has allowed himself to be second marked and, for all I know, has desires for a full marking. Romantic bonds between Fae and vampire are strongly discouraged. Feeding a vampire with our blood is absolutely forbidden and indeed, considered so repellent by most of us we were not even certain a rule was necessary. Until now."

Lyssa's gaze moved from Keldwyn to Uthe and back again. As Uthe had expected, the news he had Ennui was clearly not news at all to her. Gratitude for both her confidence and discretion gripped him. The news Keldwyn was marked produced a flash of surprise, however. She was looking toward the Fae Lord.

"For the contempt you initially showed me as a half-breed, let alone for my vampire blood, I find your decision...curious, Lord Keldwyn."

"Perhaps you could lay the blame at your own feet, my lady. You have persuaded me to view your kind with a different eye, first with your example and then through my liaison role with Council."

"I would think sitting in Council meetings would merely have confirmed your low opinion of us," Lyssa said. "In some of our meetings, I've almost agreed with you."

Rhoswen sent a sharp look her way. "You jest, my sister, but vampires are no less purist than the Fae. Do you think they will accept this match?"

"I think the Council members already have."

Uthe felt Keldwyn's surprise match his own. Lyssa met Uthe's gaze. "We've noticed the bond growing between Lord Uthe and Lord Keldwyn for some time. Initially we thought of it as a useful friendship that would benefit our two worlds, and I'm sure it has. Uthe and Keldwyn's chess games have resulted in some excellent ideas in Council. It is a good match, Your Majesty. I expect they can fight through many ideas in the bedchamber and save us endless debates."

"Yet this is always the way it starts." Rhoswen sighed. She moved up the steps to her throne, which was mounted on a domino-like arrangement of small waterfalls. She sat down on her hip, one leg tucked up underneath her, a casual pose that did not dilute the effect of her regal detachment or the coolness of her gaze. "First comes a relationship or two that seems advantageous to us. Then more rules are relaxed. That's when the infractions start, where the rules are bent more and more. What we deal with on a case-by-case basis becomes an epidemic and then, once again, the gates between our worlds must be sealed for a century or more."

King Tabor sat down at the table with Lyssa. Unlike most Fae, there was a lined, rugged quality to his face that only added to its strength. His golden hair, plaited back with earth-colored gemstones, added to his lionlike appearance and mannerisms. His expression was pensive, suggesting he was remembering the same issues that Rhoswen was.

"It is the nature of all humanoid species to explore beyond the boundaries of our world," Lyssa said practically. "To seek new ways to learn, grow and progress. That will always bring growing pains, along with the potential for catastrophic consequences. Everyone in this room, with the exception of the lovely Catriona, has lived over a millennium. Even in our different worlds, the same pattern repeats itself, over and over. We stumble, we break, we remake ourselves. Yes, by opening up your world, even in a limited way, you may start the cycle once more. But what is the alternative?"

"Oh no. Do not raise the stagnation argument." Rhoswen raised a hand. The Fae Queen, for all her beauty and the complexity of her wardrobe, did not wear any rings today, which increased the impact of her slim, unadorned hand, the expressive movements of her fingers. "There is plenty of opportunity for growth and change within our respective worlds, without ever having to cross the threshold of another. Plus, the Fae have a unique problem humans and vampires do not have."

Keldwyn said nothing. He was listening until he saw the opening that would help him accomplish what he desired, or seeing if the others would come to the conclusion he thought best on their own. It was always the preferred option for an advisor. Uthe understood that was what Kel was doing without being in his mind, but seeing it directly in his head was intriguing. Given their odd power exchange dynamic, he was glad Kel hadn't yet suggested Uthe block himself from being in the Fae Lord's mind when he desired to be there, though Uthe would respect that request if ever it came. He liked mixing it up—reading things from Kel's body language as he'd learned to do, but also having the new option of dipping into Kel's mind to gain further scope. It was like walking side by side versus being in his embrace. Both had their advantages.

"This is not the first time we have debated the subject of free will and passage between our worlds," Lyssa prompted. "But you have not isolated it to one primary concern before. What is this unique problem?"

Night's Templar

Uthe could tell from Keldwyn's impassive expression he already knew his Queen's answer, but would prefer that she not share it. A personal preference Uthe understood when Rhoswen responded.

"You vampires have adapted in the human world, because you can. You are powerful and fast, but you are not intimately connected to what you call magic. Your connection to the earth is essential, as it is for all life, but you maintain a certain spiritual detachment, just as the humans do. You can indulge in the delights of progress and still have a decent lifespan and life quality, though it would be far enhanced—and the earth and its other life forms would suffer far less at your hands—if you could see and feel what we do." When Rhoswen looked toward Tabor, the Seelie King picked up the thread, finishing the explanation for Lyssa.

"The difference between our species is that the Fae world could be ended utterly without that full spiritual connection. It was the lesson Rhoswen was trying to teach with Catriona."

When the young Fae quivered, Uthe rubbed her shoulder, a reassurance and reminder of forbearance. But he also pinned Keldwyn with a glance.

So if you allow yourself to be banished, cut off from the Fae world, your life would be shortened.

You would not get rid of me that quickly. I would have a couple hundred years before I withered. Catriona managed for twenty years.

Thinking of Keldwyn's exhaustion when he couldn't nourish himself in the Shattered World, Uthe doubted that. And Catriona had been in a dormant, near comatose state. If he was understanding Rhoswen's concern correctly, the earthly realm still had enough magic to sustain a Fae, but the Fae world had even deeper roots in that same energy flow.

He expected the Fae world provided the same thing to the Fae that an annual kill provided vampires. Without the

463

full blood sacrifice of a human once a year, a vampire would weaken and starve, becoming catatonic. It would take a few years, just as Keldwyn described his own situation, but it was inevitable.

It was as Tabor and Lyssa had both implied. None of the humanoid species were as different as they thought themselves. The methods might differ, but the intent was the same.

However, Uthe knew that wasn't what had Kel's expression turning thoughtful now. He'd drawn the Fae Lord's attention to the issue of the annual kill. For reasons even Lord Brian had yet to figure out, there were essential nutrients, a certain energy captured in the blood of that kill, a vampire had to have. Uthe had taken vampire and human lives in battle, but for a vampire of conscience, the annual kill was the hardest life to sacrifice. It had to be a human whose life had meaning and worth, whose heart was good. Perhaps it was easier for other vampires, who hadn't had the beginnings he'd had, but he remembered all of his annual kills. Almost a thousand souls. He'd learned he could push it back, stretch a kill over two to three years without his weakness becoming obvious enough he'd be vulnerable to other vampires, but the years he'd been involved with the Templars or the Territory wars, he hadn't had that luxury, full strength a vital necessity.

Keldwyn's eyes were on him now, telling Uthe he was picking up on his thoughts. Uthe didn't look away. The Fae Lord knew about the annual kill, but Uthe didn't think he'd drawn a straight line from it to the male vampire he'd claimed as his own. *A vampire is not only a predator. We are a predator that must take innocent lives, at least once a year.* The words hurt, even as thoughts. *Over the years, the bodies pile up.*

Rhoswen was speaking again, so Keldwyn turned away. His lack of response created a burning in his chest, but Uthe kept his expression unreadable. Keldwyn might be able to feel his reaction, but Uthe wouldn't show it to others. It touched on Uthe's fears about their relationship, however. The pleasures they found with one another might not stand the test of time. Even if Keldwyn chose to absent himself from Uthe when he took his annual kill, when Uthe returned to him, would he see Keldwyn's revulsion in his mind? He wouldn't be able to bear it. He'd been strong for over a thousand years, and he could continue to be strong about most things, even the Ennui, but loving someone created an inescapable vulnerably. It could crack shields beyond repair.

"Your humans have scientists dedicated to discovering survival options if the sun stopped shining, if the water sources dried up," Rhoswen said. "The Fae cannot survive such conditions physically, but beyond that, they would have no desire to continue living without a direct link to our elements. Humans and vampires see the elements as tools, resources for them to strip and use. They are scavengers. They always have been, adapting and destroying to survive, with no understanding what truly living means."

She paused, visibly steadying herself, but her voice was flat, her eyes cool now. "They're also a virus, because the more time our young Fae spend in that world, the more they are infected with that kind of thinking."

"Lest we make ourselves sound so much more enlightened than other humanoid species," Tabor interjected dryly, "I'd like to point out that our respect for the elements may be greater, but not our respect for one another. We have had several rather horrific wars, during and just before my lifespan. Perhaps, my lady, if we came up with a strategy to be more proactive in our interactions with the humans, as we have started to do with the vampires, we might exchange more of the best parts of ourselves, instead of the worst?"

"You ask for miracles. And demonstrate naivety that experience should have drummed out of you," Rhoswen said shortly. "No offense, my lord."

Tabor's smile was tight. "Your cynicism can bias you as much as my optimism, my lady. Keep that in mind. With respect."

"Perhaps the challenge is to make slight differences with every cycle," Lyssa said. "It might still come full circle, but it could become more of an upward spiral." She glanced at Rhoswen. "Together we could make this work better by building on the past and making adjustments for the future. Respond not by shutting down, but by changing the rules of engagement. We value the counsel of Lord Uthe and Lord Keldwyn. Perhaps their example can give us ways to achieve that. You've noted vampires have learned how to live compatibly in the human side of our world. We are like humans, yes, but we are also not entirely unlike Fae, because our long lives and enhanced capabilities do set us apart from humans. Your youthful Fae are curious about that world. How could they not be? Instead of denying them, making it a forbidden treasure, we teach them better how to navigate it and create a better outcome. And we don't react to every stumble as if the sky is falling and all must be changed."

Rhoswen's brow creased. "The sky falling?"

"It's a story called Chicken Little. I'll explain later." Lyssa pushed past that. "I have a more illustrative example. My majordomo, Elijah Ingram, was a military man. He has several guns. When John, his grandson, was eight years old, he showed him how to load and unload them, took him to a gun safety course, and made sure he understood the dangers and uses of the weapons. A couple years later, John was visiting a friend. The friend took him into a closet where his father's gun was, and was going to show it off to him. He knew nothing about gun use or safety, because his parents kept the weapon hidden from him and provided him no knowledge of it, which simply turned it into a mystery that could not be resisted. The child of course had figured out where they kept the gun and the passcode to the lockbox. The gun was loaded."

Lyssa shook her head. "John took the gun away from his friend, unloaded it, showed him the proper use of it and warned him of all the dangers. Then they put it away and went to play video games. John told his grandfather about the incident when he came home. In short, to John, it was matter-of-fact, no big mystery, but a very real danger he understood enough to protect his friend."

"Not all children are that mature."

"Most can be, if they are encouraged to grow up at the proper rate. Parents have one purpose—to help their children grow into responsible adults who are ready to inherit the leadership and protection of our societies. Not to keep them eternal children, overly protected and so never able to make responsible choices on their own." Lyssa softened. "I think you have reacted to the terrible things of the past, as we have, and not without good reason. The way through this lies somewhere in between our collective viewpoints. But when I am bogged down in a difficult decision, sometimes I find everything rests on one simple question."

She met her sister's ice blue eyes. "Do you truly want to lose Keldwyn's counsel?"

Rhoswen's lips pursed. "Do I have to answer that question with him standing there?"

"Whatever your answer, I will assume you abhor me as always, Your Majesty," Kel responded.

Lyssa rose and approached the throne, sitting down on the narrow steps that bisected the waterfalls. She placed her hand on her sister's ankle, tugging at it. Despite the conflicting emotions roiling in his gut, it was so much like a younger sister playfully badgering an older one, Uthe had to suppress a smile. The two queens had come far in a short time.

"We are currently examining a policy that grants further protections to our servants. It will not change the fundamental power structure of the relationship. A servant's devotion must be tested with complete capitulation to the will of the vampire mistress or master. But abuses of such a gift will be addressed. The essential form and purpose of the relationship is maintained, but there is more breathing room to deal with that issue on a case by case basis. As we have done there, why not consider Keldwyn and Uthe a test case for this situation? They will not only be an example of the further cooperation we can achieve together but, between the two of them, they have the experience and knowledge to study their own situation and suggest ways to apply it to the broader picture."

Lyssa glanced at Uthe. He didn't disagree with her. He was just wondering if all the topics being raised in this audience might end his relationship with Keldwyn before it truly began. The Fae Lord's mind was still silent to him, his focus on his queen. Uthe didn't venture into his mind now. The same intuition that guided both him and Kel as advisors told him when it was appropriate to delve into the Fae Lord's head, connect to his thoughts. That's what he told himself, though a darker part of him wondered if he was keeping his distance because he didn't want to have to suffer the pain of Keldwyn ordering him to do so.

Rhoswen shook her head. "I think no matter how we change the starting gate, it always ends up the same. King Tabor? You are uncharacteristically silent. Or are you more interested in the food and wine than the discussion?"

Tabor had propped a booted foot on the chair Lyssa had vacated and pushed his own back on two legs, a casual position that didn't dilute the sharpness of his eyes. "You like to throw darts when you realize you're changing your mind, my Queen. It is one of your many irresistible qualities."

He brought the chair down to all four legs. "Free will is a great responsibility, but one I think we can manage. We've certainly handled worse. I support Keldwyn continuing as your liaison and mine, and to the Vampire Council. He would be sorely missed by my advisors and myself."

"You would miss having him as part of your hunting

parties," Rhoswen said tartly. "Men are fairly the same across worlds."

"Just another example of the qualities that connect us all," Tabor rebounded.

"And the law about a Fae feeding a vampire, let alone being marked by one?"

Tabor shrugged. "We are not a democracy, Queen Rhoswen. Yes, we have our laws, but you have a certain amount of discretion to permit this relationship, especially if we deem it to be in the overall best interests of our people."

"Your Majesties, Lady Lyssa?" Uthe stepped forward. "May I have your leave to speak?"

Now at last, Keldwyn turned toward him, met his gaze. While Uthe couldn't read anything from his face, this wasn't about the two of them now. Rhoswen waved a hand. "There is an abundance of hot air in the room. Please, feel free to add to it."

Despite the biting response, Uthe bowed courteously. "Free will and choice, balancing that against the preservation of the species and its overall wellbeing, is the most challenging question leaders of worth face. Not changing is easiest, but change has a way of imposing itself regardless, in even more volatile ways than if it were managed. We see it happen in nature all the time, and you would have the greatest awareness of that. As you pointed out, the Fae are more closely aligned with nature than the rest of us."

When her eyes narrowed, he continued smoothly, not wanting to plant the incorrect idea he was using the Fae Queen's words against her. "That says to me, with the correct steps and measures, you may be the species most capable of managing and weathering those changes."

Well done, Varick.

He inclined his head slightly, but kept his gaze on the Queen.

"Ultimately, we come back to motive. Motive lies in

mutual benefit." Rhoswen shook her head. "Saturating our curiosity about tiny music players and indulging an addiction to French fries doesn't suggest a long term benefit to my species from contact with the human one. They, and you, could gain many benefits from your exposure to the Fae, but what do you provide us except an anthropology lesson about two other species? The history of the human world suggests those tribes living more in harmony with nature get dragged down and destroyed. Which I see as a cautionary tale for the Fae who wish to interact in that world. Since vampires fully indulge in all those elements of human 'progress,' I do not see them improving the situation."

She had him there. She and Tabor needed to do what would benefit their people the most, for the present and future. It was what Uthe, as an advisor, would counsel his own queen if they faced the same question. It was the root of what they'd discussed in the servant policy. Small or large, the issue was the same. How much change was good?

Keldwyn cleared his throat, drawing all eyes to him.

"Well, thank the gods. I was beginning to think feeding a vampire had numbed your tongue," Rhoswen said.

"I have been considering the wisdom of all sides of the argument, Queen Rhoswen. As I always do."

"And now, as usual, you are going to tell me how we are wrong?" she asked, her gaze fixed upon him.

Keldwyn shook his head. "No, Your Majesty. It is true. The Fae could provide a wealth of gifts to humans and vampires. Knowledge, magic...they would top the list. As I have noted, Lord Uthe's Ennui appears to improve after each feeding. Perhaps Fae blood has the key to that affliction, though that is a sweeping statement with no scientific backing."

"And one I would advise you to keep to yourself, for our people are not going to become a feeding trough for sickly vampires," Rhoswen said, frost returning to her expression. Lyssa's eyes cooled at that insult.

Knew she wasn't going to go for that one, Uthe thought. But Kel didn't look concerned, which told Uthe he was working his way to another point.

"I think no matter what we embrace in this life, how many marvels we learn or discover, the ability to share all that with another soul, one with whom we connect in a way that makes us feel whole, not alone... That is arguably the most precious gift any of us can ever receive. When we go on the Hunt at Samhain and see the reunions between those beyond the Veil with their family here, that connection, that love, is the essence of magic, of Divine Energy itself. If Lord Reghan found it with a vampire, if our Fae have found love with humans in the past, and we know they have, this is perhaps the most important benefit we may be overlooking with them. We need to stop looking only for the gifts we see in the mirror of our species. There are gifts we might see beyond its reflection, if we tear our gaze away from ourselves."

Keldwyn backed up two steps, pivoted on his heel. The deliberate movement kept him angled toward his monarch but turned his attention fully to Uthe, for all to see. "After these many long years, Lord Uthe has provided that for me. So if you are seeking an impartial opinion on whether we can or cannot receive benefit from our interactions with either vampires or humans, I am no longer the person to ask."

The wall came down in Keldwyn's mind and he pulled Uthe into it, as decidedly as if he'd reached out and pulled him into a physical embrace. Yet despite the storm of emotions he showered upon Uthe, the Fae Lord's expression remained mild, unchanged. As an advisor, Uthe was impressed the Fae could conceal so much from those around them. As his lover, his response was an equal surge of emotion. Kel's voice resounded in his head, reassuringly irritable.

I have offered my love to you, Varick, privately and now publicly. You think I came upon that lightly, without considering everything a vampire is? *You mistake my lack of response. It was annoyance with you, for doubting me so easily. I have as much blood staining my heart as you do. I could not protect my children, and I have lost all of them. I have made decisions that weigh as heavily upon my soul as yours do. And you, your touch, your mind, your soul...they ease that burden.*

Before Uthe could think of anything that would answer that remarkable statement, Keldwyn had returned his attention to his Queen. "Not too long ago, I embraced the idea that I was superior, merely because that was what we believe of our species. But perhaps that is the biggest danger of isolating ourselves from one another. We forget how very much alike we all are." His gaze shifted to Lyssa. "I expect that is the primary reason you, the most powerful vampire in your world, are contemplating changes to your relationships with your servants. Love is an equalizer, no?"

Marking Kel was one thing, even Kel feeding him, but the Fae Lord stating his feelings and intentions so baldly, it had a decided impact on their audience. Rhoswen went motionless, a glittering ice statue. Lyssa and Tabor also seemed to be momentarily without response. For Lyssa, Uthe suspected it wasn't the power of Keldwyn's unexpectedly forthright words. The Fae Lord had ever been clever-tongued. No. It was the emotions behind the words, emotions he gave free rein now, not only to Uthe but to their audience, letting them see his heart in his eyes.

Truth, it held Uthe pretty much frozen. He would have laughed at himself, letting the sentiment of proclaimed love paralyze a vampire as old and experienced as himself, but Keldwyn was right. When that connection was true, it mattered not if one was their age or Catriona's. The power of it was sweeter, deeper and more overwhelming than all magic combined.

Keldwyn moved forward then, to the edge of the rippling pool beneath Rhoswen's throne, the receptacle for the waterfalls' flow. Courteously, Lyssa rose and returned to her seat, clearing the area between him and his queen.

Drawing his sword, Kel palmed the blade across his body and knelt before her, lowering his head. "Our relationship has not been an easy one, my lady. We have suffered and wounded one another, mostly as mitigation from wounds left us by those we loved, whether or not that love was invited or deserved. Though I have not said it outright, you know the truth. You have ever had my fealty, which is why I've often directed you in ways that angered you. I would never do you the injustice of spending more time kissing your lovely ass than protecting it and, by extension, the world and people we love so well."

Rhoswen's jaw tightened, but she did not move. Taking it as assent to continue, Keldwyn did. "As I said, you may do with me as you will. But I ask you...beg you, not to punish Catriona for loving me too much."

After a weighted moment, Rhoswen rolled her eyes and rose. She descended the throne to stand before him. "Oh, get up. Always trying to outplay me with your smooth words, courtly airs and now romantic notions. I relied on you never to get moony about love. You have failed me utterly."

When Keldwyn lifted his head, she touched his face, a bemused contact that lingered. He dipped his head into her touch, and she sighed. "I will never welcome bridges between our worlds as you all do. I have internalized our losses and failures too deeply. But there is merit to your points. We cannot stop change; hence we must deal with how to permit free will enough rein not to hang itself. I expect there is no better choice available than you and Lord Uthe to show both our peoples how to balance the wellbeing of all with the care for the individual heart, and bring the two together as best we may."

Her expression changed then, her face getting more closed and yet more fragile at once. When she spoke, though, her voice was gentle and the touch on Kel's shoulder was firm. In that moment, Uthe saw the ruler in her that Keldwyn saw. "I will not necessarily give you my blessing, but I do offer a hope for your happiness. My father would be pleased you have found someone to love."

Keldwyn lifted his head, gripped her wrist. "I know he loved you, Rhoswen. Deeply. Had he had the freedom to show his love for Lyssa's mother, I expect he would have had far more opportunities to prove his feelings for you. Perhaps with these changes we can prevent something like what happened to him and his family from happening to someone else."

"Perhaps. Let us just not call it progress. I cannot abide that word, for all the evils it represents." Rhoswen sniffed. "Now, as to your ward..."

Keldwyn stiffened, but she stepped around him and moved to the center of the chamber. "Come stand before me, child."

Uthe glanced toward Kel as the Fae Lord rose and turned. Though the male's expression was tense, he nodded slightly. Uthe squeezed Catriona, a reassurance. The young woman moved toward the Queen with only a brief hesitation. Uthe saw her courage when she did her best to hold fast and not shrink before Rhoswen.

"You will be forgiven your transgression because of your pure intent." When Rhoswen reached out and touched the girl's face, Catriona jumped, an involuntary response, but she settled as Rhoswen made a quiet noise. "You will come to no harm from me today, Catriona. A ruler has to make difficult decisions. Regret is often part of those decisions, but it does not change why they must be done. You understand?"

Catriona, held under that piercing blue stare, pressed her lips together. When she shook her head, Rhoswen smiled without humor. "A sweet, honest child. No, of course you don't. That's the point, you see. Your world has yourself at the center, whereas for a ruler, her people always have to be at the center, even if she forgets that from time to time. I make right decisions and wrong decisions, and sometimes I don't know which is which until much further down the road. I don't think allowing you to stay captured in the human world for twenty years was the wrong decision, because it did dissuade other young Fae from making the same mistake you did. However, if I'd had another way to teach the lesson, I would have done so. A Queen doesn't have the luxury of indulging her more tender feelings."

Rhoswen stepped back, her familiar expression replaced by her usual imperious mask. "I overlook your tremendous disrespect today in exchange for your involuntary service to that lesson. Understood?"

"Yes, Your Majesty." Catriona curtsied on shaking knees. Keldwyn had approached and drew her to his side, grasping her elbow to steady her.

"Now be gone," Rhoswen said. "It would be best if I didn't see you for quite some time, because you are not on the best side of my temper right now."

Catriona looked toward Keldwyn, a quick flash of happiness for him crossing her face. She indulged a quick hug of his neck before she fled the room, likely as swiftly as she'd entered it. As she fluttered over him, one of the guards groaned, beginning to push himself up off the floor.

"Did you have to hit him like a battering ram?" Rhoswen said crossly. The Fae Lord glanced at the stirring guard.

"That one wasn't mine. Mine is the one that is still unconscious."

Rhoswen's gaze snapped to Uthe. Uthe cleared his throat, aware of Lyssa's amused look. "I did have the advantage of surprise, my lady. Else I'm sure he would have made a better accounting of himself."

"It will go all the worse for him when Cayden learns he let a vampire dispatch him." Rhoswen shook her head, waved a hand. The two men dissipated into the floor like melting ice, an alarming effect until she explained. "I've put them back in their bunks in the barracks. When they wake up, they can explain to Cayden why they are not at their posts. It's ridiculous to think I need constant protection anyway, particularly when I am meeting with the strongest allies I have."

She swept her gaze over Tabor and Lyssa. A pleased smile on his face, Tabor gave her a half bow. Lyssa blinked at her like a green-eyed cat, and Rhoswen's lips twisted at the expression. She threw a look at Keldwyn. "Since you have resolved the most important issue before us today, we can work out the details of our Yule celebration on our own. You and your vampire may go."

"As you wish, my lady," Keldwyn bowed. She'd confirmed what Uthe suspected, that they'd had weightier business on the table when Catriona had interrupted them. Despite her summary judgment upon Keldwyn, Rhoswen had intended to discuss the matter with the other two leaders for their consideration. It reassured Uthe and improved his opinion of her. However, in his short exposure to Keldwyn's mind, he'd already learned the Fae Queen was not too much different from the vampire one. They might not always be predictable and they were always dangerous. But in the end, they had many qualities that commanded an advisor's loyalty.

Lyssa nodded to Uthe. "I'll look forward to seeing you in Savannah, my lord. If your business elsewhere has been concluded."

There were a wealth of ifs involved with him coming back to Council headquarters, but it wasn't the appropriate time to discuss that. When her features softened slightly behind that regal look, he remembered her words before he'd left.

I would care for you.

Perhaps the decision they'd just argued and made could be applied to his personal situation. Sometimes it was best to put what safeguards in place one could and see how things unfolded. As he shifted his gaze toward Keldwyn and back to Lyssa, he found himself agreeing with Rhoswen.

No matter what happened, his greatest allies were with him.

Chapter Eighteen

It was fortunate Rhoswen had been in a more rational mood than she'd been when Kel had shown up in her throne room earlier, bloody and dusty and filled with urgency to return to Uthe's side. But as he revisited that fateful meeting when she'd decided not to lock him out of the Fae world, Keldwyn wondered what kind of soul searching she'd done between the two meetings. Perhaps she'd sought counsel with Cayden in a more intimate setting to purge the emotions that were getting in the way of what she'd told Catriona a ruler had to do—keeping the world in the center of things, rather than her personal feelings about it.

The right person could help a male or female think more clearly about things. Though he could also be the stubborn obstacle to what the proper course of things should be. In that case, Uthe and Rhoswen had too much in common.

As he approached the west entrance to the Savannah estate, Kel took off the gloves he'd been wearing to ride a dragon to the portal in the Savannah forest. He'd let Sandoval come through for a few minutes, because the forest was private and protected, and he'd promised John, Kane's closest friend, that he'd let him meet a dragon if he was on time. When he came through the portal, he'd wondered if the child had been camped there since school had let out several hours before.

The slim, serious boy had been charmingly goggle-eyed as he touched Sandoval's scales and scratched the offered snout. He liked science, and already dogged Brian and Debra in their lab regularly. As a result, many of his questions for Keldwyn—once he overcame his initial shyness with the Fae Lord and the overwhelming reality of facing a dragon—had to do with the hows and whys. Why did they breathe fire? How did they do it? Could they talk in their heads like vampires? How long did they live? Did they really lay eggs to have offspring?

Keldwyn had indulged a few hundred of such questions before he sent Sand back through the gate and John back to his grandfather. Dusk was coming and he had other business to handle. Despite his tension about that business, the boy's enthusiasm left him with a contented feeling. There was joy in sharing the magic of his world with the world here. And John already understood the quid pro quo of Fae protocol. He'd promised to show Keldwyn how to play Angry Birds.

Now he leaned against the archway of the stone patio and slapped the gloves against his thigh, waiting. *I know you're awake.*

My door is not locked.

I know your nightly routine. I'm saving myself a walk.

He waited, and eventually heard Uthe emerge from the trap door behind him. Keldwyn looked over his shoulder because, truth, it was a pleasure to gaze upon him every evening. Uthe closed his hand on Keldwyn's arm, a brief affection, before he moved out to the lawn. Kneeling beneath the emerging moon and stars, he bowed his head.

The vampire had started to wear clothes of the Fae world more often, since they went between worlds frequently. Tonight he wore a belted short tunic and dark brown hose that clung to his muscular thighs. Kel suppressed the desire to tug up the back of the tunic and enjoy how the fabric molded his taut buttocks.

Instead, he stood at a distance, respecting whatever prayers Uthe was offering to the Divine Energy he preferred to call God or the Lord. He listened to the prayers in Uthe's head, not to eavesdrop but to absorb the cadence of his thoughts, like music. When the vampire was concluding the evening ritual, Kel moved forward, trailing his fingers over the vampire's nape, teasing the soft hair there.

"So are you satisfied with what Brian told you?" He saw no reason to delay the discussion. He'd been thinking about it since they'd fought about it last night, and ended up in Brian's lab. They'd put the scientist in the center of a discussion heated enough Brian had probably wished he'd locked away his delicate instruments and glass beakers.

Uthe lifted his head. He stayed silent and didn't move as Kel continued to caress him. He wondered if Uthe did it because of how much it stirred Keldwyn, seeing him on his knees like this.

"Yes. And because it arouses me as well," Uthe said quietly. He paused. "I know Brian agrees with you, that your Fae blood likely protects you, the same way it will slow the effects of the disease on me. Perhaps even reverse it. But *likely* and *perhaps* are important words."

"Yes, they are. *Perhaps* I will refuse to be denied on this." Kel stepped in front of him, looking down into the Templar's serious face. "Do you want me as your third mark, Varick? A simple yes or no."

"Yes. But not at the expense of your life or sanity. The first is a certainty when I die. I am content with the binding we have between us now."

"I am not. The third mark will increase the viability of my blood upon you. Making it even more possible that the disease is slowed or reversed."

"If that happens, then Queen Rhoswen will shut the door between our worlds. She's not going to let Lord Brian recruit Fae servants for vampires with Ennui."

Kel flashed a smile. "Yet wouldn't it be amusing to watch her reaction if he comes to her with that request, with that earnest and handsome face of his?"

"Yes. Right up to the point she turns him into an ice sculpture and has Cayden smash him to bits with a mace."

"Do you love me, my lord?"

Uthe held his gaze steadily without responding. His mind was curiously quiet and dark. He rose. "Let's walk to the gardens."

They did that in silence. Most times, Kel could be very patient. Once they reached the gardens and were walking along a stone wall border for a wealth of blooming vines, he found he wasn't in that mood. He caught Uthe's arm and pushed him against the wall, sandwiching him there with his body, his face very close to the vampire's. "Do you love me, Varick?" he repeated, softer.

"You know I do." Uthe shoved against him but Kel would not be moved. "You are in my head, my lord. I do not hold anything back from you there."

"But the mind is much more than surface thoughts. That's something new you've given me." Kel eased back, but held him there, a hand on Uthe's hip, the other palm planted against the wall by Uthe's head. "I have many powers, but the ability to be inside another's mind was never one of them. Yours is as complex as a field. The nourishing soil beneath, the heated fire far, far below. Your thoughts are like plants, all shapes and sizes, moved by a direction-changing wind. But I want the constant, the heated fire at the core. Give me your soul, Varick, and accept mine. I have never been anyone's first choice...who was mine."

Uthe's dark eyes flickered. "Does your loss of Reghan impact this decision, my lord? You told me you were concerned about letting the opportunity slip by as you did with him. I would not have you rush it for that purpose."

"I am not that impulsive, and you know it. It would not have mattered if I had acted sooner with him, regardless.

He did not love me that way. I am quite capable of understanding the impact of this decision. Do you doubt it? Do you doubt me?" Keldwyn touched Uthe's face.

Uthe shook his head. "I do not, my lord. But I would not have you give your life for a shadow of the love you wanted."

He couldn't have surprised Keldwyn more if he'd turned into a toad in front of him. How had he not seen that? Since the vampire had given him the second mark, Keldwyn had embraced the intimacy it gave him, the increased bond in their more intense moments. Yet while he was learning to navigate the vampire's mind more every day, he'd learned it was nowhere as easy or open as a human servant's mind was to a vampire. Uthe left the door open, but there were plenty of rooms and mazes in which to conceal the track of his thoughts if he so desired.

"I apologize, my lord." The vampire straightened abruptly. "There are times I am far more sentimental than I should be. I attribute it to my condition."

"I don't." Keldwyn planted his other hand on the wall, caging Uthe between them. Kel was willing to turn this into a wrestling match if needed, and win. "I attribute it to your feelings for me, Varick. You want to know if I'm settling for you. If I'm so desperate for the love I wanted with Reghan that I've convinced myself I can 'make do' with yours." He paused, hoping the sparks snapping in his eyes underscored his point. "We have both lived long enough, loved often enough, to know love is not quantifiable. Reghan was then, you are now. I have not wanted to love again until now. You caused that feeling, Varick. You. I will repeat my question. Do you doubt me, or do I have to put my booted foot up your tight, devout ass to prove my point?"

Uthe smiled a little, easing some but not all of Kel's reaction. "I do not." He paused, getting a somber look. "When I get lost in my mind, you are there, with me. One day I might not be able to find my way back."

"As long as I'm there, you will not be alone. And you will find your way back. We are blood linked. You need only follow me."

Uthe lifted a hand and curled it around Kel's forearm. "Brian would say that was entirely mawkish and unscientific."

"It doesn't make it any less true. Varick, I'm not taking no for an answer, even if I have to bedevil you for the remainder of your life."

"Here I was, looking for a good reason to meet the sun, and you just gave me one."

When Kel showed his teeth, Uthe chuckled. He slid down the wall to rest on his haunches. As he fingered one of the blooms near him, Kel's brow creased. Squatting on his heels, he rested a hand on Uthe's knee. Uthe lifted his gaze to him.

"Before I decide, I would like to ride a dragon with you, my lord. More slowly this time. I would like to go to the place we were with Catriona and her friend Della. I want to lie in the field with you beneath me, your arms around me."

It was the type of thing someone would do before they said good-bye, but Kel ignored the uneasiness in his gut and focused instead on what he saw in Uthe's face, felt in his mind. It was not a yes, but it was not a no. He simply wanted breathing space. Fair enough. He hadn't given him much of that, in truth. Nor did he intend to start now.

"All right. I want something as well." Rising, he drew the riding crop out of his thigh high boot, twirled it.

Uthe raised a brow. "Did you use that on your dragon mount?"

"If I had, he'd be using my bones as toothpicks to clean a Fae lord's intestines out of his teeth," Keldwyn said dryly. "I want to use it on you. I want to see how you submit to pain under my hand."

Desire flared in Uthe's gaze before he could quell it. It didn't repel him, for certain. Kel decided to test that reaction further. "I'd also like to bind you, so tightly you cannot move, and then torment you to climax. I want you to give me the third mark when you are completely subjugated to me, completely surrendered to my will."

The swirls of color in Uthe's mind when he was aroused were like a painting, a rippling ocean of passionate red. Uthe let out a muttered curse. "You are not always fair, my lord."

"I am often not fair. It is something you appreciate about me. I also think that assumption is a wise way to start a third mark binding." Keldwyn flicked the end of the crop against Uthe's knee. "So you know if ever you slip and refer to me as your servant, I will exact revenge upon you in ways you will remember for decades. Ennui itself will be unable to dispel it from your memory."

Uthe straightened and started to move away. Kel brought him back with a show of strength. Uthe countered it, gripping Kel's wrist, his dark eyes glittering. "You will push me to this, and we will both regret it," he said between his teeth.

"No, we won't." Kel leaned in, touched his lips to Uthe's. "Give in to me, Varick. I love you, I refuse to let you go, I want your soul. If I have to give you mine to make that happen, it is a gift freely given. You have not stood in the way of God's will for centuries; the least you can do is step out of the way of mine this one time."

"For yet another of many times, my lord, I remind you that you are not on par with God." But he held onto Keldwyn's wrist. "You already know my resistance is because it is something I want as much as you do. I just do not want to make a hasty decision because I am afraid to be alone when the Ennui takes me fully."

"When or if," Kel corrected him. "Very well. So tell me why *do* you want to do it? What is the proper reason to take me as a third mark?"

Uthe's jaw relaxed. "A neat trap, my lord. Because I love you. Because I do not want to be apart from you, ever.

Because it already feels like our souls are bound, and this is simply the formality."

"So if all that is true, the other truth pales in comparison. Who is to say that kind of fear isn't part of the same package? Many people fear to be alone, but they do not make their decisions based on that fear."

"All right. Yes." As Keldwyn's gaze snapped back to his face, Uthe squared with him and gripped his shoulders. "Yes. You win. I agree."

Uthe laughed against Kel's mouth as the Fae crushed him against the wall, possessing his mouth with a kiss that turned heated in a blink. Kel's hands roved over Uthe's neck and shoulders, dropping to his waist and hips with intimate familiarity. Uthe pushed his body against him, letting the yearning take him. God above, it was an indescribable pleasure to surrender to this.

"I think it gave Helga a heart attack the other day, seeing the two of us twined together in the rose arbor," Keldwyn said at last when he drew back.

"Lady Lyssa did say she'd let everyone find out about us on their own." Though Uthe's submission to Keldwyn was something they'd not shared with Lyssa or anyone else. Most vampires would not understand it. The Council might think Uthe was compromised. Not that Uthe had asked to be reinstated on Council. He would wait until Keldwyn's theory about the effect of his blood on Uthe's Ennui was proven.

In the meantime, Lyssa had explained to the Council that Uthe was researching important matters in the Fae world, interspersed with brief trips like this to Savannah. He was still providing counsel when available, but the reduced stress from no longer actively serving on the Council also seemed to help slow the Ennui's progress.

"Helga was shocked, then intrigued. I think she wanted to join us."

Kel curved his fingers in Uthe's belt, latching on firmly. "Unlike vampires, I am very, very monogamous, Lord

Uthe. I've only just begun to take all I want from you."

Since they'd returned, Uthe had been in a state of wonder at how he responded to the Fae's desires and demands, now that he had the freedom and time to do so. In some ways, they did the same things they always did. Chess and spirited debates, and sparring with weapons and in hand-to-hand combat. The matches could quickly become far more sexual in nature, after they satisfied themselves that they remained battle ready. Though that readiness was an unfortunate necessity for both worlds, Uthe didn't consider it a burden to be prepared to defend what mattered.

Every day brought deeper feeling and meaning to the most mundane things. For instance, when Keldwyn was brought food from the kitchens and they were eating together alone, Uthe would sample from his plate, a casual intimacy one afforded a lover. He loved the simple contentment he felt when Kel stayed with him at dawn, twined around him in his bed. He might be immersing himself in the abundant sentiment available when indulging a relationship after such a long dry spell, but he gave himself the luxury without guilt, since Kel seemed to be taking an equal pleasure in such things.

The glorious excitations of love knew no age limit. It was a very uplifting thought.

Uthe wanted to be bound to the Fae Lord with the third mark. He wanted to be bound to him in many ways. When he thought of the hungers he saw in the male's eyes, instead of being apathetic or worse, repelled by it, his own Dominant nature capitulated to it, the way he might bend a knee to Lyssa. Both of them leaders, but he deferred to her as the greater power, someone whose commands he could accept and trust.

Keldwyn stepped back, his heavy-lidded look suggesting he wanted to tease Uthe to even greater heights, now that Uthe had agreed to his will. Fae sadist. "First we'll go ride a dragon, as you wish. I will race you to the portal, and I will win, because Fae are faster than vampires."

"Usually, but—" Quick as a flash, Uthe shoved him so Kel tripped over the short stone bench behind him, going ass over end like Jacques on the receiving end of Nexus's mischief. *I can't believe you fell for that twice. Literally, this time.*

Uthe took the garden wall in one lithe leap, a shortcut to the forest. He didn't expect to make tremendous headway, because even toppling in a backwards somersault, Kel would still land on his feet. But vampires weren't snails.

As he lengthened his stride, he was stronger, running faster. He thought he felt more vibrant, more rejuvenated and alive than he'd felt in a very long time. It gave him hope. Hope that Kel would be right.

He wouldn't ever think of such a gift as God's reward for his faithfulness, for returning the Baptist to the heavens or protecting the world from the demon. Those things were God's will, and he was merely God's instrument. But in one burst of wondrous energy, he knew if God had deemed him worthy of this gift, he'd never take it for granted.

Because of the second marking, he could sense Keldwyn's advance, and laughed out loud at the chase, the two of them flashing through the woods together. They flushed a deer, sent the stag bounding away. Uthe went over a log in a leap as high as the creature's, and then he was descending the slope to the portal.

Keep going. It's open.

Uthe sprang over the creek and he was in the Fae world, startling a family of gnomes. He jumped over them, calling out a laughing apology as he sprinted up the hill. He remembered where the meadow lay, unless Fae magic had changed the topography. He wouldn't put it past Keldwyn to do that, just so he could arrive there first.

I will ignore that you think I would stoop to cheating.

A piercing shriek rent the air, and a shadow passed over him. At a ruffle of wind, he glanced up in time to see Keldwyn leaning down from the dragon's back, offering him a hand. Uthe took it, swinging on behind him. It was the purple dragon again, and he was newly amazed at how it felt, the strength and life of the legendary creature beneath him.

"This is still cheating," he said in Keldwyn's ear, nipping the curve of it and tugging on one of the line of silver rings he was wearing there today. "Though I guess you needed help catching up to me."

"Beware what cockiness with your Master will get you, my lord." Keldwyn put his hand over Uthe's and squeezed. "Relax and enjoy the ride."

He did. This time, with no urgency to their flight, Uthe could experience it better, though he still kept an arm around Keldwyn as he looked around him. He'd been in a plane, but there was no comparison as they soared through the open air among multi-hued wisps of clouds. The dragon skirted the periphery of a flock of swans. Keldwyn dipped his head to several other Fae winging by, carrying what looked like gifts, in natural wrappings of overlapped leaves. They'd tied them with vines whose colorful blooms made a bouquet on top.

"Birthday party?"

"Something like that. The Fae take every opportunity to celebrate with dancing and singing."

"No offense to you and Catriona, but I'm not sure I'd ever leave this world if it was my home. I couldn't imagine any of this ever getting old."

"Why limit yourself, if you can have this world as home and explore other ones?" Kel shrugged. The dragon altered course, dipping his shoulder as he took the turn, and Keldwyn leaned with him, Uthe following the motion. Looking down upon an island with a small castle, he saw a grove of trees with fruit so bright crimson he could see them from this distance.

"Avalon. The isle of apples. The spirit of King Arthur rests there with the sorceress Morgana."

At first he thought the Fae was jesting with him, but

when he realized he wasn't, a smile split Uthe's face. "*Definitely* couldn't imagine this getting old, my lord."

Keldwyn caressed his fingers. Rather than speaking over the wind, he spoke in Uthe's mind. *You feel better these days. It pleases me to see it. I was concerned the loss of your lifelong task and quest would plunge you into a temporary melancholy. It is often that way when large goals are achieved.*

Uthe slid both arms around him, his mouth pressing against the side of his throat. "No. I've wanted to see it done for so long, all I feel is relief. Relief I didn't fail, gratitude that I had the friends and resources to pull it off. Someone to watch my back."

Kel brushed the side of his face against him, his hair whispering against Uthe's flesh. "So what will you do now? Loll about and be useless?"

"I understand there's a Fae Lord who needs a boy toy to amuse him..." Uthe laughed at Keldwyn's mock look of offense. "I'm sure there will be plenty in both of our worlds needing our attendance. There's no end to the violent or misguided mischief the Fae or vampires can devise."

"True enough," Kel said in amused resignation. "Catriona wants to go back to Atlanta. She wants me to devise her a node in your world. A place of magical energy so she can stay in the mortal world for longer periods. She could use it as her home base, to prevent the depletion she experienced on her previous explorations."

"Can you do that?"

"Probably. Rhoswen might agree to it for her...in a decade. I was thinking the club Anwyn runs in that city would be a good place, and she could be under Daegan's protection if needed. Hold on. We're landing."

The dragon deposited them on the edge of another thick woodland. When they were both on the ground, Keldwyn offered Uthe his hand. Though Keldwyn was given to more romantic gestures than Uthe, this one was unexpected. But the odd, closed look on the Fae's face had Uthe putting his hand in his without question, their fingers interlacing as Kel tugged him into the forest.

Uthe noticed the feel of these woods was different. There was a hushed quality here, fathomless and peaceful. The deeper into its embrace they went, the more the power of it increased. The dark shadows were not sinister, but they seemed to hold secrets centuries old.

They do. This is an ancient forest, one that has been here far longer than myself, than all of the Fae I know. The tree spirits here hold a great deal of magic within them.

A silver light began to track before them, Kel's doing, it seemed. A few steps later, they were in a new clearing, surrounded and shaded by the trees. Uthe was looking at a small stone cottage with a thatched roof, a design right out of fairy tales.

"This is mine," Kel said.

He'd always assumed Kel lived in one of the castles. As liaison, he traveled so much between the Fae royalty and the vampire world, it had never occurred to Uthe that he might maintain a private residence.

I cannot stay here as often as I like, but yes, this is my home. Keldwyn turned to face him. "You may stay here as often and as long as you like. If the Ennui takes more of your mind, you will always be safe here. Even if you wandered away from the cottage, all who live on the surrounding lands have regard and loyalty for me. They would care for you and bring you safely back home."

Uthe wasn't sure what to say. Kel's jaw tensed. "I know your pride will chafe at this. Maybe you'll say God does not find you deserving, but it's just as much the sin of pride to make God's decisions for Him. Your commitment deserves the gratitude of many. It also deserves the protection of those who love you well. There are many who assume when we die we go to a paradise where we will always feel safe and loved, happy and content in a way we were never quite able to claim here on earth." Kel shook his head. "I'm not so sure of that outcome. I think the Powers That Be give us a short respite before They send us back into the fray. If it is within my power to give you such a respite for a time, that is what I will do. Perhaps this is how God has seen fit to reward you—with me."

The last bit was said with exaggerated panache, a twinkle in his eye and a quick quirk to his lips, but Uthe could feel the Fae's tension at his continued lack of response. Uthe couldn't help it. He was riveted by the cottage, the peacefulness of it. Outside was a stone bench by a small pond, a place for reading, contemplating and napping. There was a comforting drone of bugs, both the six-legged kind and the firefly Fae, an appealing garden music. The sun was able to filter through the trees for light, but he needed no dagger. He was free to walk in the day or moonlight in the Fae world. He imagined the interior of the cottage would be simple and comfortable, not overly large but not crowded. Cozy for two males, with some space for the occasional guest.

He'd found his first sense of place with the Templars, and later among the vampires, rising in their ranks. He'd never turned away from any demand made of him, any obligation or responsibility that would lead to the betterment or protection of others. Not boastfulness, but penance, particularly at first. Over time, it had become who he was. He'd never thought of reward or respite. Like Keldwyn, he didn't expect there was a place the soul was given limitless vacation to do as it would, because it would not be satisfied with such indolence indefinitely. But to have a place of rest for a while... To have someone willing to give him that, who regarded him highly enough to think him deserving...

He could say nothing to Keldwyn, for there weren't words for what he was feeling. It was a release deep within him, far beyond the bottom of his soul. It filled him with quietness, and a fierce need and joy. Exhilaration was there, too, the kind that came with the lifting of a burden that could be relinquished without guilt. About what would become of him, what he would be...and to whom.

He turned, put his hands on either side of Keldwyn's face and held him with an expression he hoped conveyed all of it and more. "Thank you, Kel," he said.

Kel curled his hand over one of Uthe's on his jaw. "I am Fae, Varick. We do not accept thanks. I want your third mark."

Uthe had said he would do it. Despite that, his concerns and reservations came back to him, paradoxically because of all the Fae had just given him, proving his devotion. However, to continue an argument already resolved was an insult to the Fae's intelligence and depth of understanding. He was making his choice, and it was an informed one. If Uthe respected and loved him, he would argue no more. In truth, he didn't wish to do so. He already knew many things about Kel, but he had a feeling he'd only read the first few chapters. He wanted to swim in his mind, among all the memories and images there. He wanted to intertwine his own life and pictures with them, and then use those shared visions to move forward together and create new ones.

He wasn't sure the third mark would be enough—if soul-to-soul was going to be as close as he wanted to get to everything the Fae was.

Kel's dark gaze had become even darker, energy building around him. He gripped Uthe's hand again. "Come with me. I will wait no longer."

He drew Uthe along the path to the house, lined with random rock sculptures and dancing flowers. Uthe expected Catriona had been involved in the whimsical design. Landscaping probably wasn't a matter of labor here but of artistic desire. Everything natural seemed to fall into intriguing patterns and aesthetically pleasing arrangements. Kel spoke a word and the door shimmered. Apparently they did have security protocols, though.

"I can make the interior into whatever I desire," Kel

explained as he drew him inside. "I will show you what it normally looks like for daily living and comfort. Afterwards. I can change it then for your comfort. Whatever you need."

Everything was dim, dark and empty, smelling pleasantly of dry stone. Uthe could discern nothing in the room but them, but the shadows held weight and mystery, building the anticipation. There would never be anything to fear here, the closest thing to it the sensual anxiety Kel evoked from Uthe.

"Kel." Uthe stopped him. "Your care of me, it moves me more than I can say, but I do not wish you to become overly concerned about it. About the arrangement of the house, the care of your neighbors, any of that. I have what I need, right here." He placed his hand on Kel's chest, over his heart. "As long as this beats for me, then there is nothing more or less you need provide."

Kel leaned in and kissed him, sliding an arm around Uthe's waist to draw him closer and press thigh to thigh with him, his palm flattening against Uthe's back. When he teased Uthe's fang with his tongue, Uthe resisted the urge to pierce and draw blood. Lust and hunger started to rise together. Kel dropped a hand to grip his buttock. "I like that you restrain yourself until I bid you take from my vein."

"It is only courteous," Uthe teased him, with a spark in his eye. Kel's hand tightened to bruising strength. "And you seem overly fond of grabbing my ass these days."

"Because I see it as mine and I do enjoy touching my possessions. And *only* courtesy, Varick? I think not."

Uthe shifted, not expecting the sudden insertion of the crop between his testicles and the crease of his inner thigh. Kel levered the shaft up to put pressure on the joining point. His mouth got a set look that had Uthe's cock stiffening and increased the force of love and want in his heart.

"Say it," Keldwyn said softly.

"I restrain myself because I obey my Master's will." Uthe's voice was hoarse. In this secluded cottage, all the things they could do with one another, all the things Keldwyn could do to him, were far closer and even more real.

Kel slid the crop free. "I like you in these hose, my lord," he said. "I like you better in them without the tunic. Take it off."

He did. Keldwyn placed his palm on Uthe's chest, holding him place as his gaze roved down over the blatant erection now revealed, straining against the cloth. "You find hose immodest, don't you?"

"They are more revealing than what I usually wear."

"Be grateful I allow you to wear the tunic over them except when we are together. Though it might be advantageous to wear them with a short-tailed shirt next time you want to distract the Council members into agreeing with me."

"First you must present a point with which I agree, my lord. A rare occurrence."

Keldwyn gave him a dangerous smile. "Push the hose down to your knees. Show yourself to me."

Uthe complied, heat pumping through him. The cool air inside the cottage touched his hip bones, his buttocks. Stepping forward, Kel gripped Uthe's cock, working it in firm strokes. The decisiveness of the action, the deftness of his touch, had Uthe grabbing the Fae Lord's biceps to balance himself, his lips parting and stretching in aroused response.

"Let your fangs extend to their full length. I want to see the beast come out entirely. No holding back."

Keldwyn had realized the effect unsheathing fangs had on a vampire. Since feeding always connected to the lengthening of the fangs, over time, bloodlust responded to the act, whether or not blood was being offered. Uthe's organ twitched in Kel's grasp as his fangs curved over his bottom lip. Keldwyn's eyes glowed at the sight in the semi-darkness. "Take all of it off now."

He stepped back and watched Uthe strip. When Uthe stood before him naked, Kel prowled around him, examining him from every angle. Uthe hadn't ever been appraised in such a proprietary manner. His cock became thicker and harder, his blood coursing through his veins and heart like a tingling hot spring he could feel in every nerve ending. They pressed eagerly against the inside of his skin, wanting touch, contact. Penetration. Kel's fingertips whispered over his ass.

"I like looking at you like this, Varick. I haven't used much magic on you, but I could freeze you in place for hours, pleasure myself in so many ways upon your body. I would make you come again and again. When at last I was done and released you from the spell, I would catch you in my arms, because you would have no strength left. You worry that with the third mark you could tear apart my soul." He pressed against Uthe's back, his fingers sliding between his buttocks to tease his rim. "With the magic I have, I can do that to you with almost no effort. But we both show restraint, don't we? We want inside one another's souls, to cherish, to plunder, but never to destroy." His breath was a heated tease along Uthe's shoulder. "Except to destroy any thought of ever considering another Master but me."

Uthe closed his eyes as Keldwyn pressed his mouth to his shoulder. "So it begins with a bite, does it not? I take some of your blood first."

Uthe shuddered, a groan escaping his lips as Keldwyn bit deep with his sharp canines. He could feel the ache in his own as Keldwyn drew deep, his body against Uthe's back, the urgent strength of it. Keldwyn alternated the sucking pressure with sweeps of his tongue, his hands gliding over Uthe's arms, the flexing biceps, the corded forearms.

"You are beautiful, Uthe. Far more handsome than you've ever realized. Your body an unrelenting terrain, battle ready, yet so sensitive to touch, to stimulation." Kel brought his hands back up, this time leaving a small cushion of space between his palms and Uthe's arms. The sweep of heated magic ignited the nerve endings even further, and Uthe's cock convulsed.

"I can do that, too," Keldwyn murmured. "I can bring you to climax until you're near death—your body overtaxed, your heart ready to explode in your chest, your cock staying just as erect after every orgasm. I can keep you in such mindless, blissful agony without even touching you, but I would never deny myself that pleasure. Or torment you so far, though it intrigues me how your body and mind respond to such a threat. You want me to push you, Varick. The way you push yourself past endurance for your God, that is how much you want a lover to demand from you, isn't it?"

"Yes," Uthe growled. He wanted to fight, to surrender, to give pleasure, all to relieve the agony of want and yearning inside him that Kel was building higher and higher.

"Then go there." Kel turned him toward the recesses of the room. A filtered light made up of gleaming motes illuminated the back wall, showing Uthe an array of wooden vines sprouted from the stone and tangled together. "Stand against the wall, facing it. Spread your legs shoulder width apart, and lift your arms."

Uthe moved to the spot. The particles of light slid across his skin as he came closer. They left a trail of fire, a heated glow. Another stabbed his thigh and he jerked in reaction. "They can give you every sensation of the earth I can command," his diabolical Master said. "The prick of a thorn, as you just felt. The sting of a nettle, the teasing tickle of a dandelion, the scrape of bark. You will not be able to anticipate which comes next."

He had never trusted anyone like this. Uthe lifted his arms, spread his legs. The wooden vines immediately wrapped themselves around his arms from wrists to armpits, stretching his limbs out straight to either side of him and pressing his chest against the wall. The other vines did the same from ankles to thighs.

Kel stepped up behind him, reached around and found Uthe's cock, adjusting it to an upright position so the inflexible length of it was against rough stone. "Keep it pressed against the rock that way."

Then he moved back and struck Uthe with the riding crop in the center of his back.

Uthe flinched, not expecting the strike. It wasn't overly painful, but it shimmered through his nerve endings in a provocative way. Kel did it again, and this time it was like being struck by a barbed lash. A grunt caught between his teeth when the tip yanked at his flesh as the whip pulled away, though he didn't feel a trickle of blood. A very real illusion. Kel purred in masculine appreciation. "You should see the way your muscles in your shoulders and ass flex when I do that."

He kept doing it, rubbing his hands over the offended places when he left imagined welts. The harder he struck, the more Uthe's body became rigid with need, blood pooling into his loins, his testicles drawing up at the stimulation. Keldwyn, seeing it, alternated the strikes between teasing, flirting and painful, until Uthe had slashes of heat and feather light echoes of sensation all over back, ass and thighs.

All those secret dark fantasies about penance involving the lash came to the surface, deliciously tangled with other reasons he'd longed for them. The pleasures of punishment, which allowed a release of thought and care in full surrender to the one wielding the scourge.

The vines were drawing up, lifting him off his feet and away from the wall. Another vine wrapped itself around his throat and forehead, holding his head arched back as his legs were drawn further up, bending his knees. He was tilted until he was swaying in a basket hold, his knees spread and pressed up against his rib cage, arms out to his sides. Keldwyn came out of the shadows toward him. The Fae had stripped off his own shirt and was only in his tight, laced leggings. He was pure sin from head to toe, with his cruel mouth, fathomless eyes, beautiful hair and hard body.

Then the wooden vines wrapped around Uthe's eyes, closing them. He jerked as what felt like a handful of those light motes landed on cock and testicles and began to prick and heat, sliding down toward his anus. A curse slipped from his lips, his heart squeezing up in a kind of terror as Keldwyn made it clear just how helpless he was.

"I know your Lord is your salvation in all ways, my lord Uthe," the Fae Lord said conversationally. "But when I bring you to this room, now and in the future, there is only one way to salvation. Through my will. And who am I?"

Had Kel known taking his sight would make it easier? "You're my Master here on earth," Uthe croaked. "In this room, your will is the only will that matters."

Kel paused. He obviously hadn't expected more than a one-word answer, but Uthe had so much happening inside him right now, he wasn't willing to rein any of it back. So many things had commanded his passions for so long. He wanted Kel to be the center of those passions when it was like this between them. Had Kel intended that result, or was it a pleasurable surprise to them both?

The crop hit his vulnerable testicles, his unprotected cock. Uthe jerked, yanked, and danced in his bonds. "Agh..." He almost strangled on his own tongue as Kel slid a slick finger inside his rectum and probed. He had some of those mote things on his finger, apparently, because Uthe's channel caught fire in a heated, crazy way that had his cock twitching further. His body was lifting as much as it was able. With every movement he made, a vine came in to quell him, until he realized Keldwyn was stimulating him for that purpose. He intended to completely immobilize Uthe, as he'd stated earlier. When he gave the Fae Lord the third mark, it would emphasize this was no vampire-servant relationship. Not now, not ever.

His Master embraced pride. He was arrogant, Dominant. And his heart belonged to Uthe.

Kel slid his knuckles along Uthe's cock and trailed them up his stomach. As he moved around Uthe, the vines adjusted so he was dropped back, his body tilted so his raised and spread knees were higher than his head. The vine around his neck tightened, arching his head back further. Kel put two fingers in Uthe's mouth, making him open. He teased Uthe's fangs until Uthe bared them in warning, his animal nature rising to the top, as Kel intended. Kel was pushing against Uthe's own Dominant instincts, forcing them to give way.

A vine slid under his fangs and out the other side, curving up to open Uthe's mouth wider until he thought his jaw might crack. Keldwyn pushed his cock into that heated cavern, pressing it against Uthe's tongue to avoid the fangs. He insinuated himself all the way to the back of Uthe's throat, his corona rubbing against the flat of Uthe's tongue.

"Play your tongue over me, Varick," he commanded. "Get me slick with your own mouth."

It took effort and concentration with half his mouth restrained, but Kel wasn't in a hurry. When he at last slid free and the vine released Uthe's mouth, his fingers caressed Uthe's lips. Uthe kissed his Master's fingers, sucking on them one by one until Kel took them away. The vines raised him to that basket position again. Keldwyn pressed in between his spread thighs, fitting his cock against Uthe's rear opening beneath the fall of his heavy testicles. Uthe's cock was taut, a line of moisture at his navel telling him the pre-come oozing from the glans had smeared against his belly.

Uthe grunted as Keldwyn pushed through the outer ring of muscles. He brought his body so close to Uthe's that Uthe's cock was mashed between them, against Kel's muscled abdomen. He felt the pressure on the vines as Keldwyn used a tight hold on them to finish penetrating him to the hilt. His fingers overlapped Uthe's forearms.

Uthe couldn't move at all, and it was overwhelming, an excruciating paralysis. He let out an anguished sound as the vines wrapped around his cock and balls, cinching them tightly, rough tree bark embedding itself in tender flesh.

"A reminder that your climax belongs to me. Your thoughts, your desires, all of them are submissive to mine right now. And you only grow harder as I torment you. Ah, Varick, you are not making this easy on yourself. If I'd known earlier you would respond this way, I would have had you long before this."

Think I would have been that easy, my lord?

He couldn't form the words, all the sensory overload paralyzing his vocal chords, but Keldwyn's mind and thoughts slid around his, as much of an erotic restraint as the vines on his flesh. *Not at all. Which is exactly why you would have been that much more of a temptation. The tastiest meat comes from the hardest quarry to run to ground.*

As Keldwyn pushed in again, his mouth captured Uthe's, a branding kiss. Turning his head, he brushed his lips along Uthe's jaw, his temple. He stretched up so his cock pressed in deeper and his throat was against Uthe's curved fangs. The vines swayed with their movements.

"I want your third mark, vampire. Give it to me now."

Uthe bit, and nearly came from the pleasure of doing that, especially since Keldwyn reacted by beginning to thrust rhythmically, punctuating each deep plunge with the command in his mind. *Do it. Now.*

Uthe drank several swallows of the Fae's rich blood. When he felt it sizzling through his system, he released the third mark serum. As pleasurable as his marking of Mariela had been, it was nothing like this. It was as if the vibrant blue serum shot through the Fae's veins and turned into blue fire in both their minds. It was the color surrounding starlight, the one found in the night and dawn skies, at every layer of the ocean. The connection between their minds expanded, larger and larger, and then split open, an explosion of images and feelings that made everything their bodies were feeling all the more acute.

Uthe was moaning, snarling against Keldwyn's flesh. His fangs pressed in as far as they could get, as if he wanted to devour the Fae and give him the pleasurable agony of that penetrating pain at the same time. Kel had stilled, his cock embedded inside Uthe, heated stimulation rippling up and down Uthe's channel. His moans and snarls were near sobs of sexual frustration and anguished need.

The soul. He was in Keldwyn's soul, and he felt Keldwyn in his. It hadn't occurred to Uthe to try to block him, as a vampire could so easily with a servant. He knew it wouldn't be that easy with Keldwyn, and that was part of all this, Keldwyn's warning. It wasn't about Uthe never calling him servant. It was about never treating him as one, never shutting him out. Uthe thought of the human marriage ceremony, with its oath to be with one another, through better or worse, sicker, poorer. Kel's willingness and demand for the third marking was a direct indication of his willingness to go on that journey with Uthe.

It was too much. He was dying from the pleasure, the pain, the love and demand the Fae gave and took from him at once. It was as if Uthe was suddenly catapulted back to that time with his father, the lowest, most horrible memory of his life, where all the bad had culminated and taught him the truest meaning of despair. Keldwyn had reached back through the years and extended a hand to him. Locking Uthe into the mystery and beauty of his onyx and moonstone eyes, he simply said, "Come away from there. I'm here now."

Kel's mouth was on his face, capturing tears. There were harsh noises coming from Uthe's throat. He wouldn't call them sobs. They were too animal-like for that, the pain overcoming him. Keldwyn caught his head in both hands, and the vines released around his cock and balls. *Easy, my lord,* Kel soothed. *I am right here.*

"Kiss..."

"Anything for you." Kel kissed his mouth, his cheeks, his brow, then came back to his mouth again, delving in deep, making it last, a restorative and a way to arouse him further. It took him back up that pinnacle once more, letting him fly higher than the weight of his painful emotions. It was like he was back on the dragon, the fantasy and reality merging. Kel began to move his hips again, stroking Uthe inside as he was kissing him. The vines shortened, drawing Uthe's legs up higher, almost bending him double so Kel could fuck and kiss him equally thoroughly.

"Oh...God in Heaven..."

Now. Kel's voice was a savage whisper in his head. *Give your Master everything.*

The climax split him like a sword from throat to groin. The violence of it swept through him, pain, pleasure and joy that seared him like fire. Keldwyn closed his hand over Uthe's cock and caressed his balls, which enhanced the sensations that had Uthe shuddering in his bonds, his immobility adding to all of it. He'd never experienced a climax he was certain would be fatal, but this one swept him past any control, thundering him toward an edge over which if he fell, he probably wouldn't stop falling for days. Forever.

Then Kel came inside him, and there was no choice but to take that leap. He groaned, his release jetting from his cock, bathing Kel's hand, Uthe's belly, his chest, his chin. In this position, there was no dignity or holding back and he wasn't allowed that pride. Nor did he have the slightest desire for it. His Master wanted everything, and he gave it to him, dark and light, good and bad...he trusted him with everything he was.

When it was over, he had no sense of time. Only of the slow thud of his heart, the ache in his muscles and the spinning of the world around him which didn't seem to be stopping. The vines slowly released him, and Keldwyn's arms were there to catch him. He wasn't lowered to a stone floor, but onto a soft mattress of green leaves and flowers and rich earth. He opened his eyes, the wrap of vines now removed from them, and saw a canopy of leaves above him, all the colors of fall, in red, yellow, gold. The light motes fell from them, only now when they touched his skin, they were a mist, heating cooled and abraded flesh.

He was in the Fae's arms, his head on his chest. Kel was sitting halfway up in the bed, lying on his hip, one knee crooked. Uthe's arm was draped over his hip, the other resting on the thigh of the leg stretched out straight. For the moment at least, the Fae Lord's cock was thoroughly satisfied, but it still caught Uthe's attention, the curved length of it stretched so near his fingertips. But as many thoughts as that inspired, his eye and sense of touch were caught by something else. As he traced his fingers over Kel's hip and up his side, he figured out the shape of it. His lips parted in a painful smile.

"I didn't think it would happen. It didn't for Lady Lyssa when Jacob marked her, but..." he left that thought drift off as Keldwyn realized the same thing he did and twisted to see it. Uthe pushed himself upright enough they could both see.

"When a vampire third marks...someone, it usually leaves an impression on their skin." At Keldwyn's narrow look, Uthe lifted a hand, smiling. "I am not about to use the 's' word on you, my lord. I have been fair warned." Though since his body was still vibrating as if it had an insane desire for Keldwyn to do it all over again, he wasn't sure he might not test the Fae's reaction to it sometime.

Kel's eyes flashed in pleasurable threat...or a promise. Uthe cleared his throat. "From their shape and design, the marks come from a higher power or an elevated portion of our own consciousness. Whichever one it is, it seems to know more about us than we know about ourselves."

He didn't really know the scientific way it worked. That was Brian's area, not his, but he wasn't sure Brian knew the whole of it since there were reactions to a third mark impossible to explain in the scientific world. How the souls could be bound together, how it resulted in a permanent mark on the servant's body whose meaning was always significant and yet impossible to explain.

He and Kel looked down at it together and Uthe slid his fingers over it again. It always looked like a mix between a brand and a tattoo, with the skin raised beneath its imprint, giving it texture. He'd never seen one fade from the passage of time, and he was glad this one wouldn't. The pendant he'd always worn was gone, melted inside the Baptist's head. But what he looked at now, it was as if the metal disk had been heated and then the design branded into the Fae Lord's skin, a crisp image of two knights riding one horse. A seal of the Templars, now also representing the promise and bond between two men.

"There was a time you worried my love of God would keep you from me," Uthe said, easing back down and looking at Keldwyn's face above his own. "I saw it in your mind, the flashes of it."

"I did not know if there was room for us both," Kel said lightly. He adjusted onto his elbow so he was leaning over Uthe, fingertips playing along his chest. "Which is why I never made it a choice between me and Him. Well, except here, in this room. I am selfish. I want one place where you are all mine."

Uthe drew him down further, Kel's eyes filling his vision before he sampled his mouth once more, scraping him with his fangs, their minds twining around one another as he did it. He had never felt more content, more at peace with all he was, had been and could be, so it made the words easy to say. He let Keldwyn draw back, just enough for Uthe to speak.

"Love of God, my love for you, it's all one, my lord. All love is Divine love. Everything you've done and loved in your life, it's all part of it. There is no choice to be made. It is who we are and what we embrace, every day, for all of our lives." He smiled. "'Beloved, let us love one another, for love cometh of God. And every one that loveth, is born of God, and knoweth God.'"

Reaching up, he touched Keldwyn's face. "Though I like the way Marguerite Porete says it even better, no offense to John the Evangelist. 'I am God, says Love, for Love is God and God is Love, and this Soul is God by the condition of Love. I am God by divine nature and this Soul is God by the condition of Love. Thus this precious beloved of mine is taught and guided by me, without herself, for she is transformed into me, and such a perfect one, says Love, takes my nourishment.'"

They faced one another, reclined in a bed of flowers and leaves, with sweet fragranced mist falling around them. As Kel put his palm against Uthe's face, Uthe placed his own beneath it, cupping his knuckles, holding him there. "Your mind will never be lost, Lord Uthe," Kel said, a thick note to his voice. "Your wisdom exists through you and all around you. If ever you need a reminder of it, I will be here."

Uthe threaded a hand through Keldwyn's long hair, unbound and spilling over their bare flesh. "I am covered in my release, my lord," he teased gently. "I will soil this if you don't let me braid it."

"We will go swimming in the pond."

"In a while." Uthe drew Kel closer, his other hand moving to his hip, his fingers fanning out toward more intimate areas. As the Fae's eyes darkened, Uthe bared his fangs. "For all your wisdom, have you not learned just how insatiable vampires are, my lord? Perhaps you should learn how to tire one out."

Keldwyn's gaze gleamed, telling Uthe he was more than up to this task—and any other they would ever face together.

About the Author

Joey W. Hill writes about vampires, mermaids, boardroom executives, cops, witches, angels, simple housemaids... She's penned over forty acclaimed titles and six award-winning series, and been awarded the RT Book Reviews Career Achievement Award for Erotica. But she's especially proud and humbled to have won the support and enthusiasm of a wonderful, widely diverse readership.

So why erotic romance? "Writing great erotic romance is all about exploring the true face of who we are – the best and worst - which typically comes out in the most vulnerable moments of sexual intimacy." She has earned a reputation for writing BDSM romance that not only wins her fans of that genre, but readers who would "never" read BDSM romance. She believes that's because strong, compelling characters are the most important part of her books.

"Whatever genre you're writing, if the characters are captivating and sympathetic, the readers are going to want to see what happens to them. That was the defining element of the romances I loved most and which shaped my own writing. Bringing characters together who have numerous emotional obstacles standing in their way, watching them reach a soul-deep understanding of one another through the expression of their darkest sexual needs, and then growing from that understanding into love - that's the kind of story I love to write."

Take the plunge with her, and don't hesitate to let her know what you think of her work, good or bad. She thrives on feedback!

Joey welcomes comments from readers. Find more of her work by following her on Facebook and Twitter, and check out her website for more books by Joey W. Hill.

Twitter: @JoeyWHill

Facebook: JoeyWHillAuthor

On the Web: www.storywitch.com

Email: storywitch@storywitch.com

Also by Joey W. Hill

Arcane Shot Series

Something About Witches
In the Company of Witches

Daughters of Arianne Series

A Mermaid's Kiss
A Witch's Beauty
A Mermaid's Ransom

Knights of the Board Room Series

Board Resolution
Controlled Response
Honor Bound
Afterlife
Hostile Takeover
Willing Sacrifice
Soul Rest

Nature of Desire Series

Holding the Cards
Natural Law
Ice Queen

Mirror of My Soul
Mistress of Redemption
Rough Canvas
Branded Sanctuary
Divine Solace

Naughty Bits Series

The Lingerie Shop
Training Session
Bound To Please
The Highest Bid

Vampire Queen Series

Vampire Queen's Servant
Mark of the Vampire Queen
Vampire's Claim
Beloved Vampire
Vampire Mistress
Vampire Trinity
Vampire Instinct
Bound by the Vampire Queen
Taken by a Vampire
The Scientific Method
Nightfall
Elusive Hero
Night's Templar

Non-Series Titles

If Wishes Were Horses
Virtual Reality
Unrestrained

Novellas

Chance of a Lifetime
Choice of Masters
Make Her Dreams Come True

Threads of Faith
Short
Snow Angel
Submissive Angel

READY FOR MORE?

Check out Joey's website at storywitch.com where you'll find additional information, free excerpts, buy links and news about current and upcoming releases in the Vampire Queen series. You'll also find information, free excerpts, and buy links for all of her other books and series.

You can also find free vignettes and friends to share them with at The JWH Connection, a Joey W. Hill fan forum created by and operated for fans of Joey W. Hill. Sign up instructions are available at storywitch.com/community.

Also, be sure to check out the latest newsletter for information on upcoming releases, book signing events, contests, and more. You can subscribe at storywitch.com under the Community menu.

Made in the USA
Middletown, DE
07 November 2015